Falling Through the Night

Gail Marlene Schwartz

DEMETER

Falling Through the Night

Gail Marlene Schwartz

Demeter Press
PO Box 197
Coe Hill, Ontario
Canada
K0L 1P0
Tel: 289-383-0134
Email: info@demeterpress.org
Website: www.demeterpress.org

Demeter Press logo based on the sculpture "Demeter" by Maria-Luise Bodirsky www.keramik-atelier.bodirsky.de

Printed and Bound in Canada

Cover artwork: Erin Needham
Typesetting: Michelle Pirovich
Proof reading: Jena Woodhouse

Library and Archives Canada Cataloguing in Publication
Title: Falling through the night / Gail Marlene Schwartz.
Names: Schwartz, Gail Marlene, 1966- author.
Identifiers: Canadiana 20230569269 | ISBN 9781772584868 (softcover)
Subjects: LCGFT: Queer fiction. | LCGFT: Novels.
Classification: LCC PS8637.C59 F35 2024 | DDC C813/.6—dc23

 Funded by the Government of Canada | Canada | The publisher gratefully acknowledges the support of the Government of Canada

To my chosen family,
and to everybody who feels socially homeless: there's hope.

Contents

Stage One: The Sensation of Falling   7

Stage Two: Eye Movement Stops, Brain Waves Become Slower 131

Stage Three: Beginning of Deep Sleep and Parasomnias
(Sleepwalking, Night Terrors, and Bedwetting)   199

Stage Four: Deep Sleep (Brain Produces Delta Waves
Exclusively)   245

Acknowledgements   337

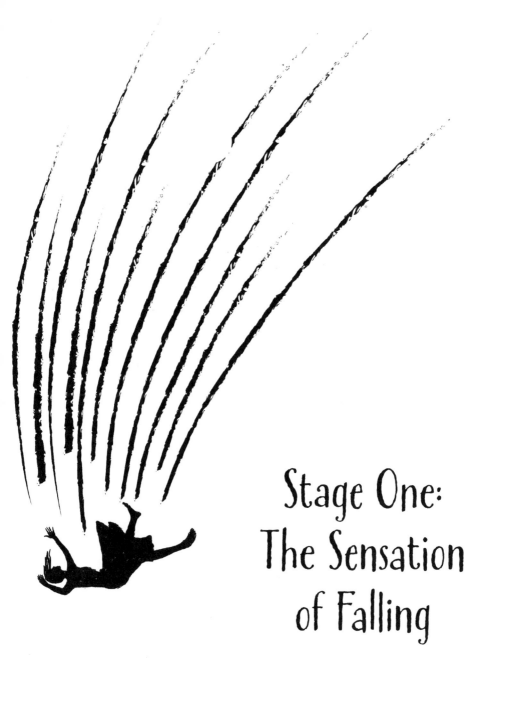

Stage One: The Sensation of Falling

Chapter 1

I t's Monday morning, and I'm ready for step one.
I'm lying in bed, staring at the water stain on the ceiling, the same one that's been there since I rented my place nine months ago. Squinting at it, I play Rorschach, and a new shape emerges: a sperm.

I glance at the rainbow rooster clock that my silly best friend, Jessica, gave me for my last birthday. 6:47 a.m.

I finger the silver Star of David pendant against my collarbone. Sharp edges poke my finger pads.

I stand, straighten the sheets, carefully refold my old baby blanket, and place the narrow rectangle back at the foot of my bed. I do a muscle scan. Jaw, neck, butt, belly, breasts, all tight. I coax my lungs to expand as I open the black eclipse curtains, the same ones that used to hang in my childhood bedroom, the first thing I'd packed when I left home. Sunshine pours in like tart lemonade, and I stand squinting in front of the window. Snow clings to the evergreen hedge and a squirrel darts up a birch tree. I wonder if she's raided her acorn stash, booty for her rugrats.

Rugsquirrels?

How does she do it? Does she ever hide in the tree next door, panicked when she doesn't know what to do, when she feels like she's not like the other squirrels and never will be?

I touch the back of the left curtain panel. Flipping it over, I grin at the familiar army of faces, all glaring up at me. Each has a unique shape, some with scrunched eyebrows, others with jagged frowns, all hideously angry. My eyes fall on the first one I created at the beginning of seventh grade, when I was first diagnosed with generalized anxiety disorder. Having an aide at school meant whispers and giggles and pointing, which soon turned dark and terrifying. Each day after school, I'd hole up in my room and use a different color Sharpie to draw one face on the white backing of the curtains. I snuck in the stepladder to reach the top. By the end of seventh grade, the faces formed complete borders around all four sides of each panel.

I pick up my phone. Notice the date. The pink Post-it note flashes in my mind like a sign at a Las Vegas casino. I put down my sketchpad and go into the office. The flimsy neon square is there, waiting patiently on my desktop screen.

"December 4, 2018: Healthy Family Project, step one."

Fingertips press into neck, pushing for softness where there is none.

What's the first step to creating a healthy family?

The doorbell rings.

Chapter 2

What the hell?

I pull jeans on under my nightshirt. As I trot downstairs, my breathing revs like a motorcycle. I open the door and my ex, Celeste, is standing there, shaking, face wet, arms and hands covered with blood. She's holding a limp black and white cat who is also bloody.

Our black and white cat. Leto.

"She got hit by a car." Her voice is a whisper. Muscles freeze. My kitty, my baby. Then slogans from my program, Wellness for Women with Mental Health Challenges, flood my brain: Boundaries. Self-care. Respectful relating. There's Celeste, with her pink rhinestone earrings and a new tattoo, a little rainbow peace sign on her wrist.

But words seem to tumble out of my mouth of their own accord. "Do you want a ride to the vet? We could go together. Maybe we could split the bill." I reach for Leto who looks stoned and cradle her in my arms.

Celeste regains her composure and rolls her eyes. "Sure, Audrey. Let's fly to Paris while we're at it with all the money left over after rent and Kraft Dinner."

I try to catch her eye, but she's looking away. So, she's still broke. But her psoriasis has cleared up. I shift Leto into my right arm and reach into my jeans pocket with my left hand, remembering I had twenty dollars left over from the Wellness retreat. I hand it to her, and she stuffs it in her purse, still not meeting my gaze.

"Your skin's better," I say. She looks so pretty.

"Fuck you," she says, finally looking me in the eye. She gives me a mocking smile, turns on her wedge heel, and marches down the driveway to her car. I try to say wait, but my tongue is stuck in quicksand. She hops into her rusty Caprice and roars off.

Leto shifts feebly in my arms. "Oh, sweet girl," I say, my eyes filling. I examine the bloody gash on her leg and immediately close my eyes. Do I touch it? Wrap it? Wash it? How am I supposed to know what to do?

My bank account. Balance: $297.83. I'll need to use my brand-new credit card at the vet's. *That's exactly what it's for,* I can hear Jessica say. A best friend thing to say but maybe the truth.

I take Leto inside, and cradling her, I tuck my phone between ear and shoulder and call my crisis counsellor, Gina.

"Audrey, what's up?"

I'm shaking. Can't speak.

Chapter 3

"Okay, Audrey, yes or no questions. Are you safe?"
Left thumb taps once.
"Is it time sensitive?"
One tap.
"Does someone else need help?"
I clear my throat. "Cat." Sandpaper voice.
"Did you call your Wellness tag team?"
Two taps.
"Okay, is that something you can do?"
Leto is squirming. I start counting to myself, one of my favorite anxiety busters. *One, two three...*
I tap twice.
"Okay Audrey, I'll take care of it. They should be there in ten to fifteen minutes."
I manage to get Leto in the carrier I'd kept forgetting to take over to Celeste's place since we broke up six months ago. Tears, muscles like ice. Finally, the green Wellness van pulls into my driveway with two women from my tag team. In less than fifteen minutes, I'm at the vet, and Leto is getting care.

*

It's a couple of hours at the vet's where they clean Leto's wound, set her leg, and wrap her bandage, and I'm relieved it's not serious. At the end of the appointment, I slip my new Visa card out of my wallet. It's white with a green stripe, and my full name is spelled out at the bottom: Audrey Lynne Meyerwitz. I have a credit card. My cheeks flush as the receptionist runs it through the system. $475.00. This is what healthy people do when they face an unexpected expense.
The Wellness women take me to the pet store before going home so

I can get cat food and a litter box. I set things up, say thank-you and goodbye, remembering the times I've supported various group members over the years the way they just supported me: Sari's home birth, Tatyana's bike accident, Liseanne's rape. It's great to have counsellors, but when we help each other as peers, everybody gets stronger.

Once Leto is settled on the living room carpet, I prepare the coffee-maker, turn on the radio, and sit at my kitchen table. The announcer describes a new situation, parents and children being separated at the Mexican border. I pick up the little pad and pencil I keep downstairs and start sketching skinny people in barbed wire pens. I hear Mom's voice, asking me why I'm drawing Holocaust images. I draw thought bubbles full of frantic words from an imaginary alphabet that looks nothing like Hebrew.

I stop and get a tissue to blow my nose and wipe tears off my glasses. I look out the window at the white birch. No squirrel. The coffee maker chugs and puffs, like the Little Engine That Could. I grab my moose mug and pour, adding soymilk and two teaspoons of sugar. Turn off the radio. Take the coffee upstairs to my office.

The Post-it note squats on the screen. We have a staring contest.

Chapter 4

I roll out my yoga mat and sit cross-legged, thinking about Celeste and me. We had started out so well. Even Jessica liked her at first. "She's honest," she told me. And then, things changed. What would make it different this time when I started dating again?

Breathing in and counting, I wonder what it would be like to wake up next to someone sane and safe and good. I close my eyes. Maybe we'd snuggle with the kids at night and read *Make Way for Ducklings*. Maybe the four of us would have Thursday movie night with caramel corn and *The Wizard of Oz*. Maybe my wife and I would be reading in bed when ...a tiny voice calls, "Mommy and Mama, I need you." I'd tell my sweetie, "I'll go this time," and pop into the bedroom with the salmon-coloured walls and a poster from *Frozen*, smile at my daughter, whose nose would be bony like mine, and wipe her tears. Her face would instantly relax, and her arms would fall open. I would lie down next to her, my body enveloping hers, and stroke her hair while I hum her to sleep.

I lie down flat on my back on my yoga mat, adjusting my shirt so it's not bunched up, and I close my eyes again. In my fantasy, the phone rings me awake the next morning, and I discover I'm in bed alone. I answer, and a man's voice identifies himself as a police officer, calling to tell me my wife smashed into an eighteen-wheeler with the two kids on the way to school and work. No survivors. The blood test for my wife was positive for heroin. Oh, and could I come to the morgue to identify the bodies?

I open my eyes, heart thumping hard. White Ikea dresser. Baby blanket. Bare white walls. Natural pine bookshelf. Just me, my clean room, and everything in its place.

Sweat trickles down my temples as I glance out the window. The sky had turned cloudy since before Celeste and Leto arrived, but a lone sunbeam pokes through the haze, and the flock of sparrows in the hedge chatter and kvetch. I stretch my arm over my side, sipping air like soda, as I encourage my muscles to relax. Jessica says a calm person is a boring person. Right now, I wouldn't mind being a little dull.

One, two, three, four, five... I sit up and reach for my sketchpad and pencil.

As I roll my head in a circle, an image pops into my head: a photographer's studio on queer family day. I flip to an empty page and start drawing a cartoon family: two moms with a giggling baby, a crazy toddler, and a sullen teenager. The moms have doe-eyes, beaming at their kiddos proudly. I add some details and shading before glancing up at the clock. Then I remember: noontime run with Jessica.

Chapter 5

"I don't understand why we have to do five miles. What was wrong with four?" Jessica says, huffing and puffing and pushing open the door to my apartment.

"Stop whining. You did great! Don't you feel yourself getting stronger?"

She takes off her scarf and wipes her cheeks. "I feel myself getting colder for longer periods of time."

I shake my head and kick off my shoes in the hallway. "Don't forget to mark it on your chart. We need extra physical points for Wellness to make up for the weekend."

Jessica drops her jacket in the foyer and takes off her hoodie, revealing a pink tee shirt with the words "STRAIGHT BUT NOT NARROW" on it.

"Isn't that the shirt from Pride last year? I thought you ended up not getting it."

"Yea, Eve bought it, belated birthday present. You know what she's like. She thinks I should wear it to work."

I laugh. "Did Sister Laura talk to that mom who complained?"

Jessica shakes her head. "She's setting up a conference with the three of us. But she says she'll back me. Apparently making twenty little braids in your student's hair isn't against the teachings of the Catholic Church. The mom actually used the word 'heathen' when she was talking about me."

She drops her snow pants and plucks off her hat. I admire, as I frequently do, her wild asymmetrical haircut, one I would be too chicken to try. The left side is shaved up to her ear and then layered; the hair gets progressively longer around her head, culminating in a long chunk on the right side dangling down to the middle of her back. Today, like most days, the long section is divided into three thin braids that she's pinned back with a turquoise barrette. Hair is just one of many things that makes her a huge hit with her second graders.

She turns to me. "Hey, did you call your mom?"

I head to the bathroom to peel off my sweaty clothes. "Yeah, it's not good. She got the cortisone shot, but her leg is still bothering her. I'm amazed she actually went to the doctor. Oh, and I forgot to tell you. Apparently, there's this thirteen-year-old who was taken into custody after he jumped off a balcony. Now that there's an open bedroom, social services has been calling like every day. She's going to take the kid as soon as he gets out of the hospital."

"What? I thought Alicia was supposed to be the last of the foster children. What about the whole 'No fostering after sixty' thing?"

"I know, right? She doesn't listen to anybody. Now she's saying it's just because of the Downs that it was exhausting with Alicia. Neuro-typical kids she can handle. Do you want the full sibling report?"

Jessica groans.

"Apparently, Ian's saving up for a hunting rifle for him and Brandon, even though Mom said they couldn't have one, and she's afraid Freddy will get it behind her back because they're texting all the time now that Ian has a phone. Chloe got a warning at the chiropractor's because she was late again, and somebody told her boss she smelled like booze. And apparently Tracy failed all her college classes except choir, so she may lose her scholarship. Mom really misses me."

I listen for Jessica's voice but only hear her belt buckle clinking.

"I'm going to drive down next Friday for Shabbat. Just a quick overnight. Can you pop in and feed Leto?"

Silence.

"Come on, Jess. Who else is going to help her? Freddy's so busy at Amherst that he hasn't answered my texts for two weeks. At New Year's, Ian spent four hours writing and rewriting an inventory of his wardrobe on the whiteboard because the letters and numbers all had to be the same size. It's incredible that Mom finds time to clean the house or take a shower."

I wet a brush, drag it through my ragged blonde hair, and make a ponytail.

"Her voice was so raspy. I think she's smoking again."

Jessica walks over to the bathroom. She leans against the doorway, crosses her arms, and looks at me. She's not smiling.

"You're doing it again. What about your class, your graphic design clients, what about dating? We've got three years of Wellness under our belts, everybody's singing your praises, and what do you do? You're packing for Albany. It's like nothing sank in for three whole years. All that hard work. Jeez." She shakes her head and walks into the kitchen.

I pull on dry sweatpants and my College of Saint Rose tee shirt and follow her.

"Mom never asks for anything."

"Because she doesn't have to. She plays that sad fiddle and little orphan Audrey comes running, still afraid she might kick you out of the nest if you put yourself first."

I slide my Star of David back and forth on its chain. Stare at the heating vent and the thick dust on top.

"Has she followed through yet on one little visit in the ten years you've lived in Burlington?"

I sit down at the table, avoiding her gaze. Jessica looks at me, starts to speak, then stops. Pours some water. Gulps it down and places the glass in the sink.

"Just promise me you won't move back to Albany. Imagine being at a gay bar and running into one of your mom's social worker buddies. Actually, that would be a really easy way to come out to your family if that ever gets high enough up on your priority list. Your life is here, in Burlington. Wellness, your business, teaching. Everything's coming together for you here. Don't screw it up."

Jessica walks into the living room and sinks into the threadbare corduroy sofa. She's in her underwear and a fresh turquoise tank top. She props her bare feet up on the glass-topped toboggan I use as a coffee table. I notice a new pinky ring, which looks especially cool with the spiderweb tattoo she has on the same foot.

She's a glamorous badass, and she's my best friend.

I wander over and sit down next to her.

"Thanks for caring."

"Part of the job description."

I remember. "Hey, I have your purple sweater from the retreat."

She shakes her head. "Don't worry about it. It looks better on you than it does on me anyway."

I squint my eyes. "But I thought that was your new favourite?"

She grins. "You're my favourite person. Makes sense."

We have bagels with light cream cheese, lox, and blueberries for breakfast. The outside world is frigid but sparkling, and we're quiet as we eat. I think about families, imagine myself holding a tiny baby. I imagine handing her to my girlfriend who drops her. My stomach seizes. *Just butterflies*, reassures the confident voice.

Jessica clears her throat. "Have you thought any more about looking for your birth family?"

"You told me you would never ask about that again. Ever."

She shifts and looks at her plate. "I know. It was a stupid promise. Because if you want a healthy family, I think it's really important to..."

"You don't get to have an opinion about that. How many times do I have to say it? You're my best friend. You're supposed to have my back."

"I can't have your back if I don't tell you something I know in my core is true. How can you make a healthy family without knowing your story? Martha's an amazing mom, an amazing person, but..."

"No buts. She's just amazing. I just don't look like her, and so what? I don't need people in my life who have my DNA to make a healthy family."

"You admitted you were curious in Wellness. So, what's the big deal? Don't you want to know if your bio mom was Jewish?"

Blood rushes into my cheeks. "Why on earth would I care about that? Who are you and what have you done with my best friend?"

"You don't need to protect Martha. Think of the stories you don't know about your bloodline. It's like you're missing all this information."

"I'm not missing anything. Mom wrapped me in that blanket upstairs when I was one hour old, for God's sake. She's Jewish, so I'm Jewish. It's that simple. We don't get to know everything in life. And yes, I do need to protect my mother. You know how my aunts and uncles look down on her because of the whole adopting and fostering thing. She had as much time with me out of the womb as they've had with their kids out of the womb. So in real life, it's exactly the same. Who cares what womb I was in? I don't want to hurt my mother. It's healthy to not want to hurt someone. Just because your mom can't be bothered to even call you doesn't mean..."

"That's not fair, Audrey, and you know it."

"So it's okay for you to tell me about my mom but not vice versa?"

She brings a tiny braid to her mouth and chews it. Shakes her head slowly.

I stare at her. "Can we just drop it?"

Chapter 6

Jessica takes the last bite of her bagel and stands up. "Are you done being mad at me?"

I smile in spite of myself. "Yes, annoying person."

"Great! It's time to go shopping."

"Forget it. Go yourself."

"Not clothes shopping."

"Then what?"

"Girls," she says, batting her eyelashes. She grabs my hand and pulls me towards the stairs.

"Are you high?"

"You want to start dating again, right? We're just looking. Does it hurt to look?" She stops at the stairs and turns to me, those big blue eyes suddenly serious.

"I'm not desperate enough to do online dating."

Jessica laughs. "Yes, you are."

I glare at her.

"You don't have to do anything. I made you a profile—"

"You made me a *profile*?!?"

Jessica shrugs. "It was fun. Just read it. Humour me. Please?"

I feel the blood drain from my face, perspiration beading around my temples. I remember that first date with Roberta when I passed out in the restaurant and the look she gave me when the paramedics hauled me off. I remember Celeste's screams during a fight in our shared apartment and the splintering of a ceramic mug I gave her as she slammed it on the floor. Maybe Jessica is right. Maybe I am desperate.

I look at my friend, at the semicolon tattoo on her shoulder. I jerk away, grab a pillow from the sofa, and smack her. Jessica shrieks. Then she grabs my hand and licks it.

"Eyew!!! Jessica Sloane Gibson, you are completely disgusting!"

"But you love me anyway, Audrey Lynne Meyerwitz!"

I wipe my hand in exaggerated strokes on my sweatpants. "Because I am a loyal friend, I will behave with gratitude instead of resistance and read the stupid profile. You have exactly five minutes." I march up the stairs to the office and sit down at my desk. Loudly.

Jessica trots up behind me, grinning, and pulls out the folding chair I keep next to the desk for visitors. "I'll drive," she says, pulling the keyboard in front of her.

She types in "SheLovesHer.com" and finds my new profile. There's a photo of me from Jessica's housewarming. I cover my eyes. She pulls my hand down.

"Stop it. You were gorgeous that night. Can you do a reversal?"

I look at myself in the vintage camisole, the thin foggy-blonde ponytail, the black nerdy glasses. I'm smiling. Thoughtfully.

"Okay, fine. My face looks...well-washed."

Jessica tsks. "You're impossible."

I look at the screen and then at my friend. "Can you..."

"Sure thing. 'Successful queer graphic designer seeks soulmate to dance with, cheek to cheek, into eternity. Smart, creative, healthy. Loves animals, art, progressive politics, and kids.'"

I look at Jessica. "That's false advertising."

She puts a hand on her hip. "No, Audrey. It is not."

I take a breath and read the description to myself. Heat rushes into my ears. Jessica looks at me intently, eyebrows raised.

Well, at least one of us is good with words.

I give her a bear hug. "Thanks. But if I end up with a serial killer, you're toast."

Jessica laughs and turns to the screen. "Shopping time."

A click of the mouse and a list of women pops up.

"Okay, how about Rusticgrrrl? She's 34, enjoys tracking, writing poetry, and spending time with her nephews."

"Tracking? Really? With those fingernails?"

"How about this one? She's getting her PhD in neurobiology at the University of Vermont, and she was a Peace Corps volunteer in Burkina Faso."

I peer at the screen. A stout woman with a button-down shirt, a brush cut, and a dimpled smile looks back at me. I shake my head.

"Yes, Audrey, she's butch, but who cares?" says Jessica. "You lose this enormous category of really cool lesbians when you refuse to date butches. Wellness was supposed to make you more flexible."

I give her the elbow. Jessica dated a woman once, in her early twenties. I've seen the photos. "We have different taste, okay?"

"Fine, fine, whatever. We'll find you an earth maiden with long flowing hair and a fair-trade sundress."

I start picking my thumbnail. "Can we broaden the search? What if we did two hundred miles from Burlington instead of thirty."

"You want to drive to Plattsburgh for a date?"

"Not sure. Maybe."

She turns to me. "What if you have car trouble? It's out of range for Wellness."

"I can get AAA. And anyway, it's not necessarily Plattsburgh. There's also Montreal."

She laughs. "What are you going to do, learn French? In between therapy and Wellness and work and teaching and doctors' appointments?"

I tap my fingers on the desk.

"You know, I've had this thought ever since we started joking about it in Wellness. Maybe I could move to Canada if things worked out with a woman.

She stares at me. "You're kidding, right?"

"Kind of, but not really. I mean, it's clearly better there, especially for having kids."

"How on earth can you know that? Did you take Canadian Life 101 in college?"

I get quiet. "You have health insurance through work. You know what will happen to me if they repeal the Affordable Care Act."

"Yes, Audrey, I know, you've reminded me every single day since the election, but it hasn't happened yet. Plus marrying someone just to get into the country is illegal. You could marry someone in Vermont who gets health insurance through their job."

"Yeah, but what if it didn't work out? I would lose my girlfriend and my health insurance. They have single payer in Canada."

She taps her fingers on the desk. "Think of how hard it was just to come to Burlington from Albany."

"I'm scared. This country is changing, and for people like me, it's not good."

"Look at me."

I do.

"Immigration is huge. If you really want to go to Canada, do it. But make sure it's based on something real. Whoever she is, she better be worth moving to another country for. You'll need to find a new psychiatrist, a new doctor, a new support group, not to mention learning French and doing all the paperwork and managing money and stress. And your Wellness sisters won't be within a fifteen-mile radius every time you have a crisis."

My shoulders tighten. I should be cleaning the kitchen. Or alphabetizing my art books.

I sigh. "Everyone has healthcare in Canada. I think if I lived there, I wouldn't be stressed out all the time, wondering if I'll still have services the next day. That could actually happen. What chance do I have of being able to work and keep my apartment without meds and therapy and Wellness and everything else? And if this potential woman lives two hours away, what's the difference between that and dating someone in Rutland? Or Albany, for that matter?"

Jessica closes her eyes and speaks softly and slowly. "The difference is a border and two countries. I don't want you to set yourself up for failure. Or for getting thrown in a Canadian jail in some frozen wasteland of a town."

I laugh. "I sincerely doubt that will happen. Can we at least look at some women from Canada? Pretty please?"

She sighs. "Fine." A new batch of profiles pops up.

We both scan the screen. Near the bottom, I notice a picture of a curvy woman with reddish-brown hair. "Her," I say, pointing.

"This one?"

"Yeah." I nudge my friend and read out loud. "'Nature and book lover seeks partner to share life and home. Enjoys hiking, music, theatre, and cooking with the woman I love. Good communication a must.'"

She sits back in her chair and shakes her head. "This feels dishonest. You can't date someone to get into another country."

"We're looking. How is that dishonest?"

"Do you want the short AA answer or the long street-smart Jessica answer?"

I look at her profile. "She's older than me..."

"Who cares? She's cute and she's a Canadian superhero, swooping in to save you from the big bad US of A." She folds her arms. I look at her and think.

"Fine. Can I bookmark her page in case I want to go back to it?"

Jessica shows me how. We do a new search with a sixty-mile radius, and I find a few women. I click on a few eyes to "wink" at them. My heart beats faster, and I count to calm down, so I manage to stay sitting without breaking a sweat.

"So now what do I do?"

She smiles. "Now's the hard part. You have to sit back and wait."

Chapter 7

Before supper, I check the SheLovesHer app for messages. Nothing.

I go back to the Canadian woman's profile that I bookmarked.

In the first photo, she's at a restaurant with some other people. Amber hair, round face, ski-jump nose. She's wearing a navy mock turtleneck, a gold chain, and small hoop earrings.

She is also holding up a glass of wine.

Red flag? I have the occasional glass myself, when I'm not with Jessica. I send the jury out to deliberate.

In the second shot, the woman is sitting on a bed, cuddling an enormous ginger cat. She looks like she's cracking up, like maybe she had lifted the big feline on a dare, or maybe someone had asked her how many cat lovers does it take to change a litter box.

Animal person. Check.

The third photo is a full-body shot. She's in a knee-length black cocktail dress. Her shoes have low heels, just enough to show off her muscular calves. The neckline is a plunging V, and I notice her cleavage. She's holding a piece of white cake. Vanilla? Coconut? A wedding? Then I see bridesmaids in the background. Definitely a wedding.

Marriage-friendly. Check.

That night, after eating a can of New England clam chowder, I take my medication, prop my pillow up on my bed, grab my pad and pencil, and start making sketches for a client who uses hot air balloon rides for conflict transformation. The ideas aren't flowing, so I draw stick figures around the edges of the page, shrivelled men and women making faces at each other.

My phone pings. A wink from SheLovesHer! My palms instantly go moist.

I check out the profile. A bikini-clad woman on a beach with a

Schnauzer and a drink topped with a pink paper umbrella. She lives in New Hampshire. I can't quite make out her face. The profile:

Spanish teacher with tons of love in my heart seeks female knight-in-shining-armour. Let's spend weekends making love and feeding each other chocolate and churros. Bilingual a plus.

I look at the photo and tilt my head. Chocolate is essential, but words in English are baffling enough for me. I peer at the screen, trying to see her face one more time, then I sigh, click "erase" on the wink, wipe my hands on my jeans, and pick up my sketchpad.

*

A week goes by, and I get a few other winks and messages, all from Americans. There's a veterinarian who wants a wife who can also do her books, and a married woman who is curious (and can her husband watch?). But a third woman from Essex, just fifteen minutes from my apartment, looks striking in her photo, dark skin with a halo of natural hair, curves in all the right places, a warm intelligent smile. She works as an engineer and does stand-up comedy on the side. We chat on the phone, a lively conversation. But she's so busy that the first opportunity to get together is more than a month away.

A consultation is in order.

Jessica comes over for Sloppy Joes and dating advice. I bring her upstairs after we eat, and I show her the woman's profile.

"She's totally hot. How was the phone call?"

"Amazing. She's funny, smart, successful, interested in so many things, tons of energy."

"Did she ask you any questions?"

"Of course."

"Not of course." Jessica folds her arms.

I sigh. "Fine, not of course. But she really did ask. It was a fabulous and balanced conversation."

"So, what's the big deal? It just sounds like a scheduling issue."

"But that says a lot about her, don't you think?"

"It says she's active and has a busy life. You want another Callie the Couch Potato to take care of for the rest of your life?"

I remember those months of trying to get Callie off welfare and into a treatment program for her Minecraft addiction.

"I want someone who has time for a relationship. It has to be a priority. And with kids, it's even more important. Don't you think that makes sense?"

Jessica shakes her head. "I think you're scared."

"Yes. I am scared. Hallelujah, you are now an honorary psychother-apist."

Jessica giggles. I don't.

"But if I'm going to do this better, I have to be deliberate. The whole online dating thing is about screening, right? So, that's what I'm doing. Screening."

Jessica rolls her eyes. "I guess us drunks are a lot less picky."

"Sober alcoholic. And how can you say that? You've turned down at least ten guys since I met you."

"That's because they were boring. Anyways, this isn't about me; it's about you. Did you send Miss Canada a wink?"

I shake my head. "You're right. My home is here. It was a crazy idea."

The next day, I wake up to my phone pinging. SheLovesHer, a new wink.

Chapter 8

I look at the profile. The woman is white with snow-coloured hair and an enormous smile. She's sitting on top of a Chevy Volt, holding the charging cord.

In a clingy exercise outfit. Cleavage and shapely girly muscles.

I look at her description.

Who are we kidding? Everyone wants to be loved. And we want to do it better than our parents. I have three mutts, a passion for movies and the environment, and miles of listening juice. Have you done your work? Let's connect!

Who are we kidding indeed.

I think of Wellness, all the years of therapy, my shelf of self-help books. I'd certainly done my work, but I was also a work in progress.

I send a wink and then after school, my phone pings again. I look at the message.

Hi, I'm Cheryl, and I'm in the New North End. Wanna grab a cup of coffee next Saturday in Burlington?

I don't think of myself as particularly grabby, but she's beautiful and introspective with the coolest dye job in town, and she lives just six minutes away. I take a few screen shots of her profile and send to Jessica. A few minutes later, she texts.

What are you waiting for?

Saturday arrives, and I meet Cheryl for coffee at Muddy Waters on Main Street. She's sitting in one of those high-backed overstuffed living room chairs, clad in clingy red yoga pants and a peasant blouse. Her smile is like the model's on my toothpaste tube, and her calf muscles look like a ballet dancer's.

"Audrey, I presume?"

I wonder if I bend down, will my shirt fall open and will she see my breasts? Do I want her to? Before I can answer, she's standing up, shaking my hand firmly, making car-salesman-worthy eye contact. My cheeks immediately redden, and I sit, dropping my purse. I look at her, and one eyebrow is raised.

I order a decaf, and Cheryl sips a reddish-orange-coloured latté. "Tell me about your art, Audrey." When she says "art," she grazes the back of my right hand with her fingernails.

"Well, it's not really that interesting," I say, sipping my decaf, trying to imagine what Jessica would coach me to do. Cheryl is staring, and the attention is nearly intolerable. She sits and sits and says nothing. I cough and adjust my chair, backing into the man sitting behind me. "Sorry," I say to him and then to Cheryl.

"It's okay if you're nervous. Maybe it's better to just say that."

My cheeks are burning. I can be honest and talk and process, just not with people I've only met once.

"Why don't you tell me about you?" I am a good listener too, after all.

She moved to Burlington six months ago. She's sharing a house with three others who are also interested in green living and the arts. She plays the guitar and her housemates have started jamming, thinking they might want to be a band someday. At several points, she touches me again, lightly, perhaps to add emphasis. Or maybe she wants to make sure I'm awake.

After about an hour, I realize I'm hungry and don't have enough money for a sandwich. I glance around the café at the other people sipping their drinks, looking so relaxed. I start counting to myself.

"I guess I should tell you something, up front. I have a disability, a...an anxiety disorder. It's under control, but I take medication and have a bunch of stuff I do for my health."

She sits back abruptly. Her mouth shifts, and one of her lips twitches slightly. "Oh. Well."

I tap my foot and pick the cuticle on my thumb. It's dry and pointy. I don't dare make eye contact with Cheryl. But even without looking, I feel her gaze boring into me like a drill.

"To be honest, Audrey, it would have been nice if you had told me this before we got together. It's an important piece of information."

I take a breath. "I...I'm just more comfortable telling people in person. It's not a big deal, but people have a lot of questions. There are stereotypes..."

"Well, thanks. It was nice to meet you." She stands, picks up her yellow pea coat and purse, and walks away.

I sit and sit and sit until my behind is burning. Then I go home and eat a pint of Ben 'n Jerry's Super Fudge Chunk ice cream.

*

That night, Jessica calls to get the report as I'm winding down doing my evening stretching routine.

"It was bad."

"How come? What did you do?"

I get up from my mat and sit on the bed. "Why do you assume I did something? Maybe we just didn't have good chemistry." Yeah, right, nice try, Audrey.

I hear her breathing. "Sorry. Tell me what happened."

My throat is prickly and dry. "I told her about my anxiety."

"What? Why did you do that?"

I'm incredulous. "You think it's morally questionable to look at a Canadian woman's profile on a dating site, but hiding an important piece of personal information is okay?"

"You're self-sabotaging. It was a first date. You don't have to lead with that, Audrey. You're more than your disability. It's part of you, not all of you."

"Well, not everybody would agree. She was pissed I didn't say anything on the phone." Tears.

Her voice evens out. "I'm sorry that happened. I just think you should wait longer next time. See what potential is there. I mean, isn't it more important to find out if the person wants kids? If they don't, what's the point in telling them anything else?"

"Maybe it's just not in the cards for me. Maybe nobody wants somebody with all that baggage. People want people who are easy. I'm not easy." More tears. In my mind, I see myself on a park bench at age eighty, feeding the sparrows by myself, wondering whether I'll find a place to sleep.

My friend laughs. "I'm not easy either, as you know. And I totally think you're worth it. Besides, I don't think easy people are all that interesting. They generally come from rich families who hire people like us to make the world go round."

I smile remembering the six months after Jessica's brother Max's death, how I took her in and for the first few weeks helped her with everything, bathing, eating, taking walks, how she cried and cried, how she slept next to me in the onesie pajama Max had given her, how she needed constant physical contact and how she eventually healed. Not easy. But I wouldn't trade that time for anything.

"Maybe you're right. Don't you have prep to do for tomorrow?"

"In-service day, so I'm binge-watching *Atypical*. Hey, Meyerwitz, go back on SheLovesHer, but this time, when you meet someone, just lead with something else. The right person will see you the way I see you, but naked. I'm sure it will go better."

Smooching sounds, and we hang up, each of us burrowing down into our single lives, propping each other up from four blocks away.

*

One morning after finishing an ad for a new app that locates holistic vets anywhere in North America, I go online several times, looking at women in Vermont. I go back to Miss Canada, to see if she's still available. She is.

I sigh and pet Leto as she slinks into the office, reminding me I need to prepare her breakfast. She trots ahead as I slip into my robe and head downstairs.

As I make my coffee, my phone rings. Jessica. Which is strange, because we normally text first before a call.

I pick up. "You're an eager beaver this morning."

She's breathing hard.

"What's wrong?" I ask.

She sniffs. "Did you look at your email yet?"

"No, I'm just having coffee. Why?"

As she says it, I walk up to my office and sit at my desktop. Click on Gmail. There's a message from our Wellness director. The program has been defunded by the feds. Wellness won't be continuing next fall.

Chapter 9

For the rest of the day, I sit at my desk, staring out the window at the white birch. I sketch a skinny woman sitting on her roof, head in hands. I draw her hair, stringy and falling to her waist. I add tiny birds like fairies fluttering around her.

But I don't have birds, fairies, or a roof I can sit on. I have an anxiety disorder and will soon be without an important service that keeps me functioning. If the feds cut the Affordable Care Act, I'll really be in trouble.

Jessica calls. I cry. She speaks softly. But there's nothing to say, so I say nothing.

Client requests come in, but I'm distracted by my life's crumbling infrastructure. I do a search for articles on the Affordable Care Act to see if there were immediate plans to axe it, but I find nothing. After a while, I start looking up information about Canada. I go back on SheLovesHer and do another search. Miss Canada is still on. I wonder if she's received my wink, and if yes, why she hasn't responded. I write her a quick note. "Hey, wanted to say hello. Hope you're having good luck on this site. And have a good day." I shake my head, wishing I had taken my mom up on it when she offered to get me a third writing tutor.

*

The next morning, my alarm sounds at 8:00 a.m. I've been up since 5:18, a rough night. I take my morning medication and check my phone.

A message from Miss Canada!

Her name is Denise, and she asks if we could chat later tonight.

My stomach lurches.

Will she run away when she finds out I'm disabled?

And is Canada really the way out for me?

The prospect of an actual date across the border becomes elephant-sized, looming. I go back to Miss Canada's profile. Cheryl seemed great, but there are certainly other fish in the Vermont sea.

I realize that in my hurry to check important dating criteria, like cuteness and the appearance of good mental health, I'd forgotten to see where in Canada the woman lives.

Back to her profile.

Montreal.

So, is it true? Canadians certainly seem better off than Americans, but can I really imagine myself living in Quebec, becoming a citizen, having children who speak French? Montreal is also a city, and I had decided long ago that urban living was not for me after visiting New York and Boston, and having multiple panic attacks during both trips. Burlington is manageable and my apartment building remote enough that there's an abundance of birds, trees, and blue sky. And a welcome absence of traffic, construction, and human beings.

I look up some basic facts. Everyone has healthcare. Daycare is subsidized and costs parents seven dollars a day. College is free for residents and university practically so. Apartment rents are much lower in Montreal than in Burlington.

But Montreal. French-speaking Montreal. And a French-speaking woman.

It's just a conversation, says the brave voice.

I know in my heart I won't have a chance at a healthy family without services. Wellness is what enabled me to climb out from under my low-functioning life. And without the Affordable Care Act, I would end up back with my mom.

I pick up my phone and message Denise my phone number.

Chapter 10

The day is the first warm one we've had, but I manage to get through it with just two handkerchiefs. That evening at home, after scarfing down some sweet-and-sour chicken leftovers for supper, I flip open my sketchpad and start drawing.

One. Two. Three. Four. Five.

After ten minutes of the birch tree and a flying squirrel, I put down pad and pencil and trot down to my utility closet. Grab the vacuum. Start on the living room rug. I spend twenty minutes, going over and over each patch, making sure the micro specks of dust and cat litter are gone. I shut it down to get a drink of water and the phone rings. I stop, check my phone. An area code I don't recognize.

"Hello?"

"Eu, may I speak with Audrey please?"

The French accent.

"Yeah, that's me."

"This is Denise from SheLovesHer. How are you?"

Startled. And something else. Charmed?

"Good!" My voice is too shiny. "Thanks for responding to my wink."

She laughs. "Internet dating is bizarre. I did it a few times since I broke up with my last lover."

Lover?!?

"Maybe you can tell me about you."

Now it's a job interview.

"Uh, well, I'm a visual artist, and I make books and collages. For work, I do graphic design, and I also teach theatre. I used to be an actor, but it was too hard on the pocketbook and the nerves."

"I love theatre. Why was it hard on your nerves?"

I wonder if I can dig the hole any deeper in the first three minutes of the conversation.

"Oh you know, lots of emotions. I'm more of an introvert."

"Did you hear of the writer Michel Tremblay? He's my favourite."

Who?

"The name sounds familiar. What does he write about?"

"Family and love relations."

A brontosaurus-sized pause.

Then, Denise cracks up.

"This is the part I am not good at, especially in English."

My diaphragm lets go, and I join Denise in the laugh.

"Me too. I wish I could sketch instead of talk. I'm so much better with pictures than words."

"What kind of pictures do you like to make?"

We keep talking—for an hour. Ninety minutes. Two hours.

"I saw you live in Vermont. Just to say, I never thought about living outside Quebec."

"It's a little early to talk about that, isn't it?" Could she know about my plot?

I pace.

Silence.

Then, I open my mouth. "I feel open to moving." Is it possible for a bellybutton to sweat?

"Really? Immigration is something serious."

I'm quiet. Such a big word, immigration.

Ignoring it seems like the ideal approach. "So, what do you do for work?" Hopefully she has a job.

"I'm a juvenile parole officer."

Pause. My mother, as a professional foster parent, has frequent encounters with parole officers. The stories I've heard about them have been less than flattering.

But I don't want to talk about Mom. "Sounds like hard work."

"Yes, but I like it. Most kids have so difficult backgrounds, and I can help them change their lives. I like to be part of that."

We somehow segue into what we love in romance. For Denise, it's preparing an elaborate and delectable meal with a fully decorated table. I talk about hand-drawn personal comics, a bouquet of papier-mâché roses, handcrafted perfume. Then I realize I just discarded three potential gift ideas in one breath.

What on earth am I doing. Canada. And I don't even know if Denise is pretty in real life.

I talk a little about my family and Leto. Denise talks about her kick-boxing class, her garden, her work friends.

I get brave. "What would your perfect relationship look like?"

She laughs. "Perfection, this is aiming high, n'est-ce pas?"

Denise is warm. I smile, imagining those bad kids melting down in front of her eyes.

"Well, whatever it means to you," I say.

Another pause.

"I think...well, for sure a shared home, a house perhaps. Sleeping together because we want to, not because one of us is needy."

"Did one of your exes call you needy because you wanted to sleep together?" I smile as I say it, imagining Jessica high fiving me.

She laughs. "You listen well, Audrey. Do you like to sleep with your lover?"

That word again.

"Well, kind of. It's nice when it works, I guess." Too early to talk about insomnia and other closet-dwelling skeletons.

"Oh, also in this perfect relationship, cooking and visiting other countries and going to concerts and plays. And we would be very silly."

"You like being silly?" Denise seems so serious.

"Mais oui. Do you find this strange?"

"God no, the opposite. My friend Jessica and I are so silly people tell us we're impossible to be around."

"What kind of a friend is Jessica?"

"Well, she's straight. We met in this program we're both in. Er, were in. But going back to the perfect relationship. For me, there would definitely be kids. At least one biological."

Denise pauses. "I like working with teenagers. I never imagined myself as a parent."

"I always dreamed about getting pregnant."

Silence.

Denise says, "I might be open in the right circumstance."

A dollhouse-sized window of hope cracks open.

Denise then tells me stories about the kids she's worked with for the past fifteen years: the anorexic girl who knifed the classmate who had bullied her, the Cree teenager who was wrongly accused of raping his white next-door neighbour, the triplets whose parents had died out in the woods hunting, and the kids who managed to stay under the radar for nearly a year, who paid for food with money stolen from teachers and other students at school. I send her a link to my graphic design website. I tell her about my exes, how Celeste initiated a lawsuit over the cat, how Callie went on welfare as a political act.

Denise laughs a lot. Which makes me smile.

When we hang up, I feel blood pumping through my body like a newly melted spring stream. I run up and down the stairs. Leto stares at me from the sofa. Then I dash upstairs one last time, throw myself on the bed, and look at the ceiling, panting and grinning.

My jaw aches. Realization: I just smiled for three hours straight on the phone with a beautiful woman. From Canada.

Chapter 11

The next day, I see my psychiatrist, Dr. Terrance, in the morning. "Tell me about your week."

I think about Denise and Canada.

"So-so. Sleep isn't great, but I've only had one panic attack since last week. Not sure if tapering the daytime dose is affecting my nights."

"It might be. But I have a new idea." He whips out his prescription pad and scribbles something down. "Take this an hour before bed with a snack. Shouldn't be any side effects. See if the sleep improves. If it does, you can start tapering again in a few days."

We map out a new tapering schedule, and he gives me the prescription with the one new med and a second with the three old ones.

On the way home from school, I buy a calling card with a special rate for Canada. I come inside, pull off my boots, and scratch Leto between the ears, using all my willpower to not check my phone. I take off my sweater, turtleneck, and bra, and then I cave. I look at my phone, and there it is: a message from Denise. "Hope your day is a good one."

My hands start sweating. I slide my Star of David up and down on its chain.

I tell Denise I was adopted, and on Wednesday, I drop hints about my disability.

"I should probably tell you that I'm kind of... sensitive."

"That's a good quality, I think."

"Well, not always."

"What do you mean?"

I think. "Let's just say I have a rich emotional life."

"I think this is great. Sometimes I don't even know what I feel. But I do cry at videos about animals."

I chuckle and exhale, quietly. Bullet dodged. "Are you afraid of mice? Or snakes?"

"Actually, mice and snakes are fine, but spiders and bats terrify me."
We talk about rural life in North America and its various critters.
Nothing more serious. Not yet.

I want to ask Denise out, but my mouth and tongue can't seem to manage it.

On Thursday, I find the words. In what turns out to be our shortest phone call yet, Denise says she already has plans for the weekend. I stay cool on the phone, wish her a fun time, but when I hang up, my insides are tangled.

Trembling, I text Jessica, who invites me to sleep over on Saturday.

*

It's raining, so we decide to watch *Jurassic Park* for the fourteenth time and make Hawaiian pizza and chocolate milkshakes.

I mix the flour and water, and Jessica chops the pineapple and ham. It's almost enough to distract me from thinking about Denise.

"Everything was going great until I told her about my rich emotional life. I'm sure she figured it out. I'm such an idiot." I stick my hands in the bowl and start mushing.

"Maybe she's going out with another woman from the ad. Maybe she met that woman first." Jessica pops a piece of pineapple in her mouth.

I keep kneading the dough. "How could it not be a rejection? I asked her out, and she said no. If you're interested, you don't say you're busy. You say, 'Not now, but how about next weekend?' If you're interested, you say what you're doing, like you're taking your Aunt Matilda to the insect museum, or you have to go watch your niece's miniature horse competition, but if you have a date, you say you're busy or that you have plans. She said she had plans."

"You're killing my fun, Meyerwitz," says Jessica as she puts the chopped ham and pineapple on the counter and starts shredding the cheese.

We get the food made. We eat and scream at the dinosaurs and cuddle up with the blanket. I do my best to push Denise into the recesses of my mind. I take my evening meds with my milkshake.

"Those the new ones?"

"Yup. But could be two weeks before I feel anything."

We stare at the screen as the guy on the toilet gets eaten by the T-rex. Then Jessica pauses the movie and looks at me.

"You're counting."

"Sorry." I give her a toothy grin. Sometimes I have no idea that I'm speaking the numbers out loud instead of in my head.

"Shush. Does Denise want kids?"

"Says she's open to it."

Then I remember.

"Hey, did I tell you I talked to Mom? She's actually coming. Here. To visit me!"

"Really? Who's going to watch the three-ring circus while she's gone?"

"Freddy and Natascha. He has to do a few days of research in Albany, and she's between jobs so they said they would come. For a whole week!"

We talk about the visit and some possible activities we could do when she comes.

"Ben 'n Jerry's? Too mainstream?" asks Jessica. We check our phones. Lots of spring events, and I start collecting URLs. Lilac Festival. International Food Fair.

Jessica looks up. "What about a tour of independent bookstores?"

I make a face.

She sticks out her tongue. "This is for Martha, silly. You don't even have to look at the books." I know she's right, but I return to my phone. Buffet brunch by the students of the New England Culinary Institute in Montpelier. Art Hop in Burlington's South End.

I look up. "It's fine if you have other stuff to do. I don't need a date to hang out with my mother." The word "date" brings my thoughts back to Denise, and I start counting again. Jessica squeezes my hand without taking her eyes off her phone. We find a few other possibilities for Mom's visit and then return to the movie.

Before I leave, I remember that next week, the last week of June, is the second anniversary of Jessica's brother Max's death.

"Are you doing anything with your family on Tuesday?" I try to sound casual, unintrusive. Jessica gets up and starts clearing dishes.

"I wanted to go to the gravesite all together. Christopher is flying in, but just for one night because he has back-to-back shows the next day. The substitute drummer has a broken wrist so he can't get out of it. That's my bro...always the hero for other people." She rinses her plate for way too long.

I get up and bring in the cups and napkins. "How about your dad?" I grab the sponge and start wiping the counter.

"He's got two pregnant cows who could give birth any minute now, so he probably won't make it. If Dad doesn't need her, Eve will come. And of course Mom, well, being Mom, she hasn't returned my calls for at least a month."

I try to catch her eye, see her expression. She won't look at me.

"Anything I can do?"

Jessica picks up the last slice of pizza. "You could come over and make my bath and read me *Ramona the Brave* like last year." She stuffs the triangle into her mouth with her head tilted back, a piece of ham dangling near her chin. I can't help smiling.

"Ramona, bubbles, whatever you want, I'll be there."

"That'd be good, Meyerwitz." Her words are barely coherent through the chewed pizza. She gives me a tiny smile, first with mouth closed, then wide open. I shriek and chase her around the kitchen island, wielding a deadly pizza crust.

Chapter 12

May arrives, and Wellness officially finishes. Everyone cries, and the leaders are apologetic. Nobody expected this. The program had gotten so much positive press as well as solid statistics about our reduced medical costs and increased functioning. We had all assumed we'd at least have another three years.

I decide to return to SheLovesHer. I had given up on Denise, but on Tuesday, she calls. She had gone out with another woman a few times, but it hadn't worked out. She suggests we meet in Montreal the following weekend. I tell her I have plans but that I would see if I could reschedule them.

I look at the clock: lunchtime. Jessica should be in the teachers' lounge after a faculty meeting. I pick up my cell and text Jessica, our secret "call me back if you're free" dialogue.

Meow.

Ssssss.

She calls right back.

I grin at the wall. "Guess who wants to go out with me?"

"I told you, Meyerwitz. That's great! What are you going to do?"

"I didn't say yes. I said I had plans."

Jessica clucks. "You're playing games? Already? What are you, twelve?"

"So, she just gets to control everything, and I'm supposed to come running like a lapdog? I don't think so."

"Okay, so call her tomorrow and say you can't that weekend, but the next one's free."

"But I want to meet her soon. I just want to do it."

"Then just do it, Audrey. What's the big deal?"

I shake my head and feel tears coming. "Forget it. I'll call you later. Smooches."

"Do you want me to come over after school?"

"No, it's okay. See you tomorrow morning."

"Smooches."

I pick up a pencil and my doodle pad and sketch two female figures. One touches the other's face.

How much can you learn about someone on a Zoom call?

I decide to call Denise.

"It's a pleasure to hear your voice!"

Words drown in my throat.

"I just wanted to say that I changed my plans."

Silence.

"Alors, thank you?"

She hates me.

I say, "Do you still want to go out this weekend?"

"Of course! Oh, yes, now I understand. This is wonderful!"

I ask, "What should we do?" It's her city.

"Is there something you haven't done ever in Montreal that you'd enjoy?"

I freeze, wondering if I had unintentionally misled Denise into thinking I was cosmopolitan enough to pop up for a weekend and take in some culture on a regular basis. The truth is, I'd been to Montreal exactly twice since moving to Burlington, and once was a full day at La Ronde, the amusement park just south of the city.

"Actually, I've always wanted to see the Holocaust Museum," I say.

More silence.

"Something more upbeat, perhaps?"

Stupid, stupid Audrey.

"Yeah, sure. How about Sunday brunch? Actually, Monday is a holiday here, so maybe we should make a reservation. Do you know a good place?"

She does, a little underground place called Café Fruit Folie. I check the weather, and the prediction is cold but sunny, meaning dry roads. We say goodbye, and I lie down on my bed. Leto jumps up and settles on my belly.

How long has it been since I'd had a vacation? I need a break, a treat. My trip doesn't have to be just because of Denise. She can be one small part of it.

I think about my new credit card. Still one thousand dollars left on my line of credit.

I hop online and do some research. I find a cute and inexpensive women's inn on Airbnb and reserve a room for three nights on Memorial Day weekend. There's an interesting photo exhibition, and I buy tickets to a new dance theatre piece about capitalism and the apocalypse. A nice getaway, full of culture and yummy food. And maybe, just maybe, the start of a new romance...and a new life.

*

"It's not about Denise, and it's not about Canada," I say to Jessica as we walk down the hall towards Immaculate Heart's exit on Friday afternoon. I had come to talk with Sister Laura about doing summer theatre camps, and Jessica had waited for me. "It's self-care. Some time away."

She smiles and shakes her head as her high heels click on the tiled floor. "You slay me, Meyerwitz," she says, pushing the three braids behind her ear. "Remember, safe sex."

I shush her, looking around for kids and nuns. Jessica throws her book tote over her shoulder, winks, and waves at me as she pushes the main door open.

When I get home, I immediately begin mining my closet for the perfect date outfit. I grab my butt-clinging purple jeans and start looking through my drawers for a top, something cool but not too dressy, since we'd be meeting for brunch.

I find a button-down shirt and a purple satin tank top and try them on with my newsboy cap.

I do a few poses and flash a smile to the mirror. Might appeal to someone. I grab Jessica's purple sweater in case it's chilly and tie it around my waist.

I restock my pill organizer and throw my cosmetic tote, pajamas, and change of clothes into my weekend bag. Leto's bowl is overflowing with extra Kibbles, and I give her backup water. She rubs my legs, and I kiss her before grabbing my bomber jacket, checking the burners, turning on the kitchen light, checking the burners again, and locking up.

The day is bright as polished silver, the roads clear and empty. I jump into my Honda Fit, pop in my iPod, and find my favourite driving music: Abba's *Gold*.

With tunes like "Dancing Queen" and "Take a Chance on Me," the two-hour drive passes quickly. I get to the Airbnb and meet the owner, who unfortunately is a smoker. I almost consult my phone for an alternative. But it's Memorial Day, and plus the place is packed with kitschy film memorabilia that keeps me gazing at the walls. In my room, there's a signed headshot of Judy Garland, curtains made with images from an Ed Wood film, and a framed still from an episode of *Deep Space Nine.*

Friday evening, I go to a hip café, Le Cagibi, that I read about online. I walk up to the counter and order squash soup and a veggie burger. When the food is ready, I grab a table, gazing at the velvety couches, the old-fashioned moldings, the 'zines spread around the built-in bookshelves, and the other patrons. As is my habit, I sketch snippets of impressions in between bites: the waiter just as he drops a cranberry muffin, twin sisters having a staring contest, and a redhead with piercings all the way up her ear cartilage, on both sides, who keeps covering her mouth as her friend tells her a long story in French.

When I leave, the air is crisp, and the passing crowds are delicious eye candy.

Saturday, I eat Portuguese barbecue at a corner dive and visit the Musée des Beaux Arts. Everything seems so chic compared to Burlington, where residents all look like they've been outfitted by L.L. Bean. The outdoor staircases, the painted bricks, the neighbourhood playgrounds and parks, it all leaves me clumsy, bumping into parking meters, curbs, and a dachshund because my eyes are fixed on some startling sight or fashionable person. This city, which feels so European, is practically in my backyard, and I'd ignored it for most of the ten years I'd lived in Vermont. I hold my head up and start feeling hip, walking amid this garden of chic and its cool inhabitants.

By the time I get back to the Airbnb on Saturday evening, I'm ready for a soak in the clawfoot tub. The owner left me a single package of lilac-scented bubble bath powder, and I sprinkle it into the hot rushing water. Even if my plans for the weekend were originally made because of Denise, it's turned into an actual getaway, the kind of treat I never was able to afford before starting my business.

Can I imagine living here? As bad as things feel in the US, the culture in Quebec is very different. But I bring my mind back to the present, stepping into the tub and feeling my muscles let go as I slide into the bubbles.

*

Sunday morning, I wake up with my alarm. I'd slept for nearly five hours straight, so I feel reasonably rested. Wondering if it's the Canadian air or my new night medication, I do some yoga, double check my phone for directions to Café Fruit Folie, and triple check my calendar for the time I'm supposed to meet Denise. It's a short walk to the restaurant in the Plateau neighbourhood, bright sunshine but chilly, even for May. I put on my date outfit and some black eyeliner. Hands shaking, I manage to pin my hair back with a silver barrette. I wonder what Denise will be wearing and whether her top will reveal some cleavage. I scold myself for being so superficial.

The walk to the restaurant takes me less than five minutes. I look around outside Café Fruit Folie and don't see Denise. I do see a menu posted on the wall, and I start trying to decode the French. A few minutes later, I feel a tap on my shoulder.

I turn, startled. It's her.

She leans in to kiss my left cheek and, before I have time to react, she leans in on the right. The two-sided kiss! My stomach does a little dance move. Denise's cheeks are ruddy, and she's wearing a blue puffer jacket with a white knit hat. She's also taller than I'd expected.

And way hotter.

We go inside. Denise tells the host something in French, and soon, we're sitting at a narrow table with clear vases of wispy yellow daisies. I ask if the waiter speaks English, and he laughs and says of course. Denise orders black coffee, and I ask for decaf with soymilk and sugar. When he comes back, he brings the coffees and menus with breakfast items described in both French and English. I say a silent prayer of thanks in case anybody's listening and choose the waffles with strawberry preserves and Beyond Sausages.

Denise has the same accent she's had during our phone conversations, but it's easier for me to understand her in person. Her auburn hair glows in a ray of light streaming through the window. Her eyes are golden brown and curl up in the corners. I imagine reaching out and brushing my fingertips against her smooth cheeks.

We talk before we order, after we order, and when our orders come. We talk, apologetically, with full mouths. We talk while trying to calculate the bill, and we talk as we grab our coats to leave.

My theatre ticket is for 8:00 p.m., and it's just 1:30 p.m. when we leave the café.

"I don't know if you have time, but there is a cemetery nearby, lovely to walk in," says Denise, pointing. "If you're not too cold. I walk in any kind of weather."

The Holocaust Museum was too morbid, but a cemetery is fine?

"Sure, sounds good." I imagine impressing Denise with how easygoing I am and manage to refocus on the beauty of the city as we walk.

We trudge up to the cemetery and continue talking. The conversation becomes punctuated with moments of silence as we push our way through snow mounds, noting names on headstones: Pierre Fontaine, Alain Couture, Genevieve Dion. Occasionally there's an English name, but most are French. I ask Denise why, and she says the cemeteries were as segregated as the living people were.

"In my parents' generation, it wasn't even possible to get served in French at a store or a restaurant. It's only since the Quiet Revolution that French is the official language, and we have now language laws."

"My God. That sounds intense. Were French Canadians discriminated against?"

Denise looks me.

"Don't they teach you about Canada in Vermont?"

My cheeks turn rosy. I realize I know nothing about the Quebec culture. I'd just assumed Canadians were pretty much like us. She tells me about the oppressive Catholic church, about how English people were the owners and employers and French people were second-class citizens, and about the Quiet Revolution in the 1960s when Quebecois people rose up and demanded that French be Quebec's official language, meaning freedom from the oppression of the English-speaking owning class.

"It sounds a lot like our history in the US. The Jews from Eastern Europe."

She stops walking. "How do you think it's the same?"

I'm in deep over my head. "Well, just that we were an oppressed minority until we, you know, kind of fought for our rights."

Something passes over her face like a gust of wind. "But for us, it was our language. Our mother tongue. Jewish people could just blend in, once the second generation was born anyway."

We look at one another and my skin suddenly feels loose, like a big mansion I'd just moved into and can't find my way around. My mouth fills with sludge and my tongue is MIA. Then I think of my great-grandmother.

"The six million who died in the camps couldn't blend in."

Her expression changes. But then she turns around and silently walks out of the cemetery.

When we get to the metro and I'm about to leave to go back to the Airbnb, she gives me a hug goodbye, a surprise.

"I...I thought I offended you," I say.

She smiles. "This is a big topic, these identities. It's complicated. This doesn't scare me, Audrey Meyerwitz."

Her eyes look like sun-drenched molasses cookies in the afternoon sunshine. I feel myself start to lean in to kiss her but remember Wellness and stop. I look at my red boots and grab my necklace. "I...I had fun too."

*

The dance theatre show about the apocalypse is fast-paced, visually arresting, and smartly acted, but I'm distracted by Denise's image. Her honey-coloured eyes, her laugh lines, her soft cheeks, her strong physical presence that says, "I'm here. You can trust me. I'm paying attention." With a French accent.

I drive back to Burlington on Monday morning, singing songs from my childhood, "Free to Be You and Me," the Peanut Butter and Jelly song, a camp tune called "Today." As the melodies vibrate through my body, my mind conjures up pictures of Denise. When I stop for gas, I text Jessica.

Amazing weekend. You'll ❤ her.

Chapter 13

The next morning, I sketch some ads for a new client marketing a solar-powered breast pump, and then I teach my theatre class in the afternoon. On my way out, I bump into Jessica who's just leaving a staff meeting.

"Hey, Miss Romance," she says, elbowing me. "When do I get the details?"

"I have a deadline tomorrow. Oh, and Mom called, surprise, surprise. She cancelled her visit because Ian got suspended."

"Jesus. I thought this time..." My friend gives me a soft look.

I try to ignore it. "Text me when you get home."

"You okay?"

I nod. She squeezes my arm as she goes. I blink back tears and watch her walk to her car, an orange Subaru station wagon. Jessica and her last boyfriend painted it when she bought it from her neighbour a few years ago. She said she wanted to feel excited each time she left her house to go anywhere. I remember visiting Max's grave in that car, how quiet Jessica was, how she talked to Max while we were there, catching him up on her life, telling him how many days of sobriety she had, how happy she was to have an orange car, and how she had found a new friend who was like a sister.

When I get home, I pick up the mail, give Leto a pat, and grab a peach. After my snack, I do some yoga, but halfway through I start crying. I grab my baby blanket and lie down on my mat, looking at my tree. I stay on the floor and skip supper.

But I don't connect with Jessica that evening because Denise calls first. I'm surprised; Denise seemed too reserved to call just a few days after our date. We also talk several times that same week, but we don't make plans to see one another again. Not yet.

*

At the end of the weekend, I invite Denise to Burlington, and she gives me an enthusiastic yes. She tells me she'll take the bus, since she doesn't have a car.

On the Friday of her arrival, my stomach is iron, but I'm not shaking or losing my words. I managed the day before with a slightly lower daytime dose, and my body is relieved today not to have to work so hard at being calm.

I take a shower and pick out my outfit carefully again. White jeans with patches, purple tee shirt, simple ponytail. I toss my bomber jacket in the back seat just in case the temperature drops fifteen degrees while I'm waiting for the bus. You never know.

It's early when I arrive at the station, but the bus is already there. *One. Two. Three. Four.* My breathing slows with the counting. Where's Denise? A woman in a burgundy fleece and sunglasses waves at me and grins, picks up her bag, and heads towards the car. It's her. Denise is still smiling as she opens the passenger door.

"Aren't you hot?" I say as I pop the trunk and grab her suitcase.

"Layers. It's good to be prepared." We get into the car, Denise double kisses me and then immediately unzips her fleece. She takes it off, revealing a low-cut black tank top underneath.

"How was the ride?" I'm trying not to look at Denise's chest but failing. She's wearing a musky perfume that isn't helping me be a gentlewoman.

"There was one lady on the bus with a hijab, so of course we all had to get off and go through the big interview. You Americans talk about how free you are here, but you have much more racism than we do." She adjusts the seat to accommodate her long legs.

"I know." I'm embarrassed. "It's pretty bad right now, especially for Muslims."

I remember I'd picked up a rose for Denise on the way and thrown it into the backseat with my jacket.

"I got this for you." I hand the flower to Denise without ceremony, hoping she wouldn't find it silly. She looks at the flower, and then at me.

"Merci!" She sniffs and smiles. "Mmm. How did you know white is my favourite colour for flowers?"

Then she leans in and kisses me, this time on the mouth. Her lips are soft and sweet, like sponge cake.

Just as I start moving my tongue, I peel apart from her and quickly start the car. There's a pulsing between my legs, and my temples are moist. What I really want to do is park with Denise behind the bus station and stay there for hours, discovering what's underneath her black top.

When we get home, I introduce Denise to Leto, who threads through Denise's legs, and I show her around my apartment, which sparkles from days of organizing and cleaning. Denise admires my Pippin poster and the framed picture of the cat, but she takes a minute and looks around. "I thought you were an artist," she says with a funny smile.

"I am an artist," I say, confused.

"Your walls are so bare. I expected more...colour, I suppose."

I wonder how I could tell her about claustrophobia, how when there's too much happening visually in a space, my body short-circuits. My cheeks redden, so I don't reply, but instead I bring her bag upstairs to the office, and I start unfolding the futon.

She follows me, and then she scrunches her eyebrows and puts one hand on a hip. "This is where you want me to *sleep*?"

Is she joking? "I just didn't want to assume anything. It's only our second date." I stop messing with the futon and look at her.

"I suppose, oui. Mais, all the time we've been talking, I think this is more like four or perhaps even five dates?" Denise lowers her head and raises those thick eyebrows.

Math is not my specialty, nor is making good decisions about sex. "Well," I say, locating my tongue, "how about you leave your stuff here, and we go hang out on my bed. You can decide where you want to sleep later."

I stick out my elbow, Denise slides her arm through, and I lead her to the bedroom. When we reach the bed, Denise stops and turns. She puts her hands on my waist. Then she moves her mouth to my ear. She whispers, "Do you want me?" I take Denise's face in my hands and kiss that mouth, long and tender. Then, remembering, I pull the shades and hit the light switch. I clap and my fake candle turns itself on. Denise giggles. I push her down on the bed. She takes her pinkie and slowly traces the outline of her salmon-pink lips. Another current shoots through my body, and Denise reaches up to unbutton my jeans. "Oh, no you don't, not yet," I say, smiling. I lie on top of her and start kissing her again. Soon our tongues are entwined. My hips press into hers, and I lean on one elbow, stroking her long neck with my other hand. I'm overcome with desire, and I already want to press my naked flesh into hers. My hand travels down past her neck, then I fondle one breast, so full, and then the other. My breath quickens as I feel Denise's nipple harden in my palm. I reach down, inside her panties, between her legs, and find her clit in so much wetness.

We don't stop until it's dark and way past our bedtimes.

Chapter 14

The next morning, I wake up first after a whopping six hours of sound sleep, and I tiptoe downstairs to make my decaf and Denise's regular. I put the mugs on the tray Mom had given me when I moved out. I grab the white rose I had given Denise and set it next to the mugs and then carry the tray up to the bedroom. Leto follows close behind me. Denise is sitting up, naked under my yellow sheets. Her hair is full of static and her mascara smudged. I want to jump back into bed and start kissing her all over again, but I find some restraint.

"Bon matin," I say, handing her a cup. "One regular black coffee, house special."

"Somebody is paying attention. She knows on the second date how I like my coffee." She takes the mug and gives me a look that can only be about one thing. I have a body memory of her being on top of me and reaching my mouth up to lick her breast.

She seems to read my mind. "You like my body, don't you, dirty girl?"

"I have to admit, I was a little surprised with the, uh, talking."

"Why?"

I blink. "Well, it's—it's your second language. And personally, I'm more of an introvert, so it's not really something I do."

She sips her coffee. "I dreamed you came while you were fondling my tits. Or did that really happen?"

I laugh. "No, I think it was you." I set down my coffee and start kissing her again. When her lips meet mine, something splits apart inside me. I reach for her breasts with both hands, and a sound comes up through my throat. Denise laughs then groans as my hand travels between her legs. We get lost in each other's bodies until it's clear we need a second coffee break.

"There's something I should probably tell you," I say, putting my mug down and bracing myself.

"What?" She leans up on one elbow, hair falling around her face. What a beauty. This is where I find out it's only a dream.

"Remember when we first talked, and I said I had a rich emotional life?"

"Yes."

"Well, it's more than that. I'm—I have a disability. A psychiatric disability. I have an anxiety disorder."

She looks at me like she's waiting for something.

"That's it. That's what I needed to tell you. What do you think?"

"I don't think anything. That's not a disability. Lots of people have anxiety."

"No, it's really a disability. I have a diagnosis, a psychiatrist, I had an individualized education program in school—"

"Lots of kids have IEPs. I've seen some in my office, and lots of them are great. It doesn't mean a thing."

"How can you say it doesn't mean a thing? You're a parole officer. All the kids you work with are criminals."

"So, I suppose you'll tell me now that you're a criminal?" She's smiling. I'm sweating.

"No, but I've had a psychiatrist my whole life. I've been on medication on and off, but mostly on since I was twelve. I receive disability benefits. Services. I'm not like normal people."

She laughs. "I'm not like normal people either. Who is like normal people?"

"What I'm saying is that normal things trigger panic attacks. Normal things like crowds and reading and new social situations and being touched in certain ways. Maybe you'll have second thoughts about being with me. Are you having second thoughts?"

"Of course not. Audrey, what is this about?"

"Well, it's a lot to take on. Maybe you'd rather be with someone without that kind of baggage."

"I don't want to be with 'someone.' I want to be with you. And we all have baggage." She sips her coffee. "Does your mom think you're disabled?"

"She's the one who got me help and thank goodness. She got me diagnosed, and she got me services. If it hadn't been for her, I would have never made it through school, or probably through childhood."

"That's a big statement. I don't look at you and see someone who's deficient."

"That's not what a disability is."

"That's what the word means, at least to me as a francophone. It means you aren't able, and that isn't true."

"It's a difference. My brain is different than yours because the chemicals aren't balanced right."

"Well, to me, you're you, and I like you as you are. Now will you put that coffee down and come caress my breasts?"

*

When the sun starts to sink behind the mountains, we break for food. I whip up some scrambled eggs with kale and garlic and cheese, English muffins with butter, strawberries, and a green salad. "Mmmm," Denise says. "Merci."

She's cute in her extra-large men's tee shirt and bikini underwear. Two bites into my English muffin, my phone rings. It's Jessica. "I have to get this, sorry," I say to Denise, asking Jessica to hold. I go upstairs to my bedroom with my phone and shut the door.

"So, is she there?" There's a smile in Jessica's voice that normally wouldn't bother me.

"Yeah, actually we're in the middle of breakfast."

Silence.

"So, why did you pick up?"

I don't know. "I wanted to at least say hi."

"Okay, hi."

"Hi."

I hear her breathing.

"Can I come over?"

I think about it. It's our second date, technically.

"Let's do it next time, if there is a next time, which I don't even know right now."

She laughs. "You slept with her, I hope?"

I don't answer. Something inside me feels sharp and unkind.

"How about I call you tomorrow night after she leaves?"

"Sure, Meyerwitz, I'm just planning for the week and watching reruns of *Mystery Science Theater 3000*. Always time for an interruption."

"Thanks for understanding, Jess."

"Smooches." I hear her waiting.

I say nothing, press end, and sit on the edge of my bed. My skin is tingly, and my breath shallow.

I put the phone on my bed. *One. Two. Three. Four. Five. Six.* When I'm in decent enough shape, I go downstairs to the kitchen table.

"Who was it?"

"Jessica, my silly friend, remember?"

Denise smiles. "The straight woman."

I look at her and don't smile. "She's really straight. And there's nothing between us other than taking care of each other's wounded soul."

"Wounded soul? Wow, that's poetic."

My voice rises in pitch. "We met at Wellness. We support each other. When my last girlfriend dumped me, and I had no money and no place to live, she took me in. She loaned me money. She helped me get my teaching job and find my apartment. It's like having a sister."

She sips her coffee, gazing out the window.

"She's been there for me more than anyone ever has."

Denise looks at me like she's searching for something.

"Why was she in Wellness?"

"She's a recovering alcoholic. Four years, two months, and six days sober." The words come out as if Jessica had spoken them, my vocal chords, her timbre.

"So why did you close your bedroom door to talk to her?"

Hot blood rushes into my face. "Look, it's a really important friendship, especially because I'm not close to my family. Jessica's there for me, and I'm there for her. It's simple and it's healthy. And," I say as I reach for her hand and look into her eyes, "I think you two will really like each other."

Leto jumps into my lap. Denise's face changes, and she blinks away tears. "Sorry."

I pull my chair over. "Did someone cheat on you?"

She grabs a tissue from the box on the table. "Someones. I am attracted to people who are attracted to women who aren't me."

My eyes widen. "But you're gorgeous. How could any self-respecting lesbian not be faithful to you?"

She laughs. "Maybe because I am a parole officer. Being around all those bad girls all the time."

"I thought you said most of them weren't bad."

"It's just play. I can't say why, but three of my four major relation-ships ended because my girlfriends cheated on me."

I put my arm around her. "You have nothing to worry about with me. I have a lot of problems, but cheating isn't one of them." Then I kiss her gently on the cheek.

She looks at me. "Tu es vraiment belle, Audrey Meyerwitz."

I don't understand the words, but I do understand that we probably would have a third date.

Chapter 15

S unday evening arrives, and it's hard for us to separate. After I drop her at the bus station, I text my mom.

Up for a chat?

She writes that she has to deal with one of my brothers but that she could talk tomorrow. So, I go upstairs to my office and Zoom with Jessica. I tell her about the weekend, and things feel back to normal. Neither of us mentions the weird phone call.

The next day when I'm eating supper, I phone Denise.

"So, I'm thinking of coming out to my mom," I tell her.

"No small talk tonight," she teases. "I would have thought you'd be out to your family."

I explain how it is, with Mom and all her foster kids and my five adopted siblings. "My mom's a save-the-world kind of woman. It makes her great in a crisis but not so great in regular life."

"Did you ever think about coming out to her when you were younger?"

I tell Denise that, in fact, I had almost told her on break after my first semester of college. It was the first time I was in love—and tormented. Sherri was my roommate, a field hockey player with tanned skin, black hair, and crazy curves. Although we had become friends that first semester, Sherri was clearly straight and had even "rushed" a sorority.

"Did she flirt with you in that annoying way straight women can do?"

"Honestly, she was from a conservative family, and the concept of our being naked together would never have crossed her mind." But it crossed my mind often back then, several times a day, French braiding her hair, listening to her tales of biology lab and sorority gossip. Sometimes I gave her massages to help her relax, and I would softly knead her neck muscles, then trace the outlines of her arms, soon moving over to her back.

"I can guess where your mind went next," says Denise.

"Yeah, but I'd never actually done it before. And, of course, I wouldn't have dared anyway. I'd have had twenty enormous fraternity guys hunting me down."

Break arrived, and Sherri was with her family at their North Dakota ranch. For New Year's Eve, Mom and her next door neighbour went out to some nonprofit fundraiser. My friends at home all had shimmery satin dresses and dates with boyfriends. I played with the dog, heated up a bowl of alphabet soup, and sat down in front of the TV. I watched Dick Clark in his silken bowtie, the performers on floats, throngs of people with paper hats, kazoos, and glitter makeup.

Then, tears.

I raided the liquor cabinet. Grabbed the bottle in front.

Chugged.

"Wait a minute," says Denise. "I thought you were against drinking."

"Not against; I just try not to make it a habit. That was the first and last time I've been drunk. After that, I just kept dating alcoholics, kind of like you with the cheaters."

I continued the story. At 2:00 a.m., I clutched the toilet bowl, stinking of vodka and vomit, skin wet with sweat, hair clumped and sticky. I heard the garage door open. Mom came upstairs and into the bathroom and rubbed my back while I continued barfing and crying. She pressed a cool washcloth against my forehead and told me everything would be okay. She fed me sips of cool water and stroked my forehead. She listened.

The next morning, I came downstairs, every cell throbbing. Mom was drinking coffee in her bathrobe; I busied myself making my decaf. She casually mentioned a New Year's Eve misadventure she once had herself with alcohol. Our eyes met for a brief but warm moment. I sat down next to her with my coffee and a weak smile while my siblings dribbled in.

"In the end, I was too afraid to tell her, because I needed her too much. So, I went back to school after break, still in the closet."

"And why now of all times?" Denise has this way of talking that makes me want to pay attention. A true seductress.

"I've met somebody pretty special, if you must know," I say in a low murmur.

"Well, is that so?"

"It is."

"You want to know what else is?" Her voice is a stand-up bass playing a solo. I know what's happening, and I step off the cliff anyway.

"What?"

"If you were here, I would take your hand and show you."

I lie down on my bed, unzip my jeans, and the conversation travels to places I've only dreamt about.

*

An hour after Denise and I hang up, my cell phone rings. I jump, body still raw.

Mom.

She's cool...all I need to do is say it. Then my mind flashes on Abigail, a lesbian from Wellness, whose parents had kicked her out of the house at sixteen when she came out to them. She had thought they would be cool, too.

Forgetting to count, I take a deep breath and swipe.

"How are things, Auddy?" The sound of a match lighting, Mom sucking in. Damn cigarettes.

"Okay." I think about telling her about my new medication and decide against it. "I mean, well, more than okay."

"More than okay? Mmmm, interesting." Another puff. There's a grin in her voice.

The phone battery is nearly empty. I grope around for my charger while trying to get the words out.

"Actually, I'm—I'm seeing someone. Like, dating."

Leto walks in. I plug the cord into the phone and into the wall. There's a pause on the other end. "Tell me more." She's still grinning. I hear it in her voice.

"I don't know if you're going to like it."

"Audrey Lynne, don't you know that your mother is a modern and open-minded woman? Tell me about your boyfriend! I want details."

I sit down on my bed near the outlet I've plugged my phone into. Leto jumps up. "I don't have a boyfriend, Mom. I have—a girlfriend."

The breath rushes out of me. There. Done.

"Really? A girlfriend. Well, I'll be damned." Her tone is the same, and she sounds genuinely surprised, not repulsed.

"You're not upset?" The cat is on my lap, purring.

"Is she the president of Exxon? Does she work for Walmart?"

"She's actually a probation officer. For kids."

"Wow," says Martha. "Well, I'll have lots to talk with her about. Good job, good values. That's all I care about. That and your happiness, of course. I'm really glad you told me."

I stroke Leto down her spine. My face is hot, but breathing is steadier.

Mom asks, "Does she want children?"

"She likes kids. I think she's open to it."

"Well, this is something you'll want to find out immediately."

Mom knows about my dream of having a family. We talk for a while. But she's spread thin and distracted, and soon she has to go help the boys with their homework.

"Auddy, I know your heart is beating a million miles an hour. I get it, but please know you're perfect with me, exactly as you are."

"Thanks Mom. I—"

She hangs up.

I lie back on my bed and feel grateful for my mother.

Chapter 16

Spring comes, and I meet Denise's older sister, Micheline, aka Mimi. She's shorter than Denise and older but built more muscular than curvy with short jet-black hair shaved above her ears. She's a successful chef at a fancy French restaurant downtown that Denise tells me all the time we have to try, that Mimi can feed us for half price. I ask Denise if she's married or anything, and Denise tells me she's never known her sister to be in a relationship. I wonder if she's asexual. When Mimi shakes my hand, she squeezes hard, avoiding my gaze. Denise says she's an introvert, even more than me, but that she has a huge heart. We play Skip-Bo on her three-season back porch and sip mojitos with a sprig of mint from her window herb garden.

July brings a family event, a poolside barbecue hosted by Denise's older brother Antoine, a tall and round jovial fellow with dark wavy hair and a full beard. He and his wife have four children between the ages of four and sixteen, so their house is not quiet. When we arrive, he gives me an enormous welcome with the Quebecoise two-cheek kiss and says, "Audrey, I have heard a lot about you. Grand plaisir de te rencontrer."

I've been practising the handful of French words and phrases I'd learned, so I'm able to say, "Moi aussi," but I'm still anxious. This brother is known in the family for making the best ribs, so the party is a favourite among Denise's family.

My girlfriend introduces me to her younger brother, Julian, and his baby and toddler daughters. They have the signature amber eyes, like Julian and Denise, and the baby is grinning and chortling at everybody who stops to coo at her, which is pretty much everybody who's there except Antoine's two teenagers, who are playing video games in the basement.

I'm able to chitchat with a few people individually in English, but when we gather at the giant table under the umbrella, the family speaks in its native tongue. My body stiffens, each muscle freezing up as I feel the conversation walls closing me out. It's a huge circle with words zooming back and forth like paper airplanes. For two hours, I'm quiet, only saying the occasional "oui," "moi aussi," or "non, pas maintenant." Sometimes the whole gang bursts into laughter, all at the same moment. I'm not sure if I should laugh with them, which is my inclination but dishonest, or ask for a translation, which I'm learning is Montreal's top way to be a party pooper.

My head throbs by the end of the evening.

I text Jessica.

Can I do this?

YES!!! Cheering u on.

*

Denise and I enjoy the summer with lots of time in bed. She's the first woman I've actually been able to sleep with, and waking up becomes warm and pleasurable instead of anxiety producing. We talk and play charades and listen to multiple versions of the same song, discussing the differences and our preferences. Denise loves the original Talking Heads' "This Must be the Place," citing loyalty to the original artist as key. I prefer Shawn Colvin's because her voice tenderizes the lyrics, the guitar riff evoking something fragile and hopeful.

I show her my drawings. She brings home bags full of books from work, since the library is next to her office: Maurice Sendak and *Better Homes and Gardens*, *French for Dummies* and an all-drawn anatomy book. I leave a blackout mask and a pair of earplugs at her place, in the little night-table drawer on "my" side of her bed. She leaves her electric toothbrush in my bathroom.

I subscribe to LearnFrenchOnline.com and start listening to thirty minutes a night when I'm not with Denise.

*

It's August, and Jessica and I are having supper at my place after a late afternoon run. "It's now clear there's been a third and a fourth and a fortieth date. It's time for me to meet Denise," she says as we eat veggie dogs and potato chips as a reward. "After all, I'm the Yenta."

"Do you even have a passport?"

"Why can't I meet her here? Audrey, for God's sake, just relax."

"We're more there than here is all."

64

Jessica cocks her head and reaches down to stroke the cat. "What are you scared of?"

I crunch a chip. "Nothing. It'll be fun. Actually, she'll be here this coming weekend. Maybe we could go to Muddy Waters?"

"How about I invite you two lovebirds to supper?"

My heart is beating fast, and I stare at Jessica's hand on the bun. She's redone her nails in chrome. "Uh, sure, I'll ask Denise." I take a bite and avoid her gaze.

Jessica leans forwards and speaks in a low tone. "If you have anything you need to talk to me about, please do. Like the Not Dogs, I will not bite."

I giggle and start to say something, then change my mind. "I got some Cherry Garcia for dessert. And I made shortbread cookies."

That night, I'm sleepless for the first time in months.

*

Saturday comes, and Denise is at my place, getting ready to go to Jessica's supper. "Help me pick my outfit," she says.

"Dress is casual, so whatever you have will be fine." I'm sitting on the bed as she unpacks her clothes. I'm in my black jeans, a stretchy black top, and Jessica's purple sweater. Denise takes out seven shirts and five pairs of pants.

"You don't have to stress about clothes," I tell her. "You look good in anything. Or nothing. Actually, better in nothing."

She flashes me a quick fake smile and returns to the task at hand. I've managed to catch up on sleep and am finding it exciting to watch my beautiful new girlfriend get dressed.

After thirty minutes of trying on outfits, she picks a rose-coloured silk tank top with daisies, white jean shorts, and strappy sandals. Her hair has been growing out since we met; I say nothing, wanting her to be free with her appearance, but I'm secretly happy it's now below her shoulders. "You look so pretty," I say. "Tout garni."

She laughs.

"What? Is that wrong?"

"It's all dressed but for pizza, not for women."

"I looked it up online." My cheeks burn.

"Mon amour, it's great, really. You're trying. This is what matters. And if you make a mistake like that, everyone in Montreal will just love you. The people who don't try are the ones who are hard for us."

She sits down on the bed next to me and gives me a slow soft kiss. "Now go do something else because you're distracting me."

When we get to Jessica's, there's a surprise: Her sister Eve's car is in the driveway.

"I thought we were three," Denise says, checking her pocket mirror and applying more lip-gloss.

"It's just her older sister, Eve. She lives in Middlebury, so she's around a lot. It was probably spontaneous. They're like that in Jessica's family. Eve is super easygoing. Oh, and she's gay."

We walk up to the building's entrance and buzz. Jessica opens the door. She's wearing a black miniskirt, a black Spandex tube top, and a chrome-colored headband.

"You said casual," I say, hugging her. My hands are shaking, and I hang on to her to steady them.

"I was going through my drawer and trying stuff on to see if I had anything to get rid of. Eve's always looking for hand-me-ups. You must be Denise." Jessica turns to my girlfriend. Just before politeness kicks in, something hard passes between them. But it's over before I can decode it.

"So nice to meet you, Jessica," Denise says, going in for the double kiss.

"Enchantée," says Jessica, all smiles. "I'm going back to my spana-kopita, and I can get you ladies some drinks if you like."

We put our coats in the closet and walk into the living room. Eve is sitting on the couch, dressed like I had thought everybody would have been: blue jeans with holes, a faded Middlebury tee shirt, bare feet.

She gives me a big hug. "Audrey! It's been forever!"

After the arrival hubbub, we sit together in the living room. I look at Jessica's glass habitually: Perrier with lime. She pours refills, wine for Eve and Denise and a cup of soymilk for me. I never drink around Jessica, which she appreciates.

We chit chat about Eve's latest construction project, an Earthship house about fifteen miles outside the centre of Middlebury. She tells us about the new calves on their father's dairy farm and how she was the midwife for the second one. She and Jessica ask Denise about her work, and Denise shares about a few of her kids: the fourteen-year-old who broke into her school and painted the words "mange d'la marde" on her history teacher's door, the two boys who kidnapped their driving teacher at knifepoint and made him take them to Quebec City, and the twelve-year-old trans girl who stuffed one of her bullies in her locker and left him there overnight.

We eat the spanakopita with a spinach salad.

After supper, Denise helps Jessica with the dishes, and I go upstairs to look at a computer issue Jessica has been having recently. My belly is rigid, and a headache is brewing. I futz with the program and get nowhere. I hear their voices get louder, more boisterous. I shut the office door and try to concentrate. It takes me nearly a half hour, but I solve the problem. I write down instructions for Jessica and head back down to join my friends.

When I come into the kitchen, Denise and Jessica are laughing as they set out dessert: brownies à la mode.

"Did you have to go downstairs?" Jessica asks Denise.

"Downstairs? I had to leave the building," says Denise. They're both hysterical.

"What's so funny?" All of my fleshy parts solidify, like the Tin Man. *One. Two. Three.* I stretch my arms, trying to look casual.

"We're just—just talking about..." Jessica is crying from laughing so hard. Denise is close.

"Don't be offended, darling; we're talking about your snoring."

My cheeks blaze, but the tension seeps out of my body. My snoring has been compared to many things, none of them cute or charming. But I'm just happy my girlfriend and my best friend are getting along.

We leave around 11:30 p.m., late for us. "C'était une très belle soirée," Denise says, reaching to rub the back of my neck. "I see why you love her so much."

We get home, and I spend the night awake, stroking Denise's hair as she sleeps.

Chapter 17

The next day, we're sipping coffee in bed. Denise suggests we get up and look at the Immigration Canada website, just to see what's involved.

"But it's Sunday morning. I thought it was a day of rest," I say, rubbing her naked back.

"That's only for Christians. For Jews and their Quebecois lovers, it's a day for research."

"Is that so?" I'm smiling, but I breathe and count, making sure it's not out loud.

I fire up the desktop and find the URL. The screen is bursting with words. It turns out that immigration, even from the US to Canada, is a big deal. I'm overwhelmed in under two minutes flat.

"It's so complicated."

She rests her hands on my shoulders, looking at the screen.

"There are people who do this who don't know English or French. We just need to follow directions. And call the number if we need help."

"That's easy for you to say."

"You can get the packet in English." She points to the screen.

"This is a big deal for me, Denise. You just don't get it." I get up, push the desk chair brusquely, go into the bedroom, and flop myself down on my bed. I try to clear my head but instead an image of the SheLovesHer app appears in my mind and the profiles of all the single women who live in Burlington, 10 minutes from my place.

*

Eventually, Denise comes back with two glasses of juice and climbs into bed with me. She pauses, eyes big.

"I'm sorry. You're right. It is a big deal. If it were me, I would be overwhelmed too. And I don't even have anxiety about reading."

She doesn't fight. She doesn't react. Instead, she apologizes.

I'm lost.

"Are you feeling panicky?" she asks.

I laugh. "Hardly. Haven't you ever seen one of your parolees have an anxiety attack?"

"Everybody's different. I just wondered, since I don't think I saw you have one yet. Is that true?"

"Oh, trust me, you'll know. I was just being a baby about the whole immigration thing," I mumble, sipping the dark purple juice.

She frowns. "Why do you say that? Of course you're not a baby. Was I making you feel that way?"

I sip again. "Nobody can make anybody feel any way."

She almost laughs.

"What's so funny?" I say, a giggle sneaking out. I put the juice down on the nightstand, and I push Denise playfully. Her glass almost tips over.

"Attention! This will make stains, you know," she says, putting down her juice on her night table. Then she shoves me. We wrestle, full of muffled screams and bumps and a few "shhhh's." Then, at an impasse, I take a chance and lean in for a kiss. Tension gone, we wrap ourselves around each other like vine leaves.

*

On Sunday night, I try for the third time to read the home page of Immigration Canada; after a few sentences, I'm shaking. That many words is bad enough, but the enormity of immigration pulls the breath right out of my lungs.

I flop down on the bed, and Leto jumps up and settles on my chest. Deep down I know I have to find a way through if I am considering a serious relationship with Denise.

I decide I need a hard copy of the application.

While waiting for the printer to finish, I remember one high school aide who passed on creative strategies for my reading anxiety. The woman once destroyed a mildewy old book, cutting the pages up into little squares so I could break down large chunks of text and understand the main point of each paragraph.

Impatient, I grab the first few pages of the instructions and take them into my office. I get out my scissors, breathe deeply, and begin cutting. Then I find a large sheet of card stock, and I gather paint pens,

69

glitter glue, a folder of clipped out magazine ads, and some stencils. Beginning with the little cut-out paragraphs, I plunge into a new collage about leaving the safety of one world for the shadowy unknown of another.

After three hours, I put the collage on the "in-progress" shelf to dry and write down what I understood about Canadian immigration. After thirty minutes, I'm startled when I look down: I've filled up an entire piece of paper.

The application process is one thing—actually immigrating is another. I close my eyes and try to imagine this new life. Honking horns. Smog. The upstairs neighbours, fighting. Smoking.

But free health insurance. Paid family leave. Seven-dollars-a-day childcare.

I open my eyes, sit down, and look out my window at the birch tree. A robin flies by. The sparrows in the bush are at it again. Music.

Montreal.

I imagine walking to my new favourite art supply store. I can't find the handmade paper, so I go up to the cashier. "Parlez-vous anglais?"

"Malheureusement, non," says the young woman.

I skip ahead ten years. There's an open house at our daughter's school. Denise and I go, excited to find out what she's been doing for the first few months. The teacher greets us with a big smile and tells us about our child in French. No translation.

My phone buzzes.

Baaa.

Jessica.

Moo.

We hop on Zoom.

"Oh. My. God. Your girlfriend is divine, Meyerwitz. Why did you not tell me? I would be with you every second of every visit!"

Nod. Can't speak.

"Now it makes sense to me why your panic attacks have dropped off. I really don't think it's the new medication. I think—hey, you okay?"

Tears.

"What's wrong?"

Shrug.

"Is it me?"

70

Head shake.

"Whew. Okay, is it Denise?"

Nod. Nose drips. Tissues.

"Can you talk? Do you want me to come over?"

"I...I just...it's...French."

She nods. "I know, honey. It's huge."

Tension fizzles out of my body. Tears fall and fall. Jessica sits with me on screen. "I've got you, Meyerwitz. I've got you."

Chapter 18

Even with fears, questions, and uncertainties, the months pass by quickly, and Denise and I fall deeper in love. In August, we visit the Montreal Botanical Gardens and attend the film festival in Montpelier. We trade stories, cook paté chinoise, play "Name That Tune." We visit with Mimi and eat her divine crabcakes. We go out for Peruvian in Burlington, for homemade ravioli in Montreal's Little Italy.

It's her birthday in September, and I take her out for a special night of Indian food and dancing in the Gay Village. Exhausted, we leave at midnight, taking the metro to Beaubien and walking the three blocks to her apartment.

We stop at the corner, and there's a home I never noticed before. "Hey, look at that house. Nice, huh? I love the balcony."

Denise looks. "It's funny because since I moved here, I always liked that house. It's warm with the wooden shutters and the window boxes."

"Can we peek inside?"

Denise looks at me, aghast. "Of course not. Somebody lives there!"

I roll my eyes. "Not in an obvious way. We can just casually walk by and pretend something caught our eye."

"It's illegal." She shakes her head, but I prepare and look around to make sure nobody is watching.

"It's also dark."

"Fine, but be subtle," she whispers. I amble slowly down the sidewalk, my head turned. I see a living room with hardwood floors and a bright rectangular garden in the back, behind a sliding door.

"Assez! They'll call the police!"

I pass the house and cover my hand with my mouth to stop the giggles. A couple walks by, arm in arm.

"Bonjour!" I say brightly.

Denise walks ahead of me, muttering something in French.

I keep walking, singing, "She loves you, yeah, yeah, yeah." My future life fantasy is growing and developing. If I lived in a house like that, maybe I wouldn't mind the city noise.

*

The next morning over omelets on her balcony, I raise the topic of children again. This time she's more enthusiastic. "What's your favourite name for a boy?" I ask.

"Definitely Felix. Or maybe Xavier. You?"

"Xavier. Isn't that Greek?"

"It's French, I think. Mimi's manager's son is Xavier."

"How about Joshua? Or Abraham?"

"Girl?"

"Charlotte. Eleanor. Talia."

"Alexia. Laurence. Éliane."

I text Mom:

Making list of baby names.

My phone buzzes.

*

One Thursday night, Jessica and I are hanging out at her apartment, playing Bananagrams, and drinking virgin pina coladas.

"Hey, did you ever call the clinic?"

"Dump." I put a tile back and take three new ones. "No, it's going really well with Denise. We talked about baby names last week."

She stares at the table, then at me. "I'm sorry. 'Siblify' is not a word."

"Of course it is, silly. Peel." We each take a new tile.

She slaps the table, which gets my attention.

"Your thirty-fifth is in two months."

My eyebrows go up. "What's that supposed to mean?"

"You need to pay attention to your biological clock."

"I just started dating a woman you reeled in for me. Whose life is this anyway?"

"I've invested in you like a corporate stock. I want a return on my investment."

I laugh. "Well, don't think you get to be godmother by trying to control things. Trust me, it will have the opposite effect."

Jessica glares at me. "I trust you. Peel."

*

Denise has a week off at the end of September, so I spend a long weekend in Montreal. Sleep has evened out, and I get close to seven hours on Saturday night. On Sunday morning, I'm lying down on her couch, reading Snoopy comics. Denise is making coffee as early sunbeams pool on the aging checkered rug.

"If you still want to, I'd like to try. To live together—if you're willing to—to immigrate," she says loudly from the kitchen. I hear the cafetière's noise build to a near whistle and the sound of the fridge opening and closing. Denise comes in with our coffees, mine with soy-milk and sugar, hers black. Her face is shiny with sweat, and she's got a tiny smile.

We look at each other, me on the couch, her standing up holding the steaming mugs.

I get up, take both coffees from her, set them down on the table, and hold her with everything I've got.

"Does this mean we can get married?" I ask the wall as the hug stretches on.

Chapter 19

I go to school the following Monday and notice my body feels different. Taller. More rooted. I'm relieved I'm down to three medications and that they all seem to be working. One of my theatre students asks, "Hey, Ms. Meyerwitz, how come you're all smiley today?" I tell him the smiles will stop if he doesn't put the Cheetos away and take out his script.

Denise surprises me over email one day with the story of her first girlfriend, all written out. Apparently, the woman was a lifeguard at the pool where Denise practised competitive swimming, and the lifeguard dumped her football-playing boyfriend to date Denise. The story gets really interesting when the football player shows up at Denise's parents' house, and he and Denise's father duke it out on the front lawn. I was half laughing, half gasping by the end.

I Zoom her immediately.

"You're amazing. Do you know that? How can you write that well in English?"

"Oh, that was nothing, just an email. Happy you liked it."

"Liked it? I think you should send it to the *New Yorker*. Or the Montrealer if there is such a thing."

"I had something in mind when I wrote it."

I look at the email and think for a moment. What am I missing?

"You're going to have to tell me."

She sighs. "I was hoping you would respond by sending me a story from your life."

I laugh. "You know how terrible I am with words."

"It doesn't matter. You're not trying to get published. Just send me a story."

"Why do you want me to write something? Can't I just tell you the story instead? Or maybe I could do it with pictures."

"We can do that too, after."

I think about it. Why is she pushing me on this? Part of me wants to tell her to go screw herself. Then I remember the new flexible me. "Okay, but there can't be a deadline."

She giggles. "Mais oui."

I feel my heart do that thudding out of time thing, and my hands start sweating. I start pacing and then bend in half, clutching myself around the middle. Leto stares at me from the couch, and I want to go to her, but I can't seem to coordinate my brain and my legs to make it happen. I get up and try giving myself a head massage, but my chest is trapped between two sides of an invisible vice. I lie down and try deep breathing but can only get a tiny bit of oxygen, like I sucked the air with a straw. I look at the entryway table where I always put my phone, but it's not there. I jump to my feet and begin running around the apartment, gasping for breath, convinced I left my phone on the bus or at the grocery store and that someone is in the process of stealing my identity and ruining my life before I've had any chance of marrying Denise and having children and grandchildren and challenging her to a wheelchair race in the old folks' home.

Like it always does, at one point, my heart rate slows enough that it occurs to me to get myself some ice water. I go upstairs with the glass and into the bathroom. I take out a washcloth and dip it in, then mop around my temples. The cold water pierces something in my skin, and things begin to settle. I hang the washcloth on its little hook, grab the glass, and go back downstairs. I sit on the couch, put my cup on the coaster, and make kissing sounds for Leto to come over and sit on my lap, which she does, purring.

I notice my phone, on the side table. I sigh and roll my eyes.

I don't tell Denise about the panic attack. Over the course of the next few nights, I jot down notes, sweating it out but making slow progress. The story takes me a week, but I finally arrive at something I'm happy with.

A Very Sad Day

I was asleep when my best friend called me. It was 2:24 a.m. I remember because I looked at the clock when the phone rang.

It was Jessica, but I didn't recognize her voice. She was breathing heavy like sobbing.

"Are you hurt?"

She said no with a stuffy nose voice. I knew I had to get a grip. I was seriously worried but didn't want to worry her with my anxiety. Instead, I told her to stay home, and I would be over soon.

When I got to her apartment, I was shocked. Jessica was huddled in a corner in just a t-shirt and underpants. She was shaking and sweating and breathing really strangely.

I went over and tried to touch her. When I did, she screamed.

So, I made some coffee and tried to think what to do.

Then I went into her freezer and got out the ice cream we bought the day before. Then I dished out a huge bowl full. I got two spoons and brought it over to her. I sat down in the corner and started to eat. I handed her a spoon. After a while, she took a tiny bite. And then she told me what happened. Her brother Max who was a drug addict had taken an overdose on purpose. He killed himself.

She cried, and I hugged her for a really long time. Then I helped her pack a bag, and I brought her to my apartment. I called the school where she worked and told them what had happened, and they arranged for a sub for a few weeks. It took a really long time, but she got better. I feel so lucky to have a friend that can accept my help like she could.

I email the story to Denise on a Friday morning. We Zoom after supper that night.

"Merci for your story. It's terrible about Jessica's brother, though. You didn't tell me before that it was from drugs."

"The whole family was in shock. I wouldn't wish that on my worst enemy. Her dad was in pieces. Well, they all were."

"You know, you aren't bad with writing, really."

I laugh. "Let's do the drawing one next and you'll see the difference."

She sighs. "It isn't a contest, and of course I know you can draw much better than me. It was kind of a test to see if the whole reading and writing anxiety thing was real. You seem fine to me, and your writing is more than fine."

I look at her. A test? Couldn't she see how hard it was for me? I want to push it, but I also don't want to have an argument, so I just smile and make a smooching noise at the screen.

Chapter 20

Denise invites me to stay with her in the country one weekend in October, in a little town called St-Armand, ninety minutes south of Montreal. We meet at the house, and it's breathtaking. On rambling hills that remind me of Vermont, the property has a renovated brick farmhouse from the 1800s. There's a woodstove, a giant kitchen with rust-coloured quartz countertops, a loft bedroom with a picture window overlooking Mount Pinnacle. There are two barns, a storage shed, and a duck pond.

"Wow," I say as Denise leads me around by the hand.

"It's Antoine's sister-in-law's. This is their country place, can you believe it?"

I settle in quickly, thrilled to witness the warm light and foliage display. I sketch barn swallows, Denise skipping stones, and a splash of black-eyed Susans before supper.

"This kitchen nearly cooks for you," Denise says, carrying out steaming plates of linguini with shrimp and scallops. I breathe in garlic and admire the asparagus, sautéed with slivered almonds, the salad with cranberries and toasted almonds, the mahogany silk tablecloth, the yellow beeswax candles. A Billie Holliday mix plays in the background.

After supper, we get a fire going, and Denise cracks open an expensive bottle of wine that she'd been saving. We serve ourselves some apple crisp and kick back and relax. Our conversation is full, slightly sexy. She changes the music, a group from Quebec called Beau Dommage, and then lays down on the billowy sofa. The couch is flanked with pillows with needlepoint cats, and Denise tucks her long legs under a crimson throw. I notice tiny flakes of dried skin on her lower lip. I wonder if they would come off if we kissed.

Denise leans forward to pick up her glass, sips and smiles, adjusts the pillow so she's upright. She speaks, first in English, then in French.

Instantly, I'm hyperaware of my body. There's a clutching and then a slamming sensation, and the warmth from the fire and ease of the rocker become distant, historical. I'm following her. I understand, really I do. I know those words she's speaking, but now I'm on the clock, with the appearance of the first two tiny words, "un peu." I've punched in, and now half of me is outside the conversation, working hard, tracking, studying, resisting the urge to interrupt her and ask for a translation.

I pull the rocker closer to the wood stove. The blood drains from my toes, and I prop my feet up on a dusty ottoman to get them closer to the fire. I listen diligently, disciplined in my nodding and uh-huh-ing. I look at an antique painting on the wall and imagine French Canadian ancestors filling the living room. It's no longer a date but a Quebecois family reunion. A stout woman slices a tourtière, and a girl with a pearl necklace offers me a piece of sucre à la crème. A few couples are dancing, and everyone is talking and singing. What's the word for shy again? Timide. But that's not quite it. How can I translate my internal experience into French when I can't yet translate it into English?

In my mind I'm staring at all those ancestors clustered around the woodstove. I listen to her, to them, swallow to get rid of the catch in my throat. I nod, smile, feign connection. I watch the ancestors warming themselves, laughing incomprehensibly.

I listen to her, to them, holding back tears.

Denise finishes her sentence, refills her glass, adjusts the red throw. The fire snaps.

"Mon Dieu, did I just talk in French all that time?"

But I don't hear because I'm lurching towards the bathroom. I slam the door, sweating, and fall onto the toilet. I'm panting.

Back at summer camp, I'm twelve years old and breathing hard on another toilet, this one in a cabin in the Maine woods. Three girls perch on the rafters; they are looking down at me in the bathroom and laughing. One has a camera in her hand, and flash bulbs pop every few seconds.

The girl with the camera yells, "Hey freakazoid, show us your poop!"

Another one laughs and says, "Smile at the camera, psycho!"

The third adds, "Yo, stinky, don't you pee standing up?"

My hands cover my short curly hair as paper airplanes, spitballs, and wads of chewing gum sail down from above. Two girls lurk outside the bathroom door in case I try to leave. Hands over eyes, my brain plays happy pictures of my room at home, my birch tree, my teacher, Mrs. Scanlon.

The jeering fades.

"Audrey? Are you okay? Please, say something, anything."

I cradle my face in my hands, silently.

"Please, Audrey, I just want to sit with you."

I stand. Step into bathtub. Lie down.

Close shower curtain.

The door opens.

"You're in the tub?"

GO AWAY. Can't speak.

She opens the curtain.

"Don't!" Hands to face.

"I'm sorry...I...I don't know what's happening. I want to help. Can I help?"

Hands away. Her eyes. I look. Cry.

"Take my hand, Audrey."

Hand out. She pulls. Move. Bed.

Lie down. She tucks. Crawls in. We're on our sides. We look at each other. My eyes burn. Fists unfurl. Breathing deepens. Denise edges towards me. She drapes her arm around my waist.

"That was a panic attack, right?"

I clasp her hand around me, pulling her tighter.

"You don't have to talk, but can I ask questions?"

I nod.

"Was it because I was speaking French?"

I think. The answer is more complicated than I can explain. I shrug.

"Why didn't you just ask me to speak in English? I honestly wasn't aware."

Tears.

"Sorry." She starts rubbing my back again. I smile and close my eyes. A few more tears come out.

"I don't know what to say, Audrey. I love you, but I'm a francophone. I just can't worry that every time I speak French you're going to be upset."

My body instinctively moves away from her. Eyes open wide.

"I don't know why it's so upsetting. It's just another language. There's nothing bad happening to you."

I thought she was on my side. I thought she understood. I clear my throat and start formulating my thoughts. "It's...it's a trigger."

She nods. "What is it triggering?"

I wipe my eyes and look around for tissues. "Times I was...excluded."

She looks at me expectantly.

I shake my head. The mountain feels way too high. Unscalable.

She reaches out for my hand. "I want to understand. But you have to know that the language issue is a trigger pretty much for all francophones in Quebec. You know a little about our history. Having the right to speak in our native tongue is important. And I can speak English most of the time, with you, but I can't do it all the time. I don't want to do it all the time. I need you to make at least a little effort."

"I am making a little effort. I'm learning French. I do a half hour every day online. Are you saying that's not good enough?" My words are back, running on the fuel of anger.

"Of course not. I'm not saying anything like that. I love how much French you're learning. I just can't deal with big reactions like this from me speaking French for five minutes."

I get up and walk back into the bathroom. She follows me. I turn slowly and put my hands on her shoulders. "My feelings won't make sense to you. But they're real to me, and they make sense to me. I need to do some yoga or something, and then I'll come to bed. Maybe we can talk more tomorrow."

She nods, kisses me softly on the cheek, and turns away. Her eyes are shiny, and I wonder if there are tears.

*

The sun rises in the morning, casting a golden haze over the hills. Despite barely sleeping, I'm breathing, and my body is less rigid as I sip my decaf and watch the sky.

Denise stands by the big picture window in the living room, staring at the mountains, steam twirling up from her coffee mug. "I was scared last night. I didn't know what you would do."

I say nothing. Wait for the breakup I'm sure is coming. It doesn't. I put my mug on the little table and go over to her. "I'm sorry. I had no idea that would happen. It's been such a long time since I had one like that."

I wrap my arms around her, and she tips her head back so it's resting on my collarbone. I sit down and tell her about the bullying that left such a mark on me.

Later, we walk in the local bird sanctuary, spotting a grosbeak, several hummingbirds, and eight turkey vultures. We stop on the way home for maple creemies, soft serve ice cream swirled into a wafer cone, and catch a glimpse of snow geese headed south.

Chapter 21

In November, we're still visiting every weekend, bouncing back and forth between Burlington and Montreal, Jessica being a trooper and taking care of Leto as needed. A university friend of Denise's invites us to a party. "Marie-France's husband is British, and he knows a lesbian couple near me, on the other side of Parc Pére-Marquette, on Chambord. Just think," Denise says, being the extroverted soul that she is. "Another lesbian couple like us! Claire is francophone, and the other, I can't remember her name, but she's anglophone."

I wrinkle my nose. A social event with no structure gives me hives. "So, because they're another bilingual lesbian couple in Montreal, we're supposed to become bosom buddies?"

"Mon Dieu, just meet them. If they smell bad or if they talk compulsively, you can excuse yourself and go eat some chips."

I shake my head. I know making friends in Montreal is a good idea, but I would always rather stay home and draw than go to a party where I can't figure out what to do with my hands.

But Denise is so enthusiastic that I cave, and we go. And incredibly, we have wonderful conversations with francophone Claire, a veterinary technician, and anglophone Sabrina, a research scientist. They are both so warm and easy to talk to that I don't think about my hands once. Claire is the more outgoing of the two, with brown hair cut in a pageboy style and hazel eyes, dressed in bright blue cotton pants with zigzags all over them and a baggy yellow blazer. In a mix of French and English that's so common in social situations in Montreal, she tells us stories about the pet owners and the animals she hangs out with at work each day. Occasionally she stops, remembering me.

"Oh sorry, am I losing you, Audrey? Tell me please if I go into French. Truly, half the time I don't know what language I'm speaking!"

Sabrina is softer than Claire. She has short straight hair that's cut in layers, dark brown eyes with wire-framed glasses, large hoop earrings, and a dimple on her right side. She seems more inclined to ask questions than talk.

"How long have you two been together?"

"Do you know Montreal well?"

"Did you study French in school?"

It's a relief to listen to English from someone other than Denise. Sabrina tells me she grew up in Toronto but moved to Montreal fifteen years earlier to follow a girlfriend. She fell in love with the Quebec culture, broke up with the girlfriend, and has been here ever since.

Her neuroscience lab is researching the impact of mindfulness meditation on people with chronic migraines. "It's very promising," she tells me, her eyes animated and her voice nearly a whisper. We talk about Oliver Sacks, cultural differences between anglophones and francophones, and the best places for Indian food in Rosemont, Denise's neighbourhood.

"We'll definitely have to get together when you're in town," Claire says as the party winds down. We program in each other's cell numbers and say goodnight to our hosts. I notice that I had only eaten some salad, too taken with my new friends to think about food.

We walk back with Claire and Sabrina, taking a short detour to see where they live.

"This is amazing," I say. "It's less than a ten minute walk from Denise's!"

In the end, it's twelve minutes, but still, having nice English-speaking neighbours within walking distance of Denise's place who are potential friends is big news.

That night on Denise's short double bed where I normally lay restless, my body melts into a profound and still sleep.

Chapter 22

I wake up the next morning, refreshed from my night. When I open my eyes, Denise is sitting on the edge of the bed with her coffee.

"We both have to ask, and we both have to say yes."

Huh?

"Getting married. You asked me a few weeks ago if we could get married. Well, I think we both should propose and see what the answer is."

I laugh.

"Did you make my decaf?"

But she isn't kidding. And I realize it makes sense. To want and be wanted. So, after coffee, lounging in her Montreal apartment listening to birds and buses, I tell my beautiful girlfriend she's got a deal.

*

The next Friday brings warmth and clear roads to Burlington, warm for December anyway, so I ride my bike to and from school. Denise had arrived the night before on the bus. When I open the front door to my apartment, it smells like Thanksgiving.

"Cooking, already? It's barely 5:00 p.m.," I say, wheeling my bike into the living room. "What's for supper?"

"Nothing special, just a chicken. How was class?" Music is playing, the mix I had made her a few weeks ago with Macy Gray, Tracy Chapman, Kyra Shaughnessey. The cat trots over and says hi.

"I hate them all. I think every problem child in the third grade signed up for theatre. Corey and Megan still don't have their lines memorized. Alexandra dropped potato chips on the rug and crunched them with her heel, on purpose, when I was busy yelling at Liam and Jerusa for putting tiny bits of chewing gum at the ends of Gracie's braids. I don't know why I keep doing this." I take off my windbreaker and sunglasses, blow my nose.

"Ready in half an hour," says Denise, clanging around in the kitchen.

"Need some help?"

"Non, ça va, just relax."

I notice that the table is set. A yellow tablecloth I don't remember owning. She's put out crystal goblets and my favourite April Cornell print napkins.

"What's all this?"

"You told me Friday nights are special for Jewish people," says Denise, coming into the living room with a platter of chicken surrounded by orange, yellow, and dark purple root veggies. She sets it down and grabs my three-wicked beeswax candle.

"Sweet. Actually, we use special candlesticks and special wine and special bread, but we can say 'Shabbat Shalom' without any of that." I walk over to her and kiss her. "Thanks for being so thoughtful." I try counting in my head to get rid of the image of potato chips ground into Sister Agatha's classroom carpet. On my watch.

I turn to sit down. In the centre of my plate stands a tiny glass bottle with an even tinier cork. There's some sand at the bottom, a few miniscule seashells, and on top of them a small rolled up piece of paper. I look at it for a few seconds, puzzled.

"I don't—"

"Open it," she says.

I uncork the bottle and slide out the message.

Audrey Lynne Meyerwitz,
Je t'aime.
I want to spend the rest of my life with you.
Be my family.
Be my wife.
Will you marry me?
If not, I prefer to stay alone on my desert island.
Ton amoureuse, Denise

I read it again. Look at her. She's red faced. Eyebrows raised.

I don't cry. Don't get up and embrace her.

"Yes. Yes, I will marry you." Voice flat.

"Wonderful!" She looks at me, my face still frozen. "Are you happy?"

"Of course." Cough. Laugh. Look for Leto.

We eat. "So good, sweetie."

Quiet.

"Are you okay, Audrey?"

"It's—it's just so perfect. I don't know what to say." I finger the tiny bottle. "Where did you find this?"

She smiles. "If I tell you, the magic will disappear."

*

The next Monday during lunchtime, I'm eating with Jessica in the staff lounge at school. She's munching on cookies as I slurp Ramen noodles. I tell her about Denise's proposal and warn her not to do anything stupid, like a bridal shower.

"Boy, you sure know how to take the fun out of a friendship, Meyerwitz. Is there anything I get to do to enjoy this? Pick out your dress? Recruit bridesmaids? Hire a plane to write 'I love you Denise' in the sky?" She bites into a cookie.

I wonder if she's talking too loudly. I look around. It's just us and the ninety-year-old German teacher who refuses to retire.

"Don't you read, Jessica? Don't you know anything about being a woman and not acting like Barbie?"

She rolls her eyes. "When women get engaged, their inner bridezilla always comes out. It's in the x chromosome."

"Ick. Can you please clean up your cookie crumbs? Sister Agatha is going to leave me another nasty note. Anytime she finds crumbs, anywhere in the school, she assumes it was me."

I brush my fingers on the table and catch the pile of crumbs in my other hand. I look out the window and notice it's snowing. "Hey, what are you doing for the holidays?"

Jessica rolls her eyes again. "My sister is having her big shindig, and if it was anybody else besides Eve, I'd skip it...I kinda need to make an appearance, for her. But I'll probably spend most of the day in AA meetings. You?"

I scratch my head. "No idea. I don't have the energy for Ian and Brandon making latkes, and Mom doesn't care if I come or not. Do you want to do Jewish Christmas with me and maybe Denise if she doesn't go to her sister's?"

Jessica smiled. "Chinese food and a movie. So much better than going to meetings."

"I'll ask her tonight when we talk."

I suddenly remember that if we're going to get married, I still have to propose.

*

The next Saturday, we're out walking in Denise's neighbourhood enjoying the Christmas lights, and we run into Sabrina. She's in front of the Depanneur, holding a leash with a small black poodle on the other end. Claire comes out a second later.

"Hey!"

"Hey, wow, it's about time we ran into you!"

"How are things?"

They introduce us to their dog, Hercule Noirot, and we chat happily in front until the storeowner asks us to move because we're blocking his customers.

"Does anybody want to get some gelato?" asks Sabrina.

I look at Denise. "Isn't it a little cold?"

Claire leans in. "It's the best time of year to go because there are no lines."

"Do you mean that place at the Jean-Talon Market?" Denise asks. "That's pretty far."

Sabrina smiles. "But so worth it."

So, we hop on a bus, Sabrina with the dog in her handbag, and we get fancy ice cream with our new friends. We sit on a bench, licking cones as the snow falls, cars zooming by and a brave guitarist on the corner playing "Ch-ch-ch-changes."

We talk about what we're doing for the holidays. Denise had invited me to be with her family at Mimi's, but I tell her I need to hang out with Jessica because the holidays are hard for recovering alcoholics. Denise tells them that she proposed, which delights them both, and Sabrina tells us she and Claire are going to Cuba to celebrate their fifth anniversary—which happens to be today.

"Happy anniversary, my love," says Claire, who then plants a chocolatey kiss on Sabrina's pale cheek. They tell us about their commitment ceremony, which they had created themselves.

"We're not legally married because we didn't want the state mixed up in our personal lives," explains Sabrina. "Plus, there's so much patriarchy in the institution of marriage."

"Here," says Claire, "I have a few photos on my phone."

We cluster around the Samsung and see a beautiful space with yellow walls decorated with candles and daisies and fairy lights. Sabrina is wearing a yellow dress with an antique yellow hat. Claire has on white pants and a mock turtleneck camisole with a golden jacket. Their friends and family hold a homemade Chuppah, the canopy under which Jewish couples stand during the wedding ceremony. Sabrina explains it was constructed from broom handles from her mom and squares cut from Claire's mother's bridal gown.

"I mean, it's not like I would ever wear the thing, can you imagine?" Claire laughs, catching a drip of chocolate at the tip of her cone. "A childhood friend is a seamstress, so we got a gang of women together for a few evenings, hacked it up, sewed the squares, and the whole thing just came together. It was a real community event."

I eat my raspberry sorbet as I look at the photos. Claire and Sabrina, visions of loveliness, gazing into each other's eyes, surrounded by crowds of adoring friends and family.

Sabrina turns to me.

"Maybe we could help you with your ceremony?"

I look at Denise.

"Actually, we're only half engaged right now," I say, standing up and not making eye contact with anybody.

Denise giggles. Claire and Sabrina look at each other uncomprehendingly.

Denise and I take the bus to the Rosemont metro station and start walking back to her apartment. As we wait at the corner for the light to change, I clear my throat.

"Denise?"

She's watching a little girl playing with an old man in a bowler hat. The little girl goes in close, and then the man sticks out his hat to try to "get" her. Each time, the girl screams in delight, throws her hands up in the air, and scoots away. I finger my Star of David, sliding it back and forth on its chain.

"Yes?"

"Denise, please look at me."

She turns. I take a deep breath.

"Denise, will you marry me?"

There's a beat of nothing, and then she laughs, so hard and long that I can't help laughing too, and before long, everybody around us is smiling. The little girl and the old man and all the commuters leaving metro Beaubien and the people in their toques and boots stopping for food turn to look at us, two women torn apart with laughter, eyelashes thick with snow and happy tears sliding down our cheeks. Periodically, Denise leans in to whisper in my ear, but every time she cracks up and can't finish her sentence.

We walk back home and manage to get up the stairs and inside the apartment, breathless and crossing our legs because we have to pee so badly. After we both use the bathroom, I close the curtains, and then she pulls my arm and looks me in the eye.

"Oui," she says, and then she kisses me like she means it.

Chapter 23

Jessica and I make latkes for Denise on the first night of Hannukah in Burlington, and we introduce her to the dreidel game. Then in Montreal, Denise and I go to Provigo and buy a Christmas tree that we carry back to her apartment on our shoulders. We decorate it with a tiny collection of ornaments from her parents that she keeps in a shoebox. Our plan is to host Jessica for brunch, serve meals at the local church, and then do the traditional Jewish Christmas.

"Next year, we should really celebrate the holidays together, maybe have a big dinner or something, go to Mimi's..." my girlfriend says as she clips a blue jay ornament on a branch.

I'm quiet as I decide where to hang a wooden nutcracker. "It's nice being laid back though, don't you think?" I slide the fellow on halfway down the tree.

"It's okay, but Christmas is social. It's about love and families and making a joyful noise as they say."

I laugh. "What book did you read that in?"

"It's from a piece of choral music I sang in university. 'Make a joyful noise unto the Lord.'"

I stopped. "You sing?"

"Just for fun. Three of my friends did it, so I signed up. It was for one year."

"Can you sing me a song now?"

She laughs. "What kind of song?"

"How about a French Christmas carol."

She sits down, and her eyes dart from one wall to the other. Then she looks at me.

"This is an old one."

She stands up. "This is 'Bel astre que j'adore.'" Her voice is clear but thin. The notes leave her mouth and flutter around the modest apartment with the worn grey rugs and the tangerine loveseat. I close my eyes and feel the song wrap itself around me like the baby blanket Mom took me home from the hospital in. I'm warm and happy, and it strikes me that Denise is singing in French, and all I feel is pleasure.

*

We celebrate New Year's in Montreal at Coin G, a restaurant near Metro Jarry. On the way home from supper, Denise asks, "Who do you think should marry us?"

I hadn't thought about it.

"Can't we just marry ourselves?"

Denise shakes her head. "It would be strange. We're the ones making the commitment. We'll be nervous. Somebody else should be in charge. Qu'est-ce que t'en penses?"

I consider this and nod. She's right. But who? We want our ceremony to be ours, to be personal, to be interactive. We don't want to hire some unknown authority figure, certainly not a rabbi or a priest. Denise's parents died before I met her, and although Mom would be happy for me, it's quite possible she might not even come because of parenting responsibilities.

"How about Mimi?" I suggest.

"Mimi, vraiment? In front of a crowd? She shines in the back, like in the kitchen."

Then it hits me.

"How about Claire and Sabrina?"

For a flash, she looks impressed.

"But you have to ask them," she says.

"Why? Why me?"

"Because...you're the...enthusiastic one."

"Oh, no, you don't. I think you should ask because you're bilingual."

We continue until we're arguing and squealing, and she's shushing me, and then I fart and start cracking up as we stroll down the slushy streets, houses laced with lights and flanked with balloony Christmas characters our neighbours hadn't taken down yet.

*

We finally decide we'd ask our new friends via email after supper on a Saturday in mid-January when I'm with Denise in Montreal. We're two eight-year-olds, hiding behind giggles, screens, anything we can find. But our adult logic says if they want to say no, this will give them the space to say it. Make it easier. For them.

We sit on the couch with my laptop in front of the big picture window in our living room, the neighbour's fence dappled with flickering lights. We craft the note together and try with each and every cell of our anxiety-riddled beings to keep it simple.

We send the email at 7:09 p.m. I'm sitting on the sofa with the laptop as she washes dishes when a message pops up on my screen. It's from Claire. For a second, I debate waiting to read it so Denise and I hear the news at the same time, but my impulses get the better of me.

"We would LOVE to officiate at your ceremony! Thank you so much for the honour! When can we come over and start talking about the details? Love C and S."

I scream.

Denise runs in shushing me and then grabs the laptop. She reads the email then looks at me, her face bright as a jingle bell. She grabs my hands and pulls me into a happy dance, one of her hands covering my mouth. Apartment-friendly jubilation.

The next night, a Sunday, Claire and Sabrina come over to talk and plan. They ask lots of questions. What are our goals for the ritual? How do we want to involve friends and family? Do we want to borrow from our cultures and traditions? We ooh and aaah, give each other awkward looks, say a few vague and superficial things that don't exactly reflect how we feel. A start.

After the conversation, we serve them the first of many suppers we insist on offering as part of the process, since they refuse to accept payment. That first night it's chicken breasts stuffed with chopped prunes, toasted almonds, and goat cheese with a side of Brussels sprouts pan-seared with garlic. Clearly no kissing would be happening in either household.

They leave, and we start the dishes, Denise washing and me drying.

"It has to be in both languages," I say, rubbing the flowered ceramic salad bowl with my dishtowel. I sneak a look at her in my peripheral vision, hoping she's impressed with how far I've come.

"Oui, mais, it'll be too long if everything is translated." Denise raises her voice ever so slightly over the sound of running water.

"I definitely want a Chuppah, maybe something personal like they did. It can be made out of anything, really. I made the one for Freddy's second wedding."

We talk, share photos, dreams, memories. Before getting concrete, we talk about what kind of experience we want. Our strongest desire is that our ceremony reflect who we are, that it be an invitation to friends and family into our lives as our community. We want to make promises we can keep, so we decide that each of us will write our own vows. We think into the future, imagining babies, sleepovers, Halloween with orange lights, singing folk tunes around the piano, playing Skip-Bo, playing dress-up.

One day, I text Denise at work.

Favourite colour?

Five minutes later, my phone buzzes.

White. I told you on our first date.

No, she didn't. She told me it was her favourite colour for flowers. And it was the second date.

Then I think, white and purple could be beautiful colours for our ceremony.

*

I hop onto Zoom with Jessica on Monday after school.

"It's happening. Like, really happening." My foot is bobbing up and down as I sit at the computer.

"What is?" She's wearing a ski hat and drinking something in a mug. It's not steaming, and I briefly wonder if it's something alcoholic. Of course not. Pure paranoia.

"Claire and Sabrina. They're going to officiate at our ceremony. Why are you wearing that hat?"

"Because my heater's out downstairs. Doesn't it have to be a judge or something?"

"Claire is ordained in the mail-order ministry. She can do it."

"Hey, did Martha tell her brother and sister?"

"What, about me being engaged to another woman? Mom's not an idiot. Her siblings are snobs."

"So, you're not going to invite them?"

I finger my Star of David. "Hadn't thought about it. I have to check with Mom. I doubt they would come."

"But you went to two of their kids' weddings."

I roll my eyes. "Jess, it's a different world. They have money and normal jobs. They're normal upper-middle-class Jewish families. Martha's always been the black sheep."

"But Audrey, don't you want to do this family thing right? You can't just leave them out because they're snobby. Think of how Martha would feel."

I shake my head. "I'll talk to her, but she's never seemed that invested in us having any kind of close relationship with them."

She sips her drink and looks at the wall. "So, did you tell Denise?"

"Tell her what?"

"Tell her that this is what you wanted. To marry someone from Canada to escape the big bad US of A."

My foot stops bobbing, and my mouth hangs open. "But that's not true. I mean, I thought that at first, but when I saw her photo—"

Jessica shakes her head. "If you want a healthy relationship, you need to tell the truth."

My face pinkens. "There's nothing to tell. It was a thought in my head. It wasn't like I was scheming the whole time and that once I get my citizenship, I'm plotting to leave her."

She shakes her head. "I really like Denise, and I love you. But if you don't tell her, you're lying."

My fingers grip the edges of my desk. "That's not lying in my book."

Chapter 24

I spend long hours in the dark wondering if I've deceived Denise and if I need to explain why I first discovered her profile. Does a healthy relationship mean you tell the person every single thing? Fortunately, between design work and preparations for moving, immigration, and the wedding, I'm keeping busy, and soon I forget all about it.

The next time Mom calls, I remember what Jessica had said about her siblings.

"Mom, do you think I should invite Esther and Josh and the cousins to the wedding?"

She chuckles, and then I hear rustling. Cigarette. The flick of her lighter, the soft whirr of her exhale. "That's up to you, Auddy. You know they probably won't come, and you know it's not about you."

"I know, Mom, but we all got invited to their kids' Bar and Bat Mitzvahs and weddings. It would seem strange if they found out about ours without getting an invitation. They're your family, after all. Your blood family." The words surprised me and their roughness even more.

"Audrey Lynne, this has nothing to do with biology, and you know it. Family is..."

"Who shows up, yes, I know, Mom, but you show up for them."

Silence.

"I'm sorry I brought it up."

*

The next week, I'm home, and I have my appointment with Dr. Terrance. He gives me a few names of psychiatrists in Montreal, telling me it's best to get on a waiting list as soon as possible.

"What if I can't do that until I've officially immigrated?"

"You'll still have status here, so I can see you until that point. No worries." He smiles, gives me my prescription, and we say our good-byes. My hand holding the prescription is sweaty, so I stuff the little white rectangle into my back pocket.

The next week is slow for client work. I have a few sketches I'm working on for a new vegan line of chunky sweaters, but Cabaret is over, and Scene Study doesn't start for another two weeks. The drive between Burlington and Montreal feels like a piece of cake compared with immigration, which I've started gathering paperwork for.

I go to school to teach and come back home to eat cheese toast and drink a mug of hot chocolate, and I start lazily doodling in my sketch-pad. Leto rubs against my leg, and I reach down absentmindedly and scratch her head. Much to my own amusement, I draw a cartoon version of Denise holding a bouquet. I couldn't imagine anyone who would be less inclined to hold flowers ceremoniously. Then I start drawing little stick figures sitting in the chairs, each of them holding a flower, looking at Denise. I jot down this idea with the others in my notebook.

Chapter 25

One Saturday evening in mid-April, we're in Montreal, walking home from supper at Claire and Sabrina's, and we see a for sale sign on the neighbourhood house we'd been admiring since we got together.

We look at each other.

"Bad timing," I say, shaking my head.

"What do you mean, bad timing? It's perfect timing!" Denise's eyes are huge.

"You amaze me, Denise. How on earth can we buy a house?"

Denise rolls her eyes. "We can try to come up with that money. We don't know if we don't try."

When we get back, we look online. The list price for the Montreal house is very reasonable. And between what we make per year, Denise persuades me we could afford a mortgage, if some bank was nice enough to give us one.

Denise looks at me with concern. "What's wrong?"

I fan myself. "Why do we have to buy a house? What's wrong with the apartment?"

She gets up and stares at me. "I thought we both wanted to share a home."

"Yes, an apartment is a home. A home you don't go into massive debt to have."

Her eyebrows tightened. "So, admiring that house was just an act? You were just pretending to go along with it?"

I get up, feeling heat rising inside. "We were just imagining. I didn't think you wanted to do it right now."

"Well, how about a year from now? Will you still be fighting me then?"

I feel my chest muscles constrict. I sink into the couch. "We're planning a wedding, I'm doing the paperwork for immigration, and I'm moving. So, we don't have enough to do, let's buy a house? You're looking at somebody who has lived in one apartment my whole adult life."

Denise stomps into the bedroom and slams her door.

Shaking, I pick up my phone and text Mom:

She wants to buy a house. Is she crazy?

You have an anxiety disorder. Keep it simple.

Chapter 26

I drive back to my apartment on Sunday evening, and as soon as I stop to pick up the mail, a text comes in from Denise.

Can't do this. Can we take a break?

I stand in my bomber jacket in front of the building's mailboxes, staring at the message. Take a break? Break as in breakup? Is she backing out? She wanted to buy a house. Does she want to break up because I don't?

Put phone in pocket. Car. Drive to apartment. Armpits dripping. Reread. Call? Everything off?

Breathe. Wellness. Wait twenty-four hours. Sit. Just—

One. Two. Three. Four. Five.

Phone buzzes. Jessica.

Oink.

Tweet.

I grunt. Upstairs. Phone.

We connect on Zoom. Her desk. Cluttered. Lesson plans. Tupperwares with Thai noodles.

Amstel Light.

Can't look.

"Oh my God, are you okay? Did somebody hurt you?"

Still crying. Jessica looks...

I point to beer bottle. "What's that?"

"Please don't. It's no big deal. You're the one in crisis, so please just tell me what's happening. If that bitch did anything to you—"

"She's not a bitch, Jessica. God, why do you always have to do that?"

Her face. Shock.

"Audrey, what happened?"

"She texted—" Crying. "She's dumping me."

"Forward me the text."

I do.

"She's not dumping you. Did you tell her you were pregnant or something?"

"No. There's this house near her apartment that we both like and a for sale sign went up yesterday. When we walked by, she was all like, 'We should buy that house.'"

Jessica's eyes get big.

"So, what did you say?"

I scowl. "What do you think I said? I told her she was crazy."

She puts her hands on her hips. "Literally?"

I roll my eyes. "No, I just told her we were doing all these major life changes and why should we have to buy a house to be happy?"

"You are a piece of work. Do you get that this is your fault?"

"How can you say that? I listen to everything she tells me and remember it. I always show up early. I research places to eat to make informed suggestions. I do her laundry."

"And now you're being stubborn. You go back and forth between two extremes."

I look at her, swallowing the sting in my throat. "Who are you, and where is my best friend?"

"You've been the one doing the entire relationship all this time. She's doing nothing. You're immigrating. You're fitting into her life. You're making her life easier. What has she done to make your life easier?"

I'm silent.

"Then she plants a big idea that actually might not be a bad one, and you're completely inflexible."

I do something I've never done before: I hang up on Jessica.

Fifteen minutes later, my doorbell rings.

"Open up!" Jessica says, too loudly. I do it, not wanting anyone to file a complaint, even though my neighbours all know Jessica. If I were being honest, I would admit I didn't want anyone to suspect she'd been drinking.

She comes inside, pushing me back, eyes rabid. "What the fuck is your problem?"

The booze? The conversation? I've never seen her mad like this.

"You're my friend, Audrey, and that means we don't hang up on each other. You know who hangs up on people? My mother. Your ex.

Not us!"

She throws her purse down and goes into my kitchen. She grabs a glass of water. Silence, sipping sounds.

"I'm sorry, Jess."

She sits on the couch and downs the rest of the water. "I know you are."

This cracks me up. I smile. She starts to grin but then turns away. "Goddammit, now you've got me fucking laughing."

I sit next to her on the couch, and Leto jumps up onto my lap. I poke Jessica's ribs. She shrieks and drops the glass. If not for the rug, it would have shattered.

"Stop that! Stop! Help, somebody. Crazy woman at large!"

We're both laughing so hard we almost forget we're in a fight.

I sit back and wipe my face with my sleeve. I grab her glass, go into the kitchen, and refill it and then grab a towel. I come back and she's checking her phone.

"Please tell me why I shouldn't worry about the beer." I give her my sternest and most serious face.

She puts her phone away. "Audrey, I'm sober. AA isn't right about everything. Now and then, I have a beer after a long day. You've just never seen me do it. That's all."

I stare at her.

"Believe what you want, but that's the truth. Besides, you're the one who's nutso at the moment. I think my beer is a convenient way for you to avoid your own shit."

I think about this. She's right.

"I don't want to be dumped again," I say quietly.

"Yeah, you, me, and the rest of the world. But everyone is allowed to feel like the other person's pace doesn't work for them. It doesn't mean she's dumping you. Maybe you're just stalled because of this house thing. But even if she does want to break up, that's love. You say you want a family, a healthy family. Even healthy people dump each other. They just do it more politely."

I cross my arms, sulking. "Healthy people stay together. Period."

She shakes her head. "Remember in Wellness that thing about relationships having lifespans like people? We never know what's going to happen. Let's say our friendship ended tomorrow. Maybe I steal Denise away from you. Do you think that would mean the friendship was unhealthy?"

"But you wouldn't steal Denise, and we wouldn't stop being friends tomorrow."

"How do you know, Audrey?"

I take a big breath. "I think about buying a house, and all I want to do is stick my head in the oven. How am I supposed to get over that and smile and say, 'Sure honey!'"

Jessica shakes her head. "It's not about what you do. It's about how you do it. Give her space. Or call and ask her what she means. Maybe you don't buy this house, but you look into doing it next year after you have time to get settled in Montreal. Or maybe she means taking twenty-four hours to process. Maybe you talk to your mom. It's a text. How are you supposed to understand what she means? Healthy is about communication, right?"

I take a sip from her glass. A window cracks open in my psyche.

"You're trying to make something you've never seen," says Jessica, more gently. "I know you don't want to hear it, but I think the whole adoption thing is very deep. And your mom never dated. So here you are, an orphan raised by a single woman, trying to make a healthy relationship and have a baby. It's like going to Croatia and running for president. Or prime minister. Whatever."

I smile. Jessica isn't slurring her words, and I don't feel worried about the beer. "But I could never be president of Croatia. Maybe I can never have a healthy family either. Maybe it's impossible." Emptiness floods my brain.

"Maybe. But I don't think so. And I don't think you think so."

We sit for a few more minutes, breathing together, drinking water. I futz with my Star of David. She holds my other hand.

"I do think it could help if you..."

"I know, find my bio family, yes, yes, I get it. So, tell me, all knowing one, what would that give me that I don't already have?"

She bites one of her nails. "Knowing where we come from is so basic. Maybe you'll find out you come from a family of famous artists. Maybe they all have anxiety. I don't know. I just think not having all the pieces can't be helping."

"What is that, a quadruple negative? I want to get better and better, and that's about looking ahead. I can make choices I haven't made yet. This has nothing to do with my birth family. So drop it, okay?"

She tells me fine, that she has to finish her lesson plan and call her sister and get to bed before the witching hour. I hug her, and she kisses my cheek, just one side.

"Don't screw up this relationship. Denise is gold."

"You called her a bitch before. Which is it?"

But she's already gone, whistling as she swings her purse, headed for the orange Subaru.

*

I go up to my room, change into my pajamas, and text Denise. Carefully.

Space is fine. What do you need?

The phone rings five seconds later.

"Hi," I say, voice wobbly.

"Hi," she says.

Silence.

"Sorry Audrey. I...I got too excited about the house. But I shouldn't have sent that text."

I smile. "Can we talk tomorrow?"

We say goodnight.

I prop myself up in bed that night and sketch. I draw the house and fill it with children, grapes, a fireplace, trunks full of art supplies, an attic with secrets. As I fall asleep, I think I hear footsteps. I try to move but can't, realizing I'm dreaming but with some of my physical reality intact. I feel somebody sit on the corner of the bed. The presence feels female. I try to scream. Then I hear Denise's voice, as if she were falling over a cliff.

I sit straight up. Look at the clock. 5:00 a.m. Monday morning.

Might as well get up.

Chapter 27

In between design work in the morning and theatre classes in the afternoon, I start doing research about home ownership. I go to therapy and talk to Jessica and my brother Freddy, who owns his own place. Mom suddenly gets busy, too busy to talk, and I get that this is something she doesn't think I should do. Denise and I talk but avoid conversation about the house until several days later when I call her.

"Is the house still for sale?" Part of me is praying it isn't.

Pause. "Er, I think yes. Why?"

Inhale. "I think I can do this. Dr. Terrance thinks so and Freddy too. I think it would be okay. If I want to."

"I thought you didn't want to."

"It's the biggest purchase I will ever make in my lifetime. My three cars have all been used. I have anxiety. It's a big deal with lots of other big deals happening."

"We can just let it go, darling."

"I don't want to live like that anymore. I'm in this for life. You're my partner, and we're making a life together. We love the house. So, let's try."

"Mon amour," she murmurs.

I try to breathe and feel a piercing in my side.

*

Then I start asking for help. I start with Freddy. He says it's a good time and that the market in Montreal is deflated. He tells me he'll give us one thousand dollars and lend us another three.

Then I talk to Mom.

"Audrey Lynne, did you discuss this with Dr. Terrance?"

"Yes, he thinks I can do it. He sees how much better I'm doing. I think I can do it, Mom."

"They didn't raise you. They didn't go through your adolescence and the nightmares and the panic attacks and the stress headaches. To be honest, I think you're making a big mistake."

My cheeks feel hot.

"But I will say, I have been thinking about the wedding and I wanted to offer you and Denise five thousand dollars to help pay for expenses. You're free to use that money for whatever you like."

"Including the down payment?"

Silence.

"You're a grown woman, Audrey. Use it for whatever you and Denise would like."

Denise asks Mimi, who offers us fifteen hundred, and her bachelor uncle, who tells us he's happy to give us five thousand and that real estate is one of the best investments there is.

Friday, we go to the bank and visit the house on Chambord. Saturday morning, we make an offer. Saturday afternoon, the owners counteroffer. Saturday night, we walk over, sign the papers, and give them our deposit check.

I try to be okay.

I cry and tremble on and off during the negotiations as we move through each contingency. Denise gets that we're at different stages with this thing: I've never owned my own home before, whereas Denise had gone through the same process with the condo she owned with her ex.

But when it's over, when we finish the closing and the notary hands us the keys, I can't stop smiling. We walk over to 6273 rue Chambord, between Beaubien and St-Zotique.

"Do you mind?" I ask shyly, pointing the key at the door. The spring sun is especially bright, and the birds are tweeting up a storm. Denise nods and grins. I put the key inside the door handle and push open the door to our new home.

"Merci pour ta patience," I say, kissing her in the foyer.

We look around. The house looks different with no furniture. But everything we loved about it, the shiny wood floors, the open layout downstairs, the spacious basement, the three balconies, and the perennial garden out back, it's all there, and it's all ours.

I stand in the centre between the dining and living rooms.

"This is a cool spot. Maybe we should get married here."

Denise laughs. "C'est trop petit. We'll be a fire hazard."

"Just come over here."

She steps carefully on the floor and arrives by my side.

"Oh," she says, looking around. "I see what you mean."

"It's perfect. And think about how much money we'd save." There are windows on either side of the long expanse of wood planks on the floor. "I think if thirty-five people sat on either side of us, it could work. And if the weather is nice—"

She shakes her head.

"May in Montreal? Not realistic."

I walk around the whole perimeter.

"If we opened the upstairs and the basement for people, I think it wouldn't be too crowded. Really."

Denise walks through the whole space. I trail behind her. We go out onto the front downstairs balcony, the backyard balcony, the back and front balcony on the second floor, all three bedrooms, the basement. I follow her back to that central spot on the first floor, where I imagine our Chuppah. Denise takes my hand, strokes my arm, and smiles.

"Yes. I want to marry you here. In our home."

Chapter 28

We move Denise's stuff into the new house and mine into Jessica's garage. Leto and I are officially Jessica's roommates until my immigration papers go through. Luckily, I'm allowed to stay in Canada as a visitor for weeks, months even, as long as I have work in the US, maintain an address in the US, and come back to the US every six months. But I'm actually back more often than that, for teaching, therapy, haircuts, and hanging out with Jess. Once my permanent resident papers come through, I can move everything from Jessica's to the Montreal house and officially "land."

As the planning gets more and more detailed, and the reality of our buying a house and getting married becomes more concrete, I begin waking up at 2:00 a.m. with a thumping heart, a constricted throat, and sweat chilling my underarms. I dream I'm thrown out of a station wagon, chased by a snarling ogre, stuck alone in the ocean on a small piece of ice and watching it melt before my eyes. Tums and valerian tincture are purchased and ingested. Restorative yoga is practised. Breaths are counted. Leto is petted. Runs are ran over and over and over.

Somehow, I manage to stave off the panic attacks during the day. Dr. Terrance is encouraging, and Jessica tells me daily that I'm her hero. But I don't feel like a hero. I feel like a frightened disabled girl who's playing the part of a normal person and not doing a very convincing job.

Spring sun makes the piles of snow disappear as we continue preparing for the wedding. It seems we make progress on one front each day as May nineteenth draws nearer.

One Saturday when I'm in Montreal, I return from my run to find Denise at the dining room table.

"You know what we haven't thought about?"

In front of her is a plate of scrambled eggs and baked beans.

"What are you eating? It looks like what Mrs. Allenbrook had in the terrarium in third grade."

She dips in with a fork and offers me some.

"Eggs and beans."

I make a yucky face. She pops the forkful into her mouth.

I look at her enjoying it. "Really? Baked beans? With the eggs?"

I get out some corn chips and salsa. Vermont-made salsa. I plop down next to her at the table.

"You're such an American," she smiles. "Do you give up about what we didn't think about yet?"

Yes, I give up.

"Kissing," she says, barely understandable with her full mouth.

"Kissing? What do you mean?" I ask, taking another chip.

"You know, after the talking part, when they say something like 'Now you have to kiss the bride.'"

I stop mid-chomp.

"It's 'Now you may kiss the bride.' But I'm not kissing you in front of a big crowd, especially if my family is part of it. Sorry." I crunch a chip for emphasis.

"All couples that get married kiss at the end of the ceremony," she says. "It doesn't have to be a big one."

I laugh.

"Right. Claire will say the magic words, and then we give each other two little French Canadian pecks on the cheek," I say, shaking my head.

"We can practise," says Denise. "We can get it just right. Just a hint of romance..."

"...but not so much that people are thinking, 'Get a room!'"

She nods. "How about now?"

I shift positions, clip the chip bag, and put the jar of salsa back in the fridge. "But I'm all sweaty."

"So?" She puts her hands on her hips.

"Fine, so show me," I say.

She's wearing a hunter green t-shirt, which brings out her golden skin tone and auburn eyes. Her hair is shiny, and she's wearing a bit of rouge and lipstick. I decide I wouldn't mind kissing her, no matter what the reason is or how sweaty I am.

We both stand up and get awkwardly close to each other, like posing for a photo shoot. She leans in, pressing her breasts against mine, and I instinctively flatten myself against the wall.

"Too fast!" I yell and she laughs.

"Just relax, Audrey. Come on."

We kiss, softly, but far from a peck on the cheek.

"That's nice," I say. "But nobody's here. I'd never kiss you like that in front of a crowd."

She stands up. "I have an idea. So, say what Claire will say at the end."

"I think it's 'By the power of their commitment and their whole community's support, we now pronounce Audrey and Denise as married.'"

She takes my hand.

"We'll be holding hands and looking at each other?"

I nod.

"Alors, after Claire speaks, we do the thing with the glass under our feet?"

I nod, smiling.

"Bien, et après ça, I put my arms around your waist, and you put your arms around my shoulders, and we give them a suggestion of a big kiss."

I scrunch my eyebrows.

"How do we suggest a big kiss without actually doing one?"

"Like this," she says and leans in again. Our lips meet and soon we clearly exceed the bounds of suggestion.

I pull out first but not happily.

"I think we should go into the bedroom for a more in-depth exploration about the various ways to suggest a kiss," I say, lips buzzing. I grab Denise's hand and start giving little nips to her fingers.

She jerks away. "I'm serious, Audrey. We have to figure this out because it's not a regular kiss. We have to practise."

I groan. "Can't we take a break from preparations? It's been so long since we've had a good roll in the hay." I pick up her other hand and start kissing it. Then I see her expression.

"Okay, fine." I drop her hand and fold my arms.

"So, let's pretend Claire is finishing. We're holding hands and gazing into each other's eyes. Now—"

She grabs my waist. I put my arms around her shoulders, which feels like elbowing somebody standing too close on the metro.

"Really? Like this?" I wiggle and adjust, trying to find something that feels natural.

"Great, let's try the kiss," she says, looking at me seriously.

We look at each other. We crack up and lose it. We take a breath and try to be serious. We lean in and smooch, the kind of kiss your Aunt Evelyn from the Bronx with department-store perfume might give you after a few years had passed.

"Everybody will think we're long-lost sisters," Denise says. I keep laughing and breathing, trying to get my lips to be still and cooperate.

We lean in again. This time, there are tongues.

I give a little moan. She stops.

"Non!"

I feel the heat building inside me and wonder if I should suggest the bedroom again, hoping that we would be hopeless at a suggested kiss and we would quickly move on to the real thing.

But I take a breath and think about that day when we'll be surrounded by seventy people, all expecting a kiss at the close of the ceremony. I sigh and assume the position.

After twenty minutes, we find it. The trick is less actual lip-to-lip contact and a slower approach and retreat. We get out my phone and tripod and videotape ourselves to check how things look from the outside.

"Ugh, my hair," I say. "And look at those eighteen chins."

Denise shakes her head. "It's the angle. Me too. But look, I think that kiss is perfect, n'est-ce pas?"

It's the nicest suggestion of a kiss I'd ever seen.

We move into the bedroom to continue the exploration.

*

We meet several more times with Claire and Sabrina to finish creating the ceremony. We've settled on half English and half French with no translations except of the actual marriage words. Denise has agreed to a Chuppah that Freddy offered to make from trees on his land and fabric from Mom's old aprons. But I wonder about other Jewish rituals. I ask Denise about it when she's visiting one weekend. I'm taking a bath that she's drawn for me complete with scented bubbles and a candle, her effort at bringing more calm into my life.

"I'm Jewish. I mean, I was born Jewish. It's not like I believe in the Bible and all that; it's more the cultural stuff. Remember when we walked in the cemetery? You were telling me about francophones and how they were second-class citizens. Jewish people have that history, too."

She dips the washcloth in and rubs my naked shoulders. The warm water spills onto my breasts. "I know there is a history. But the two cultures are so different."

I open my eyes. "Well, yeah, but what I'm talking about is the same. Being oppressed."

She looks at me and then away. "Language is very particular, darling. When you are denied the right to speak your mother tongue, when it's always in danger of being lost, there's an edge to your existence. I feel it even though things are so different than they were for my parents and grandparents. Look at us. If we decide to have children..."

My eyebrows lift. "If? I thought it was when?"

"Yes, when, sorry. Do you think our child will have French as a first language, with us speaking English all the time?"

I splash water on my face. "We get to decide that. What we don't get to decide is what language she'll go to school in. And how do you think that makes me feel?"

"Audrey, your first language is English. You have never worried about it disappearing for one minute, for one second, in your entire thirty-four years. Isn't that true?"

She's right, but I don't want to be wrong yet again. "What does that have to do with anything?"

"It has everything to do with everything. I'm trying to get you an idea of what it feels like to be a francophone. You told me about those bullies in camp when you were on the toilet or in school when they would dump your lunch tray. Imagine you walk into the cafeteria, and everyone is talking a language you can't understand. And they tell you they won't talk to you unless you learn it."

I sink down lower under the bubbles. My brain is rogue, flashing images of Denise telling me she doesn't want children because they might be anglophones. "Can we talk about this another time?"

She sighs. "I'll go put my pj."

Chapter 29

The weeks fly by, and our wedding weekend in May arrives. Jessica is the first to show up at our Montreal house on Friday morning. She knocks on the door around 11:00 a.m., armed with two suitcases and a backpack.

I go to hug her, and we press together. As I breathe in, I smell alcohol. For a second, I freeze, like I'd walked into a spider web. But I quickly recover and grab her shoulders instead, swallowing my reaction. We both yell "AAAAAHHHHHH!" and then we hop up and down, hugging and hopping, hopping and hugging. Denise sneaks up on us and says "Boo!"

We scream and then pull her in, hopping and hugging in trio.

When we pull apart, I see that Jessica's eyes are glassy.

"Oh no, you don't," I say. "I refuse to have body paint streaming down my cheeks because my best friend can't keep her tears in her head."

"Body paint? What..."

We both grin at her but say nothing.

"Ohhhh, I get it. This is why Audrey wouldn't tell me what you guys are wearing. You're going nude with paint? You two are wicked badass!"

"Not naked," I say. "Just silk tank tops and pants. White for her, purple for me."

Again, Jessica's eyes look glassy. She turns away from us. Denise frowns at me. I go put my arm around Jessica's shoulders.

"I'm really happy you're here," I whisper in her ear. "My guest of honour." Her tears spill out onto her cheeks, and for a second, I'm not sure if she's crying because she's happy for us or for some other reason. I look at her questioningly, and she gives me a playful slap.

"Okay you two, let's go have some classic American PB & J. There's

113

a lot we have to do today," Denise says, suddenly in task mode. I look at her to see if she had noticed Jessica's breath. I can't tell.

"What are you talking about, Denise? Our list is all crossed off!"

She shakes her head.

"We didn't buy the shrub, and we have to confirm the folding chair delivery from the rental company for tomorrow, pick up the tables, and print out the schedules with everybody's name and tasks. I think there are a few more."

I sigh, grab Jessica's bags, and head upstairs to the guest room. I hope she hasn't brought any marijuana or booze and find myself jostling the bags to feel if there are any bottles. I tell myself to chill out and be kind.

After lunch, Jessica and I fill our water bottles and head out in my car. First, we go to the garden store and pick out a lilac shrub, and then after putting it in the back of the car, we go to get the tables. In the car, we talk a lot. We hadn't spent much time together since my unofficial move to Montreal, other than shlepping my stuff into her garage and a few suppers. We talk about being friends and how we don't want that to change. She asks me if Denise and I are planning to have children.

"We talked about it when we first got together, and it's in the ceremony. But I don't know." As I say it, I remember the conversation in the bath. The fact that we're getting married without a definite "yes" from Denise suddenly hits me hard. She's good at getting what she wants. What if she ends up just saying no?

Despite two hours' worth of Friday afternoon traffic, we manage to get the tables, squeeze them into the car, and return home in time to choose takeout dishes from the Indian restaurant near our place. It feels cozy, the three of us, and I put the question about kids out of my head, at least temporarily, until our guest goes to sleep, and Denise and I are tidying up.

I run the sponge over the table, several times.

"Ça va?" Denise asks, wiping the counters dry with a dishcloth.

I nod.

"Just tired—and—"

I try to keep it down, but it has a life of its own—an idea baby who refuses to go down for her nap.

"I just keep thinking about the kids thing."

Denise stops wiping and looks at me.

"Now?"

"I just...need to know if you're still open to it. Soon."

Denise comes over to me.

"Depends on what you mean by soon."

"Maybe in a few months?"

She sighs.

"Yes, we can start thinking about it in a few months. But I think a break is in order, don't you? Why don't we have nothing for a while. No special projects. I want to live together in a normal rhythm. You know, like go to work and come home, go to parties, be spontaneous, be bored. Wish for the weekend and stay in our pj all day."

I wrap my arms around my wife to be. But I don't squeeze her tight.

Chapter 30

The next day, we wake up almost at the same moment, in the bed facing each other. Our eyes get big at the same time.

"We're getting married!!!"

Denise covers my mouth with her hand.

"The neighbours!"

I bite her finger.

The day unfolds with each element gently falling into place. While we eat our homemade cherry granola with yogurt and coffee, the white folding chairs arrive. Then I bring out long strands of paper-chain ladies with purple and white outfits—a little project I'd pulled together in the week prior, since we'd only lived in the house for a month and hadn't had time to decorate. Denise is enchanted, looking at each one of the differently patterned dresses. The ceremony area, with the white chairs and the purple and white ladies dancing, now looks like a magical portal into a new reality where art, community, and love meet.

Around lunchtime, the bell rings, and it's our body painter, Fawn, about fifteen minutes late. She had told us it would take her about two hours for each of us to get painted.

"How are you doing?" she asks, cradling my hand again. She's holding an old-fashioned valise and a fishing pole.

I look at it and then her.

"Are you going fishing after the wedding?"

She gives a mysterious grin. "Is Denise home?"

I frown. "Sadly, Denise changed her mind at the last minute and is at the airport catching the next flight out to Buenos Aires."

I lead Fawn upstairs to the guest room, where Jessica is sitting in a bra and slip with six old-fashioned pink curlers in her hair, reading *Moby Dick*.

She looks up and says hi. "It's actually very exciting." She holds up the book. "I only read the cliff notes in high school."

Silence.

"Sorry, is there something I should be doing right now?" asks Jessica.

"Jess, this is Fawn, our body painter."

Jessica looks at Fawn who sets down the valise and the fishing pole. Anything at all could happen.

Jessica stands up. Puts *Moby Dick* down on the computer table. Shakes Fawn's hand.

"It's so nice to meet you. I'm looking forward to seeing your, er, work."

Fawn bows, smiles, and closes her eyes. It's barely lunchtime, and I'm already fighting urges to run away screaming. Jessica excuses herself to go get dressed. Denise is downstairs organizing.

"Have a seat, Audrey. I just have to unpack."

Fawn sits me down, sets up her portable studio, and starts.

I hear the bell ring around 1:15 p.m. and know it's Claire and Sabrina, but Fawn insists on absolute stillness, so nobody is allowed to come upstairs and talk to me. Fortunately, sound travels easily through our new house, so I can make out their voices and hear their excitement. They're ooh-ing and ahhh-ing over Freddy's Chuppah. Sabrina asks about an iron.

As Fawn runs a delicate brush across my shoulder, I hear a light tinkling. "Do you hear that?" I ask her. She giggles and shows me one bare leg: She's wearing an anklet of tiny bells.

I hear Denise's coworker Pi arrive. Fawn asks me to close my eyes, and I take the opportunity to do a quick body scan. I count nineteen knots of tension.

Denise comes up at 2:00 p.m.

"Mon Dieu," she says, looking at me.

Denise asks Fawn if she could show me a mirror.

I'm startled by my reflection. I look like I stepped out of a fairy tale. What's better: it looks nothing like bridezilla and everything like how I feel about Denise.

I thank Fawn who bows. I stand up, and Denise takes my place for her turn.

At around 2:30 p.m., I hear Claire's musician duo arrive. A lesbian couple from Manitoba, Miriam and Samya, had snuck out of their native

Iran before anyone could discover their relationship. We'd heard their CD and fell in love with their sound, strong female voices unafraid of vulnerability.

Once Denise's paint is finished, we go into the bathroom to check ourselves.

I turn on the mirror lights. Both of us have makeup on our faces, around our necks down to our chests, and covering our backs to our camisoles. My theme is the sun, orange-rust streaks with purple and yellow, with a swirl around my left eye topped with glitter and a few tiny diamonds. My back has a beautiful mountain range, covered with sparkling snow. Denise is the moon, and on her face, Fawn had painted a half-moon surrounded with rhinestones and thin lines of colour. On her back are the same mountains as mine but at night, the snow glowing in the moonlight.

We look at each other's reflections in the mirror. The doorbell rings and rings as guests arrive, and Pi and Claire greet them and lead them to the seating areas. The musicians set levels with their amps and equipment in the corner of the entryway.

"Turn around," suggests Denise.

We do. She gives me the hand mirror Fawn had brought.

"She may be strange, but she's an incredible artist," whispers Denise.

I laugh. Then I check myself in the mirror.

It's really me, an anxious disabled girl from Albany who never thought she'd get anywhere or be anybody, nobody who anybody would want, besides my bleeding-heart mother. Me who immigrated, me who is learning French, me who is marrying the most beautiful woman I'd ever met who pays her own bills and is nice to me nearly all the time.

Just then, things downstairs get quiet. I hear the musicians play the setup cue.

I grab Denise's hand and squeeze. She squeezes back.

I start to go downstairs, pulling her hand, but she doesn't move. She just shakes her head and mouths, "J'peux pas." I can't.

"You have to. We don't get to eat the gorgeous meal unless we go down and act like we want to marry each other. Just think of the salmon en croute, the mushroom caps with crabmeat, the mousseux."

She takes a breath, then a step.

Miriam and Samya are playing a medley of "Home" and "Le Toi Du

Moi." I keep Denise's hand locked in mine. I glance at her. She looks like she's going into shock. I just keep moving, slowly, the lining of my pants rustling with each step. I notice our white leather flipflop sandals and our painted toenails, Denise's white and mine purple. As we descend, the light in the stairwell hits Denise's shoulder, where Fawn had painted an ocean and brushed it with glitter. We step and step and step, and finally we hit the ground floor.

Miriam and Samya grin as we pass them. Then we turn to look at the guests, our Chuppah held by Mom and Jessica and Mimi and Antoine, the room that had been so empty and bare now filled with everyone in our life and our creations.

I hear Denise gasp when she sees everybody and when everyone turns to us. Seventy people, each holding a flower, white for those who knew Denise first, purple if they knew me first. I give Denise a little push towards the dining room while I make the rounds in the living room. The first person I see is my brother Freddy with his wife Natascha, grasping his arm. He stands up to give me a hug, and I notice tears running into his moustache as he gives me a purple iris. I look into his eyes, and something happens between us, something effortless and unfamiliar. Then I see my sister Chloe next to them, with lilac cuttings and a giant new tattoo of a pentacle on her shoulder. I hug her, and she doesn't smell like booze. Then I look at my mother, clutching her pole to hold up the Chuppah. She's crying and smiling. She pulls me into her and whispers how proud I'm making her.

I stand up and see Denise's brothers and their wives and Mimi, all holding white flowers. Then I see my six Wellness sisters, each holding two flowers, one white and one purple.

I hug, kiss, and receive purple flowers from nearly twenty people.

After covering the room, I can barely wrap my hands around all the blossoms. I look across the space to Denise, and she's stunning with her massive white bouquet, Calla lilies, a rose, babies' breath, carnations, all glowing white next to the moonrise painted on her back.

By the time we meet in the middle, we're hearing sniffles and seeing people wiping their eyes.

We arrange all the flowers in the middle in a vase that Sabrina had bought us as a gift.

Claire and Sabrina are under the Chuppah, with us and the pole holders. We move through each part of our carefully planned ceremony:

the May Sarton poem, the candle lighting, the wishing tree, readings about the responsibilities of communities in supporting new partners and new families, and a tribute to those who had passed.

We then each read our vows. Denise goes first.

"Finding Audrey last year was a turning point for me. Audrey, you help me challenge myself. You help me let go of fear, sometimes even forcing me to let go when all I want is to cuddle up with it and close my eyes. I want to live passionately with you, taking chances in life, in love, and in friendship. I want to share a home and maybe children. I trust you, and I feel so grateful and honoured that you trust me. Please be my conjointe, now and forever."

My tears start again, and I bite the inside of my cheek to stop them. Jessica hands me a tissue. I catch a glimpse of Fawn out of the corner of my eye. She's glaring at me.

When Denise finishes, she picks up the little box of rings on the little table. Claire touches her arm, indicating it isn't time yet. Denise turns to one side of the audience.

"But I want to marry her NOW!"

Everybody laughs.

I compose myself and reach into the pocket of my pants and pull out a folded-up piece of paper.

"Marie Véronique Nicole Denise Beauregard. My first promise is that I will never forget any of your names, nor will I mix them up when addressing you. When you first explained to me that in your generation, all the girls were named 'Marie' and all the boys 'Joseph,' I thought you were joking. Now I realize, as I have grown to realize over the past year, what different cultures we actually come from. You've taught me so much about openness, strength, loyalty, and being willing to collaborate, to learn about other people and other ways. Yes, it's harder to marry somebody from a different culture, but it's also a great adventure. My second promise is to learn as much as I can about Quebec and to learn to speak French so I can join you fully in your life and your culture. I promise to be faithful in all the meanings of the word. I promise to be there for you in sickness, health, and all the grey area in between. I promise to laugh at your jokes. I promise to be my authentic self with you and to accept who you are. I promise I will push myself to grow, to go to more parties and make more speeches and try to like people. To quote somebody who wrote something on my brother's fridge: 'Come marry me! The best is yet to be.' I love you Denise, will you please be my wife?" I look at Jessica, my ghostwriter, who winks at me through her tears as she holds her Chuppah pole.

Claire reaches down for the rings and first hands Denise mine. I notice tears on her cheek. Denise slides the ring onto my finger. I glance at Jessica who blows me a kiss. Then Claire hands me Denise's ring. When I reach for Denise's hand, mine are shaking. I manage to slide the band on her finger, her white nail polish and body paint creating a perfect backdrop for the golden twisted vines of her new wedding ring.

Sabrina reads the portion of the service where we marry each other.

"Marie Denise Beauregard, do you take Audrey Lynne Meyerwitz as your conjointe, in sickness and in health, from now until the end of your days?"

I look at Denise who nods. "Oui."

"And Audrey Meyerwitz, do you take Marie Denise Beauregard as your conjointe, in sickness and in health, from now until the end of your days?"

"I do."

Sabrina and Claire each turn to one side of the audience and speak in unison, one in French, and one in English:

"And you, the community and family of Audrey and Denise, do you promise to support this couple and help them in difficult times, celebrate with them in happiness, and provide the acceptance and love that enables a couple to flourish?"

A sea of ouis and yesses.

Claire wraps the cheap wineglass I'd purchased in a thin towel on the floor. I go to stomp on it but accidentally step on Denise's foot instead. For a second, I think I really hurt her because she looks like she's crying, but I realize that she is laughing hysterically, trying to muffle herself. The crowd is roaring. On my second try, it's clear that the glass isn't going down without a fight. So, the third time, both of us stomp with all our weight, and when the guests hear the shattering sound, they all applaud.

The kiss we had been rehearsing for weeks is next. I take Denise's hand and go to wrap my arms around her shoulders. Just then, I hear "NO!" from the back of the dining room.

It's Fawn, gesturing wildly, a light tinkling of bells sounding as she hops up and down.

Huh? I look at Denise, who isn't bothering to contain her laughter.

She then reaches her hands behind her, leans in her and gives me the most minimalist kiss in the history of humankind.

"No smudging here," she whispers.

Chapter 31

W e go upstairs for a quick pee break and eventually find our way back down to the party. Events move smoothly, from the toast to the buffet supper, speeches and gifts, the cake-feeding ritual, which we do with our mocha fudge cupcakes. The wine and beer and champagne flow, and many of us are a little tipsy.

Including Jessica.

She tumbles over to me in the kitchen and flings herself over my shoulders. "Mrs. Meyerwitz. It's a sincere pleasure."

I recoil. "How much have you had to drink?"

"Dunno—not much. It's a wedding. It's your wedding. Shouldn't we be celebrating?"

The paint on my face hides the redness as I work to stay calm and measured. Just then, Pi grabs my arm and whisks me away to the dining room to answer a question about whether the couscous salad is gluten free.

The photographer comes over with Mom and says we need to do group shots. I glance at Mom, and she puts on her diplomatic face: "Twenty minutes, just twenty minutes, and then you can do whatever you want." She hugs me then pulls away to look at me, her face like a four-year-old who just wants one more piece of candy. So, I nod, and she rounds everyone up, Freddy and Natascha, Chloe, Ian and Brandon, Charlie and Chelsea, Leo, aka the balcony jumper, and even Tracy, who had made the trip from Boston with her new Irish boyfriend. As the photographer organizes us, I realize we've never had a photo taken with all of us before. Mom looks a little stoned, happy the way you're happy on the first day of a vacation—when you walk out on the beach barefoot, and you smell the ocean and feel the waves tickling your toes.

I poke Ian, telling him to take off his baseball cap. He rolls his eyes but does it. Chloe is standing behind me, and she squeezes my shoulder, giving me a shy smile. Mom puts her arm around me on one side of her and Denise on the other: "My new daughter-in-law."

The photographer tells us to say cheese. At that moment, Jessica leaps in front of us, hamming it up just as the shutter clicks. She looks back at me, and I can't help cracking up. My siblings are all laughing, too.

We smile and smile and smile. Then, we do the same with Denise's family, sweating and hungry but knowing we're going to be happy later when we can visit this moment anytime we want.

Meanwhile, Fawn is upstairs in the office, and there's a line down the hall of people who want face paint. She gives each kid an animal, a fox, a lion, a raccoon, a fish. Several adults get in on the fun, too. At one point, the kitchen is full of painted people. Every time the photographer sees us, he clicks his shutter. A few times he asks us to pose. Denise puts her pinkie in my nose, and I pretend to be eating her hair.

Miriam and Samya DJ, and we use the centre and living room areas for dancing.

Sweaty from doing the Macarena, I go into the kitchen for water. Jessica is there with one of Denise's nephews, flirting. She's blitzed and can barely stand. The nephew stares at me, a quiet call for help.

"Jess, I think you should go up to our bedroom and lie down," I say, trying to be smooth. I pour her a glass of water.

"I don't need this, silly. Where's the champagne? Maybe this nice gentleman will pour your guest of honour some more bubbly? S'il vous plaît?" She leans into the nephew, who immediately excuses himself to go find his girlfriend.

Denise walks in. "What's happening here?"

Jessica manages to go over to Denise without falling down. "Your wife wants me to drink some water. Don't you think your guest of honour deserves champagne? You're a class act, Denise, show 'em how it's done."

Denise looks at Jessica, then at me. Her mouth is a tight line, and her arms are crossed.

"Come with me," says Denise quietly to Jessica. "I'll set you up." Jessica, thinking she's being escorted to a secret stash, grabs Denise's arm. Denise takes her to Pi, and they have a conversation in French. Then Denise goes to the fridge and writes something down on a piece of paper and gives it to Pi. He sticks it in his back pocket, nods his head, grabs his keys, and takes Jessica outside.

I make my way to the front of the house where Denise is standing, looking out the window.

"What did you say? Where is he taking her?"

"I gave him my credit card. He's bringing her to the Marriott. I don't want her in my house."

Blood rushes to my cheeks.

"Why didn't you talk to me first? We could have figured out something else."

"There isn't anything else, Audrey. It's one thing to be tipsy at a party. But she's drunk, and I'm not going have her making our guests uncomfortable, and I also don't want to be responsible. I didn't consult with you because you told me she was sober."

"She is sober. She's just celebrating our wedding. I guess that's not allowed in your rule book." I jerk away and hurl myself downstairs into the basement where the kids are playing Twister. I plunk myself down in a corner where nobody can see me and try breathing slowly. You don't just send your wife's best friend to a hotel during your wedding reception without a talk, even if she is drunk. Images of me driving off, leaving Denise and the party, play in my mind.

Claire finds me eventually.

"I heard what happened. Are you okay?"

My hand covers my face, and I feel sticky paint on my fingers.

"It was a terrible position for both you and Denise. Your friend needs help."

I look up. "She has help. She's sober. She's just enjoying our wedding. Is that so bad?"

Claire sat down next to me. "What I think doesn't really matter. It's for Denise. You two need to talk."

She persuades me to go upstairs. Lots of people are gone. The fairy lights in the backyard glint against the dark backdrop of the night. I see Martha with Ian and Brandon, two of the Wellness girls, Claire and Sabrina, and Denise. I manage to avoid my wife and pretend everything is okay. When I do find her, we open a few presents before realizing that we are exhausted. I give my mom a big hug, and she tells me she's happy for me and so proud. I collapse into her arms and whisper, "Does it get easier?" She laughs and tells me to call her tomorrow, and she'll have an answer. She leaves and I fall onto the sofa. Denise is on the blue

Ikea chair with her feet up on the ottoman.

We sit in silence.

She looks up first. "You okay?"

"Not really. You?"

"Same."

I think of Jessica on her own, sleeping it off at the Marriott. "She's my best friend."

"This is my house, too, Audrey, and I don't want drunks in it. I thought we were the same on that."

I'm quiet. "You should have talked to me. We should have figured it out together."

"But I knew you would never agree to her spending the night somewhere else."

I sigh. "Maybe we should talk more tomorrow."

She nods and heads upstairs. I follow.

On the hallway floor is a trail of red rose petals.

"Oh my God. Who did this?" I ask, turning to Denise. Her face is suddenly bright, like a bike bell.

"Pas moi."

We walk into our bedroom, and the bed is covered with crimson petals. There's the chain of paper ladies I'd taped downstairs and a piece of purple velvet fabric tacked up on the window. Two candles with glass covers provide just enough warm light. Instead of a bare room full of boxes waiting to be unpacked, our bedroom is a romantic honeymoon suite, thanks to some creative phantom on our guest list.

We change into our pajamas and each get into bed on our respective sides. We fall asleep back-to-back.

Chapter 32

The next morning, I wake up at 7:30 a.m. thinking about Jessica alone in that hotel room, the day after my wedding. I call the Marriott, but she doesn't pick up. I decide to go talk to her. Denise is still sleeping, so I leave her a note.

I walk down the hall and find the room number that Pi had written down for me. I knock on her room door and hear "Hang on." There's a softness to the voice, like dandelion fluff you blow to make a wish. I imagine white downy scatterings in the air that give Jessica a gentle wakeup.

The door opens, and I'm shocked to see Eve, Jessica's older sister from Middlebury.

She whispers, "Hi. I figured it was you."

She gathers me into a hug. Speech seems a distant memory.

"I'm so sorry about all of this, and at your wedding—"

I break out of the hug. "Is Jess here?"

"She's sleeping it off. But I found her another rehab place, so don't worry."

"How—"

I see Jessica sleeping in the bed and remember to keep my voice down. "Can I come in?"

"I think it's actually better if we talk in the hallway." Eve checks for her key card and closes the door slowly behind her.

"Pi called when he got her settled in. Apparently, Denise gave him my number and asked him to stay with her until I got here."

Denise hadn't said anything about Eve.

Eve looks at the floor. "I'm so sorry my sister ruined your reception."

"No, she actually didn't, not at all. I was just worried. Why do you think she has to go back to rehab?"

Eve smiles and cocks her head. "Audrey, come on. She drank. A lot.

That's breaking sobriety."

I think about the beer bottles and Jessica's insistence that AA isn't right about everything. I wonder if Jessica had been drinking and driving this whole time. I think about the accidents that could have happened if she had been. I think of how much I knew and how little I did in response.

"Do you think she'll be okay?"

"Sure. My sister's an ox, but I have to keep an eye on her. I've been working so much I've been a little out of touch. And it's different with you in Montreal now."

"You think this is my fault?"

"Of course it's not your fault. Don't misunderstand me. It's just that you and the Wellness girls were Jess's primary support for three years, and those were probably the three best years of her life. You gave her so much that it's an adjustment for her without Wellness every week and without you in walking distance. She has to find other friends now, friends from AA, which of course she resists."

"She has a sponsor." I need to defend Jessica. "And she has other friends, teacher friends. And there's a couple of women from Wellness she's in touch with." But even as I say it, I know Eve is right. Jessica isn't close to anyone in the way she's close to me. I need to make more of an effort.

"Why don't you go home and be with Denise. There's nothing you can do here. When she wakes up, I'm taking her to rehab. It might be better if she doesn't see you."

I breathe in and try to think. Rehab, for a second time? But she was definitely drunk. And Eve and Christopher can afford that kind of expensive treatment, so why not?

"Okay." I hug Eve. "Tell her I love her. And tell her it was fine, that the reception was fine, that Denise and I are fine."

Eve touches my cheek and hugs me again. "I'll email you the address of the place, and you can tell her yourself. This place forbids patients from sending and receiving emails, so you'll have to put pen to paper. Maybe you could send some drawings or something." She gives me a tired smile, goes back inside the room, and then turns. "Oh, and the flower petals in your bedroom? That was Jess. But don't tell her I told you."

She slowly closes the door as I stand there, trying not to cry.

*

When I get home, Denise is sitting in the living room in her bathrobe, sipping her coffee. I take off my shoes and go to join her on the sofa.

"Where've you been?"

"The Marriott. Eve was there with Jess."

"I know."

She sips her coffee. I look out the window and see three girls across the street jumping rope. The peonies in our front garden had bloomed overnight.

"I'm going to make some decaf."

"Your mom called."

"What did she want?"

"She offered to take us out for brunch. She and the kids were heading to L'Oeufrier in le Plateau."

I count out three scoops of decaf, dump them into the reusable filter, and fill the pot with water.

I go back to the living room and sit in the blue chair. "How come you didn't tell me about Eve?"

Denise sips her coffee. "Not sure."

"I'm sorry about Jess. I should have seen it before. Eve's got her back in rehab."

She looks at her mug.

"Are you still mad at me?" I ask.

"No, but it's—concerning."

Divorce.

"I just think you need to be more realistic. You want to see the best in everyone, which is great, but sometimes it's not great. She was propositioning all the male guests. At our wedding."

"I know, Denise. I get it now. I made one mistake. I said I was sorry. What do you want from me?"

She takes her coffee and goes upstairs.

We don't speak for the whole day. I lie down on the futon in the room that's going to be my office and listen for kitchen sounds. When it's quiet, I make food, go to the bathroom, take a run.

Then on Tuesday, she knocks.

"Come in," I say, tapping my pencil against the sketchpad.

"J' peux pas," she says. "Can we talk? Or agree to disagree?"

I nod. "Let's have some fun and try talking later. It's supposed to be our honeymoon."

The fact of the matter is that we completely neglected to think about what might happen after the wedding. Denise is on vacation, and I'd cleared my calendar, but we hadn't had one conversation about what we would actually do.

"You know that hotel downtown, Beaux Voyages? The one with the pool on the roof that's open all year around?"

"Never heard of it," I say.

"They're having a May mid-week special. Two nights for the price of one."

I pull up Beaux Voyages on my phone to check prices and availability. "Looks like they have a bunch of rooms open. Are you sure you want to spend that much time in an enclosed space with me?" I'm half joking.

She smiles. "As long as you don't mind me wearing my new Victoria's Secret lingerie."

Now she has my attention. "Who gave you that?"

She looks away. "Jessica."

*

We put extra food and water down for Leto and go to the hotel. We spend most of the two days sleeping. When we return home, we put away gifts and don't talk about Jessica. We hang around in our sweats, eat scrambled eggs and fruit and peanut butter toasts, and occasionally throw on clothes to go grocery shopping. Some days, I practise yoga. But mostly, we allow ourselves the rest we hadn't gotten for the past six months.

And on the last night, we find one another's bodies in the pitch black of our bedroom.

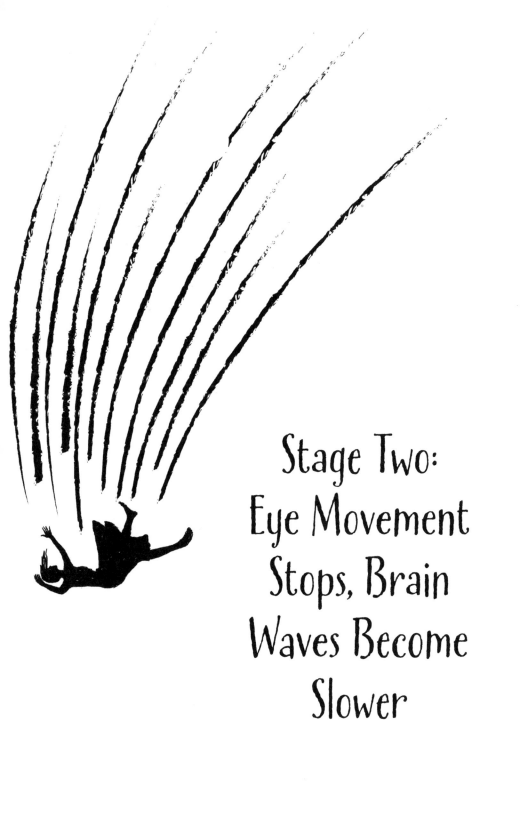

Stage Two:
Eye Movement
Stops, Brain
Waves Become
Slower

Chapter 33

Life settles. Other than a trip to see Denise's cousins in Ontario, we spend June at a neighboring public pool, barbecuing with Claire and Sabrina and occasionally with Miriam and Samya when they're in town, taking walks in different Montreal neighbourhoods and setting up our new home.

Now that the wedding is over, Dr. Terrance suggests getting involved and meeting new people in Montreal. Claire had told me about her British friend, Patti, who volunteers at the Humane Society, something I'd done for years in Albany. She suggests I see if they need any help. So, one day, I stop by.

I walk in and take off my sun hat. I pray I can find somebody who speaks English. The first person I see is a short round woman with dyed magenta hair. She's shouting instructions about setting up new dog cages to someone in another room in a booming voice. In English. I put my hands on the counter and smile.

"Uh, bonjour," I say, my voice soft and high pitched. I get her attention, and she stops shouting and turns to me. "I'm Claire's friend?"

She looks up. "Is it Audrey? So great to finally meet you." Her face explodes into a grin, and she comes around the counter to give me a bear hug. I feel myself stiffen. "Claire told me about you. Congrats on your marriage! Brilliant news."

She has freckles and a nose ring. Her eyes are enormous, and she looks ridiculously happy to see me.

I tell her about being new to Montreal and ask about volunteering.

"Actually, we just had one of our volunteers leave so your timing is perfect. I came here four years ago from the UK, so I understand it takes time to settle in and meet people and what not."

We chitchat until it's time to feed the dogs. Patti hands me a bag and a scoop. She says officially I have to take a volunteer training session, but they have several coming up, and it isn't a big deal if I want to help a little now. We lug the food bags into the dog room and are greeted by a chorus of twenty-five canine vocalists. I pop in my earplugs and get to work.

By the time I leave, I'm signed up for a training session in two days, and I have a possible new friend in Patti.

*

At the end of June, my permanent residency papers are approved, and Jessica comes home from rehab. I spend a weekend with her and Eve in Burlington before I move all my belongings to officially "land" in Canada. They surprise me with a Canada-shaped cake, vanilla frosting with a red maple leaf in the middle. I give Jessica a little gift for her work in rehab: a mixed media collage I'd made using the letters S-O-B-E-R and photo transfers of her at different ages when she'd looked healthy and happy. She cries and apologizes, over and over, for the wedding. I reassure her, over and over, that it's not a biggie.

"Denise probably hates me," she says after supper on Saturday. "I don't even remember getting from your place to the hotel."

Eve's setting up *Jurassic Park III* on the big screen. "Isn't there an AA step where you have to apologize to everyone you've spent time with since you started drinking?"

Jessica rolls her eyes. "Yes, Eve. I did it last time, and I'll do it this time. Can we just talk about something else? I've had months of it, and I need a friggin' break."

I look at Eve, who shrugs.

"Come up for a weekend when you're feeling better," I say. "You and Denise can talk. She forgives easy. I promise."

On Sunday, they help me pile all the boxes I'd been storing at Jessica's apartment in the moving van. The process is laborious, with the government requiring a list of each and every possession that is landing with me. Denise meets us at the border with Claire. Incredibly, the guards don't even look inside the van.

The officer who fills out the paperwork reads me the speech that all new permanent residents hear. He talks about Canada being a welcoming nation and says that being a permanent resident comes with rights and responsibilities. I'm exhausted and not listening very carefully, but Denise is. When he finishes, and I say the equivalent of "I do," Denise's eyes well up.

I look at her and squeeze her hand. Her sensitivity touches me, and I realize I've done most of my life milestones with no witnesses. But as grateful as I am, I'm also sweaty and weary. For me, this step is just another item to cross off on my to-do list.

What the website doesn't say is that when you land, there are still oodles of administrative tasks you have to do to become fully functional in Canadian society. I wait until my official permanent resident card arrives, and then I apply for a health insurance card, find a doctor, and take a driver's license exam. I also get a library card and fill out change of addresses for the governments of the United States and Vermont, the credit card company, my former utilities, my high school and university alma maters, the six charities I regularly support, and random others.

Once my health insurance card arrives, I sign up with a local doctor at the CLSC, the public health offices, and am referred to a new psychiatrist. Dr. Couture is bilingual and warm, and she has a special focus on anxiety. Together, we review my treatment plan from Vermont and decide to continue on unless there's any indication that there's a problem. I'm able to tell her honestly that my sleep isn't great but that for the first time in years, I'm consistently getting four to five hours in a row and, patched together, often between six to seven hours in a night. My panic attacks seemed to have subsided now that the bulk of immigration is finished.

I continue my graphic design work but decide to end my after-school theatre program in Vermont. Jessica organizes a good-bye shindig at Immaculate Heart of Mary on a Friday afternoon in July. She prepares little triangle sandwiches on Wonder Bread, plump green grapes, almonds, heart-shaped sugar cookies. I'm relieved to be at a party and not to have to worry about Jessica drinking. Sister Agatha gives me a painted ceramic plate made by some of the older Sisters of Mercy. Jessica got a bunch of the parents and teachers to pitch in, and they present me with a gift certificate to Second Cup, where I'd hung out so many times already, drawing or meeting up with Denise or Claire or Sabrina. Voice cracking, Jessica explains to the nuns and the parents that Second Cup is the Starbucks of Canada.

Chapter 34

Back in Montreal, I spend most of the time when Denise is working at home with Leto. I decide to increase my hours at the Humane Society to two days a week. They start a new project I'm helping out with: constructing a new outdoor play area for the dogs. One day, a woman brings in a white Chow-Chow/Samoyed mix named Mira and says the dog barks all day while she is at work, and she is constantly fielding complaints from the neighbours. But Mira is so quiet at the shelter that most volunteers don't even notice her. She spends most of her time shaking silently in the back corner of her cage. When I first meet her, she doesn't move from the corner, doesn't stop trembling, and pants so much I'm sure she'll keel over.

I start arriving fifteen minutes before my shift to hang out with Mira. I go into the dog kennel area armed with my earplugs and a large piece of cardboard cut from a moving box. At first, I put the cardboard down in front of her cage and just sit. I talk with her about the stress of moving, the stress of not having a home and a family, about getting used to a place that is profoundly different than where we used to live. I offer her treats from my pockets, which she ignores.

Then one day, I get the key and open her cage but then sit back down in front of the door as I'd been doing. I speak in low tones and avoid eye contract, not wanting her to perceive me as aggressive. I continue talking to her quietly.

I initially avoid mentioning Mira to Denise, as I remember our vow of no new changes for six months. But after one volunteer session, she seems curious.

"You sure seem in a good mood," she says, kissing me as she walks inside after work.

"Oh, I am," I say. "But I'm sure you don't want to know why."

She looks at the mail but smiles, shaking her head. "How can you be so sure of what is happening in my head?"

"Well," I say, doodling in my sketchpad, "there's this new dog who is totally gorgeous and totally traumatized. But I've been getting to know her, and I think it's helping."

She looks at me and smiles. "I love your heart, Audrey." We had talked about a dog someday, maybe even to doing animal therapy for disabled kids, but I had figured it was too soon. Now that she seems open, I know it's okay to at least talk about it.

From then on, any progress that happens or doesn't happen with Mira, I report to Denise. One day, I snap a photo of the dog with my cell, and I use it as my phone's wallpaper. I show it to Denise, hoping for an "awwwwww." Instead, she looks at me with lifted eyebrows.

I put my hands on my hips. "What? What is that look? I'm just hanging out with her. That's all."

Denise shakes her head. "She's beautiful, for sure. But no big changes for six months, right?"

"Absolutely." I dash upstairs and look at the calendar. That leaves several months during which Mira would undoubtedly be adopted or worse.

I make peace with the fact that Mira will eventually disappear. But I gaze at her delicate image on my phone whenever I have the chance. And I start taking more photos of her each time we get together. Quietly.

And one day at the Humane Society, when the rest of the dog residents are quiet, I sit in my usual spot on the floor on my piece of cardboard, and I see Mira get up and sniff in front of her. I slowly reach into my pocket, pull out a heart-shaped dog treat, and place it inside the cage, in the space between us. She sniffs some more and then, for the first time in weeks, she looks at me and stops trembling.

During my shift, I can't think of anything else as I slap primer on the new fence, shovel poop into the dumpster, and take several dogs for a stroll. I come back the next day, even though I'm not signed up for a shift, and sit with Mira for hours. I bring a book and sit there reading, my pockets stuffed with treats. In between chapters, I fantasize about Mira and me together, going to residential programs for kids with mental illness and giving them love and delight.

Obviously, there's a lot of work that needs to happen first.

I throw caution to the wind one day: I open the cage, crawl in, put a treat in the middle, and close the door. My legs start getting cramped, and I'm about to change positions when out of the corner of my eye, I see Mira get up, hesitate, then stretch her neck as far forward as she can, soft black nose in the lead, and when she's close enough, a black and pink tongue emerges and sweeps the treat into her mouth. She quickly goes back to her corner, chomping with crumbs flying out like dust from a construction project.

That night at supper, I stick a toe in the water.

"Honey, I know we said no changes for six months, and that's fine. But I wanted to at least tell you this." I sit down with a glass of grape juice and fizzy water. "Mira has been at the Humane Society for almost a month, and nobody has adopted her yet. She growls, but she's not violent. She's just traumatized."

Denise looks at me. Sips her soup.

"We both want to adopt a dog eventually. We can wait. But I wondered if you might want to see a video I made of her today."

More soup sipping. No words.

I scooch over, and we look at the miracle on my phone. Mira's stunning with her white coat and black spots.

After a few minutes Denise's face relaxes. "She matches Leto."

I grin. "Yeah, right?"

The next time I work, I text my wife a video of Mira wagging her tail. I send her Snapchat images, Mira sleeping in her corner, relaxed. Mira walking with me on the leash. One day in August, Patti takes a series of photos of us together. Mira actually approaches me, takes a treat from my hand, and then licks it. Another day, Patti takes a video on her phone of me inside Mira's cage, lying down next to her on the concrete floor, our sides pressed together. At one point, Mira licks my face.

We all crowd around Patti's phone in the shelter's kitchen.

"Send it to Denise," suggests one of the volunteers. Patti's laughter fills the space, and she immediately obliges.

Now every evening at supper, Denise asks me how Mira is doing. But she asks in a polite, impersonal tone, like how you might ask about someone's aunt whom you met at Thanksgiving last year. So, I finally ask her one weekend if she'd like to go to meet Mira in "person." Her mouth distorts, like she's trying to keep something in there. She says yes, no harm in meeting her.

I call the Humane Society before we leave, just to make sure nobody is walking her. Somebody is.

"Audrey, you better come quick," says Patti, "because there's a guy with his bratty daughter who thinks Mira is pretty like her doll. You don't have a hold on her or even an open file. Come now, mate!"

I tell Denise that Mira is about to be adopted by an Aryan Nation family who are planning to use the dog to sniff out liberals and communists and that it was our duty as compassionate citizens to ensure that this did not happen.

"Why do I feel like I am going into a conspiracy of many against lonely little me?" she says, her eyes warm as she gets into the car. I realize we are doing a role reversal from before the wedding, when Denise wanted the house. I wonder briefly about power and influence in a family. Is it healthy to persuade her to do something she doesn't really want to do?

When we arrive, Patti is with the man and his daughter, who is crying. Patti is shaking her head and apologizing.

"We just can't predict when there's been a big trauma like Mira's. The right circumstance will eventually present itself, and I have no doubt she could bite under stress. This is just not a dog I can recommend with children. Terribly sorry."

The little girl is wailing, "No, no, no, it's not true what that lady says. I want Mira, Daddy. I want her. I want her. I want her!"

The man sighs, picks up the little screamer, and slowly walks out of the shelter.

Patti has a hint of a smirk on her face when she sees us.

"What?" I ask, forgetting to introduce Denise.

"You owe me. That was almost really bad."

What she told the man wasn't true. I'd spent hours at a time with Mira in stressful situations, and I knew she was a submissive dog. She would retreat before biting anybody. My friend had lied to help me get Mira, without even knowing what Denise would say. I feel soft in my belly, looking at Patti.

I snap out of it and remember my manners and introduce Patti to Denise.

"I've heard so much about you, Denise. C'est un vrai plaisir."

Denise smiles and does the double cheek kiss but says nothing.

Patti goes to get Mira. When she emerges from the dog pen, she's wagging her tail even as she pants nervously. But strangely, she immediately approaches Denise, ignoring me completely.

"Whoa, bonjour toi, quelle belle fille Mira, plus belle que ta photo." Denise is scratching Mira behind her ears. Mira's whole body wags.

Denise stands up and looks at me. She has tears in her eyes. I look at Patti who is looking at the three other volunteers standing around grinning.

For now, anyway, a happy ending.

Chapter 35

Mira comes home with us on a Friday, and by the end of the weekend, neither Denise nor I can imagine life without her. She and Leto sniff one another, and on Sunday afternoon, Leto meows as she walks underneath the dog, rubbing her back and tail on Mira's ribcage.

This gives me some confidence to start researching the very complicated adoption laws in Quebec. Knowing the process would take much longer than six months, I download a PDF online for lesbians looking to make a family in Quebec. I take the time to cut up the pages into small chunks of text and put paperclips around sets of three so I could take frequent breaks.

On a mid-August weekend, I get to page fifty-three. On that page, I learn adoption isn't an avenue for hopeful moms with psychiatric disabilities. I'm ineligible. Period.

My fingers go numb. I stare at the word "ineligible" on the page. The house is silent other than my office clock which ticks and ticks.

For days, I barely sleep, but I manage to appear cheerful. Denise doesn't ask, and I don't tell her anything. But I know at that moment that the only hope I have of becoming a parent is pregnancy.

Putting family planning on the back burner, I continue volunteering, but I cut back to a saner schedule of one shift per week. Things are quiet, given it's after July 1st, the provincial moving day.

"But why does everybody move on the same day?" I ask Denise.

"Well, some people say it's so anglophones can't celebrate Canada Day."

"Isn't there a shortage of moving vans?"

Denise chuckles and says something about Americans being too literal.

*

Patti and I sit at the desk in late August, updating files and occasionally bringing out a cat who needs socialization. I tell her about growing up in Albany, about graphic design, moving to Vermont, running my afterschool classes, and performing with a small professional theatre company.

"I had no idea," she says. "I'm a performer too!"

"Totally makes sense. I bet you're amazing."

"I used to perform with two companies, actually. But it was too much so I just do one now. Good stuff."

"I'm impressed."

She brushes off the compliment. "I just love to improvise and experiment. I can see you doing that kind of work if you wanted to."

I shake my head. "I don't perform anymore. Just doesn't agree with me emotionally."

She laughs. "What's that supposed to mean?"

"Too many late nights."

"What kind of work did you do when you were performing?"

"I've done some classics, but what I loved was developing a piece with a group, something original, related to social issues. It has to mean something important for me to really get into it. I did a play with a group in Vermont based on the lives of three gay couples who wanted to get married when the movement for civil unions was happening."

She looks intrigued. "You should check out my old company. It's that kind of thing precisely and they're bilingual, though they mostly perform in French. I know the director, Stéfanie, was looking for someone to replace me. You should give her a call. I can make the introduction if you like."

I think about it, and my heart rate immediately quickens. Performing—and in French. But it would probably be a great way to develop my language skills. And the new friends thing. Most persuasively, I would be contributing to my new community.

I get the information about Patti's old group, Théâtre de la Prochaine Génération, and when I get home from my shift, I go up to the office and fire up the desktop. Leto jumps into my lap as I look at TPG's website. The website is only in French and out of date, with too much small text and no design at all. On the home page are three photographs of the company performing, but they are abstract and fuzzy. There's only one headshot, a stunning woman with an intense expression. It's the company's director, Stéfanie Olivier. Her bio is a whopping six paragraphs long, with what I assume are impressive credits from shows in Quebec. I can't find any names of the rest of the company.

I study Stéfanie's picture. She has a square-ish face with wavy black hair and dark eyes flanked with thick mascara. Her gaze bores into me, and she looks like she could step out of the screen as Lady MacBeth. "Come, you spirits / That tend on mortal thoughts, unsex me here."

I talk it over with Jessica. She has some opinions.

"She's way too hot. Don't do it."

"I'm not going to date her. I'm happily married, thank you very much."

"You are now, but I know you and beautiful women. Besides, why would you start performing again? You were so unhappy the last time you did it. Maybe you should teach instead, like you did here."

"There's only one English theatre school here, and I already applied. It's very competitive. And I'm interested in the work this group is doing. It's political. It's not just Stéfanie; it's the whole company."

"Not from what I see on their website."

"Come on, Jess, you know how it is. Some artistic groups just don't have the funds to update their sites, especially the ones trying to do good in the world. It doesn't necessarily mean anything."

After our chat, I decide to be brave, and I put in a call to Stéfanie to let her know I'm interested in auditioning. I pet Mira who pants and licks my wrist. I'm happy somebody approves.

Chapter 36

I pop down to Burlington to visit Jessica on Labour Day weekend, and when I get back, I check email and Facebook, and there's no message from Stéfanie. I get my sketchpad where I wrote down the number for Théâtre de la Prochaine Génération and call again. This time I get a live voice.

"Théâtre de la Prochaine Génération, bonjour."

"Bonjour. Parlez-vous anglais?"

"Sure. This is Stéfanie, how can I help you?"

No accent in English.

"Hi Stéfanie, my name is Audrey Meyerwitz, and I volunteer with Patti Clarke—"

"Oh, Audrey, I am truly sorry," she says. "I've been swamped with production details and haven't had a minute to return your call. Patti told me all about you, and I'm so happy you're interested. Is there time and day week that we could get together for a coffee?"

"Well, I'm pretty sure I'd like to audition," I say.

"We have a process for new members and a coffee meeting is the first step."

I never heard of that way of working, but I remind myself I'm the new flexible me, so we make an appointment for next Wednesday.

That evening at supper, I tell Denise about it.

"Sounds great," she says, nursing a beer. "Do you have time?"

"Think so. It'll be great for my French, too."

Denise tilts her head. "Do you really want to perform again?"

"I wouldn't have made the appointment if I didn't."

"Okay, franchement. I'm just trying to help you."

"Sometimes, believe it or not, I don't need any help."

She eats the last bite of tilapia and puts her plate in the dishwasher. She walks upstairs without saying another word. Mira trots up after her.

I wonder if I should go, too. I ask myself what it is about performing that's pulling me so strongly. I decide to go up and talk with my wife. She's lying on the bed, facing the window.

"I'm sorry, honey," I say, sitting down next to her on the bed. "If you don't want me to do it, I won't do it."

She doesn't turn towards me.

"Is it because you want me to have more time for us?"

She rolls over. "Of course I want time for us. But more important is you told me yourself that performing isn't healthy for you. What am I supposed to do with that? I am watching you doing something that could be risky health-wise. Do I just shrug my shoulders and say, 'Oh well?'"

I feel myself gearing up to defend myself. Instead, I take a big breath.

"No, you're right. I would probably feel the same if I was in your shoes. And I don't know why, but something is pulling me. Maybe it's wanting to be part of a group like Wellness."

"Why don't you just look for a therapy group or a support group? I think there's an English women's centre in Westmount."

"I talked it over with Dr. Couture, and she encouraged me to join groups for regular people. If I start getting panic attacks or whatever, she has some ideas. Anyways, thanks for caring. And sorry I got defensive, if that helps." I give her a hug.

She smiles. "That helps. A lot."

*

The next afternoon I'm on Marketplace posting an ad for my old red corduroy couch, which didn't end up fitting in the living room with Denise's. The photos are taking forever to upload, so I start poking around the events section to see if there's anything that looks interesting. Leto is sleeping on my desk, and I hear kids laughing and singing outside. I look and notice three girls across the street playing hopscotch. I'm thinking about Denise's concerns about the theatre and looking for other ways to meet people and make friends. I see a post in English for a picnic "for lesbians and their friends who want to meet new people" at the Parc Mont Royal that Saturday.

I forward it to Denise, who is more cautious about getting involved with things via the internet.

"C'est bien. Mais, what if it's a serial rapist?" she asks me that evening, drying the teapot with the pink dishcloth.

"It's a picnic. On the mountain. If there's a problem, all we have to do is scream."

"Alors," she says, putting the teapot back on its little shelf near the window, "will there be potato salad?"

I call Claire, but they have choir practice and a party. But Patti is free and up for it, so we organize to meet there on Sunday.

We wrap up a bunch of sandwiches, and I make Denise's picnic favourite, cold potato salad with bacon and pecans and chives. And we meet Mireille, the organizer, who brings muhamarra, baba ghanoush, and St-Viateur bagels. Nobody else responded to her ad. So, the four of us have a feast on my old camping blanket, listening to the tam-tam drums, getting to know one another, and laughing.

Mireille is from France and doesn't speak English very well, so Denise and Patti translate. She's a soft-spoken wiry woman with frizzy hair from a northern French village, and she explains that she moved here with her sister who got transferred for her high-tech job. Mireille is a sign language interpreter.

"Good on ya, mate," says Patti. "You're gonna love it here." I look at Denise. "Oh, shit, je m'excuse," says Patti, and the laughing begins. I watch Patti laugh and notice her holding long gazes with Mireille, so different than how she is with me.

After we eat several Mae Wests for dessert, Denise wants to get closer to the tam tams, so she and Mireille go, leaving Patti and I to talk.

"Meant to ask you mate, I'm looking for a flat closer to work and on the subway line. Maybe Villeray, Rosemont, somewhere in that area. That's near you, isn't it?"

I sit up. "There's a four-and-a-half for rent a few buildings near metro Beaubien, just two blocks from our place."

"You're joking."

"And you know Claire and Sabrina live around the corner?"

The next day, she sets up a meeting with the landlord, and we exchange multiple texts. I promise to help with the move and in less than twenty-four hours, everything is settled.

I send her a final text.

Did you get Mireille's number?

Don't you know it! 😊

Chapter 37

After such a great weekend, I'm excited to meet Stéfanie for our coffee date. My Montreal life is growing, and I'm starting to believe there's a chance I might build a healthy life here that could include theater, friends, and maybe even children.

It's September, and the city has come back to life after the sleepy summer. The metro is packed, but I arrive at Café St-Henri fifteen minutes early. When my chocolate croissant and mocha latte are ready, I pick a small table near the window. The place is busy even though it's 11:00 a.m., too late for breakfast and too early for lunch. I overhear several conversations in French and try, as I always do, to figure out what the people are talking about. A conversation about a retirement party and somebody's cousin and being included or not. Then another person mentions a hair stylist who might or might not be a colleague. I sigh. My French is improving, but I have a long way to go.

My cell phone says 11:08 a.m. and no sign of Stéfanie. I feel my insides tighten. Hanging out at restaurants, on street corners, in conference rooms, and outside people's apartments, waiting for friends and lovers who were perpetually late had been a big part of my life before Wellness. Moving to Montreal and marrying Denise meant a clean slate. If this is par for the course with Stéfanie and her company, I know I'll turn around without looking back.

At 11:20 a.m., just as I'm about to leave, Stéfanie rushes in. She's breathing heavily, toting a large black leather bag in one hand and a neon green floor lamp in the other. Her sunglasses are on top of her head, holding back her thick dark hair, and she's wearing a knee-length black miniskirt. Her lipstick is bright red and some of it was smudged in the right-hand corner of her mouth. Her dark eyes are larger and kinder in person than on her photo on the website.

"Je m'excuse. I'm so sorry Audrey," she pants, organizing the bag and the lamp and herself in the crowded café. I move a few of my things so we can fit at the table.

"Do you want to sit somewhere else?"

"No, this should work." She gestures to the lamp and laughs. "I saw this in a friperie, so I was delayed. It's perfect for our show going up next month." She goes and gets her food while I manage to cram everything in the tiny space we have. Stéfanie returns, taps the table with both hands, takes a breath, and then looks straight at me. I feel something unexpected in my belly and try to conceal it. I smile and extend my hand.

"C'est un vrai plaisir," I say, grateful I'd practised at home with Denise.

"Oh, so you do speak French?" Her hand is warm. I hold it just a few seconds too long.

"Not really." I look down at my empty plate, wishing I had ordered two croissants. "I'm still a beginner. Well, maybe advanced beginner." My mug is empty, but I take a sip anyway. "Do you live around here?"

Stéfanie grins and gathers her hair into a yellow scrunchy she has on her wrist.

"C'est toujours chaud ici, je trouve," she mutters. "And no, I don't live in this neighbourhood but not so far. Rosemont. You?"

I nearly choke on my invisible coffee. "I live in Rosemont, too." Her face lights up. We compare addresses. We are about a fifteen-minute walk from each other. Stéfanie takes a bite of her tomato mozzarella sandwich on baguette. We chat and eat and smile a lot.

"What kind of theatre do you do?" she finally asks.

I tell her.

Her face beams. "It's amazing. Our work is so similar. So, a bit about the company. We have a regular rehearsal each week to stay in shape and keep our performative cohesiveness. Then when we're in development, it moves to twice a week, and if we're in rehearsal, three times; typically, one of those is a Sunday afternoon or evening. I have a country house, and I'm there most weekends, which is why it has to be later on Sundays."

"Wow, that's so great that you have a place in the country. I just moved from Vermont to Montreal and our house is smack in the middle of all the noise and pollution." That sounds so ungrateful. "But Montreal's wonderful. And the schedule seems fine for me. I'd love to come check out a rehearsal," I say.

"Actually, we have a process for new members that I'll ask you to follow," she says, talking with her mouth full. I excuse it and notice her eyes, rich brown like fresh organic soil. "First step is a coffee date with moi, so you can check that off. Next, you'll meet with two company members, and they'll ask you some questions, and you'll do some improv together. If that goes well, you'll audition with the whole company, usually the first forty-five minutes of a rehearsal. The company can take up to two weeks to decide. If we're unsure, we may ask you to be a 'visiting member' for several months, after which, if all goes well, you'll be invited to full membership."

Big pause.

"You'll understand better when you meet the group. It's a very intimate process, the work we do," she says, washing her last sentence down with milky coffee. I can tell she's given this speech often. My heart is jogging, and I'm sitting on my hands. But finally, I pull out my calendar, smile, and say I'd love to book step two.

I leave the café, body pulsing with energy.

*

That night, I tell Denise about the coffee date, about Stéfanie, about the theatre company. "She's different. But clearly intelligent and committed. And she has a doctorate. And she teaches at Université du Québec à Montréal." Denise rolls her eyes as she organizes her pillows.

"If she's insane, it doesn't matter if she teaches at Harvard."

"I don't think she's insane. She's intense. Sensitive. Careful. Those are good qualities in an artist."

"You're already defending her," Denise says. "Maybe you should watch one of their shows before you do anything. And since they're so professional and have all these steps, they must pay the actors. Did she tell you anything about salary?"

I'm silent. The question had completely slipped my mind.

Chapter 38

A t the end of September, in between the many steps to audition for TPG, I help Patti pack and move into her new place in Rosemont. Since the picnic, we talk, text, or visit daily. We have Shabbat supper with Claire and Sabrina at our place, and Patti brings Mireille, with whom she's had several dates. We fill the evening with songs from our various cultures, with Claire playing her accordion, Sabrina on the drum, Patti in her knock-'em-dead Broadway-blasting alto voice, me and Mireille doing harmonies, and Denise picking up a tambourine or a shaker egg.

After the jam, we relax with glasses of wine. "We should take our band on the road," I say playfully.

"We'd need a name," says Sabrina. "How about the Sabbath Starlets?"

"Too much like Black Sabbath," says Denise, giggling.

"The Rosemont Rockers?"

"The Sassy Soubrettes?"

We continue drinking, laughing, and coming up with group names. It feels like what family should be, like a cozy log home with a green painted roof and a slight French accent.

*

I discover unexpected pleasures of city life. I rarely drive and I lose ten pounds just from walking from one place to the next. Our new home is a subway ride away from most anything we'd want to do and walking distance from grocery stores, bakeries, restaurants, a hardware store, a seamstress, even a cobbler.

The leaves on our street become yellow, red, orange. The air is chilly at night, and Denise and I stay cuddled up under the covers one Sunday morning in late October. I'm tickling her bare back.

I take a big breath. "I've been thinking about the baby thing."

Silence.

I continue tracing imaginary flowers on her petal-soft skin.

"Maybe I should just make the first appointment. There are four clinics in Montreal—"

Denise flops over onto her back and pushes away this short lock of hair that always gets in her face. Her eyes have bags under them.

She sighs.

"I thought you wanted to run off and join the theatre."

"Can we have a serious conversation, please?"

"You're sure about this?"

I sit up.

"Yes, of course I'm sure. You're the one who's not sure."

She props herself up on one arm.

"How can anybody be sure about a baby?"

I lie down next to her and close my eyes.

"I see a little girl with big green eyes and thick, messy hair. She's trucking towards you on the floor and you're speaking to her in French, in that high-pitched baby voice that moms use—"

Denise interrupts me. "I'm not going to talk in a baby voice."

I swat her with a pillow. She swings hers towards me, and I shriek. She cups my mouth with her hand.

"It's Sunday! The neighbours!"

"I think our neighbours should send us a fruit basket for how quiet we are. Nobody else in Montreal tiptoes around like we have to."

I sulk.

But the next day, when Denise is at work, I make the appointment, in very broken French. It's a month away, just enough time to be completely eaten up by anxiety. Fortunately, with Mira and Leto, the theatre, new friends, a few solid design projects, and volunteer hours at the Humane Society, I find it relatively easy to keep my mind off my ovaries.

Chapter 39

Patti and I grow closer with regular contact. She's very different from Jessica but shares her loyalty and willingness to commit in a friendship. Getting together with Patti is spontaneous. We'll text the other at all hours and then head out, usually meeting at the park where Patti smokes, always blowing it away from me.

One evening in September, we both can't sleep. We text at 3:00 a.m. and decide to drive up the Mount Royal and watch the sun rise. We have two camping blankets, a thermos of coffee, and Patti's cell.

"Whose idea was this?" I ask Patti's phone as we walk from the parking lot. She is videotaping for posterity.

She laughs, having trouble holding the phone straight.

"It was yours. I'm quite certain," she says in her thick British accent, cracking up.

"So, how's it going with Mireille?"

She turns off the phone, looks at me, and then cracks up.

"What? What's so funny?" I say. She starts wheezing from laughing so hard.

"Are you okay?" She's folded in half, gasping for air. She holds up her pointer, and then she's bent over again, tears streaming down her face and squealing. I'm laughing at her laughing. We start to calm down, then glance at each other and lose it again.

"Suffice it to say," she says, when she catches her breath, "that we've been warned several times by her landlord about excessive noise ...and shaking the downstairs neighbours' ceiling."

We tumble onto the ground laughing, and I feel a bit of pee leak out. When we stand up and calm down, I ask her what Mireille is like. She tells me she's very direct, quick with one-liners, and extremely easygoing.

"With a voracious sexual appetite. She's positively unstoppable. I thought I was extreme."

I'm amazed. Mireille seems so quiet.

"Do you think you guys will move in together?"

"She likes it over in Rosemont, but she has a lease until the end of the year. We're trying to experiment with being in my new place together. One thing's for certain, she'll need to pick up after herself, or else I'm not interested."

I look at Patti. "That's pretty rigid. Don't you think? It's not like she's a liar or a drug dealer."

"I don't deny it mate, I'm a hard ass about certain areas. Being inconsiderate is a deal breaker. And having dirty dishes and washing all over common areas isn't considerate. It's that simple."

"I'm glad I'm not your girlfriend." I cup my red nose with one hand. When the hand gets cold, I switch to the other one. "It's freezing. Must be barely two degrees. What are we doing out here in the middle of the night?"

"Trust me. it's worth it. I saw a bunch of guys doing Tai Chi up here last week," she says. "Pure magic."

I grab the phone, turn the video on, and point it at her.

"Tell the camera about the magic," I say. In the corner of the frame, I see moving shadows in the background. I push stop.

"Oh my God. Look!"

We're snickering again, but this time we muffle ourselves. Sure enough, there's a pack of senior citizens jogging, looking like marathoners with matching wick-proof sweat suits and headbands. We look at them, then at each other, in our toques and scarves and blankets. We're out of control, slapping our hands on the other's mouth to try to stop it, but failing miserably.

Eventually, we reach the summit, drink coffee from the thermos, and watch as the deep-blue sky gradually lightens, with rays poking out from the horizon like lasers. I can't feel my fingers or toes, but I feel the beauty of Montreal and the warmth of a growing new friendship.

Chapter 40

I meet with two TPG members and do my little improv session. I seem to have passed these steps because Stéfanie invites me formally to audition. There are three men and seven women, three Quebecoises, one anglophone Canadian, one guy from Guatemala, one woman from Syria, two women from France, as well as me and Stéfanie. One of the French women, Rebecca, leads us in a warm-up in a circle. We stretch our bodies and then our voices. We toss around a mimed ball. We pass energy around the circle. We say our names with a gesture and a particular vocal inflection that the group mirrors. Then we play an improv game actors love called "Freeze." It's mostly in French, but a few times, when the other anglophone actor was onstage, I hear some English. When forty-five minutes pass, Stéfanie, first in French then in English, thanks me for coming, and says the group would consult, and they'll have an answer for me in two weeks.

Walking to the metro, I realize I had forgotten again to ask about payment.

Two weeks come and go, and I don't hear anything. Then four. I count the days until our first appointment at Clinique Cigogne, but I also want to know if I'm in or out of the company. Sleep is hard to find, and a few nights I give up, quietly leaving Denise and going to my studio to sketch or read. The theatre company takes up all the space in my head, and even my drawings reflect that—a big-breasted diva singing an aria, acrobats standing on one another's shoulders, a group of aliens performing a revival of *The King and I*.

Five weeks after my audition, I come home from walking Mira to find a message from Stéfanie.

"Bonjour Audrey, c'est moi, Stéfanie, from TPG. The group was impressed with you, and we think you will make a wonderful new addition to the company. I congratulate you. Please mark your calendar.

We'll have two rehearsals next week, a performance a week from Saturday, and then the following Sunday morning. À bientôt!"

I dance around the living room, and Mira comes over and joins in, whining and barking.

"Qu'est-ce qui ce passe?" Denise comes downstairs.

"I made it! I got TPG! I'm an actor again!" I skip around the kitchen with Mira nudging me and crouching into play position.

A sunbeam catches the reddish highlights of my wife's hair. "What were all those dates?"

"Oh, that was the rehearsal schedule for the next couple of weeks. And they, I mean, we, have two performances too."

"She just expects you to be free?"

"That's the professional theater world. They're serious." I'm imagining a scene in French, me in a pivotal role, the audience riveted. "There were probably ten other people who they could have chosen."

"Were they all at the audition?"

"They do it one at a time so they can really get to know each actor."

"So, you don't actually know if there was anybody else."

"What difference does it make? It's great news." I walk over to her and put my arms around her. "It's just these first few dates. After I've been there awhile, it will settle down. They don't have shows all the time, so mostly it will be one or two evenings per week."

She hugs me and then goes into the kitchen, pours herself a glass of milk. She sits at the kitchen table and Leto jumps up into her lap. "So, what are you being paid for this very exclusive contract?"

"I'm not sure. But honey, this is going to be my French class. I'll have to get up to speed, much faster than if I just sat there for three hours. And anyway, the immigrant classes are five days a week for like four hours a day, which I can't do if I'm working."

Denise strokes Leto and gives me an edgy smile. "Ok, félicitations."

*

At my first rehearsal in October, Stéfanie gives a little speech, and then each company member comes up to me and honours me with a sound and a movement. Then Carlos brings out a cake that he had baked with blue-frosted letters: "Bienvenue Audrie." I don't say a word about the spelling. We eat cake and chitchat about the script that's in process. It's about a murder trial that had ripped apart the Montreal community several years before. A francophone man was accused of killing his

155

anglophone wife. Mixed into the case were years of tensions between the two language communities.

I learn that the upcoming performances are a different show. They created this piece the year before about a Muslim girl who played on a soccer team that tried to forbid her from wearing her hijab during games.

Before we all leave, Stéfanie pulls me aside.

"Audrey, can you help me with something? The guy who's supposed to run lights has an emergency. I know you're an actor, but if ever you would consider stepping in and doing the lights, it would be so great."

"Of course," I say, without hesitation. "I was just going to watch anyways. Do you have a lighting script?"

She hands it to me, and I take a look. "I've never run a light board before. Can I come to the rehearsal before?"

"Yes, that would be required of course. That's Friday evening, from six to eight."

"No problem. My wife is really flexible, and we don't have plans for that night anyway."

Carlos sends me home with leftover cake, which I give Denise.

"Myam myam! They gave you cake for joining the company? This is sounding better already," she says, mouth full of frosting. "Did you eat any?"

"I actually had three pieces already. Oh, and I have one extra rehearsal because their lighting guy was in an accident or something. So, I have to be there Friday evening and one hour earlier on Saturday for the show."

My wife looks at me like I had slapped her.

"That's five times this week. And a Friday night. Shabbat."

"It's just this one time, honey. I have to get up to speed."

"But you're supposed to be acting, not doing lights."

"It's a collective. We all have to pitch in when there's an emergency."

I give her a hug and slip my hands under her shirt to feel her soft warm back with my palms. She shivers, then looks up at me, sighs, and presses her lips into mine.

Chapter 41

The next day is our first appointment at the clinic, and I'm up all night. I sketch old-fashioned spotlights and actors standing in circular pools of light. One is crying. One is nursing an infant.

*

In the morning, Denise is well rested but quiet as we drink our coffee. On the drive to the clinic, I focus on rehearsal to stay calm. Denise is staring out the window.

"The whole francophone-anglophone thing is pretty intense," I say, putting on my blinker. "Stéfanie's grandfather was the head of a department store, and he could only speak English, even on his lunch break."

Denise doesn't look at me.

"What's wrong, honey?"

"Nothing, just nervous about the appointment."

I reach over and hold her hand. "It's going to be okay. I promise."

She turns her head and gives me a tiny smile. I start stroking her thigh, remembering the night before. She gently places my hand back on the steering wheel.

When I open the door for Denise to Clinique Cigogne, we stop in the lobby, mouths open, staring. It's not just the plush grey carpet or the hanging Mason jar lighting. It's not just the overstuffed teal upholstered couches and the charcoal loveseats. It's not just the staff, who all wear suits, even the receptionist. It's the effect of all this grandeur on a simple lesbian couple wearing tennis shoes, mine purple and Denise's white, two women who just want to make a baby together.

"Est-ce que je peux vous aider, can I help you?" asks the smiling receptionist. My armpits dampen. I open my mouth to speak, but nothing resembling French or English comes out.

"Oui, nous avons un rendez-vous," says Denise, taking control. The receptionist directs us to sit in the lounge, then offers us a cup of tea or some spring water.

We sit down and notice the glass coffee table in front of us. I take off my fleece and look around the waiting room. There are two white heterosexual couples and one mixed race lesbian couple. The woman closest to me is Black, and she's speaking to her partner with an accent I don't recognize.

"Paris?" I whisper to Denise.

She shakes her head, grabs the pen and notepad she knows I keep in my backpack, and writes "Haiti." I've been in Montreal for a year and am starting to understand some French, but recognizing accents is still beyond me.

The two women stop chatting and begin reading "Fertility Today." The other partner is pale white with light blue eyes and an athletic build. I wonder if she's Norwegian. Then I wonder if she's wearing coloured contact lenses. At one point, she looks up and catches me staring. I immediately turn to the table and grab a magazine.

Once we finally get in to see the first nurse, she gives us a binder with twenty-five pages full of information. In addition to two pages of tests I need to take, we also have to meet with a psychologist and start charting my ovulation and menstrual cycles. Depending on when my periods arrive, I would need to come in to be poked, prodded, and eventually harvested (my eggs, anyways). The sweat production under my armpits amps up every time the woman opens her mouth.

"Now, are you currently taking any medications?" she asks me, with only a hint of an accent.

"I'm taking three for anxiety and a sleep disorder. I wrote them down on my intake form."

The nurse looks at the file and nods. "The Ativan you'll want to cut. Are you still taking one milligram only?"

"Actually, I went off that one since I met Denise."

"That's great because you really don't want to have any of that stuff in your system if you get pregnant. I suggest you try herbs or melatonin in small doses if the Amitriptyline doesn't do the trick."

"Do I need to get off the Amitriptyline too?"

A pearl of sweat trickles down my left temple.

"Some studies have shown a slightly larger percentage of babies having birth defects with mothers taking TCAs; other studies didn't show any difference. If you're taking a reasonably low dose, which you are, you should be okay."

I give Denise a huge smile, which she returns. We had both been worried about the medication. With the final hurdles crossed off, we were in sight of my dream. If only my heart would slow down...

Chapter 42

At home, Denise and I organize our fertility project as we'd organized the wedding and immigration processes: lists and binders, with plastic tabs and labels, coded with different colour inks, and a special calendar dedicated to baby making. I make sure to photocopy everything, punch three holes, and properly classify each piece of paper in the binder.

One of the first decisions we need to make is about sperm. Since it's illegal to buy or sell sperm in Canada, our choices are limited to using "Canadian compliant" online donors or have a man we know personally who would need to do it for free. Like many future lesbian moms, I had dreamed up the perfect scenario by which to orchestrate our family as soon as I realized we couldn't adopt. We would find a gay male couple who likes kids but isn't committed enough to become parents, and then we would use the most virile and handsome partner's sperm to create our family. The child would have full access to both biological parents plus our partners, providing him or her with the added bonus of four role models with at least two different genders.

So, with images of apple picking and acorn squash in fall, sledding and snow forts in winter, piano recitals and pizza parties in spring, and sandcastles and splashing in summer, I approach our number one choice for this fertility adventure: the best looking, warmest, and most successful gay male couple in our lives. Who also happen to be the only gay male couple in our lives. My friend Jerome, with whom I used to do children's theater, and his husband, Kevin.

I call Jerome and Kevin who live in Burlington and arrange a supper at The Daily Planet, one of my favourite Burlington restaurants, on a Saturday evening in early December. Denise and I arrive early so we order melon daiquiris at the bar, which is packed with voices, laughing, exclaiming, joking, even singing. The guys walk in, and I practically melt.

I jump off my barstool and go hug them both.

Kevin, who is both authentic and socially gifted, introduces himself to Denise. When the hugging and introducing ends, we switch.

"Let's see if we can get a table in the main room," suggests Kevin. I hold Jerome's hand tightly. He pulls his away before I'm ready to let go.

Once we're installed and the server takes our order, the moment presents itself. I scratch my head, noticing my scalp is sweaty. Denise reaches for my hand under the table. She looks at me: my country, my lead.

"So, guys, Denise and I have started the process of becoming parents."

Jerome's eyes get big.

"Mazel tov, that's amazing, Audrey. When are you due?"

I laugh, feeling insanely serious.

"Oh, we're not even close to that yet. We have to make some, er, big decisions first."

I feel Kevin take a step back psychically. He had donated sperm to a lesbian couple who had a daughter. The moms wanted him involved but were difficult and controlling people with whom Kevin had never quite found peace. Of course, I had imagined it would be different with us, since we were, in contrast, easy and delightful people with whom the guys already felt peaceful.

I look at the cliff and step off it.

"We wondered if either of you would consider being our donor."

My face throbs with heat and now sweat covers my neck and bra line. The men look at each other and then back at us, smiling the way that people do when they have to tell you something you don't want to hear.

"Sorry," says Kevin. "You know my situation, and it's not something I could or would want to do again. I'm flattered to be asked, though."

My mouth is slightly open and my body frozen in place.

Jerome pipes up.

"Did you know that Kevin sits on panels advising lesbian couples against using a known donor?"

Nope.

I dig my thumbnail into my leg to stop the tears.

Jerome looks at Kevin to make sure he's finished and then he speaks.

"For me, it's more about not wanting to contribute to overpopulation of the planet. That's the generic reason I would say no to anybody. But I would also worry about our friendship. I saw what happened with

Kevin and Monica and Sherry. I would never want that to happen to us. But I feel like Kevin does, the being flattered part."

Jerome gives me a sad smile. I try to see him through my tears. He leans over and hugs me.

"It's big, baby stuff. I give you both a lot of credit."

I wipe my eyes.

"Even if you think we're ruining the planet?"

He looks at me, and we both start laughing. I know it will be okay in a while. I'm grateful we have a delicious restaurant meal coming to change the vibe.

It never occurred to me or Denise that both men would politely decline our fabulous invitation, especially since one had already given this gift to another lesbian couple thirteen years previously. This seemingly simple gift, which cost almost nothing in time or money, apparently meant a lot more to them than we'd expected.

Only mildly miffed, we dust ourselves off and next approach one of Denise's nephews, Jacques, somebody we knew was not planning to have any children of his own. How perfect—our child would be a blend of Denise's genetics and mine! We invite him over for tea and pastries. He stops by on a Sunday afternoon.

"Hey, bonjour," I say, opening the door. Jacques gives me a quick smile and a polite two-cheeked kiss. "Ça va, Audrey?"

"Great. Come on in, Denise is making tea."

Jacques hangs up his jacket and looks around. He'd been at the house once before, for the ceremony, and comments on our artwork and painting. We sit in the living room and wait for Denise.

"So, how's work?" My voice is bright, like a hostess.

"Good. We're interviewing for a third attorney, which is necessary, since all of us are working too many long hours."

"That sounds productive."

He nods and looks down at his feet. I look at the clock. "I think I'll go see what's keeping Denise."

I practically bump into Denise who carries a tea tray into the living room. We laugh nervously, and I go back into the kitchen to bring in the plate of chocolatines from our local bakery. I place it next to the tea tray as Denise pours each of us a small sky-blue ceramic cupful of Earl Grey. Leto strolls in and rubs against Jacques' shins. He reaches down and pets her.

We all look at each other.

Denise sighs. "Alors, maybe you know or not, but Audrey and I want to have a baby."

Jacques smiles. "Je sais."

We smile back at him. I reach for a chocolatine. Then a napkin.

I nod at Denise. Her lead.

"We need to find someone who is very generous to help us with this project. A male someone."

He looks at the door. I bite into my pastry. Denise looks at me, her face crimson. "We thought maybe we could ask you."

Jacques laughs. "It's nice, I suppose, being asked. But I wonder if you two have thought seriously about how the child will feel and do. Like is it good for the child?"

Denise and I look at each other. She picks up her teacup and looks at him. "What do you mean?"

He crosses and uncrosses his legs. "A child should have a mother and a father. I know not every child grows up like this, but that's what's natural. Think about how the child will feel at school, when the kids see two moms come in and no dads. I think it would be a very hard life, not healthy for a developing person."

My mouth is stuck mid-chew. Leto jumps onto the couch. Denise slowly puts down her teacup. Neither of us says anything. Mira comes in, panting, and pokes Jacques with her snout. He's startled and then he laughs, strokes her between her ears.

"No offense. I don't have anything against gay people. I have gay friends, and it's not a big deal. But I wouldn't want to be part of something that might be harmful to a child. I think you're both great, but I don't think it's a good idea. Sorry."

My wife and I just stare. Leto jumps down and Mira sniffs her butt. Jacques picks up his teacup and makes a soft slurping sound.

"Well, I guess we can just agree to disagree," I say, gobbling the rest of my chocolatine, reaching out to pet Mira who is leaning against my knees.

Denise is not so diplomatic. "Je pense que tu devrais partir," she says coldly, standing up. Jacques shrugs and smiles. "Just telling the truth. Je m'excuse." She escorts him out of the house. I hear the door shut.

She comes back and looks at me. We sit there for what feels like ten minutes. Then we go upstairs and silently get ready for bed.

Chapter 43

We're out of options for a known donor. We talk it over on Shabbat just before the holidays with our friends.

"I know a bunch of couples who've used sperm banks, and their kids are lovely," says Sabrina, bringing out a platter of salmon. Claire bought a new striped tablecloth, and a glass vase holds a bunch of daisies from Mireille. "When I was single and thinking about doing it, I had decided to use a sperm bank."

I stare at her. "You wanted to have kids when you were single?"

She smiles and nods. Then she looks at Claire.

"It's me," says Claire, shrugging her shoulders. "No babies."

"Why not? You two would be the best parents in the world." As I say it, my brain is already working on a sketch of the two women with a sizable brood.

Claire shakes her head. "I took care of my two brothers and sister after my mom passed away, when I was ten. I've already been a mother. Not something I want to do again."

I look at Sabrina. She's smiling politely, but I see her eyes get glassy. She excuses herself and goes to the bathroom. Claire follows and closes the door.

The four of us don't say anything. Then Patti pipes up.

"Honestly, mate, I think sperm banks aren't a bad way to go. Kids are kids. My brother's best friend got knocked up at a bar. She didn't even know the guy's name. Her daughter is strong and gorgeous and smart."

I look at Patti. "Do you think kids should have a mother and a father?"

"Bollocks. Kids can be raised by aging aunties if they're keen on it. It just matters that they're raised by committed adults. Why, did some-one say that?"

I tell her about Jacques. She shakes her head. "Homophobia, that's all."

I look at Denise. "I don't know. I mean, the whole idea is to have a healthy family. What if it really is better to have one male and one female parent?"

Mireille clears her throat. "They say parents should be man and woman and that this is healthy. But many men and women have children, and many unhealthy things happen in this family. It is bonds matter for health of baby. This is all."

Claire comes back to the table. "She'll be okay. We go through this every now and then. She's fine with it, but sometimes she has to grieve." She pours wine into our glasses. We watch her carefully.

"But about the sperm, I think you have to be careful. I mean, I wouldn't want to pick just any guy off the street. At least with the sperm banks, they give you some information, don't they?"

I nod. I'd spent hours the day before researching sperm banks. I couldn't tell one man from the next by the time I was finished. "I guess we have to figure out what our priorities are." Part of me is stepping into Sabrina's shoes, imagining marrying someone who doesn't want kids. Then I realize I wouldn't have done it.

Sabrina returns, and Claire gives her a kiss. She goes to sit back down, and I catch her eye, checking to see if she's okay. She winks at me. My breathing eases.

Claire starts pouring water. "This kind of thing makes me wonder. I mean, the whole selection process. It's kind of like trying to play God, isn't it, if you think you're screening for certain physical traits or personality characteristics?"

I shake my head. "Maybe some people do that, but we're not. I just want someone without a psychiatric history."

Mireille asks, "What if the donor is adopted like you, Audrey?"

"We're given medical records. I'm sure they know what they're doing."

Denise says, "Nobody has much control in baby making."

"We're all just mere mortals, girls," says Patti, rubbing Mireille's neck.

Mireille turns to her. "Scratch my back?"

Patti laughs. "Not mere mortals but itchy mortals!"

Claire's eyes widen. "That's it. The name of our group!" Sabrina nods with a smile. "The Itchy Mortals."

*

Our spirits are only temporarily lifted. The bizarrely anonymous sperm bank is now our sole option. One evening, we make mojitos and go back online to look at profiles of Canadian-compliant sperm donors. White male, 6'1, Italian descent, physician's assistant, heart disease on mother's side, favourite food, strawberry sundaes, favourite season, summer. Hispanic male, 5'6, pianist, graduated from college summa cum laude, male-pattern baldness on paternal grandmother's side of family, bucket list items include writing a score for a feature film, climbing Mount Kilimanjaro, studying engineering. African American male, 5'11, graphic designer...

"So," says Denise, "we can have somebody who's gifted in the arts but who might have a heart attack at fifty. Or a guy who's not so great looking but who has fabulous eyesight and grandparents well into their one hundreds."

After an hour, it becomes one big mushy indistinguishable pile of potential sperm. We decide we must go out for ice cream sundaes immediately.

We come home and narrow our search to three men, all of whom appear good looking, sane, and in reasonable health. When I call the company the next day, they only have vials available from one of the three. So, we choose him. Our donor is thirty, 6'1, green eyes, and blonde hair, of German and Swedish descent, a computer programmer, and a self-described Renaissance man. He already has a daughter with his girlfriend, and in his essay says he's donating because his best friend went through fertility problems, and he wants to help couples struggling to have a family. He goes to church, loves his parents, and is a volunteer tutor at the local elementary school.

We fill out the form, send it in, and cc Clinique Cigogne.

Chapter 44

We take a break from the baby project for the holidays. Mimi throws a family party on Le Reveillon, Christmas Eve, and I get to taste some traditional Quebecois food, like tourtière, bûche, ragout de boulettes, and pattes de cochon. Sabrina and Claire host a Hanukkah gathering for the Itchy Mortals. On another night, Jessica pops up. We light my menorah, and I make my mom's famous latkes, leaving our house smelling like a greasy spoon for days.

In mid-January, I work the light board for TPG's performance of *Nabila Scores* at the Greek community centre in Parc Extension. It's a family show, and the audience loves it. I only make a few minor errors which Stéfanie notes for me after the show. The actors and the script are top notch. But afterward, there's tension in the group that I don't understand.

I ask Carlos and he rolls his eyes. "Drama, drama, and more drama. People think us queens have drama, but actors are far worse."

"What do you mean?"

"Well, François going missing for starters, leaving you to do the lights."

"I thought he had an accident or something?"

Carlos laughed. "Uh, no, he lives down the street from me, and I saw him yesterday, smoking a joint and making out with a sixteen-year-old girl."

I say nothing. Then I look over at Stéfanie, who is deep in conversation with two actors. "She told me—"

Carlos gives me a hug. "You're a good sport Audrey. I'm glad you're here."

*

In February, TPG rehearsals resume. The company is in a development period, so I'm out Monday and Wednesday evenings. My French improves, but oftentimes I ask Carlos for a whispered translation if we're working with a transcript. I warm up with the group and do some exploratory exercises, then I usually watch. François hasn't rematerialized, and nobody mentions him.

On the fifteenth, Denise and I have our psychological assessment at Clinique Cigogne. We have a meeting with a Madame Boisvert at 3:15 p.m. on Wednesday. Denise has to take more time off from work, and her boss isn't happy, so she's in a sour mood when I pick her up.

"I hope she's bilingual," she growls, "because it's impossible to translate and be assessed at the same time." I kiss her and offer the pear I'd brought for her snack.

After we arrive and give our name, we barely have time to sit before we're invited into the office by a friendly-looking woman who introduces herself as Madame Boisvert. She's wearing an olive pantsuit with wide lapels, a white blouse with brass buttons, and plastic framed glasses with a cord around her neck. She's also wearing heavy black eyeliner and coral lipstick that seem to be from a different movie.

"Audrey, Denise, thank you for coming in. Merci d'être venues aujourd'hui."

I catch Denise's profile out of my peripheral vision. Barely detectable lip muscles suppressing a giggle.

"Would you prefer English, français, les deux?"

We look at each other and Denise answers.

"English, please."

Madame Boisvert takes off her glasses and offers us plastic bottles of water, which we take, despite our new campaign to only drink from the metal bottles we have at home.

Once everyone is settled, Madame glances down at our file.

"So, Denise, Audrey, tell me a bit about yourselves."

Denise starts. She talks about growing up in Montreal with her two brothers and one sister, her parents who were always very supportive though not emotionally expressive. She talks about working as a probation officer for twenty-two years. She talks about volunteering in a nursing home for ten years, keeping residents company and reading them French poetry and literature. She tells Madame that her life had become much more exciting since meeting me, which was both wonderful and exhausting but perhaps most relevantly excellent training for life with a newborn. She tells her about travelling to Italy,

New Brunswick, and New York City with her mother, just the two of them. She says she loved both parents very much and misses them since they've passed. She says she's happy with her life and with me, and she thinks we have a lot to offer a child.

"And you, Audrey? "Tell me about your family."

I hold up one finger and slide out of Jessica's purple sweater. I wipe my sweaty hands on my jeans.

"Well, my family is—er—I'm from the States, from Albany, New York. I'm adopted. I have four siblings who were also adopted, and Mom is still fostering. She's in touch with all the kids who lived with us, so her life can get kind of unmanageable at times. I help her out when I can, when I'm not too busy. My youngest brothers Ian and Brandon are a handful, but they're actually really creative. They make these giant sculptures on our lawn every Halloween. This year it was a zombie with an ax stuck in its skull with red paint for blood all over the place. Somehow, they got it to pop up from behind a big rock on the side of our house. You should have seen it. The neighbourhood kids were terrified. One of them even peed his pants. There were hardly any trick or treaters it was so scary. Ian and Brandon were out of their minds. They kept high fiving each other and throwing themselves on the ground screaming."

I giggle. Madame Boisvert and Denise don't.

"My family is really busy, so I just don't spend much time with them. My sister Chloe is a part-time receptionist for a chiropractor in Albany. She's an alcoholic, but Mom pays her rent so when she misses work, well, let's say this is the longest she's held onto a job. Then there's Freddy, the oldest. He's a scientist and his third wife, Natascha, is also an academic. She's really the one who calls the shots in their relationship. Freddy still smokes cigarettes behind their barn, which he supposedly does behind her back, but I think Nat knows and doesn't say anything because she's a hoarder, and he doesn't confront her about that or anything, really. I mean, obviously she can smell the smoke on him—well, I can smell it on him, that's for sure."

Madame Boisvert clears her throat. Denise gives me a thin smile as she sips her water.

"I'm hearing that your oldest brother is the sibling you're closest to. Is that right?"

"You could say that. It's not like we text each other every day but he's a good guy."

"He's been married three times?"

I nod. "He's optimistic."

Denise coughs.

"Was it difficult for you, when he got divorced?"

"No, it was a huge relief, at least the first time. They broke up just as I was going off to college. He was having this affair with his graduate student for like six years. His first wife, Brenda, found out about it one day when she found this fur coat that wasn't hers in the trunk of his car. Both of them were a mess. Glad I missed that one."

Both women are staring at me. I pick at fraying threads on my jeans at the left knee. A phone rings in the office next door. Someone answers it, "Clinique Cigogne bonjour." Madame scribbles some notes.

Denise pipes up.

"Audrey has some amazing friends."

I look at her, then at Madame Boisvert.

"Why don't you tell me a bit about yourself," she suggests, adjusting her glasses.

"I'm an artist. I do graphic design and teach for money, I mean, not lots of money but enough to pay the bills. But my real work is being an artist: performance, handmade books and collages, comics, things for friends. I'm also a new member of a professional theatre company here in Montreal. It's like, art as activism. I don't think too much about money. I want to make the world a better place."

They both look at me, expressionless.

"I'm good in the kitchen. I bake these pumpkin muffins. Maple syrup, no refined sugar. And walnuts. You know, essential fatty acids and stuff."

Any social compass I might have had walking into the clinic is long gone. No matter what comes out of my mouth, I dig myself deeper and deeper into a hole where no child would ever be conceived.

"Denise is my healthiest relationship. That's why I didn't do this on my own. I know we can do it much better together."

My throat constricts, and my eyes fill.

"Please believe me." I look into Madame Boisvert's eyes. She looks down at her notes.

Denise takes my hand.

"I'm not going to evaluate whether you'll be nominated for mother of the year, Audrey," says Madame, putting down her pencil. "It's clear you're intelligent, driven, and sensitive. My job is to provide support during what is most certainly a stressful process. You and Denise have a lot to offer a child. You both cleared any sort of minimum standard, in my mind anyhow, so please relax."

Denise sighs. My shoulders sink down. Breathing becomes possible again.

"What you must know about this path is that it's difficult and seldom comfortable. Your emotions will be stretched beyond the limits of anything you've experienced prior. Don't fool yourself into thinking you have something under control, like knowing a statistic. You'll either get pregnant, or you won't. And then you'll need to decide if you want to go through it again. IVF is extremely expensive."

Denise interrupts.

"Oui, and we are both committed to trying only once."

"Don't make fast decisions about any of this. Use your supports. If you want to talk, you can make an appointment with me. You'll have to pay the fee, but it can be well worth it."

She hands Denise her card because clearly Denise is the stable adult in the relationship.

They stand up, shaking hands and exchanging niceties. I get up, a beat behind, bundle up, mumble merci, and bee-line it for the exit. I run towards our snow-covered Honda Fit.

"Audrey, what's wrong?" Denise is chasing me, her blue puffy coat flapping unzipped. "I have to go pay. Come inside. We can talk later."

I get to the car and lean against it, hiding my face with my mittens. Hold my breath. She unlocks the doors, and we both get in. I take off my mittens and wipe my cheeks with my hands. We sit in silence.

"I can't be the poor mentally ill immigrant in this relationship," I finally say. She takes my face in her hand.

"You aren't. And you never will be." But I'm imagining our baby at five, crying for Denise in the dark, at ten, asking Denise about menstruation, at seventeen, getting Denise's opinion about colleges. French colleges.

We pay, go home, and turn on a Netflix nature film about cheetahs.

Chapter 45

In late March, I begin hormone shots.

Our first clue that the stakes are higher is filling our prescription. The nurse explained about the process and what would happen, but nobody mentioned anything about cost. When we go to the pharmacy, we assume it will be high, maybe even several hundred dollars. I stand at the counter, which is overflowing with rectangular-shaped boxes, each with tiny bottles of daily injections and syringes. The pharmacist places all of it in a big pink and blue shopping bag and takes it to the register.

"That will be $5,873.95. How will you be paying today?"

I ask her to please repeat herself. Must be a translation problem.

"$5,873.95. What method of payment, please?"

I turn to Denise who is having a petit mal seizure. Quickly I race through the balances I'm carrying on my old credit card from the US and the new one I'd gotten when I opened my Canadian bank account and realize I have enough left on two if the total can be split. The pharmacist informs me that yes, it can.

I manage the transaction, only occasionally glancing at Denise who has taken on the role of hood ornament. When we finish, I take the bag, smile, and calmly offer a "merci." Looping my arm through my frozen wife's, I return us both to the car. Maybe the process is just stressful. Maybe we can take turns being strong.

*

The next evening is day one of the injections. I keep track of two cycles, and Denise begins administering the hormones designed to help my ovaries go into mass production mode. There is a seventeen-page instruction booklet and a DVD, which I refuse to watch because how complicated could it be? Not only does Denise view it, but she also takes notes.

That evening, at exactly 7:30 p.m., she rereads the instruction booklet, her notes, and lays the whole kit out on the bathroom counter. There are several vials, syringes, a needle, a mixing jar, and then a marker to pick a spot on one of my fleshy hips for the injection.

"How are you doing?" she asks.

"Fine. It's you I'm worried about."

She opens the vials and attaches the needle, mixing and pushing and several times referring back to her notes. She takes a breath. "I think I'm ready."

Her hand is shaking as she positions the needle on my hip. She pushes tentatively, and her face cringes.

"Just do it," I say, the injection site burning. And she does.

It becomes clear on that first night that going faster feels better, and she improves with practice. After a week, when her technique had been perfected, I videotape our ritual, narrating each step to our future child.

Just as Denise injects me full of hormones, I aim my phone at the bathroom mirror.

"We're making you," I say, smiling. We both look at the other's reflection in the mirror and stop. I imagine a third presence behind us. It feels, I decide, like hope.

*

At the end of April, TPG has a meeting about the fall and starting the process of booking the new show we're creating. In a rare moment, I offer my opinion that the company's website needs an overhaul if potential clients are going to take us seriously.

Stéfanie nods. "Je sais. Unfortunately, nobody in the company except François has the skills for that. And we definitely don't have any money in the budget."

Silence.

I pipe up. "What's the deal with François?"

Stéfanie says, "He's in a burnout."

I laugh. "No, but really, what's wrong with him?"

Everybody looks at each other but nobody speaks.

Stéfanie's voice gets chilly. "Vraiment, he's in a burnout."

"What does that mean?" Smoking joints and fucking sixteen-year-olds isn't the picture I envision for someone who is burned out.

"He's struggling with questions of identity, vocation, spirituality, many things. C'est vraiment un chemin difficile."

"So, nobody knows when or if he's coming back?" I'm trying not to look as shocked as I feel.

"The company needs to be supportive of all its members and their needs. We're choosing to be patient."

"Well, I'm going to assume he's out, so maybe I should just do the website. I can even do a logo. I'm a graphic designer." Everyone is looking at me and then at Stéfanie.

Stéfanie smiles. "That's quite generous, Audrey. Thank you. I want to honour François's tenure with TPG and his commitment to the website. Carlos has contacted him a few times. Carlos, would you feel comfor-table trying once more?"

I feel weightless and disembodied. I see the circle of us, the company, from the ceiling. I see Stéfanie's dark roots.

Carlos steps up. "I think if Audrey's offering, and she's a professional, we should just let her do it."

Stéfanie looks to the others. "Anyone else willing to connect with François?"

"Je peux essayer," says one of the francophone women.

"Merci, let's do that. Next week, we can reassess. And if you do reach him, let him know I'd like to meet him face to face, to discuss things. In a gentle way, d'accord?"

She nods. We all get up and do our closing exercise: each of us does a gesture showing something we'll take from the rehearsal out into our lives. Then we hold hands and pass the squeeze.

I get home and wonder if I should tell Denise what happened. When I come inside, the lights are off, and she's already asleep. I put my backpack in the office and quietly put on my pajamas.

*

When I wake up the next morning, I make my decaf and remember what happened at rehearsal. Little prickers jab at my ribcage. I guess François is more professional than I am, more talented, more experienced. It's just as well. The baby-making project and my own clients will take most of my time and energy anyway.

Denise and I quickly realize that preparing for IVF, unlike making love, is complicated, with the spotlight on my innards. It's shots, clinic appointments, shots, clinic appointments, more shots, all of which builds to the climax of three events: egg retrieval, fertilization, and transfer. The doctor originally tells us I am very fertile, that she sees fifteen eggs produced in my follicles on the ultrasound. But the day after the retrieval in June, the nurse on the phone reports that there are only five.

After the call, my confidence collapses. I go down to the basement amid the still unpacked boxes, sink down to the cement floor, and drop my face into my hands. Slowly, I lower myself from sitting to lying down, warm cheek against the cold concrete floor, and imagine a childless life. Still living paycheck to paycheck. Still that troubled adopted girl with the anxiety disorder who's always in and out of doctor's offices and hospitals. Now this, which had so much promise, becomes yet another piece of evidence that, indeed, my story is true, consistent, inescapable.

I stay down in the basement for the rest of the afternoon. Mira and Leto come down, taking turns snuggling, licking, or lying with me. I intend to come up before Denise returns to freshen up and start supper, but I lose track of time. The animals rush upstairs when she opens the door. She says my name, but I can't answer.

Eventually she finds me.

"Wanna talk about it?"

I sit up, shake my head no. The tears make a track on my dusty cheek and fall to the cement floor where they form a tiny pool.

Denise's rubs my shoulder. She waits until the tears slow down before she speaks.

"There's a message on the landline. Did you hear it?"

I shake my head and tell her about that morning's phone call and the measly five viable eggs.

She grins. "Three are apparently growing. It's possible they could transfer all of them into your uterus. The nurse said it looked very positive."

I'm silent. My nose runs. My ribcage is sore from lying on the concrete. I'm suspicious about hope's return. Denise reaches out her hand, and I take it, and we slowly make our way upstairs.

*

The three days between retrieval and transfer are long, but Denise and I stay busy. Keeping my hopes in check is another matter. I Zoom with Jessica.

"Hey, remember that kid at school whose mom died last year?"

175

"Yeah, that was awful. Did the police ever figure out what happened?" I start doodling a spiral staircase.

"Not sure. Anyway, I ran into her dad at the gym. I didn't know it was her dad until I told him what I did for work. He's totally hot, and he's starting to date, and he asked me out. So, I said yes!"

I look up. Her eyes have a technicolor glow.

"He's actually got another kid, too, a four-year-old. He just finished a six-month grief group yesterday, and he's celebrating. I get to tag along."

"Really?" I ask her. "Are you seriously up to being a stepmother to two traumatized kids?" I bite into a banana as I watch her put on make-up for her date.

"Do you think blue mascara looks cheap?" She holds it up to the camera.

"You're gorgeous no matter what you do. And if you wear the blue skirt, it will look intentional, which gets you extra points."

She rolls her eyes, then holds up three other mascaras.

"My middle name is intentional. And you have nothing to worry about. Bill isn't even looking for a relationship. I plan to seduce him with no strings attached and enjoy each and every minute." She grins and raises her eyebrows. I see a beer on the side of the sink, but I say nothing.

"Are you doing okay with all the fertility crap?" She takes a break from getting ready and looks at me.

I bite my banana.

"Whatever."

*

Denise and I go back to the clinic for the transfer the next day. We dress in gowns and shower caps. I had requested anaesthesia, so once they take us into the OR, and the doctor gives me some gas. I'm only half there, laughing and talking about Robin Williams dying and gluten-free pancakes and why it's a good idea to carry a whistle while hiking alone. Denise tells me later that the doctors and nurses were amused and wondered if I had done stand-up comedy or theatre. I say it figures my best performance was neither videotaped nor televised.

Chapter 46

The next week at rehearsal, we learn that nobody has succeeded in reaching François, although Carlos saw him wearing a suit and getting into a Saab over the weekend. I volunteer again for the website, making sure they know I'd do it for free, and again, Stéfanie says we need to wait and give François a chance. I finally give up. The company deserves the best, and I need to step out of the way with my good but misguided intentions.

Denise makes the appointment for a pregnancy test on July eighth, two weeks after the transfer. Fortunately, it's a weekend, so instead of going crazy, we watch *Jeeves and Wooster* and *South Park* and all of Margaret Cho's filmed stand-up performances. God bless Netflix.

For supper on Sunday, Denise serves a breast of chicken with primavera sauce on a bed of pasta.

"How do you feel?" she asks, yet again.

I look at my plate. "Like I'm about to get my period."

During the following days, my back throbs, my abdomen is wracked with cramps, and I tear up every time I go on Facebook. My body seems to be preparing for the biggest menstruation of its life. I poke around online and find many similar stories from other women trying to get pregnant. Some who thought they were getting their periods did end up getting them. Others, in fact, were pregnant. I give up my search for the truth and focus on logo design for a company using recycled human hair to make wrapping paper. Tears come and go, along with picturing myself old and senile, without children or a successful art career, homeless on the streets of Montreal, unable to find the shelter because my French hasn't progressed from very shitty to mildly shitty. I finally settle in at my computer, and Leto jumps up to help by curling up on my lap for a snooze.

On blood test day, I wake up with clenched teeth. I ask Denise if we could skip the appointment. I ask her if we could pretend none of this had ever happened. I ask if I could eat the meatloaf she's prepared for supper as my breakfast. The answer is "no" to all of my questions. Finally, I climb out of bed and haul myself into the kitchen for decaf and granola.

Our appointment is at 8:30 a.m., so we decide to delay Mira's walk until after we get back. At the clinic, the nurse who takes my blood asks how we want to receive the news. Denise turns to me.

"Voicemail, please." I certainly don't want any witnesses when I find out I've failed yet again. The nurse smiles politely and makes a note in our chart.

"It probably won't be until the afternoon," she says. "The lab is pretty backlogged."

We get home a little after 9:30 a.m. We do the dishes together, and then Denise takes Mira for her walk. I go upstairs, boot up my computer, and check my to-do list. One file is open on my desktop—a drawing I'd done for an organic florist of a little girl tossing flowers up in the air, arms stretched open, face full of delight. For twenty minutes, I stare at her. If I were the girl's mom, perhaps I'd come outside, tell her how lovely the blossoms are, and help her gather the flowers back up. Or maybe I would join her, bringing out my own bouquet that I'd toss into the air, watching her shrieking and laughing at my mirror performance.

My mind attached itself to the baby project like super glue and simply refuses to give. Maybe I could convince Denise to try again. Maybe we could get an egg donor. Maybe—

The phone rings.

My head falls into my hands. Probably my new client from Delaware, the Golden Doodle breeder. I glance at the clock and see it's a few minutes past 10:00 a.m. I look at the caller ID on my desk phone.

Clinique Cigogne.

Already?

It rings again. Somehow, I can't will my hand to pick up. The ringing eventually stops. I count out one minute. I then go onto the second-floor balcony. No sign of Denise and Mira. I amble back to my office.

What the hell.

I dial *98. Then our passcode. A woman's voice delivers the message.

"Bonjour, this is Marie-Josée from Clinique Cigogne, calling for

Audrey and Denise, just to say congratulations because you are pregnant. Please call back to set up your eight-week ultrasound. We're very
happy for you. Bonne journée."

A clicking noise. A dial tone.

I call voice mail again and listen again. Two more times. Three. Then
I scream without a single thought of the neighbours. I nearly run over
Leto tearing downstairs, needing to find Denise that second.

I go to open the front door, and it's dead-bolted. From the outside.

Denise, in her commitment to security, had locked the upper lock
from the outside, with me inside. My pocket, where I normally keep
my keys, is empty.

I start bopping around the first floor, looking in the front hall closet
on the little hooks, in my coat pocket, on my bed, and finally I look in
my drawer where I keep extra sets of everything. I unlock the door and
dart out of the house, yelling at the top of my lungs.

"Denise, we're pregnant!"

I trot by several neighbours, one who's weeding his garden and
another reading on her balcony. A guy leaning against his fence gives
me a thumbs-up sign. Another shouts, "Felicitations!" But I am
running and running, and I still don't see Denise or Mira.

Finally, I get to the end of the second block and go down a cross
street we don't normally take. As soon as I turn the corner, I see them.
I wave my arms big, like the guy with the batons on the airport runway.

"Denise! Denise! We're pregnant!" She isn't moving, which makes
me scream louder. I eventually reach them. Mira jumps up and licks
my chin.

"We're pregnant!" I say to both of them.

Denise looks down.

"You're not wearing shoes."

I look. She's right.

"But we're pregnant. We're going to have a baby!"

Denise's face is blank. She attends to Mira but sort of ignores me as
we make our way back to the house.

"You locked me out," I say matter of factly.

"We both have keys."

Her face is still blank.

When we get home, we listen to the message together on speakerphone. Denise begins to sob. I hug her. She sits down on the couch.

I bring her a glass of iced tea and some tissues.

"Merci." A few sips, and she's calmer.

"Are you happy?"

"Of course. Mais, c'est beaucoup. I need time for it to sink in."

*

Our first ultrasound happens at eight weeks. The tech rubs jelly on my belly, and a tiny pulsing heart appears on the screen.

And then another.

Two bodies. Two heartbeats.

"Well, well," says the tech, "Looks like twins! Let me move around here to see if there may be a third."

I look at Denise whose face is green. I tell her to sit down. She looks like she might bite someone.

But inside, my soul is doing somersaults. Twins. Not only would we have a baby, but we'd have two, so one would not have to grow up alone. Certainly, life as a twin has got to be better than life as an only child. Lying still for the tech takes all the discipline I can manage.

"Nope, it's just two."

Denise exhales loudly.

"Do you want to hear their heartbeats?" she asks.

We nod because we are too stunned to do anything else. The tech flips a switch on the ultrasound, and we hear a little rat-a-tat rat-a-tat, fast beats that are unmistakable.

"I just heard my babies' heartbeats," I whisper.

"Actually, that was just one. Here's the other."

The room is silent except the da-DUM, da-DUM, da-DUM. Life. Two lives. Inside my body.

We walk back to the car slowly, silently, holding hands.

Driving home, I ask Denise how she feels.

"Vraiment, the second she started looking for the third, I wanted to punch her."

I giggle.

"It's not her fault your wife is the reproductive equivalent of a Lamborghini."

Chapter 47

At home that evening, we celebrate with flowers: two yellow mums for them, a white for Denise, and a purple for me. We light candles, hold hands, weep for joy.

I step on the scale.

161.

No weight gain yet.

Denise brings piles of books on pregnancy back from the library, and I spend half my days reading and studying. Some of the books are about raising twins. But one gets my attention. It's simply called *The Baby Book*, by a doctor named William Sears. The book is written about a special practice called attachment parenting.

"Hey, did you look at this one?" I ask Denise one night as she's finishing the dishes.

"Not yet."

"There's all this stuff about how mainstream North American parenting deprives babies of their basic needs."

Denise looks at me dubiously. "Like?"

I skim the book. "It's pretty extreme. You're supposed to keep your baby in your arms for the entire first year."

"Oh sure, so there's no brushing teeth or cooking supper or cleaning or food shopping, or—"

"Hang on." I spend the next several hours absorbing this idea that new parents are meant to respond to babies' cues, get lots of touch or "skin-to-skin," as Sears calls it, carry their babies or "wear" them in something called a sling instead of putting them in a stroller, put them to sleep in their parents' bed instead of a crib, and nurse them until they're not interested anymore, at least two years.

"This is not a book for parents of twins," says my wife.

"There's actually a whole chapter about twins and multiples."

I call Mom and she poo-poos it. "Sears is a sexist pig. He's done no research at all, and he's religious. It's all about keeping the women at home, barefoot and pregnant. Take care of your kids like you want to, Audrey, and take care of yourself while you do it."

"But what did you do with me? Did you do that skin-to-skin stuff?"

"All I can say is that I cared for you the best I could. I had Freddy and Chloe to worry about and fostering. And I worked. I had lots of jobs so I could buy food and toys and pay rent. You turned out fine, so I don't really understand why you'd do anything differently."

"I wouldn't say I turned out fine, Mom. I have a psychiatric disability for God's sake. Maybe there are reasons for that."

I hear her light up a cigarette and take a puff. "I've been over this with you throughout your life, and I'll say the same thing every time you ask. You have a chemical imbalance in your brain. You have a physiological problem that your medication corrects. End of story."

I hear tension in her voice, weariness. I had never thought about how I'd been parented as a baby. I certainly never thought that it could have had an impact on my development. I'd always believed that I had been born disabled.

The book opens a door in my brain to terra incognita. And I am terrified. Because in the innermost shadows of my soul, I know I want to be this kind of mother.

Unfortunately, Denise doesn't share my newfound enthusiasm. She sits in the office alone after supper while I'm downstairs drawing. She cries at night in bed and only occasionally lets me rub her back. She asks me if we can have "time off" from pregnancy, since it's the only thing we talk about or think about. It's counter to my nature, but I say yes. I want her to be happy, but I understand she is where she is and that we have to make space for the hard stuff.

One evening after rehearsal, I find her sitting upstairs reading a book I'd finished the night before, *The Continuum Concept*. "This book was written in the 1940s, way before Sears. But she explains the theory based on actual research with a tribe in South America."

I smile. "Are you convinced?"

"The tribes that she studies don't have conflict. The five-year-olds watch over the younger ones, and the younger ones watch the babies. It's hard to imagine, but if it's true, it's very persuasive." She puts down the book. "How was rehearsal?"

I sigh. "Stéfanie asked me to do the new logo and website."

"Non! What happened with François?"

"He finally went to meet her, and he's taking an official leave of absence from the company. She made sure he knew he would be welcome whenever he feels like coming back."

"Franchement. So you're going to spend work time on this thing you've been volunteering to do for weeks, and they've been saying no, and now that you're pregnant, and the guy who can't communicate decides he's on leave, they want you to do it?"

I shake my head. "Once I have it done, that will be the end, and the group will have a professional online persona. It won't take long."

We cuddle up in bed like spoons. Denise puts her hands on my belly. "Feels the same to me."

"In the first trimester, nothing shows. Seems like such a long time," I sigh. My wife's arm is warm, and even with the heat of the summer, I feel comforted.

*

I watch a video of a woman giving birth in a tub at home with a midwife and immediately decide that this is what I want. I call a midwifery clinic. I tell the woman on the phone about myself, that it's my first pregnancy, that I'm carrying twins, and she laughs. Apparently, twin pregnancies are high risk. Quebec law requires me to be followed by a doctor and give birth in a hospital.

I put down the phone. The piece of the puzzle where the baby exits my body through an orifice smaller than my mouth is something I'd shoved to the side, rationalizing I would be fine when the time came and that women have been doing this same thing for millennia, however strange and ridiculously painful it seemed to be. But having a bunch of drugs on hand in case I'm wrong doesn't seem like a bad idea, even if it's not what attachment parenting recommends.

The first person I tell, if course, is Jessica, on Zoom while she washes dishes.

"Did Denise okay your telling me?"

"No, but how could I not?"

"Wow, Meyerwitz, you're actually doing it! Is this, like, step thirty-nine of the healthy family project? How does it feel?"

"I'm—well, I'm playing 'L'Chayim' from *Fiddler on the Roof* over and over and over."

"That's kinda manic."

"It's celebrating. Shouldn't I be celebrating?" I sip my kiwi berry smoothie.

"Most people don't say anything for the first three months. I think you should lay low in case something happens."

"Yeah, that's what I thought at first, but I didn't think it would be this hard not to talk about it."

And then Patti calls, and I let it slip. She tells me she has a pregnant friend who is further along than me with twins who goes to the Twin Clinic at the Royal Victoria Hospital. I call and book my first appointment at week ten.

In the meantime, life continues. I read everything I can about pregnancy. I stop running and start doing yoga. Client work is normally slow in the summer, but I'm branding a horse farm doing therapy with homeless children, and with that and the TPG website, I'm plenty busy. On breaks, I sketch women with pregnant bellies in different poses in different places, the beach, a park, in bed. Another day, I begin sketching my future children. One boy, one girl. They would be creative of course. Beautiful. The boy would be smart, maybe good at math and music. The girl would love reading and drawing.

Neither would have an anxiety disorder.

One morning, I wake up, go down for my coffee, and suddenly rush into the bathroom and throw up.

Jessica texts several times a day.

Eating your veggies?

Need a barf bag?

Taking your folic acid?

Loving food the way I do, I wait for cravings, but none arrive. Aversions, on the other hand, blossom. Lasagne. Brussels sprouts. Peanut butter. A slice of key lime pie. To say this is disappointing doesn't begin to scratch the surface. Knowing the importance of good nutrition, I force myself to eat regardless of how I feel. And oftentimes there's a mad dash to the bathroom involved.

Chapter 48

The next weekend, Denise is at Mimi's helping her move, so I take a break from the horse farm logo and the TPG site and go to Burlington to see Jessica. During our last few Zoom conversations, she was drinking and even smoking cigarettes. She seems happy with Bill but overwhelmed by the kids and their intense needs. She's not the type to ask for help directly, so when she suggests that "it might be fun" to babysit together for a few hours on Saturday, I know I'm needed. I also know Eve is going to be in Burlington with her new girlfriend and staying with Jessica. Eve and I had been emailing about the visit and Jessica's using, deciding we needed to make time for a one-on-one talk about intervention.

I arrive in Burlington and park on the street in front of Jessica's apartment, grabbing my backpack. When I walk up to the door, a tall slender woman with thick lips, a miniskirt, and heels answers. "Hi there, you must be Audrey," she says in a jazzy tenor drawl. "I'm Abigail." She looks at me, and for a few seconds, I just stare, unable to speak. My hands tremble. I force myself to maintain eye contact to stop looking at her breasts, which are ample with hard nipples pushing through the fabric of her tank top. Then I remember that Eve had tried monogamy, and it had never quite fit. I imagine grabbing Abigail around the waist, pulling her into me, pressing my lips to hers—

"Nice to meet you," I say casually. Think networking event.

"Eve's told me a lot about you," says Abigail in that voice.

I hear shrieking in the back of the apartment.

"Audrey's here, Audrey's here!"

Jessica skips to the front of the apartment and jumps on me, something between a tackle and a hug. Then she grabs my backpack and prances around the apartment, singing her sentences in made-up tunes. Somehow, I find a way to break out of my gaze with Abigail and follow Jessica into her room.

"I can't believe you never told me about her before. What's that about anyway?" Eve is known for favouring women with cropped hair-cuts and big biceps.

"Not sure," says Jessica, pulling out an under-bed storage box. In it are five bottles of vodka. She grabs one and pushes it back under. She opens it, grabs a shot glass on her dresser, pours, then chugs.

"Love love love that you're here, Meyerwitz!" She hops up on her bed and starts jumping.

"Watch your head, Jess." In the five years we'd known one another, this was the first time I've seen her jump on the bed. The booze, on the other hand, is becoming increasingly familiar.

"Maybe we should wait until dinner for cocktails?" I suggest as lightly as I can.

She makes a face at me. "Such a stick in the mud!" She pours herself another shot and passes me the bottle.

I shake my head. "Doesn't go with pregnancy."

We end up staying in and ordering pizza. The wait is long, so we play jacks, Spot-It, charades.

Saturday with the kids is low key. We take them to the science museum and then have a picnic lunch and a wild Frisbee game in Battery Park. After we drop them off at their aunt's, we go running, stop back at the apartment for a shower, and go to the movies. Jessica doesn't say much about Bill, but he calls or texts constantly during the three days I'm there. Jessica doesn't pick up, but she always texts back. She also doesn't mention anything about my meeting him, and I don't ask. That kind of self-censorship is contagious. By Saturday evening, I'm ignoring the vodka every time Jessica takes it out.

On Sunday night, Eve and Abigail go to Pat's Parlor, the local gay bar. Before they leave, Eve asks me to come look at her new car, a Volkswagen New Beetle convertible. Eve knows Martha had had a red Beetle when I was a child because she'd seen the photos of five-year-old me, helping my mom and my brothers wash it, waving from the driver's seat, and sticking my torso out the window on the passenger side.

"It's sweet, Eve. Love the flower holder."

"Thanks. Yeah, I like it too."

We sit in silence.

Then I look at her.

She shakes her head.

"I just don't know what to do." Eve looks down.

"I didn't know it was this bad," I say.

"You talk to her all the time. How could you not know?"

I'm silent.

"She was doing great after rehab this time. She was going to meetings four times a week. And then, there's this fuckwad, Bill, and bang, she's drinking again. It's like it happened in five minutes. How can it happen in five minutes?"

"You know what addiction's like. It's a monster. And it's fast."

We're quiet.

I look at her. "Have you met Bill?"

She shakes her head. "It's weird. My sister always drags her boyfriends to me in the early days of knowing them. This one's different. I have a weird feeling, but it's probably because of the drinking. Maybe it has nothing to do with him, but it's an odd coincidence." Eve wipes her brow. "I'm sorry, Audrey. I shouldn't dump this in your lap. She's my sister, and I obviously haven't done a good enough job taking care of her. Forty-five minutes is not that long. I should be in Burlington at least once a week."

I shake my head. "Don't do that," I say. "It isn't true, and it isn't helpful. She's a grownup. You have responsibilities."

A few seconds pass.

"Did you say anything to your dad, or to Christopher?" I ask. Jessica and Eve's musician brother drinks, but not like Jessica.

Eve laughs. "Chris never calls back. And Dad's either in denial, or he's still so traumatized by Max's death that he won't go there with me."

She looks at me. Her forehead is moist, and her lower lip trembles.

"Take care of her the best you can, okay, Audrey?"

I nod. And wonder how.

Chapter 49

Concern about Jessica fades into the background as Denise and I relax into the rhythm of regular life in Montreal. My TPG colleagues like my work on the website. Stéfanie and I meet a few times at a coffee shop to work out the copywriting. She smiles more around me and develops a habit of touching me casually as we work. I start doodling primitive sketches of us holding hands. In one, we are sitting side by side, leaning our heads together.

*

At the next pregnancy appointment, our ObGyn, Dr. Lu, gives me screening tests, and afterwards she sits us down; she's concerned about the nuchal translucency test, which indicates that Baby B has a thirty-three percent chance of having Down syndrome. She strongly recommends an early amniocentesis, which would be close to definitive.

"I could do it tomorrow," she says. Ninety-five percent of women who get this news choose abortion, she tells us, and if it's necessary, sooner is better for the healthy twin.

"Take a few minutes to think about it, and I'll be back," she says, shutting the door behind her.

My whole body goes numb.

Denise and I sit in the office. A fluorescent light buzzes. The intercom calls Dr. Berkowitz, Dr. Berkowitz to cardiology. Hospital staff walk by in the hall, chatting in French and English. Finally, I look at Denise.

"I think we should do the amnio."

She nods, face white.

We make an appointment in a few days to give ourselves time to think. The doctor says that the genetics department would follow up to make a counselling appointment. I look at Denise and then at my doctor.

"I don't want a counselling appointment."

She shakes her head.

"It's a free service, and they'll be able to answer questions specific to your situation."

I don't say anything, but I feel a concrete wall go up in my psyche between us and the genetics counselor. This is our choice, our family, not the province of Quebec's. Already the doctor is ready to abort the second baby, and she hasn't mentioned anything about potential complications for the first.

I cry silently in the car going home, wiping my cheeks and nose with the grey fleece of my jacket.

I weigh myself three times during the week.

165

165

168

More fantasy children visit my mind. Two girls. One olive-skinned, with dark hair, like Denise, and one fair one with pale skin and light hair, like me. Smart. Talented. Successful. People who other people cherish. People who care for the world and make me proud.

Girls. Girls who resembled me, who would have their bio mom to grow up with.

Neither fantasy child has Down syndrome.

168

169

166

Slow. Special needs. Mentally handicapped.

Someone whom ninety-five percent of pregnant women choose to abort.

Someone who is disabled.

Like me.

I remember a foster daughter my mom took care of when I was in high school. Jenny was older than me, but because she had Down syndrome, she was developmentally much closer to my brother's age. She laughed a lot and was always picking daffodils in the yard and bringing them to Mom.

She needed help wiping herself when she went to the bathroom.

No, this news does not fit into my plans at all.

171

170

171

Suddenly I want to tuck myself into the corner, under the loose floorboard in our bedroom, where nobody can see me.

Weekdays, I work on the horse farm branding and the TPG website. In the evenings, one of us makes supper. We eat quietly. The other cleans up. I walk Mira and Denise feeds both animals. On Monday and Wednesday evenings, I go to rehearsals.

When we talk about the pregnancy, the conversation is choppy. Lots of pauses. Often one of us cries. We go around and around, visiting and revisiting feelings and ideas and decisions.

Me: "I'm a damaged person. Of course I have a damaged child."

Denise: "I think we could do it. Downs kids are sweet."

Me: "If Mom can deal with special needs kids, plus all the others, I should be able to handle one Downs child and one neurotypical one."

Denise: "I want to be a loving, accepting parent, no matter who my kids are."

Me: "What better rite of passage could there be to finally heal old wounds?"

Denise: "I miss my mom."

Me: "I wonder if my bio mom gave me up because of my disability."

Denise: "This is big, way too big."

Me: "How can I have a business, two babies, one disabled, and an art career?"

172

170

170

Denise stomps around and Mira cowers in the corner. I lay on the couch and weep while Leto settles on my chest, purring. When an old high school friend sends me a batch of photos of her twins whom she'd had by IVF, I immediately delete the email. Denise talks about her lack of experience, her fears. I talk about of my birth mother's decision, the years of bullying I endured, the nagging little thought that perhaps those bullies were right.

Jessica calls but I don't respond. Claire and Sabrina come by, but we don't answer the door. Patti texts. Stéfanie hugs me both before and after rehearsals and continually asks if I'm okay. Mom leaves two messages. Part of me doesn't want anyone to know and the other part needs to talk. But I can't find my words.

170

173

172

My brain does somersaults around the one in three odds. Sixty-six percent of the people who get this news have normal kids, I reason. Medical doctors are such alarmists. Two out of three, two out of three, two out of three.

I see a new mom pushing her twins in a double stroller down the street. I turn around and cover four extra blocks to avoid her.

I finish the TPG website. The company is thrilled.

After a week, we're one step closer to a decision. We are startled to realize we feel like parents already, and we know that abortion is not an option for us. We find a nonprofit organization online whose goal is to support both birth parents and adoptive parents in special-needs adoptions. Some of the wording on the site indicates a religious bent, but I'm desperate to talk to someone other than the genetics counsellor, someone who knows more than we do. Someone who doesn't have a stake in our decision, who isn't going to try to convince us of anything.

Monique, the director, makes an appointment to visit us. I slip into Jessica's purple sweater and pace around the house, waiting.

"I wonder if she's going to lay on the religious guilt," says Denise, making coffee. "Well, we have to talk to somebody, and at least this is a step removed from the government."

The doorbell rings. When I answer and see Monique, I'm shocked. She's wearing cowboy boots, has black highlights in her hair, and is wearing a jeans jacket. She's nothing like the prim, conservative, Christian woman I had been expecting.

"Bonjour, hello, you must be Audrey?"

I invite her in and shake her hand. My face goes calm and kind.

Denise introduces herself, and the two of them speak French. I ask Monique if she would like coffee or tea.

We sit down, and I instantly start crying. Monique nods but says nothing. Denise puts her arm around me. The dog comes in and flops down at my feet.

"C'est pas facile."

I look at her. She hands me a tissue.

"My English is not so good, but I think this is important that we all understand together," says Monique. "I do my best like you do your best."

We sit together for two hours. She tells us she never judges anybody but rather sees her role as helping families reach whatever decision is right for them. I ask her about the genetics counselling, and she indicates that, as I'd thought, it wasn't unbiased. For once, I'm glad I followed my intuition.

"What I can tell you is that Downs babies are easily adoptable by families who feel called to raise special needs kids. With prenatal testing as accurate as it is, ninety-five percent of Downs babies are aborted. So, your baby is like a precious diamond. I could have ten families lined up at your door, ready to adopt your baby tomorrow."

Denise and I look at each other with wide eyes.

After she leaves, I inhale deeply, oxygen pouring into each extremity. Denise and I fall asleep holding each other that night, her arms wrapped around my slow-growing belly.

I weigh myself again and again and again.

173

173

172

Halloween arrives. We spend hours on our costumes, Denise a witch and me, the Headless Horseman. We make an orange-themed dinner for the Itchy Mortals, sweet potato fries, pumpkin soup, cheese puffs. We light candles and carve intricate designs into pumpkins à la *Country Living*. We invite our friends over–Claire and Sabrina, Patti and Mireille–and we tell them what's happened. They hold us in our silly costumes and cry with us.

172

175

175

I'm easily winded on the stairs, and I start going back to bed after breakfast. I sometimes stay there until lunch. Leto stays with me, on my stomach or on Denise's pillow.

175

176

175

We go for the amniocentesis. I do an acting exercise beforehand to prepare. It's about centring yourself so you have the strongest and most grounded energy field in the room. You empty your soul and put your own emotions on hold. The goal is to maintain stability and calm, like a trained police officer talking to the guy about to jump off a bridge. The confidence is initially fake, but it ends with the actual feeling if you do it right. One of my counsellors had studied drama therapy, and she had shared this technique with me when I was dealing with bullying. I've also used the technique before on stage, and it was powerful.

Several people walk in and out during the procedure: nurses, interns, medical students. I breathe evenly and ask them all how they are. I am unfazed. Denise is pale sitting in a plastic chair, head leaning back against the wall.

After the poking and needles and fluid are finished, Dr. Lu comes in and hands us a package.

"Just take this across town to the lab, and they'll analyze it and let me know, after which point, I'll give you a call."

We both look at the package and then at the doctor.

"What's this?"

"It's the amniotic fluid. I know it can seem, er, unconventional, but the hospital saves a lot of money this way. Just make sure you have her do it," the doctor says to me, indicating Denise. "You should be resting."

She shakes our hands, opens the door, and leaves.

The bag is brown, not unlike the kinds of bags I used to bring my lunches in to school. We're in an Ed Wood film where an alien is about to crawl out of the bag onto my hand. I give the bag to Denise, shaking my head.

"This would never happen in the States."

*

We deliver the goods and go home. As we walk into the house, my message tone rings. Jessica.

Gold necklace from Bill. Gorgeous. Call soon. Smooches.

I press delete and forget about it as I go upstairs to lie down.

Chapter 50

The doctor calls two weeks later with the results of the amnio. Baby B has Down syndrome.

The waiting is over.

I spend the day with Denise. We cry and hold each other as we wander around the house. I look for something to fill myself with. Flax toast with peanut butter. Semi-sweet chocolate morsels. Lucky Charms Cereal with rice milk. A Granny Smith apple and some cheddar.

The gaping hole remains in the depths of my pregnant belly.

In the evening, I make the mistake of calling Mom. She listens silently for a moment before speaking.

"You'll learn how to parent him or her. Down's children are lovely. Remember Jenny?" There's a pause.

"We're still figuring things out, Mom."

I hang up quietly and lie down on the couch and stay there, staring at the window, until morning when the sun rises over the row houses in Rosemont.

We talk at breakfast before Denise leaves for work. We know down deep that we cannot provide for Baby B. My anxiety and career are reason enough; I don't even have to face my initial shame.

179

177

178

I float out, further and further from my people. I'm too broken to manage others' reactions, judgments, even their clumsy kind offers of "Is there anything I can do?" I write an email to Mom to tell her we decided to give Baby B up for adoption.

179

180

180

I spend more and more time in bed.

Quietness. Emptiness. Agony.

My belly pushes out, more and more, and I sleep in short spurts. My maternity pants keep falling down, and I can't walk to the corner without feeling breathless.

No word from Mom.

We find out Baby A is a boy and Baby B, a girl. We decide to name them: Baby A is Adam, our son. Baby B is Brianna. We use their hospital initials to honour their time as twins, kicking, elbowing, and hiccupping inside me.

Jessica and I chat, but she's quiet about her relationship drama. "I want to be there for you, Auds. This is really heavy stuff."

"I love you, and what you're going through is just as important."

She smiles. "Another time."

182

183

184

Claire and Sabrina host a baby ritual for us. Patti and Mireille come and Mimi and even Jessica. Sabrina tells me she'd invited my mom, but she didn't hear back from her. I say nothing.

The celebration is a flurry of colour and sound, poems in French and English, gifts. We open tiny red overalls and a ladybug teething toy and lime-green pajamas with purple puppies. Our friends bless us, feed us, drum for us. Jessica crouches down, puts her mouth to my belly, and softly sings "The Wind" to the babies.

Each friend ties one delicate red thread on our wrists representing one wish for us as new parents: Humour. Patience. Compassion. Humility. Appreciation. Trust. When we look at the bracelets, they explain, we'll remember we're not alone. Then they toast us with sparkling purple juice.

After we drink, each woman kisses us, first me, then Denise. I notice the warm grapey smell on their breath, and a few of them whisper words I love and can't quite understand.

*

The next day, I finish up an ad for an all-queer whale-watching outfit in Provincetown, my last contract before the birth. I shift on the chair, feeling both babies move. I glance down and see something elbowlike poke out and disappear. Kicks. I breathe deeply and shut down my computer.

Nothing left to do.

Between week thirty-two and thirty-three, the adoption proceedings begin. We shed tears of relief when our social worker tells us there is a family waiting for little Brianna. Monique emails to see how the social worker appointment went. As always, interacting with her is both light and grounding. She holds us steady in the midst of the howling storm.

Repeated questions about us being sure of our decision are difficult. We are sure...and we are sad.

No word from Mom.

185

187

187

Movements inside my belly surprise me, moments of pure joy. But unyielding tornados of the mind still sweep me up as I walk through my day. "What if something is wrong with Adam?" "What if something happens at the birth?" "What if I am a terrible mother?"

Elbows and heels glide across my middle. The fear retreats into the shadow of the miracle and loosens its grip on my soul.

190

191

192

At thirty-six weeks, Dr. Lu tells me I am having light contractions and that Brianna's heart rate is dropping dangerously low with each one. She suggests going ahead with an induction, knowing how important a vaginal birth is to me.

"We can always wheel you across the hall to the OR for a c-section if there's any problem."

My eyebrows scrunch together. "But couldn't Brianna die quickly with stronger contractions?"

She just looks at me and finally shrugs. And in a flash, I understand. My doctor is thinking only of Adam. She is willing to sacrifice Brianna, seeing her like most of the outside world will see her.

And then I see my own birth mother, talking with her obstetrician. Did she have some kind of test? Did she know I had an anxiety disorder before I was born?

My mind flashes on Dr. Sears's book, remembering all the reasons c-sections are bad for babies; this is not how I want Adam to enter the world. But at that moment, I am Brianna's mother too, her birth mother. Like me, she is disabled. And like me, she deserves as much of a chance as a baby without a disability.

I tell my doctor to go ahead with the c-section, and the nurses begin prepping me for surgery.

I tell the nurse I don't want to see Brianna at all. My focus must be on Adam, and I can't get bogged down in grief.

Shivering, they wheel me into the OR in my gown. Someone sticks a needle in my spine and slowly sensations in my bottom half fade away. They rig up a curtain, so I can't see what's happening down there. Denise comes into the OR in her scrubs and shower cap, and she holds my hand. At some points nausea almost overcomes me; the resident says it's because I'm losing a lot of blood. Finally, they pull Adam out, and I hear him wail. The nurse puts him on my chest for a few moments, but between the fluorescent lights, my scrubs, and not having my glasses, it's a brief meeting with little emotion. Somebody whisks him away to be cleaned. They take Brianna out next and quickly bring her elsewhere. She isn't making a sound.

When we arrive in the recovery room, both babies are there. It seems the staff had forgotten my request. A nurse takes Adam away for some extra oxygen, and Brianna remains in her little plastic bassinet, quietly smacking her tiny lips together. Denise wonders out loud if she's hungry. I throw caution to the wind, take her in my arms, and give it my best effort: my first moment of breastfeeding. She latches on and nurses like a pro while maintaining eye contact.

Her eyes are dark and warm, like hot chocolate, and her movements are punctuated and full of life, like a baby Charlie Chaplin. Her new lips feel strangely capable on my nipple.

Her gaze meets mine, and I whisper, "Well hello, Brianna," my voice grainy from the surgery.

I nurse her hello, and I nurse her goodbye. I haven't seen her since.

Stage Three:
Beginning of
Deep Sleep and
Parasomnias
(Sleepwalking,
Night Terrors,
and Bedwetting)

Chapter 51

After supper that night, I'm sucking ice chips while Denise holds Adam topless, practising skin-to-skin. My body trembles as the anaesthesia wears off. My lips are cracked and bleeding, and my tongue is gritty, sticking to the roof of my mouth. What I want more than anything is a big meal, but the nurses tell me I have to wait until the next day to eat.

My blood seems to be pumping through my body in fast motion. I hope the baby doesn't cry because that will mean I have to try feeding him, and I'm doubtful I'm strong enough to support his seven pounds.

A nurse comes in to take my blood pressure, and then she checks the staples on my stomach.

There's a knock. All eyes turn to the door. It cracks open and some-one peeks in.

Patti.

Despite my compromised state, I start giggling. In a tiny voice, I say, "My sister!"

Patti keeps a straight face. Barely.

"Downstairs they told me family is welcome," she says in her thick Cockney accent.

The nurse says it's fine with her if it's fine with us.

She refills my cup with ice chips, and when she leaves, Patti and I lose it. Denise wants to know what's so funny.

"Audrey and I figured out a way for me to visit first off," says Patti. "We decided to say we were sisters. We'd sussed out the details, how we had the same mother but different fathers, how our mother left Audrey's father in the US, and she moved to England and met my father, who's from Egypt."

Anybody who'd studied high school genetics would call our bluff immediately, but the nurse didn't notice or, more likely, didn't care.

"How's it going, Mum?" asks Patti, rubbing my arm.

"Eh."

Denise grins as she strokes Adam's cheek.

Patti approaches Denise cautiously. "Can I hold him, Mum?"

My wife is still in the rocker, singing a little French folk tune called "La Laine des Moutons."

"I'm really happy to share if you call me Maman. She's Mommy. No Mum," says Denise.

Patti gathers Adam with the blanket that's around him. She looks afraid. "What if I drop him?" Denise gets up and shows Patti what the nurse had shown us a few hours ago. Patti shakes her head and hands him back. "Maybe when he's older, and he can hold his head up. Need anything?"

"Sleep and an instruction booklet," says Denise.

"How are Mira and Leto?" I ask. Patti says both animals are getting used to sleeping in bed with her. I begin laughing but stop when my incision cite starts to burn.

*

The first night the nurses keep Adam so I can sleep; Denise stays over on a five-foot plastic sofa bed. It's easy during those twelve blissful hours to forget that we now have a tiny being who is dependent on us for his very survival. Every second of every minute of every hour.

The second night I'm lying awake, staring at the hospital ceiling, stomach in knots knowing Adam would wake up any minute to feed, and it occurs to me: I've never asked Mom anything about my birth.

Of course, she might not know, but maybe the social worker told her. Maybe my bio mom had a c-section. Maybe this was a factor in my developing a mental illness.

*

The next day, we're moved to our own room in the maternity ward. We'd paid for a private room, one of our best decisions yet, and I am grateful for the horse farm contract that allowed for extra funds. Denise posts on Facebook that the baby was born, and everything is fine.

Our social worker comes by and updates us on Brianna. She isn't well, heart problems being common to Down syndrome infants. Denise goes to visit her twice, since legally we are still her parents. She returns crying the second time.

"I'm sorry honey," I say, taking her hand and kissing it. "I wish I could come with you."

"I feel sorry for her. She doesn't get to nurse or do skin-to-skin with anyone." I tear up picturing her face, her eyes gazing into mine during that first breastfeeding.

In contrast with his sister, Adam struggles with nursing, as I struggle to function on little sleep. Nurses tell us to aim for eight feedings a day, two at night, and three rounds of pumping in between. Exhausted, I can barely remember my name and where I am half the time, but I aim high and muscle through.

People call: Claire, Mimi and Denise's brothers, Patti. Our next-door neighbour texts, saying she would let our other neighbours know. I check my email and Facebook and had a bunch of congrats, Freddy and Natascha, an e-card from Jessica and Eve, a bunch of "likes" from TPG members, even Stéfanie.

Nothing from Mom.

*

On day three, in the afternoon, there's another knock at our door.

Claire and Sabrina!

I'm breastfeeding when they come in, and they immediately start oohing and aahing. "Oh, he's beautiful. Can I hold him?" asks Sabrina, looking like a child herself.

"Sure, just wash your hands." A tiny yellow and blue knit hat from hospital volunteers covers Adam's head. He's wearing a onesie and a diaper. He looks like an ancient monk.

I wrap him in his receiving blanket and hand him to Sabrina.

"He has wavy hair, just like Audrey!" says Claire, snapping a photo of Sabrina and Adam with her phone.

"It was actually curlier when they first pulled him out. Maybe from the humidity."

Sabrina nuzzles Adam and lets him grasp her pinky. She looks so natural with him.

"Hm. Now that I'm closer—he actually kind of looks like Denise," says Claire.

I look at my wife. Two other nurses had made the same comment.

Jessica calls again. She tells us the school found a sub for a week so she could come and stay at our place, help out with the baby. She tells us on the phone that she would drive up the next day so Denise could get a full night's sleep before we leave the hospital. Our stress level drops for the first time since the delivery.

Chapter 52

The third night lingers like a week, knowing as I drift off that in just two hours, I need to be awake and upright to nurse my baby. My ribcage turns to steel as I peer at the tiny body in the little bassinet, making sure he's still breathing.

I sketch. I problem solve. I pray. I cry a lot and ask Denise if things will get better. While Adam sleeps, I tell myself stories in my head, inventing two characters, two young lovers named Agnes and Belle. Belle lives a cosmopolitan life as a journalist in Manhattan. Agnes is an organic farmer in upstate New York. The various scenarios I concoct mostly have to do with the two of them finding the time and space to be together in ways that make sense. Occasionally I try old breathing techniques from anxiety treatment, but Belle and Agnes are a better distraction.

At 3:15 a.m., I'm awake and stare at the hospital ceiling, the stucco finish, the vent on the right side, the square translucent lighting fixture. Brianna's image pops into my mind, and for the first time, I wonder if we'd made the right decision. Maybe her health issues were about not being with me. Maybe I should have asked Monique if I could see how things went first, take Brianna home, see what it was like. I hear noises from out in the hall, the click click click of high heels, a page for a doctor, two nurses chatting in French. I turn on my side to try for sleep again, tears on my cheeks, heart still pounding.

On our fourth day at the hospital, the staff paediatrician comes to see if Adam is ready to leave. He grabs him, slaps his back, and handles him like a football.

I sit on my bed, staring. Words are a distant world I cannot access. Denise has gone to get me some juice. The paediatrician gives me a thumbs up and drops my son into my lap.

When Denise comes back, I'm sitting up in bed, nursing Adam, staring out the window, face pale.

"What's wrong, darling?" Denise pours juice in my glass and puts her arm around my shoulders.

"The doctor. He hit Adam. And I just sat here. I couldn't speak. I'm a terrible mother."

Denise laughs. "You've been a mother for seventy-two hours. How terrible could you be?"

I feel my eyes water. "You know what I mean. He was awful."

Just then a nurse came in to take out my catheter. "Sorry to listen, but were you speaking about Dr. Archambault?" Her accent was thicker than most francophones.

I nodded. She shook her head. "The nurse complain and complain, but nothing happen. Maybe you can write a letter. Maybe you help get this guy out. It's no good for the little ones."

But activism is as far away as my mother. It's my job to protect this little helpless baby, and I've already blown it.

Chapter 53

A dam's voice is getting stronger and more difficult to listen to. I can't find a moment to pump because I'm either nursing or trying to sleep. The fourth night is bleak, with Adam crying almost every hour. The three of us cuddle together in my little bed, Denise and I gazing at Adam who is relaxing between us. I glance at the clock: it's only 7:30 p.m. It feels like midnight.

Somebody knocks.

"Anybody home?" We look up: Jessica. It's like the first warm day after an Arctic winter. The transition team of one has arrived, and we wouldn't be alone for another ten days. Jessica is in her black jeans and University of Vermont tee shirt, black leather overnight bag slung over her shoulder. Denise jumps out of bed and hugs her. Jessica goes to break away, but Denise is still hanging on. Then Jessica looks at Adam and me and says, "Holy shit." Her face flushes, and her expression goes soft. "Can I hold him?'

"Of course! Just wash hands first." I scoop up all seven pounds of baby with the receiving blanket. Jessica comes out of the bathroom drying her hands and takes him, clucking. I turn to Denise.

"We should record the kinds of sounds people make with Adam as a sociological performance art project."

"How about after the nurse removes your catheter?" my wife suggests brightly.

Jessica asks me how the walking is going.

"Rough. But not as bad as sleeping."

She looks around the room. "Is that blood on the wall?"

We look. It is.

She peers into the bathroom. "This is disgusting. Has anyone been in to clean while you've been here?"

We look at each other, then shake our heads, like guilty children.

"Socialized medicine is fabulous, but if you get sick at the hospital because they don't have enough staff to clean, it's not worth much."

"I'm just glad we didn't have to pay for any of it, other than the private room," I say, "with all the money we had to shell out just to get pregnant. We wouldn't have been able to do this if we'd been in the US."

Jessica looks at me, starts to speak, and then stops herself.

I look at her. "Did you bring the necklace?"

Her expression changes and her face goes white. "I lost it."

I roll my eyes. "You should have given it to me for safekeeping." I smile, trying not to laugh. "How's Bill?"

"What are they giving you to eat?" She's looking out the window.

Nothing great.

"I'm going to walk around outside and see if I can scrounge up something with taste, ideally something with a nutrient or two. Any requests?"

"Pepperoni pizza, Chunky Monkey, and a beer," I answer. Denise asks for a steak, medium well. "Anything you find will be better than what we've been eating," I say. Jessica looks at me in the bed with the baby and whispers.

"You did it, Meyerwitz. You did it."

I look at our son and think, yes, but we did it. I mouth "I love you" to my best friend and kiss my wife.

Then I wonder, again, about Bill.

*

The fifth day is our last at the hospital. We're grateful and terrified. We've gotten used to having lots of people around who know about babies. Us? We've just read a few books. I don't even feel particularly bonded to Adam, which I tell nobody. That electric connection I experienced in just a few minutes of nursing Brianna was dramatic and visceral. Now, Adam just seems like a nonstop bundle of needs, which only my battered and bone-weary body can fulfill.

Denise updates me on Brianna. "The nurse told me she's out of intensive care. The adoption is on hold until after her health status is updated. But she's definitely better."

I shift and notice the pain where the catheter had been. "Do you think we're doing the right thing?"

Denise sits on the edge of the bed. She looks out the window and then at me. "Je pense que oui, mais…" She shakes her head. "Part of me wants to just go scoop her up and bring her home. But it's not realistic, Audrey. I'm already overwhelmed, and we have an entire hospital department helping us."

Hearing Denise say she's overwhelmed helps me relax and not believe it's my fault. I once again think of my bio mom, and a new thought appears: Maybe my birth mother was disabled. Maybe she thought she couldn't handle me, and that's why she gave me up.

It's March and still winter in Montreal. When we're discharged, Jessica goes back to Rosemont to do some grocery shopping, and Denise brings the car around while a nurse wheels Adam and me to the hospital exit. I hadn't been outside for days and didn't realize there had been a snowstorm. I gather Adam closer to me, hoping the warmth of my body, the hat, and the blanket I'd wrapped him in would protect him from the frosty wind.

We get home and there's Jessica, in the process of cooking salmon, sweet potatoes, and cauliflower leek soup.

Gifts flood the downstairs spaces. Our next-door-neighbour, Marie-Claude, calls to say she put up a sign on our door that she would receive things for us and that when she heard we were coming home, she brought everything into our place. There's a balloon arrangement, numerous potted plants, six vases of flowers, even an edible bouquet of fruit. I'm touched by people's generosity but so wasted that I collapse on the sofa and tell the other two to wake me only if I'm needed. Which I am, fifteen minutes later. I sigh, take Adam from Denise, and put him on my breast.

*

Jessica takes care of the three of us as we slowly start adjusting to life as a family. She helps us diaper and dress our baby. She cooks and cleans while Adam and I figure out breastfeeding. She makes several daily trips to Pharmaprix for diapers, shampoo, nipple cream, milk storage bags, wipes, and elephant-sized sanitary napkins. She goes to the used clothing store and returns with piles of onesies and receiving blankets. She uses her minimal French and her charm to improvise public transactions. She refuses to take our money and wakes up for a few night feedings so we can sleep longer. At no point do I smell alcohol on her breath. Neither does Denise.

"What will we do when she goes home?" asks Denise one night as Adam sleeps in the middle of our bodies. "Can we kidnap her?"

Chapter 54

The next day, we try giving Adam a bath. When water touches his body, he screams like we're breaking his arms. Slightly traumatized, we put it off twice until Jessica finally insists.

"Unless you want me to tell everyone you named him Stink Bomb," she says, munching on some grapes. I'm snuggled down into the blue chair in my Snoopy shirt and size forty-eight underpants. Denise is trying a new onesie on Adam because he's already outgrown most of the outfits we'd bought for him before the birth.

I hear water running in the bathroom. Apparently, Jessica is filling up Adam's baby bath in the tub.

"Do we have to?" I ask Denise. She finishes snapping the orange onesie around Adam's diaper and stands him up for my approval.

"C'est un beau garçon!" she says to Adam, conveniently avoiding my question.

We are teenagers, so we do what we're told. We bring the victim into the torture chamber.

This entails disrobing him, which is annoying, given the cute new outfit and the fresh diaper.

"Save it," I say. Denise picks up Adam, takes the outfit and diaper out of the bathroom, and comes back. Jessica and I are around the tub where she's finishing filling up the baby bath.

"Okay, pass me the wunderkind," she says, on her knees armed with baby shampoo and a soft washcloth with a zebra on it. Denise starts to give Adam to Jessica, but for a second, she hesitates. Reluctantly, she hands him over.

The second Adam feels the water, he shrieks. Just like the first time. It's so disturbing I climb onto the small sink vanity so I can see over Jessica's head to monitor exactly what she's doing to him.

"He sounds terrified," I say, doubting myself even as I say it.

"Oh," says Jessica, rubbing him down with the cloth, "he'll get used to it."

"Here," she says to Denise. "Why don't you try."

Denise looks at me. She's crying.

"I'd like to try, actually," I say to Jessica, "and maybe Denise, you could go make me a mango spritzer?"

Denise slips out without Jessica seeing her tears. I squeeze around my friend as she backs up so I can take over. I grab the towel hanging on the bar and put it around my sobbing infant.

"But you're not done," says Jessica. "You need to soap his hair and body and then rinse it."

I ignore her and wrap Adam in the towel, murmuring to him. He stops crying almost immediately. "I have a different idea. Maybe you could go with Denise and make a little snack?"

I know in my bones that I have to make Adam's bathing experience less awful for him. The fact that he's only two weeks old doesn't mean it's right for me to hurt him, despite what ninety-nine percent of adults might think.

Denise comes in and gives me my drink. I tell her my idea. She smiles and nods. "Can I take him while you get set up?" she asks. I hand Adam to her and take off my clothes. I remove the baby bath out of the regular bathtub, empty its water, and set it down on the sink. Then I run a lukewarm bath in the tub. When the water's a bit higher than two centimeters, I step in.

"Now, give him to me." Denise lowers the baby down slowly. I take him in the nursing position known as the "football hold" and put him on my breast. He starts sucking happily. Denise places the shampoo on the side of the tub and tosses in the zebra washcloth. Slowly, as Adam nurses, I begin dipping the washcloth in and wetting his skin. If he starts to cry, I stop. This continues for fifteen minutes. Eventually, I get to his hair. I'm able to wet it, but I need Denise to do the shampoo. She does, and although he fusses, he's far less distressed than when he was there by himself experiencing all those strange sensations apart from me and my body.

I look at Denise and breathe, my first real exhale since my son's birth.

*

The week flies by, while the hours seem to crawl. Our lives are no longer broken up by day or night, just three-hour cycles. Between Denise and Jessica, there's very little required of me besides attending to Adam, and every day, I hug and kiss them both, letting them know how grateful I am. But new motherhood is still more than enough. With a completely screwed up sleeping schedule, I feel my sanity slipping away, while many moments are sheer delight, gazing into Adam's eyes when he's awake, petting his head and snuggling him against my body when he's asleep, which is still most of the time.

It becomes clear that he knows me, and one day when I'm changing him, we make eye contact. "It's me, little one. I'm your mom. Nice to meet you," I say as we look at each other. I gently kiss each of his cheeks.

Brianna's face haunts me, often when I'm nursing Adam. Monique calls one day to update us. She tells us Brianna had to go back into intensive care. Monique says she's requesting that the adoption proceedings be rushed, so her adoptive parents can be with her at the hospital. She says she'll keep us posted.

That evening, Jessica's last with us, Denise makes a tourtière, the Quebecois dish we ate last Christmas. She puts out our one tablecloth and two candles. Adam sleeps in the sling wrapped around me, and we have a warm and cozy supper, reminiscent of those normal days before March 28.

Adam wakes up after about fifteen minutes, fussing, bobbing his head, opening his mouth.

"Already?" I sigh. "You guys don't mind if I nurse him here, do you?"

They both laugh.

I feel my eyes tearing up.

"I'm going to miss you, Jess," I say.

Denise nods. "All of us will."

*

The next morning, as she gets in her car to go back to Burlington, we ask her if she would be Adam's godmother. My beautiful badass Jessica weeps and weeps, hugging all three of us against her bright orange Subaru.

As she pulls away out of the spring slush, we walk slowly back to the house, me wearing Adam in the sling, Denise sighing. She looks depleted. I decide it's time to call the real parents and tell them that the jig is up: We're not qualified to provide long-term babysitting, so please come pick up their kid immediately. It's not funny anymore.

Chapter 55

It's May, and seven-week-old Adam is suffering terribly with gas cramps. Each time we nestle together in the blue chair—his mouth pursed around my nipple and his twelve-pound body flopped over me—he finishes, rests, and then, a minute later, clenches in half, reddens, grimaces, and shrieks. My own stomach tightens, and I begin, again, to try to soothe my baby. I clutch at my Star of David around my neck and shift him from my right shoulder to the left.

The crying rages on.

Denise is back to work, and it's a huge adjustment. We're doing sleep shifts so each of us can get at least four hours in a row, the amount we've decided is necessary for basic sanity. Not the amount required for good health or good mood, but what you need to prevent psychosis. Sometimes we don't even get that much. Those days, I go into my medicine cabinet, grab the bottle of leftover Ativan, and sometimes I put one of the .5 milligram pills in my hand. I think about tossing it onto my tongue and washing it down with water cupped in my hand. But then I visualize the medication flowing into my breasts and Adam sucking and sucking. The pill always goes back into its plastic bottle.

I pick up Adam and sway with him in my arms. My phone pings. I walk over to the table. Jessica.

Meow?

Arf.

I go to my desktop and open Zoom. "No school?"

She clucks. "Memorial Day. Already you've forgotten?"

"It's Victoria Day here. But Denise has to work anyway. Hey, do you think girls cry this much? I wonder if Brianna is a crier. I always wanted a girl. Is that mean?"

"You're a lesbian and a feminist, Audrey," she said, sipping a glass of something the colour of thinned blood. "It totally makes sense."

"Is that wine?" A peach pit rattles around in my stomach.

"No, it's extra rain from my rain barrel," she says with a grin. Adam starts doing this bird imitation he'd been working on all morning.

"Let me see the holy child." Jessica subtly moves her glass away from the computer's camera so it's no longer in the picture.

I hold him up. She makes cooing noises. Adam blinks and drools.

"Any news about Brianna?"

I bring Adam back to my shoulder. "She's still in the hospital. Denise went yesterday to visit again. They're transferring her to Montreal Children's tomorrow where they have a guy who specializes in infant heart problems."

"Are the adoptive parents still going to take her?"

"Yeah, but the legal stuff is stalled, which is why Denise goes."

She nods. "Not that you asked, but I'm sure you guys made the right call."

"I know one professional foster parent in Albany who wouldn't agree." I kiss Adam's head and rearrange him in my lap.

There's a pause. "No word?"

I shake my head and bite my lip. "How's Bill?"

She smiles. "Great! I had the kids last weekend at my place because he had a conference. They're starting to trust me. We stayed up until ten and played Twister and drank milkshakes."

"We'll make a mother out of you yet," I say, teasing. She seems much more relaxed about Bill. "Did you find the necklace?"

"No, but it's no biggie. He actually got me something else." She raised her eyebrow.

"What?" I look around in her room but don't see anything I don't recognize.

She goes into her drawer and pulls out a black teddy with red trim.

"Holy shit, Jess. That's seriously sexy. Did you try it on?"

She does a little dance holding it up to her. "You'll have to use your imagination."

"Eeeyew! No thank you." She laughs.

I adjust Adam and play with my Star of David. "I've been thinking about my birth mom."

Jessica gasps. "No way!"

I smile. "Don't get all excited. She's just been in my head. Wondering if maybe she gave me up because she was disabled. Wondering what she's like. Just that. Nothing big."

Jessica has a big smile. "Do you want to start looking?"

"Of course not. But with Martha out of the picture, maybe I would be more open if she came knocking on my door, or if we accidentally met up."

Jessica shakes her head. "Ain't gonna happen."

"Well, it's fine because I have plenty to occupy my time at the moment."

"You look so sweet with him." Her face is different. Fragile, maybe.

"I was actually thinking last night," I say, shifting him in my lap. "I let this dude, this male person, suck my friggin' nipples, but we never chose each other. How weird is that? It's like going to the market, covering your eyes, and pointing to find your next best friend. Who makes important life decisions that way?"

Silence.

"Get some sleep, Meyerwitz."

We make smooching sounds and end the call.

Now I'm aware of murmuring in my stomach. Adam starts crying again, but I get up and go to the fridge. The only interesting thing I find are two drinkable yogurts, which I open and consume in four seconds. I go back into the living room to sit down to feed my baby, who turns his head to and fro and sounds like he's about to sneeze. He nurses for a while before screeching and hunching over again.

Then he gets the hiccups, wet sobby little hiccups. I sing "The Wheels on the Bus" as I carry him to the kitchen and turn on the water. For a minute, he's distracted by the faucet, and it seems like the crying might pass. But as soon as I turn it off, a new scream ripples through his torso and out his mouth. Every inch of my skin prickles and my throat tightens like a violin string being tuned.

The doorbell rings.

I set down the mug and keep the melody going with "lalala" and head for the door. I shift Adam onto my other hip, moving the lacy curtains on the door back to see who's there.

Claire and Sabrina, smiling and waving.

I open the door and immediately start bawling. Sabrina gently takes Adam and heads for the sofa. Her head brushes against the wooden bird mobile, a baby gift that Denise's brother had brought back from Cuba last winter. Claire hugs me tight.

The burst of new energy and Sabrina's animated face distracts my crampy baby who is now all coos and giggles.

Claire takes off her jacket and leads me back into the kitchen...the white flecked vinyl floor tiles that are chipping around the edges, the white Danish modern island with a blue accent piece in the centre, the glaring track lighting with three bulbs out. The renovation we said we'd do when we bought the house is now clearly in the distant future. Food particles have gathered and smooshed into the corners on the floor, and the cupboards are streaked with dark spots from hands.

Claire opens one greying cabinet door and grabs a glass, one of the ones with Daffy Duck that I found at a garage sale in Burlington. She fills the glass with water, hands it to me and holds my hand as I cry, giving me tissues from her jeans pocket and asking if I've eaten anything. I lean against the crumb-laden countertop, notice the opened plastic bag with the cheap Provigo bread, and continue crying, covering my face with my hand. I hear Sabrina talking to Adam in her high-pitched baby voice, the one Denise insisted she would never use, wiggling his red cloth ragdoll, Emile. His own baby voice warbles with delight.

Claire embraces me and whispers that I'm going to be fine, that this moment will pass, that they have our backs.

Later that afternoon, Patti calls, asking if we want to order takeout pizza. Denise returns from work with more milk bags and groceries. Mireille arrives a half hour later and then the delivery guy with three hot and cheesy pizzas, Patti right behind him. Once the supper and the friends are all inside, Patti tosses Adam high in the air while I check to make sure his head doesn't hit the ceiling. Claire shows Mireille photos of this ostrich she took care of at work the week before. Denise holds up Adam's new tiger pajamas, striped sun hat, and orange summer onesie she found at a consignment shop, and Sabrina ooo-s and aaah-s. The noise level is decibels above Adam's crying, but my nerves settle, and I smile watching the scene.

My eyes land on a photo of Mom and me with my siblings at our wedding on the piano. We've been home from the hospital for seven weeks, and my mother is still MIA. I almost start crying again, but when my eyes leave the photo, I see the four warm, loving women who are here, present, and helping.

Ironically, maybe Martha was right. Maybe healthy family really is who shows up.

I wonder for the first time what type of man Adam will become. He won't have a father to be like or to rebel against, but he will have these women who nestle up against us, prop us up when we wilt, nourish us when we're depleted, and make us laugh when we despair. His village may look different from the mainstream, but it's solid and plentiful and loving.

Patti returns Adam to me. I tuck him into the sling, and he falls fast asleep, against my beating heart.

After everybody leaves, Denise and I get ready for bed, and I nurse my boy, the last feeding of the day. Like earlier, he eats well and then, minutes later, wails with cramps. All the unanswered questions recede as I take my boy in my arms, bending my knees in a colic dance, trying, gently, to release the gas from his tender anguished belly, both of us fumbling our way together, supported by our chosen family, through the long darkness of the night.

Chapter 56

Early parenthood is like boot camp. You're allotted the absolute minimum of time required of your body to sleep, and each of your waking hours is spent in service to someone else's needs. Activities that were on that list before baby are now on the other one labelled "optional"—items like exercising, bathing, and food preparation, beyond pouring cereal into a bowl. You see how lax you are allowed to be in your relationships with other adults and how much time each person gives you to slack off before dumping you as yet another child-obsessed helicopter parent who doesn't even respond to texts.

In June, we see a doctor, a lactation consultant, and a naturopath to get help with Adam's painful belly. The paediatrician says he'll grow out of it, the lactation consultant says he has an incorrect latch, and the naturopath suggests that I eliminate gluten, dairy, and bovine products. We work on the latch and implement the diet, and I drop ten pounds in two weeks, putting me at fifteen pounds below my pre-pregnancy weight. Any edginess I felt before from hormones and sleep deprivation is magnified as I wander through my days, looking for nourishment in the kitchen and finding only quinoa crackers and apples that never seem to fill me up.

Adam's nipple-worshipping relationship with breastfeeding contrasts greatly with mine, which varies between spacing out, eye rolling, or, if things go on for too long, teary despair. I finish serving up each marathon feast, knowing he could be ready to go again in just thirty more minutes. White-faced, I hand him over to Denise after feedings so she can take care of his other needs. Our nicknames are now "Breast Mama" and "The Rest Mama". I fantasize about a one-way ticket to Key West and leaving my spit-up stained wardrobe and stain maker safely at home.

Denise looks at me on the couch after a two-and-a-half hour feeding session. I'm watching reruns of *Grey's Anatomy*.

"We have to switch to formula," she says, replenishing my glass of mango juice and spring water. I focus on the beautiful Meredith Grey. My eyes fill with tears, but I pay little attention, wiping them away quickly, grabbing a tissue to blow my nose.

"It's not a big deal, and you'll feel so much better," my wife argues into the void. "Adam needs you more than your milk, and you don't want much to do with him when he's not nursing."

"When is he not nursing?" I snap. "During the three hours out of twenty-four that exist in a day, I should probably be trying to sleep."

Denise shakes her head. "I'm on your side, Audrey. You need more of everything—more sleep, more food, more freedom."

I cover my eyes with my hands. I think about Dr. Sears and Jean Liedloff. Infancy goes by in a flash. Nursing, like baby wearing and co-sleeping, is time limited. Something I read described it as a sprint. But to me it feels like a full marathon, and the most I've ever run is ten kilometres. I have nothing left to give. Between no sleep, no food, and no second twin, I'm completely empty.

I remember another passage in an attachment parenting book. If you do just one thing for your baby, nurse him for two years minimum. Immune system, bonding, nutrition, brain development, environment... there's nothing else that gives so many benefits in one parenting choice.

I calm down, wipe my face, blow my nose. "Sorry honey. I just have to muscle through."

Every day, Denise suggests feeding formula. Jessica asks about it when we talk. Patti tells me all of her siblings, eight in total, were bottle-fed and the four who are parents are now bottle-feeding their kids and everybody is fine. But I continue nursing and nursing and nursing.

At twelve weeks, Adam begins drinking so much that I am unable to pump extra milk during the daytime, which had been buying me that four-hour sleep shift tucked away in our basement, earplugs firmly in place. Having the extra pumped bottle allowed me to mother the next day without bawling or considering a leap in front of the #31 bus.

I hit the wall.

I'm lying down next to Adam, nursing him. He is sucking in his sleep, sucking, sucking, sucking, forty-five minutes, fifty, sixty. His breathing is even, but I know if I take out my nipple, he'll wake up. I've been awake for close to forty hours. My hands tremble, tiny micro shakes. My body now feeds mostly on itself since the new diet. I lie there feeling like a starving animal being eaten.

I tell myself to breathe. *One, two, three, four...*

Something catches on fire inside my chest. The harder I breathe, the harder I try to push it down, the hotter and more furious it burns. It spreads to my stomach, heart, intestines, and soon it's warming my blood, pushing out of the veins into the skin.

I rip the nipple from the baby's mouth and start howling. My fingers clench my oily hair as Adam's eyes pop open. He's pulled into my storm and joins me wailing and screaming. It's like we're two infants, desperate and uncomprehending, swallowed up by the tidal wave of present meets past.

Denise rushes downstairs.

"What happened? What is it?"

Adam is on the rug, and I am lying face down on the couch, trying to muffle my cries with the pillow.

She picks up the baby, cuddles him against her shoulder, and gets him calmed down. Then she sits down tentatively beside me on the couch.

"Can you please talk to me so I know what's going on? I can't help if I don't know." She rubs my back.

"When do I get to eat what I want? When do I get to walk normally? I want my old life back." I cry and cry until the pillow is so wet, I have to flip it over.

She gets Adam into the sling, wears him into the kitchen, and I hear sounds I don't recognize. Then I hear the click of a can opening and a glug glug glug.

I don't have the strength to resist.

I want permission to fall apart. I want my mom. I want my medication. I want to sleep eight hours in a row. Anything to make it stop.

Denise returns to the living room and feeds Adam with the bottle of formula. The quiet and his gulping bring us back together. Full-time nursing is no longer an option.

The next day I call my psychiatrist and ask about medication, my old one or any new ones that could help me sleep. There are some risks involved with nursing, so we decide that each morning, I would pump and toss that milk, waiting until the medication is out of my system before the first nursing of the day. I decide it's a compromise I can live with.

I begin feeling stronger almost immediately. Diaper changing and dressing become part of my baby-care activities. I invent a new kissy-kissy game: Adam blinks his eyes and purses his lips when I smooch him, which makes me eager to do it again. I draw some black-and-white geometric shapes on an old white sheet for him to stare at because I read infants like stuff like that. I even start cuddling him when I'm not nursing. I take photos, sniff his head, and lie down with him for a nap after supper, with Denise sometimes, instead of trying to get something done in the house.

I pick up my phone to call Mom and almost do it. Then I think about how long it's been since she called or responded to my messages. I think about how Adam is her first grandchild.

Hands quivering, I go into the contacts screen on my phone and erase "Martha Meyerwitz."

Chapter 57

Jessica notices my newfound energy on Zoom early in July. It's evening, and Denise is taking a walk around the neighbourhood with Mira, wearing Adam in the sling.

"Wow, Mama, you're getting some colour back in those pale cheeks. Did you take Boy Wonder to the beach?"

I smile and tell her about using formula a few times a day. She grabs two dishtowels and does a cheerleader routine. I scan for alcohol and see a bottle of vodka on the little table behind her desk. I don't say anything and just let her be happy for me.

"Hey, speaking of congrats, Bill asked me to move in."

My mouth drops open. "I thought he didn't want a relationship."

She grins. "I'm like opium. He can't get enough."

"Is that really what you want to be for him?"

"It's a joke, Audrey, jeez. Burst my bubble."

"Sorry. So, what are you going to do?"

"I'm thinking yes but later. Maybe in the fall. I'm with the kids pretty regularly now, so in a way, it would make things easier."

I wonder where I've been lately. "What's happening with the kids?"

"They're really amazing, but they're still grieving. I pick them up from day camp, so they're with me until Bill finishes work at 7:00. Patricia is having nightmares, so sometimes when I'm at their place, I go in and cuddle with her until she relaxes. Sam throws tantrums, so I do silly things to change the dynamic like I do at school, and sometimes it works, sometimes not. Sometimes I just have to be there when they cry. I get it, so maybe it helps them a little."

"That sounds hard. How do you have the energy for that?"

She laughs. "How do you have the energy to nurse twenty hours a day without any sleep? We just do what we have to do, I guess. Bill doesn't have any expendable cash, so they can't afford therapy. I've been picking the school counsellor's brain for interventions I can do at home as kind of a substitute for therapy."

"That's great for them. But what about for you?"

She tilts her head towards the right and then left shoulder, indicating "so so." Then I see her eyes get watery. "Hang on, gotta take the chicken out of the oven."

When she returns, she looks fine.

I realize she's getting in deeper and deeper. I hadn't voiced my concerns about her love life since last time when she made it clear she didn't want my opinion about her drinking. And I haven't seen her drink since then. But hearing about her taking care of the kids and getting a glimpse of the vodka puts a stitch in my side.

At night in bed, I tell Denise as we lie next to our sleeping baby.

"I'm worried about Jessica," I whisper.

"You're always worried about Jessica," says Denise, abruptly sitting up. "Why don't you tell her instead of me? You say you two are so close, but who's going to help her if nobody is honest about what's going on? Frankly, I'm worried about you worrying, especially on so little sleep."

Denise has dark rings under her eyes. How come I hadn't noticed?

"I don't know what to do," I say. "Nothing works."

Adam shifts in his sleep, and Denise and I turn away from one another. The conversation is over. I brace myself for the darkness and pray for four consecutive hours, enough to have a little time with those elusive delta waves.

*

It's a beautiful August afternoon in Rosemont. Denise is at the grocery store, and Adam and I are up from our before-supper nap. We're playing peek-a-boo with the sheet on the bed, and Adam is beside himself with giggles.

My phone pings. Jessica.

Chirp.

Cocorico.

HUH?

Quebecois rooster.

I turn on Zoom on my phone. Jessica is laughing and eating Ferro Rocher chocolates, blue, red, and gold. The wrappers are scattered over the desk and some on the floor.

I'm sitting up in bed and hauling Adam onto my lap. I smile at my best friend. "So good to see your gorgeous face."

"Hey, immigrant mama, what's happening? You look grim." She unwraps another chocolate. "The child is clearly not starving. Hi cutie, wave to Auntie Jess!" She makes kiss-kiss noises. Adam looks at the screen. Maybe he's looking at the chocolates. Maybe I'm looking at the chocolates.

Then I see her arm. Bruises, wrapped around her bicep, like the sleeve of a tie-dyed turtleneck.

"What happened to your arm?"

She grabs a cardigan sweater. "We had this self defense workshop at school, and Charlene grabbed me too hard during one of the exercises. Good old Charlene, the pit bull who thinks she's a chihuahua."

"I'm worried about you, Jess." The words fall out of my mouth.

She slips into the sweater.

"Ah, pishaw," she says. "You of all people should know I'm made of rubber. And did you know rubber is an ecologically sound alternative to plastic?"

I try to find my breath, but it's stuck somewhere between my lungs and my chin.

"I want you to go to rehab again. I'll set it up, I'll pack for you, whatever you want, just say you'll go."

Her expression changes on a dime. I backpedal.

"I'm saying it because I care about what happens to you."

She doesn't move or speak. Adam fusses, looking for my breast. I adjust and put him on my right side.

Then she laughs.

Opens another chocolate.

"Audrey, Audrey, Audrey, with your perfect little life in perfect socialist Canada," she says, grabbing a bottle of vodka that she'd had out of my view. She pours some in a glass and drinks it in front of the camera, eyes on me the entire time. "The rest of us have to have stress outlets. Remember that from your days of slumming it down here with me?"

I stay quiet and focus on the wall behind her, the photos hanging. In one, we're singing "The First Cut Is the Deepest" at the Wellness retreat. The other is from my wedding, us both crying and laughing, arms around one another. Then I see a third picture, one of her and Bill under a beach umbrella. I realize that not only have I never met Bill, but I've also never seen a photo of him. Scanning the last months, I realize I had never asked. I think of her creating my dating profile, and my face flushes.

"How are things with Bill?"

"No," she shouts, pointing at the camera. "You can't condemn me one minute and be my buddy the next. Make up your mind, Audrey. Are you my judge or my sister? Wait a sec, forget it. I already know the answer."

She disappears.

Chapter 58

I call Jessica the next day, and we both apologize. She says she's been in a bad mood because one of the nuns wrote her up. She doesn't say what for. But she convinces me, one more time, that she's fine. I tell her I'm sorry I've been so preoccupied, and I ask to see a photo of Bill. We both laugh and make smooching sounds before hanging up. I breathe in, and my lungs fill up like bagpipes.

Before long, it's mid-September. Adam starts solid foods and sleeps longer stretches, and I start marketing for new clients and begin TPG rehearsals. Stéfanie and the other actors are happy to have me back, but my French is extremely rusty. I jump into warmups and begin with the company to explore the political romance and heartbreak story we'll be telling our audiences in January.

Canadian Thanksgiving is in early October, and my mind is working on some kind of gratitude event. I imagine Jessica and Bill and his kids integrating into the Itchy Mortals, and an idea is born.

I toss it out to Denise over a pancake breakfast.

"Maybe we should have a celebration for Thanksgiving. You know, not 'glad we stole the land,' but gratefulness and the harvest, that sort of thing."

Denise picks up a box of Corn Flakes. She approaches Adam's highchair and drops a bunch onto his tray.

"Pas sure. We're still not showering on a regular basis. Un souper d'Action de grâce? Might be too much."

"Okay, but if we don't try, if we don't superimpose normalcy onto our infant-centred lives, we might never get it back."

She bends over and gives Adam a zerbert on his cheek. He shrieks and bangs his hands on his tray, grinning. "Mommy has big plans for us, grand garçon." Then she gives me a smile I haven't seen in months.

So, we send out Evites to Jessica and Bill and family, Claire and

Sabrina, Patti and Mireille, and Denise's siblings and their partners.

The next day, on a whim, I send one to Mom.

No response.

Every time I feel at the end of my devastation, strong and settled in my chosen family, another blast of sadness rises into my throat. As we prepare for the celebration, I'm full of memories from a favourite time in my childhood. On American Thanksgiving, I would wake up to the smell of Mom's cinnamon buns in the oven, a crazy blend with the scent of turkey and fried onions that she always starts at the same time. We'd come downstairs, and she'd make us hot chocolates while we all watched the Macy's day parade with whomever Mom was fostering that year. The coffee and buns tasted so much better with my siblings and the parade and the promise of pumpkin pie later in the day.

I push memories to the side and focus on Adam and preparations. Denise and I make the menu: an eighteen-pound turkey, tofurkey, slow-cooker stuffing, green beans amandine, maple-orange cranberry sauce, and pumpkin pie. We also create a gratitude installation. We invite guests to send us words and phrases that express things they feel grateful for. I then take the words and use my gold paint pen to write them with little line drawings on collected autumnal leaves, which I press between heavy books. I discover an old white tablecloth and use it as a base on which to scatter the leaves on the day of the meal.

While I'm transforming the leaves, I think about what I'm grateful for. I think about my friends who have been there beside me, every step of the way, how starting my family life only worked because of them and because of Denise, whom I would never have met but for Jessica's pushing me to do online dating. I also notice that I hadn't done much appreciating since Adam's birth. When parenting days are hard, when I'm nursing every few hours from 5:00 a.m. until midnight, unless I'm making a big effort, I can only focus on what's in front of me and getting through it, on a good day without crying more than four times. It hasn't occurred to me to be grateful until this moment.

It could have gone the other way. I might not have gotten pregnant at all. And I might have fallen apart in those first few months.

I even think about Mom and how she was there for me for most of my life. She certainly taught me about love and embracing people who aren't biological relatives. I couldn't have made it this far as a person with an anxiety disorder without her organizing services for me throughout my life.

*

I'm preparing the tablecloth and napkins, and I think about a question Jessica asked me the other day: What exactly do I do with all my time that I can't text, call, or Zoom with her? If Jessica and I talk, it's because she reaches out. I love my little boy, but the nothingness of daily life often wastes me, leaving me with both too much space and too little, too much quiet or too much noise, one profound connection and too much disconnection from what I had so recently gained and held so dear.

Motherhood with an anxiety disorder.

I ask Denise what she thinks.

"Frankly, if all the kids in the world had Adam's childhood, there's no question in my mind that we would achieve world peace in his lifetime."

That night, I go to sleep with Adam's heavy breathing on my right, in between Denise and me. I think about those moments, all held together by something intangible that we call family. I breathe in the wisp of wind that blows through the window. I imagine myself before I met Denise, standing outside the mosaic, longing and lonely. Now I'm part of it, one of the morsels in the frame, one of the mortals. Am I all better? Is mine a healthy family? Maybe I can begin to see the full picture that the mosaic makes—to start understanding that all those nothing minutes during my days could be a precursor to a large and lovely something.

Chapter 59

Jessica and Bill cancel at the last minute, but we still manage to pull off Canadian Thanksgiving. Along with our menu, Patti brings a chocolate fondue with fruit, Claire makes asparagus spears with garlic, Sabrina bakes gluten-free oat bread, and Mireille makes a sweet potato casserole. Patti holds Adam for most of supper and then when we're singing, she passes him off to Sabrina, and when Sabrina goes to help Denise with the dishes, Claire takes him.

In the middle of the evening, I hear my cell phone ping in my backpack upstairs. Normally I turn it off for dinner parties, but I was so focussed on the event that I'd forgotten. I excuse myself and dash upstairs. Jessica.

Call ASAP. Need you. Xo.

I call her immediately but get bounced to voice mail.

"What's happening?" I turn to see Denise in the doorway. I freeze, not wanting to give her more information about Jessica's problems.

"Hang on."

I turn back to the phone. "I'll try you tomorrow. Have a nice evening."

She looks at me and frowns. "It's Thanksgiving."

"Yeah, that was an American client. He had a last-minute edit for his logo that we have to discuss before I send it to the printers."

She looks at my face like she's trying to figure something out. I look down at the phone. "Let's go back downstairs with our guests, okay?"

She turns around and leaves. I follow, making a mental note to try Jessica after the Mortals leave, and Adam is asleep.

But after company and a big meal and dishes, I'm too exhausted to do anything besides fall into bed in my clothes. The next day I have an appointment with my psychiatrist, which means getting everything prepared for the babysitter, and then, like most things, returning a phone call completely slips my mind.

*

By mid-October, all the leaves have fallen, exposing bare tree branches and long Vs of geese flying south. It's a stark muted time of year that I feel at home in, and with Adam hitting the eight-month mark, our little family starts moving out of three-hour cycles and toward something that vaguely resembles normalcy.

I text Jessica a week after Thanksgiving and don't hear back. She's probably busy with the kids, I think, and I shouldn't push.

Rehearsals become intense, and I suddenly have three branding contracts. I do everything when Adam is sleeping, which means I can't work at the speed I'm used to, but things get done, somehow. Compared with my American friends, whose babies go to daycare at three months old, I know I'm fortunate. Denise and I study our attachment parenting books, continue wearing Adam in the sling, doing skin-to-skin, and responding faithfully to his cries. He's pushing himself to standing and even taking wobbly steps. With teething, his cheeks flush, and he often needs to chew. I try frozen washcloths, teething toys, rubber baby flatware, and colic water—all of this helps, but none takes the pain away completely. So, we do lots of walks, hugs, baths, and, of course, nursing.

With the company, Stéfanie works with us on tension. "We need all the looseness and flexibility of each muscle, so it is available to us to create our characters," she says. I roll my neck around and knead it, pushing fingertips into the bands of tension gripping the muscles. I shake out my arms and legs, practise yoga before rehearsals start, and breathe deep. But my anxiety has taken my relaxation hostage and won't budge.

One evening after we're finished with rehearsal, she comes over to me. I'm loading my script and pen into my backpack and taking out my scarf.

"Audrey, ma chère, I would like to work with you individually on tension. I have some ideas, so let's plan for an extra rehearsal one-on-one." I'm looking for my boots in the church foyer and not finding them.

"I'm busy with Adam and work…"

She smiles. "This is your real work, and you'll love the difference it'll make in your onstage experiences. How about Thursday afternoon?"

I find my boots and my cheeks flush with heat. Who would I get to babysit?

Mireille has Thursdays off from work, so after she agrees to stay with Adam, I email Stéfanie and confirm. On Thursday, I trudge to the metro, kicking a stone with the metal toe of my boot. I hadn't wanted to leave Adam as he was fussy and not happy to see Mireille. At the same time, the idea of spending one-on-one time with Stéfanie made my heart beat louder, faster, and stronger. I think about what Jessica said about me and beautiful women, and then I dismiss it. I'm happily married.

I get to the church, and Stéfanie is waiting for me. She's wearing this pink scarf wrapped around her head and a low-cut black tank top. I slip out of my boots, and she comes up to me and kisses both cheeks.

"Aren't you freezing?" I ask her. I'm wearing my SUNY Albany sweatshirt and a turtleneck.

"Warm-blooded. Must be my mom's Spanish stock."

I look at her thick dark hair. "I didn't know you were Spanish."

She grins. "My mom came here when she was a teenager. I actually learned Spanish before I learned French, and English only started when I was ten."

I walk into the centre of the space and raise my hands up, stretching my shoulders. We do some warming up and then she comes over and gives me a mini massage. Her fingers are surprisingly strong, and each poke against my tense back makes my body let go, one tiny push at a time.

"Okay, so, when you're working onstage, you must stay connected to the breath. I watch you, and I see someone cut off from the neck down. Not always, but often when your characters come in close contact with others. Do you know what I mean?"

Sure. It's called social anxiety. "I haven't really noticed."

"I want you to focus on the breath while we work on an improv. Let's say you're my co-worker, and you see me steal something. You're close friends with the owner of the store where we work, but you also know I have two little kids and not much money. While you improvise, try to stay conscious of your breath rising and falling. See how it affects your character, your experience."

She brings two chairs onstage. My stomach seizes up, and I try to let it go while sipping breaths. I wiggle my shoulders and walk onstage.

Stéfanie sits and mimes taking inventory. "Hey, how are you," she says in character, not looking up.

I mime folding shirts. "Good. How did it go with the kids last night?"

She makes a face. "Pierre didn't get home until close to midnight. And Valerie was up with a fever until way past 10:30 p.m."

My consciousness splits, moving back and forth between my chest rising and falling and the scene. Something is different, but I can't identify exactly what.

"Do you feel like a coffee? Sabine made some just a few minutes ago." I move an imaginary pile of folded shirts. When I turn back toward Stéfanie, I see her slip an imaginary object into her pocket.

Immediately my chest freezes. I try to breathe and get distracted. "I..." Words disappear.

She drops her character. "This is the first step—identifying when it happens. You see, it's an emotionally charged moment. We go into habit onstage at precisely those times when we are most in need of flexibility."

My throat is dry, and tears seep into my eyes. Stéfanie sees them and smiles. "Yes, it's emotional what we do." She stands up, comes over, and wraps her arms around me. My weight shifts, and all of my cells press into her. She's soft and fleshy, and I don't want the hug to end.

"Okay, back to work!"

*

With rehearsals in full swing, I start making friends, occasionally going out after rehearsals with the other actors. Sometimes Stéfanie comes along, and we talk a lot. When we're having drinks together, she stands closer to me than most colleagues would. She touches me a lot as she tells me stories, and when she kisses each cheek, she seems to linger.

One day, I notice she smells like cotton candy.

At home, Denise and I are both wasted with exhaustion. We squabble as we take care of Adam and the house. When Mimi comes over for our weekly date, we stay in the neighbourhood and mostly talk about the baby and being mothers. Sometimes we don't talk at all. During those times, I often look out the window onto whatever street in Rosemont we're on, thinking about connections and health and desire.

One night as we're falling asleep, Adam between us in bed, I ask her.

"Are you still attracted to me?"

She sits up. "Mais oui. Toi?"

"Calm down, I'm just asking. Yeah, of course. I just feel like my body has been temporarily put on hold for anything other than nursing. It's better, but right now, I think it's possible I could go the rest of my life without having sex again."

She shakes her head. "So, it's not about me at all, is it?"

My hands clench. "Of course not. But maybe things have changed for you. It's not like you're making passes at me or anything."

She sighs and turns over. "I work early tomorrow. Good night."

Chapter 60

When the landline rings close to midnight, I sit up and gasp.

"Honey? It's me." Eve's nose is congested, her words dull, her voice flat.

"No," I say. "No, no, no—"

"I'm sorry, Audrey. The neighbour found her unconscious on her back patio. By the time the paramedics got there, she was gone."

"How?" I whisper, knowing the answer.

Eve pauses. "Alcohol poisoning."

I drop the phone and collapse onto the floor, keening.

Chapter 61

The next day, Eve scans the note Jessica left and texts it to me. "Can't live this addict's life a moment more. Nobody's fault. Love love love." I print it out and take the piece of paper to bed and moan for an hour, clutching it to my ribcage.

Later in the afternoon, I numbly help Eve plan the memorial service by phone. Jessica was an organ donor. She wanted to be cremated. I'm underwater, sounds distorted, objects fuzzy, time functioning like lack of gravity. A world without Jessica makes no sense.

I think about loss. I think about my old Wellness friends, how after the program, it was like they had died. I think about my bio mom. I wonder if she's dead or living. I think about Mom.

I cry and cry and cry.

Denise takes Adam to Mimi's because my weeping is upsetting him. I am relieved not to have my son's emotional health to consider as I move through the unimaginable.

In the fridge, I find a leftover piece of quiche. I take a bite, put it back. Grab the jar of pickled herring.

At the kitchen table, trying to force myself to chew, I hear the doorbell ring. Mira and Leto come running and Mira barks a few times, something she rarely does. I go to the door and peer through the lace curtains.

Mom.

Her head is encircled with smoke, and I see her look down. Putting out the cigarette.

My hand is on the doorknob, but I don't move. What do I say to her? Screw you for judging me and ignoring me while I brought your first grandchild into the world? Thanks so much for being absent during his first six months when I needed you most?

Instead, I open the door and collapse into my mother's rock-solid arms.

At first, I can't speak. We spread out on the couch, and she just holds me. I occasionally sit up and notice her face full of tears. I remember that she loved Jessica too, that our grief is shared.

When the big waves pass, I ask if she wants a coffee, knowing she does. I go into the kitchen, and she follows me, sitting down at the dining room table while I prepare.

"Sweetie, I know—I realize I did a lot of damage recently."

"Wait, loud noise." The grinder.

"I think your decision...it was..."

"Mom, forget it. You're here now. No worries. I'm over it."

But am I? I scoop the coffee into the filter.

"Auddy, you were pregnant, and I stopped talking to you. You had a baby, and I was nowhere to be found. This is big stuff. It's important we—I—make the repair."

I measure the water as she talks. Big stuff. Make the repair. Foster parent jargon.

"I realized on the drive up that it felt like a rejection. Of me."

I pour the water into the machine and stare at the wall.

"I'm the one who takes kids that bio parents don't want. When you told me about the amnio, I got excited, in a weird way. I thought it would be something we could share, raising a disabled child."

I press the on button on the coffee maker and lean against the counter. I feel wetness on my cheeks. Mom stays where she is, head in hands.

We take our coffees to the living room and sit. She's in pain. She wanted to be close, and my decision prevented that. Part of me wants to go hold her. Then I remember being in the hospital, sucking on ice chips and trying to release my terror enough to rest. The months of sleep deprivation. Nursing problems. Fighting with Denise. Wondering where my mother was. And now I find out that she was sitting around judging us and feeling sorry for herself.

"Can you tell me about my bio mother?" The question springs out of nowhere.

"Honey, you know those records are sealed. I wish I could tell you something, but the system was really different back then."

So much space around my body. I'm the opposite of a magnet, an invisible force field, pushing everybody away.

I take a breath. "I'm not you, Mom. I just couldn't do what you do.

Denise couldn't either."

She's staring out the window. "When I found out about the adoption, I fell apart. You've never seen me that way." She gets up and starts pacing. Her left hand reaches to her back pocket. No cigarettes. Her right hand wipes her eyes. And I realize something: I can't remember when I last saw my mother cry.

"I...I judged you guys. I thought you and Denise were being selfish and cowardly. It reminded me of my own siblings and how judgmental they've been about my adopting disabled kids. That prejudice. It was like a betrayal, somehow. Of me. It took a while before I could see myself. And believe me, I wanted to connect." She looks at me, and I fight the urge to comfort her.

"Every single day since I hung up that phone I've wanted to get in the car and come to you. Which is why when Eve called, I got organized to come up. I knew I had to make things right between us because I knew you needed me."

I want to throw my arms around her. But she is sitting in my living room, far away in her own suffering. I look out the window and see the three girls across the street walking home from school. One of them keeps dropping a book she's carrying. Their mother is on the third-floor balcony, gesturing for them to hurry up.

I imagine my bio mother making the decision to give me up, tearfully telling her own mother. I wonder if her mother, my biological grandmother, comforted her.

I look at Mom with a half-smile. "I'm glad you came." Then I go to her, and we fall into an embrace.

*

Denise and Adam stay over at Mimi's to give Mom and me time together. When they return the next morning, it's a big lovefest. Mom holds Adam in this way that experienced mothers do, no doubts about her capacity, understanding exactly what micromovements will make him giggle. She changes his diaper and dresses him in a pair of blue overalls and a tee shirt she brought for him, which amplifies his cuteness, as was surely intended. I check Denise's reactions to Mom but can't get a read.

When she leaves, I cry, holding Adam and waving his pudgy hand at the car. Denise wraps her arms around us and joins the waving.

That night, we're getting ready for bed. I'm nursing Adam to sleep, and Denise is sifting through the pile of magazines on her side. When our baby drifts off, she turns to me. "So, did you let Martha know how hard it was for us during her silence?"

I gently pull out my nipple. "We talked. Things are fine now."

"What did you say?" Her voice is squeaky, like her vocal cords are being pinched.

"I don't remember, just that we knew we couldn't do it, that we weren't her, something like that."

She stares at me for a few seconds. "You didn't say anything, did you?"

"What do you mean?"

"You didn't let her know how much she hurt us. What a terrible thing she did. How she should have been here, helping you, helping us."

"That's not fair, Denise. Martha doesn't owe us anything."

"Merde. So typical. You need to learn to stand up for yourself and your family, Audrey. Talking about healthy, this is part of being healthy. What are you afraid of? You let her and Jessica and now Stéfanie, everybody, just walk over you and you keep smiling no matter what they do."

I shake my head. "I can't do this, Denise. I'm sorry. I have to try to sleep now."

I lie back down, my back towards my infant and my wife, wondering if I'll ever get it right, wondering if I'll ever be well, wondering when Adam would wake up for his first nursing of the endless night.

Chapter 62

I arrive at Eve's place in Middlebury to a meeting about the memorial service on Friday. The minister is there with the small group who would attend the funeral.

When I first walk down the muted grey hallway to the living room where everyone is sitting, I want to bolt. There's Eve and brother Christopher. Jessica's mom and her boyfriend are there and her dad, Frank, on a recliner.

And, big surprise, there's Bill, across from me on this single section of the sofa. By himself. When I first look at him, I think I see handcuffs on his wrists. But then he reaches for his glass. Of water. I hate that I check, but I check.

I want to jump in my Honda Fit and hightail it back to Montreal, cuddle with Denise, nurse my baby, hide in my basement, sketch cute kittens. Instead, I make the mistake of holding eye contact with Christopher who looks like he's been crushed underneath a Zamboni.

I walk over and collapse into Chris's arms. All of us—except Bill— sardined together, taking comfort in each other's warm bodies. Bill is sitting in his bubble, weeping and weeping. I think of leaving the warmth of Christopher to comfort Bill, to include him somehow. But there's something about his energy that keeps me away.

I look at him, and he glares back. My heart speeds up, and I have no idea what's going on.

The minister talks and talks, but I can't pay attention because of the emotional intensity in the room. Ripped apart people. I want to attend to them, feed them something just by being there, like passive solar energy. Sit, breathe, emit love. Maybe somebody feels a tiny moment of relief.

Christopher releases his arms, and I get dizzier and sweatier, so I switch spots and mush myself next to Eve. She clutches me. I think about the intervention we never did. Does she blame me? Do I blame me? But I don't get too far into the questions. Losing Jessica is an experience so magnified that every other impulse, thought, dynamic, or subtlety is crowded out of my heart. All I can be is devastated.

That first afternoon is when it becomes real for me. Everything in that room is vivid, unrehearsed. Simple, even, if coming together to mourn Jessica at thirty-three could ever be simple.

The next day at the small graveside funeral, I read a poem I'd written the day after she died. Christopher wears black sunglasses, and a tuft of chest hair sticks out above his white button-down shirt. Eve, spiffy and tailored as always, is wearing a black linen pants suit with a V-neck.

But I don't see Bill.

I ask Eve.

"I told him not to come," she whispers.

"Why?"

She makes a sign that I know means "later."

I notice Eve is wearing the silver locket she'd given Jessica for her fourth birthday. The locket was the subject of a conversation with Jessica the first time we had supper at her place. I'd asked her what was in it, and she told me the story of Eve being ten years old, begging her mom for a little sister. A year later, Jessica was born. Inside the locket was a photo of Eve holding baby Jessica, smiling like she'd just been picked from hundreds of other children to swim with dolphins.

I take one look at the shiny silver against Eve's chest, and I crumble. Eve grabs me before I go down, and we clutch each other, weeping. A crow caws. The minister reads a prayer. A balding man at a nearby plot plants red geraniums. Two children play hide and seek among the trees and headstones.

*

At the reception, Eve comes over, holding a mini quiche in a bright orange napkin.

"I got orange because of the car." We both smile.

She looks at me. "I need to tell you something hard, Audrey, and I don't know quite how to do it."

I squint at her. "Just tell me. I won't break."

She shakes her head. "You might."

"Just say it."

She takes a breath. "There were bruises all over my sister's body when they found her."

What?

"We think it was Bill."

"No way. Not Jessica. She's much too strong for that. She would have told him to go fuck himself. Maybe it was something medical?"

She looks at the floor. "No, nothing medical. My pathologist friend examined her as a favour to me. He said it's classic patterning for abuse."

Thousands of invisible bees sting. My skin erupts in flames. The room shakes, and my eyes go blurry. I run out of the reception room to the bathroom, lock myself in a stall, and try to breathe.

Chapter 63

Grief crashes down against the borders of my body, tidal waves that come from nowhere and then disappear. The pit deepens each day, and it's harder and harder to draw, eat, parent, or walk down the street. I go to bed after morning coffee. I move Adam's play area to our bedroom. Then the television. I start napping twice, then going to bed right after supper. At night, I wander through our dark house, arms folded, lungs struggling to bring in tiny sips of oxygen. I review our texts leading up to the suicide every day, many times a day.

I could have saved her. But I didn't.

*

The weeks pass, and I start feeling afraid of leaving the house. Dr. Couture gives me a new medication. I go to rehearsal and break down, once, then twice. Stéfanie suggests I take more time. I quit the Humane Society. I get several requests for design gigs and turn them down.

Patti comes over and takes Mira and me out for walks in the morning. She's gotten into the habit of saying, each time she sees Adam, "So, when will you start talking to me in proper English?" Adam just giggles. Sabrina stops by on her way home from work, checking on us, holding Adam for a few minutes so I can make a meal. Adam delights everyone around him, flipping over onto his stomach, hoisting himself to standing, and even taking some wobbly first steps. His face is easily coaxed into expressions of joy, and he's even laughing those full-throated belly laughs that nine-month-olds are so gifted at.

I don't laugh with him. I start seeing Jessica in the house. Sometimes she has a black eye. Sometimes she is screaming my name, and she disappears when I actually respond.

Patti calls one afternoon to see how I am.

"All I had to do was call her back—"

"Don't do that to yourself. You had no idea she was in such bad shape."

"Actually, I did. I knew, and I knew for a while. I didn't want to admit it because it was inconvenient, but I knew. I didn't know Bill was hurting her, but I knew something was wrong. Eve and I even talked about an intervention. I said no. What kind of a friend says no?"

Patti sighs into the phone. "A friend who just had a baby, perhaps?"

Tears. "I can't keep using that as an excuse. How long before I'm held to regular adult standards of judgment? She asked for help, and I ignored her. It doesn't get much simpler than that."

Patti gives me a number for an English support group for family and friends of suicide victims. The next day, I go. Most feel guilty and responsible, to some degree. And I see in other group members that those feelings, like old jeans, can fade.

I wonder if that's a good thing.

I say nothing about Bill at the support group.

When I return home, I take out Jessica's sweater. I fall on my bed hugging it tightly to my chest, staring out the window at the wispy clouds sailing past.

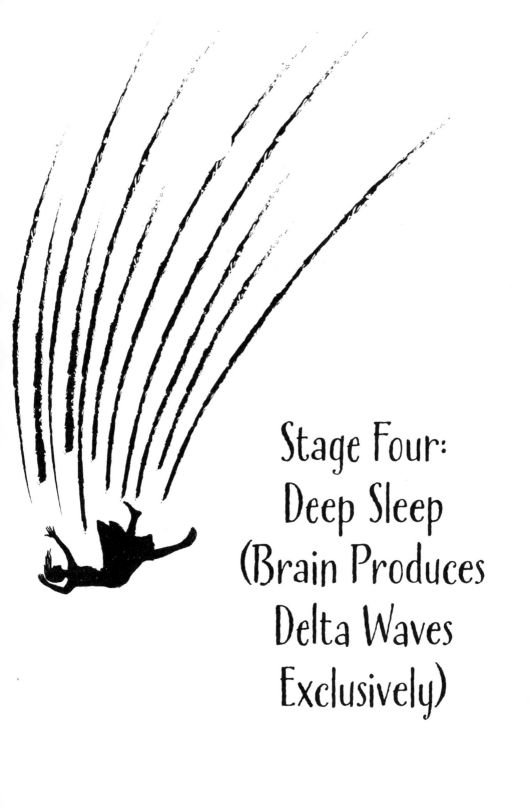

Stage Four:
Deep Sleep
(Brain Produces
Delta Waves
Exclusively)

Chapter 64

Summer is relentless, with the pavement absorbing the sun's ferocious heat. After a few months of grief support, I start taking baby steps toward normal life. We discover the outdoor wading pool at Parc Père-Marquette, and I start going there most afternoons with Adam. After work, Denise walks to the park to meet us, sometimes bringing food for a picnic. A few times, the Mortals gather for a cookout and volleyball game.

August arrives, and one night Denise curls her body against mine in bed. The air is sharp like a slap, and I relax into her warmth.

The next day I decide to go back to the Humane Society. Patti is there and gives me her classic mummy hug. "So good to have you back, mate." We break apart and her eyes are glassy. We let the dogs out and start cleaning cages.

"I'm back at rehearsal too. Stéfanie's been amazing."

"Did you get the website revisions up, finally?"

"Yeah. I just had a few tweaks left before Jess died. I went in last week and made sure everything was set. We're actually getting bookings for the new show."

I dunk the mop into the yellow janitor's cart. Grey water sloshes onto the floor.

"Are you performing?"

I shook my head. "Not for now. But Stéfanie wants to do some individual training with me to work on my breathing. She seems to think more relaxation will help with my physicality, which is kind of stiff."

Patti laughs. "How do you train a person with an anxiety disorder to relax?"

I giggle. "Yeah. She could make so much more money as a therapist."

Fall sneaks up on us and then winter. I take new contracts and do my individual training. Denise's younger nephew gives us a bunch of his son's old clothes, and Adam is walking without holding on to us. I still nurse but just once, before putting Adam to bed.

But despite being almost two, he's not speaking. Not a word.

One evening after supper, I raise the subject with Denise.

"I think something's wrong. He isn't saying anything."

"I think I heard him say 'Eera' the other day while he was petting the dog." She zips up her fleece with a shiver.

"He's almost two. He should have a bunch of words."

"Every child is different. You yourself keep telling me that when I say we should wean him."

"It's just—" I'm interrupted by a gleeful shriek. Adam found a fork on the floor. I grab him and tickle him and slip the fork out of his grasp.

We don't resume the conversation. But I'm online researching, hour after hour. Often at night, when sleep just won't come.

*

One night in February, Adam wakes up screaming. For ten long minutes, I try figuring out what's wrong. His body thrashes and stiffens, his head jerked from side to side with wailing. I go through every possible thing, but I can't it figure out.

If he had words, he could tell me.

Denise is staying over at Mimi's, and I had wanted to spend my evening doing sketches for my new client, a wild dolphin research excursion outfit in Florida, but that doesn't happen. Instead, I sit with my son while he cries, telling him stories, cuddling him, helpless with no information about his suffering.

I give him ibuprofen, and in twenty minutes, he's asleep. I go down and start working. Later when I join him in bed, I drift off and then wake up with a jolt.

"Generalized anxiety disorder," I say out loud; if I can name my problem, maybe he can learn to name his. I look down at him. He's still, eyes closed, lightly snoring.

*

Dr. Couture changes my daytime antianxiety med, but I feel the same. I go to therapy faithfully and exercise every day.

So why can't I get my act together?

The old question is like a wool sweater on bare skin. Sometimes it helps me shift gears. But mostly I just scratch.

My son, the other side of my brain argues, is surrounded by vast numbers of chosen family, including Mimi and Claire and Sabrina and Patti and Mireille, Denise's family, our neighbours, and the many other adults who make time and energy for him. The ibuprofen worked. It was probably just a fall, something muscular, a headache.

He wakes up again, shrieking. I nurse him, which worked in the past. But this time, he's inconsolable. I put him down on his side and begin massaging him, squeezing and pushing down with my weight. After a few minutes, he stops crying. I nurse him and he settles, shifts, and gets sleepy. I lie down with my arm around him, and we snuggle together, my boy nestled along my left side.

I try to remember my toddlerhood with Martha. Did we lie down in bed or on a couch? Cuddle skin-to-skin? Do emotion coaching?

The next day, Denise returns and tells me that Adam was wearing his old sneakers from last year, the ones that don't fit, when I took him to the park yesterday. The ones that make his feet hurt.

In the morning, I toss the sneakers in the trash. Then I make French toast for my tiny family.

Chapter 65

I wait for words, but none come. The babbling continues, with little shape around it. I see Dr. Couture, and we talk about daytime medication. She's got a new one to try, and she writes out a prescription. I leave her office, grateful.

The weeks pass, and as the weather gets colder, words seem more and more scarce. The knot in my stomach persists, even after I run five days at close to eight kilometres and yoga every night. I want to take action.

"Everything I read says there should be words by the second birthday," I say as we sip glasses of cider one night in November after putting Adam to bed.

"Yes, and everything I read says speech like so many things is individual. All the moms at the playground say there is nothing to worry about."

"I'm not saying to worry. I'm saying to take a few action steps, that's all."

"Going to a specialist will be expensive unless we get a referral. And I asked the paediatrician when we were there, and she said to wait until he's three."

I get up and start pacing. "If Mimi suggested this, would you do it?"

She shakes her head. "Audrey, this isn't personal. We have a disagreement, just that."

"You think it's because I have an anxiety disorder." I give her a hard stare.

"Well, you have anxiety, and you are quick to worry about many things that are not a big deal."

"A speech problem can be a big deal. All the experts say if you catch it early, the prognosis is much better. What's not a big deal is one appointment with a speech pathologist. I'll do all the leg work. And I'll take on an extra contract if it's really expensive."

She puts down her glass. "Fine. But you're in charge of this one."

*

In December, I find a woman with a home office in Rosemont who has twenty years of experience and a reasonable rate. After the assessment, the woman tells me she's ninety percent sure he has a condition called childhood apraxia of speech, or CAS. It's not a cognitive functioning problem but more like what happens to a person after a stroke.

I ask her if there's anything to do.

"The government doesn't start paying for services until he's three," she says. "But getting a head start on speech therapy and supplements would give him a huge advantage." She explains that there's a study showing that kids with CAS who take essential fatty acid supplements do much better. She suggests sign language and is also willing to work with him until his third birthday. I ask about a reduced rate in exchange for graphic design work, and she agrees. I quickly calculate and decide we can put groceries on the credit card for a year if necessary. This is important.

It's also a disability.

When I get home, I give Denise the sheet of paper on apraxia and go upstairs to our room to sit quietly. I imagine texting Jessica with a *roar* and then hopping on Zoom. She would tell me not to worry. That I can handle it.

I wonder if she's right.

*

The days that follow are tense. Denise is quiet. She talks to herself in French but says little to me or Adam. I ask her what's wrong, but she shakes her head and says, "Rien." I hold myself back from saying anything about my being right. But I'm also secretly waiting for her to apologize, to thank me, to realize that sometimes...my concerns do, in fact, lead us to better decisions.

Chapter 66

Adam prances up to me as I sit at the kitchen table sipping coffee. He stops and stares, like Snoopy doing the vulture. My toddler is wearing nothing but a diaper. He sucks in a little air and opens his mouth.

"Eeeeeiiiiiigggggghhhhh!"

It's a definite "wow" moment, and I reach down to grab him, the skin of my arms melting into his warm back.

"Horse! You did it, Boy Wonder! Where'd you get that neigh?"

But he doesn't answer; instead, he breaks out of my corral and gallops around the living room, tracing the walls and furniture with sticky fingertips, eeeiiigggghhing and squealing. I almost tell him to wash his hands but stop, basking in his joy instead as I return to my coffee and my view of Rue Chambord.

It's been six months since we started speech therapy, and now that Adam is three, we qualify for public services, a big relief for our budget and for Adam's progress. Each week, Denise brings him to occupational therapy, speech therapy, and a sign language class. I work on making sure I get out for my runs and my yoga and relaxation exercises. The thought of Adam with a lifelong disability feels like enough to unravel any progress I have made since Wellness.

Our days are full of "oof oof," "haaam," "oooo," and now "eeeiiigh." Adam is dying to make animal sounds. But as the speech pathologist explained to us, the neural pathways between his brain and his mouth are missing so he's unable to produce planned speech. Therapy involves cuing him physically to create those missing connections. Parents of kids with CAS are advised to learn and teach the child sign language so basic communication can happen quickly. Teaching a kid with apraxia to speak is a lengthy, complex process that Denise and I feel grateful we've begun early.

Since starting treatment, we notice sounds everywhere we go. During our camping trip in the summer to Ste-Agathe in the Laurentians, we're treated to warbling wild birds, bellowing bullfrogs, whispery winds. In the evenings, Denise stays inside after supper.

"Come with us, honey," I ask, feeling strangely guilty.

"Go play. The sunshine won't last forever," she says, winking at me and giving me a thin smile.

Adam and I push through the screen door, leaving space for Mira. She chases a bright yellow ball I toss, and Adam lurches after her, shrieking and growling. At night, we squeeze into the only bed, which creaks with each micro movement. The night's thick darkness seems to amplify the sounds: peepers croaking, crickets humming, and snoring, snoring, snoring. I shove my earplugs in and make the best of it.

When we return to Montreal, I receive a notice that I've been accepted at a two-week artist residency in January that I had applied for on a whim. I call Freddy and Natascha, who say Denise and Adam can visit them at their timeshare in Florida during the time I'll be gone. One Wednesday in August, Denise takes Adam to the library. They return carting canvas bags full of Florida books. Denise smacks a kiss on my lips.

"Voilà," she says, dumping the books on the kitchen table. "J'ai soif." I shuffle into the kitchen and return, offering her a glass of water. She takes it with a quick "merci" and looks at Adam across from her, sifting through the books. He finds something: *Florida Flora and Fauna*.

I haul him onto my lap and start reading. His hands push mine away, rustling through the pages, skipping jellyfish, parrot, orange blossom. But he stops cold at crocodile. He points at the picture of the scaly reptile. He looks at me and makes the sign for "speak." He simply wants to know.

"Pas sure," says Denise. I'm not sure either. I think about his nightmare with the swimming monster from last week and cluck my tongue, considering. Adam hops off my lap with the book and holds it out to his Maman, pointing and tapping at the crocodile. "Auh? Auh?" I hold back a grin.

"How bad could it be?" I wonder out loud, feeling myself cave. Denise sees my almost smile, rolls her eyes, and shakes her head.

"Have you ever heard a crocodile talk?" she asks. "I have a feeling it's not soft and sweet." Adam runs with the book over to the blue sofa and opens my laptop on the coffee table.

Apparently, a decision has been made.

I sit down next to him and do a Google search. I notice Denise is wearing the amber t-shirt I gave her for our first Valentine's Day together six years ago. I remember standing at the register at Village Value in Longueuil with three pairs of jeans over my arm, noticing the t-shirt on a return rack. *It's perfect for Denise*, I remember thinking, *because the colour matches the honey tone of her eyes.* I was right. Now it's faded, and there's a small hole in the left side, just under the armpit. But it still warms her look, reminding me of that feverish feeling I'd get in our early days together.

Denise, still sitting at the table, sighs, pushing back a piece of hair that insists on curling at her right eyebrow. She does this repeatedly, daily, refusing the indignity of a barrette. I've stopped suggesting.

I scootch closer to Adam on the couch, so my legs touch his, and I find a YouTube sampler of crocodile sounds. My arm winds protectively around my son as the crocodile appears. We listen. I'm shocked at the variety. A rattle. A snarl. And something that sounds like—a toilet flushing? I hear a rain stick turned upside down, amplified. I look at Adam whose gaze is locked onto the screen. Is it possible—Darth Vader? A grunting pig? One reminds me of Denise's uncle burping.

But it's the scariest one by far that my boy likes best: a cross between a lion roaring, a lawnmower revving, and the finale of a fireworks display. He keeps moving my hand on the mouse and we listen to that sound, over and over. After six times, Adam tries it himself. He puts some meanness into his face, tips his chin to his chest, and lets some saliva build up to make a gurgly growl.

A work in progress.

This heightened attention to sound follows me outside my home and into the places where I'm separate from my family. It's a muggy September evening, and I'm at rehearsal. Stéfanie has us improvising a scene. My character has been struggling in her marriage to Pierre's character for years: alienation, apathy, affairs. In this scene, she finally decides to leave him. For weeks, I'd been searching for how to express the depths of her despair. Reliving old breakups, researching why marriages fail, and inventing various given circumstances had all been dead ends. On this night, I decide to just wing it.

I start the scene silently, staring at Pierre. But when he starts begging me to stay, I feel a rumble inside my belly. It grows and grows and then out it bursts, a grief-stricken wail, leaving me parched, shaking.

Pierre stands up slowly. His armpits are wet. He doesn't speak. I turn to Stéfanie, who is looking at me curiously. Her face is relaxed, and her mouth is slightly open. Finally, she nods, mouthing "Oui, oui." Something in my chest inflates as I wipe sweat off my temples.

After rehearsal, Stéfanie gives me a ride home. I grab the door handle of her old Celica and feel my insides crack, like a light bulb dropped on a ceramic floor. She parks the car outside my house while the engine and my nose both run.

"I'm lonely with Denise."

"Oui, c'est comme ça. I've been with Brian for twenty-five years, and we move through cycles. Maybe I'm happy half the time. Maybe I'm angry twenty-five percent of the time. And the other quarter, well, sadness, loneliness, everything."

I pull a tissue out of my backpack. "But do you think every relationship is like that? I want to be in a healthy relationship, and I'm not even sure what that is."

She looks at the murky night through her windshield. "Intimacy is like the ocean, immense, infinite. It contains everything possible between two people. That's all." She reaches over and gives my neck a little squeeze. When I look at her, she smiles.

Her ease slips inside me like a junco's song. When she drives away, I'm whistling.

Inside, I hang up my fleece, drop my backpack, and go find my wife. She's sitting at the dining room table with the Florida books spread out around her. I notice the dirty dishes in the sink, but I don't mention them. I just kiss her forehead and ask her those Wednesday night questions about supper and bedtime. Later, we climb into bed together. We're both naked, back-to-back, and I feel a warm spot on her spine.

"Love you."

"Je t'aime."

*

The next day, I take a few hours off to work with Adam. The speech therapist stressed that it has to be a game. The second our boy feels forced, stress will shut down the possibility of progress. We're playing with some chunky wooden beads, stringing them onto a shoelace.

Adam turns to me. "Eh? Eh?"

I smile and touch his cheek. "Bead? Bead?" I make the sign and then do the gesture the speech therapist taught us for the "b" sound. He ignores me, takes another bead, and then throws them both up in the air. Cackles. He's right. It is funny. I wonder, again, why he doesn't seem frustrated. He surely has lots to say. But his sounds are full of might, and we nearly always understand. I imagine climbing into his mouth, moving his tongue and his lips around to show them what they're supposed to do. I sigh and throw a few beads up.

He claps his hands as they fall. "Aaaahhhh!"

We roll on the floor together, a tangle of giggles.

Denise returns from the Marché Jean-Talon with leeks and creamy orange daisies poking out of the canvas bag she's carrying. Some red and gold leaves follow her inside. She gives me a smooch.

"How did it go?"

"He just wanted to play with the beads. I tried a few times…"

She laughs, putting a bunch of beets in the fridge. "Not the right time, I guess." The kiss, the questions, and the answers are habitual. No roar, no passion, just the ever-repeating sounds of elevator dings.

"Did you go to the park?" Ding.

"No, I thought I'd take him after lunch." Ding.

"Did you remember his vitamins?" Ding.

The dissonance creeps up from my navel to my throat. I eat a plum-filled jelly doughnut that quiets things down.

For now.

In the evening, Adam brings us to the computer and finds the You-Tube video with the crocodile. The sound is so astonishing, I realize, because it is simply absent from North American kid culture. Find me a kid who doesn't know "moo" and "neigh," "quack" and "cluck," "woof" and "meow." You could blame it on geography, but the kids also imitate lions, elephants, even dinosaurs.

So why doesn't anybody know the crocodile?

We stare at the screen and listen. Our boy tightens his grasp around my arm but stays put. We click on another video that provides some information. Did you know that crocodiles are genetically closer to birds than lizards? It seems incongruous that this monstrous teeth-filled killer could contain any trace of the delicate fluttery creatures we feed in our backyard.

A solo flute in a sonic boom.

A week passes. I trudge to Station Beaubien amid the fall foliage, passing Parc Père-Marquette, Café El Coyote, the Moroccan place. The platform is almost empty until the train screeches in, dumping out the commuters coming home to Rosemont from downtown. I step into the car and sit down next to a fair-skinned woman with braids and ripped jeans reading Marie-Claire Blais. With my iPod on, I stare at the poster for language classes and listen to my heart vibrating through the headphones, mentally reviewing my interaction plan. It's designed to fix the distortion Stéfanie brings to my soundscape. First, I'll pretend not to see her, focussing on the other actors. She'll either greet me first, or not. Fussing with my bag, my script, my hair, I'll be far too busy to think about anyone in particular.

But then I arrive at the church and the plan fizzles. She's laughing with Pierre. I smile in their direction, far warmer than I'd planned, and then feel heat radiating in my middle; Stéfanie returns the smile, clearly happy to see me.

I start stretching on the stage, but secretly I'm paying more attention to Stéfanie. Pierre is telling her a funny story about his niece meeting his dog for the first time, and Stéfanie is cracking up. Her laugh is exactly like her hair only fuller. Her words come out rich, sounds that spin and roll and pulse in mid-air. I want to wrap myself up in her voice.

I know this crush experience. It's wired into my brain like church bells, car alarms, and camera clicks. The time she introduced me to David's Tea. The time I trimmed her bangs with my craft scissors. And then the theme yields fantastic variations I compose in my head. Whispered phone calls. The sounds of lips meeting lips. Holding hands looking at a blood moon, its reflection rippling on a pond.

Denise and I must have had a moon. But I can't remember it. Maybe it's the new medication.

Stéfanie calls me forth like a shofar. I twist my mind, fighting my feelings with logic, interpretation, analysis. I don't want this attraction any more than I wanted it when I was thirteen, twenty-three, thirty. The women live inside me, emotionally concentrated, like a tune you can't get out of your head. I tell myself that if I sing something else, if I crowd the space in my head with other sounds, maybe I can stop it. Maybe then I could jam with the crocodile in the elevator.

The next day, I'm getting Adam ready for bed. He's in the bath, rubbing his cheek with a sopping washcloth. He looks at me and makes a sound. At first, I don't connect the dots. "Mmm-ee," he says, dropping the washcloth. He murmurs, then looks at me, making the sign for "understand." I don't. So then he extends his arm forward, raises the left one, curls his fingers, and brings his hands together with a smack and then some chomping.

Crocodile. We'd learned that sign yesterday. Of course. Crocodile.

I finger his hair. His warm damp scalp takes me back to my own wet head, in the bath when I was small. We had one of those waterproof radios attached to the wall with suction cups. I was turning the dial back and forth, seeing if I could make it go so fast that the static and the voices and the music would all blend together to make a wild cacophonous stew. In the middle of trying, Mom, probably wrecked with lack of sleep as she frequently was, burst through the door and lunged at the radio, at my hand.

"Stop it! Stop it! Just stop—" I froze and felt the "dun, dun, dun" of my heart under my ribs. Mom ripped the radio off the wet tiles and hurled it onto the floor with a splitting crash. My small body hiccupped in the water, and I stopped breathing. She looked at me, mumbled an apology, shook her head, and slipped out.

As the door closed, my mouth was still hanging open, a skinny string of saliva dangling into the bath water. I remember physically pushing my chin up with my hand, the "chank" of teeth hitting teeth, the splash of my hand falling back into the bath.

That same hand now moves from Adam's scalp to his body, and I caress him with a damp washcloth. I sing the melody from "Winter Wonderland," even if it's autumn, and he chortles. My body vibrates as I exhale, loudly, like we do at rehearsal.

And in the breath, I hear Stéfanie's laughter. Her face is creased with lines as she gazes into my eyes. She's earnest, like an awkward prepubescent girl with braces, argyle socks, and an asymmetrical smile, the girl you know in three years will be a knockout. Her hair is coloured a bright mahogany shade, definitely the wrong choice, which makes me love her even more because it tells me she's not shallow.

"Ow?" "Ow?" My son's voice. Ow? He points at me kneeling next to the bath.

"Ow…" I say it and point…out! Out of the tub, of course. I say it back to him but add the word's consonant sound and the hand gesture for "t."

"Ow-t?"

He grins and tries.

"OuTAA?" Out! He said out! I repeat, overwhelmed, and he says it again, laughing and smacking his palms on the surface of the bathwater.

"OuTAA! OuTAA!" I stand and pick him up, soaking wet, and draw him into a full body hug, twirling around, his damp face pushing against my neck, mouth moving, vocal cords vibrating.

After I get him up to bed, I text Denise, but she's at the movies with her phone off. Still excited, I call Stéfanie. "Hey, it's me. Guess what Adam just did? I was—"

"Sorry, Audrey, it's not a good time," she interrupts.

I stop.

"Just quickly, I had him in the bath—"

"I really can't talk now. It's the weekend, and I'm with my boy-friend. I'm sorry. We can talk on Monday."

I whisper an apology and hang up. Tears push against my eyelids, threatening. "Boyfriend?" Such a teenage-y word, full of hormones and sex and wildness. How about "husband?" With "boyfriend," I could only sit, alone with my house's quiet murmurs, trying to remember that I have a wife and a son and am not thirteen, or twenty-three, or thirty.

I look around the kitchen and open the buzzing fridge. The forced hot-air system mutters. I let the cat out, and a plane thunders by. Somebody's car engine revs but won't start. I close the door and return to the fridge.

Not everybody can bring you to that place where your ego lies abandoned on the side of the road, your hair flying in your face. You're breathless, speeding down the highway, speakers blaring. Stéfanie is driving the car and I know I should get out, but I can't.

I go to my computer and Google "elevator," just for fun. I'm surprised that elevators have been around since 250 BC. I'm intrigued to read two alternative descriptions: "lift," "flying chair," "ascending room." I listen to some dings on a sound effects site. A Tibetan bell. The gentle ting of spoon on glass. I'm so immersed in the sounds that I don't hear Denise when she returns from the movies.

She kisses me, and I tell her about ouTAA.

"No!" she says, with excited half disbelief. "So, is that why your sweater is damp?" I pat my chest and am surprised to feel the fabric is still clammy. She asks me if I called my mother back. I say "no" and collapse on the sofa. I surprise us both when I start crying. She sits next to me and puts her arms around me. I'm thinking about my son, about apraxia, about being small and scared.

I hug my wife until she pulls away.

"I'll bring you a dry shirt, d'accord?" she says, heading upstairs.

The next day, I take a run in the park. I finish my eight kilometers and, huffing, start to walk home. I'm breathing and calm amid the yellows, the reds, and the oranges on the trees. A tiny chickadee sits on an evergreen branch. A flash: the bird opens its beak, revealing hundreds of craggy teeth, and bellows, a sound that echoes down Montreal's alleyways, over the flat roofs, above Mount Royal.

The chickadee closes its beak and flies away. I stand on the sidewalk. Look at the space where the bird was. Wait for something to happen. For a sound.

I hear the highway in the distance, humming.

My feet start walking, and I think about inviting Denise out for a ride. Maybe our modest Honda Fit could transform into a yellow convertible Porsche with throbbing speakers. Maybe I could open the door for her and jump into the driver's seat. Maybe I would feel the smooth heat of the new key before sliding it into the ignition. Maybe I would laugh at the engine's rumble, and maybe Denise would too. Maybe we would fly down route ten, cranking up the radio, clapping, singing into our soda can mikes.

I walk inside our home, and there she is, sitting and laughing with Adam at his toddler-sized wooden table. They're both colouring, furtively.

"Tell Mommy...Go on..." Denise whispers. Our son grins and shakes his head, flirting. Then he looks up at me, crimson crayon in hand, opens his mouth and speaks.

"CWOCK-OH-DYE-UW!"

He throws back his head and roars, nothing at all like the beast, but so utterly and stunningly like himself.

Chapter 67

Adam talks. A lot. Every day brings new words, and a party has taken up permanent residence in his mouth. Amid the joy, Denise and I find a closeness we'd misplaced, and we even make love in November when it's cool enough to close the windows.

We spend Christmas with my family and New Year's with hers. Adam is old enough to understand Santa Claus, and we leave out cookies for St. Nick, carrots for the reindeer. I stitch funky stockings using some antique fabric remnants I find at a thrift shop. We hang them stuffed with goodies, which Adam tears into and devours.

In January, TPG opens our new show. The press is interested in the historical angle and the anglophone francophone element. I try to keep things cordial and professional with Stéfanie, but she continues to throw her arms around me at strange moments, give me neck massages, and once she even braids my hair.

After an especially exciting performance and an interview with the CBC, we go out to a bar in the Old Port near the theatre. I take off my coat and grab a seat between Pierre and Anastasya. In five minutes, Stéfanie arrives and asks Pierre if he would mind switching seats with him. It's a big table and lots of noise, and I'm soon overwhelmed and wishing I could rest.

"Come outside with me, d'accord?" Stéfanie asks me. She wants company while she smokes, I think. But I am ready to leave anyway, so I say goodbye to the others and follow her out.

We stand on the sidewalk, letting people pass by. I watch my puffy exhales under the streetlight. She takes off her mittens, gets out her smokes, lights up, and looks around. "Were you happy with your performance tonight?" she asks, leaning against the building.

I shrug. I'm wondering if Adam went down on time.

"Are you okay?"

I nod. "Tired."

She finishes her cigarette and comes over to me. Puts her arms around me. Presses our bodies together.

Lots of seconds go by. Her scarf scrapes my cheek. At first, I'm rigid, trying not to enjoy myself. Finally, I give in. Her breasts push into mine. She breathes into my ear.

We pull apart and she holds my gloved hand, looking at me. "Go home and rest, ma chère. Oh, and don't forget to upload the English translations of the bios and the company history pages. We have an English gig coming up, and I want to make sure they can access all the information in advance."

I swallow. When did that task end up on my list? But I smile despite myself. She's holding my hand and gazing into my eyes. I squeeze back, wrap my scarf tighter, and head for the metro. A big stone is lodged in my gut, and it jiggles as I walk.

When I get home, the house is quiet and most of the lights are out. I take off my winter gear as quietly as I can, but I wake up Denise anyway. She comes out of the bedroom with a flashlight. She's wearing her sister's old red bathrobe and her blue fuzzy slippers.

She smiles as she comes down the stairs. "How was the show?"

"Good. Sorry I woke you up." I brush snow off my jacket before hanging it up. I go to her, and we kiss each other's cheeks.

She looks at me closer. "You look pale."

I pick up my backpack. "Just exhausted. How was bedtime?"

"He fell asleep while I was reading. Must have been the walk. We bundled up and went all the way to Marché Jean-Talon and back."

Once my coat and scarf and hat and gloves are off, I lean against the wall and sink down to the floor. "Stéfanie has me doing the website translation. I have to do it before Thursday."

Denise looks at me. "What do you mean by 'she has me?'"

I start crying. "She made it sound like I had offered but I'm sure I didn't. Well, not a hundred percent sure. My memory is so terrible. I can't trust anything, and my body should be back to normal by now."

She comes and sits down on the floor next to me. "Audrey, I hate to say this, but I think Stéfanie is using you."

I'm silent.

"I think you should quit, frankly."

I want to lean on her, but I can't.

"Please trust me. This is highly a dysfunctional group."

I take a breath. Then I walk upstairs and set up the futon in my office as a bed. I take my medication, brush my teeth, and close the door.

*

I see Dr. Couture, and she suggests that Denise and I start counselling.

"How's the anxiety?"

I think about it. "Maybe three panic attacks this month. Two were triggered by memory lapses. And the mornings now are all hard. I'm fighting off a nap most afternoons."

"And parenting?"

"It's amazing. He talks. We never expected it to happen. We're over the moon. I think that's why Denise and I had sex after not not touching each other for so long. But it didn't last. I have no idea why she's all up in arms about TPG, but since that performance, we've been sleeping in separate beds and not talking much."

She writes down a name and phone number. "My colleague Gretchen Moisan sees couples, gay and straight. I think she might be able to help you and Denise."

I take the paper, we schedule next week, and I take the metro home.

Chapter 68

It's March, and Denise and I have been seeing Gretchen for a month. We're communicating, but things are still difficult. There are so many layers, and despite everything I've managed, all I can do is think of Stéfanie.

The performances continue, as does Stéfanie's flirting. I'm doing all the translations for press releases. During one therapy session, I tell Denise she may be right about the company being dysfunctional. But I can't quite believe that Stéfanie's affection is just about control and getting what she wants. She seems to genuinely like me.

March 28th arrives, Adam's fourth birthday. At his party, Patti gives him a set of Lincoln Logs. As soon as the wrapping paper is off, we help our son open the cylindrical-shaped container. Denise begins stacking the tootsie-roll pieces in earnest as I study the instructions for model number one.

I high five Patti. "Totally great. Thanks so much."

She's doing her silent laugh thing and puts her hand to her mouth. Grabs me and we turn away from the child. "Hours of fun for you and Denise," she whispers, and soon we're both choking back the giggles.

Adam runs to the kitchen, scoops out handfuls of cheese puffs, and chases Claire around the table. Sabrina is chatting with Mireille on the couch, and she interrupts their conversation to tell Claire to slow down before someone loses an eye.

Claire stops and sticks out her tongue playfully. "Party pooper."

Sabrina wrinkles her nose. "I want him to live to see his fifth birthday."

Denise is down on the floor, immersed in the Lincoln Logs. "Come play," she says to me. We construct eight different cabin models. Adam stays away, involved in an elaborate game of hide-and-seek with our neighbour's twins, bouncing back and forth between hiding, ripping open presents, and pawing his cake.

After a while, he's sweaty and breathing hard, and he hops on Sabrina's lap for smooches. "I can't believe you're four, big guy. You know I held you in my arms when you were just a few hours old?"

He collapses into her chest, and they wrap their arms around each other.

I stand up, lean against the living room wall, and look around. As usual, my mom cancelled at the last minute, in crisis mode with Ian, but Denise, Claire, Sabrina, Patti, and Mireille are all here. My heart is full, my breathing deep, and despite the rockiness with Denise, I feel part of something solid.

I find my wife by the snack table and join her, grasping her hand in mine. She sees my tears and laughs, handing me a tissue.

*

After the party, the guests go home, and I leash Mira, slip into my bomber jacket, and head out for the evening walk. The air is moist, a hint of a kiss, and I notice purple crocuses poking out of the neighbour's garden. I smile, images of Adam with frosting surrounded by his favourite people replaying in my brain.

Mira stops and hunches over. I grab the plastic poop bag in my coat pocket and wait for her to finish. At that moment, I notice a couple pushing a stroller across the street with a Bernese Mountain dog. I remember Tilly, the dog Martha had for years when Chloe and Freddy and I were little, and I smile at them.

Mira finishes, and I clean up. I head towards the couple who are approaching the little park on the corner. I toss the baggie in the trash and smile again.

"Bonsoir," I say. "Est-ce que votre chien est méchant?" I'd learned to ask about petting a dog early in my French studies.

The man chuckles. "Non, pas du tout," and as Mira goes over to sniff the other dog's behind, I notice the little girl in the stroller. She's bigger than most toddlers, and she has lovely blonde hair. Her eyes are widely set, and her head and facial features are small. There's something about her that's striking.

I ask them if they live in the neighbourhood, and they tell me no, that they're visiting the man's sister. They live up north, near Trois-Rivières.

The little girl grunts, and her mother gets a doll from her purse. She gives it to her daughter who laughs, then takes it and hugs it. There's something odd about her that I can't quite grasp.

I pet the dog and wish them a good night. And when they go their way and I go mine, it occurs to me: The little girl, who looked around Adam's age, has Down syndrome.

I come home and with a shaking hand, unleash Mira, and take off my jacket. I come to bed and mutter a quick goodnight to my wife.

*

That night, I come downstairs, half asleep and hungry, and inadvertently knock all eight cabins over. The destruction is complete and instantaneous. In the night's thickness, notched wooden pieces are scattered across the playroom like branches from a hurricane. My breathing accelerates, and I spend the next ten minutes picking up as quickly and quietly as I can. At one point, Denise whisper-yells from upstairs, asking if I'm okay. I'm not. But I manage to get all the pieces back inside the tubular container and go back upstairs.

The rest of the night I'm wide eyed, staring into our bedroom's fuzzy greyness, neck muscles clenched, eyes dry.

*

April arrives with a fresh dump of snow on Montreal. TPG's show is reviewed positively in the *Montreal Gazette*, and we've booked three additional shows for May.

On a Monday evening, while Adam sleeps, Claire sends around an email to the Mortals. Sabrina's doctor discovered a mass in her right lung. I take off my glasses and read it again. The words stay the same. I run upstairs, two at a time, to my wife.

"Mon Dieu."

We sit on the edge of our bed, facing the big picture window. Our neighbour across the street is scolding her youngest in Arabic for going out on the balcony. She takes the girl's chubby hand and pulls her inside, while the little girl's other palm remains outstretched, reaching for just one more snowflake. I close my eyes. Denise leans her head on my shoulder. It's the first time we've connected physically since she told me to quit TPG.

"Maybe we should put our camping trip on hold," she says, lightly stroking my thigh.

I stand up quickly and start pacing. "We don't have to make any big decisions yet. I mean, doctors find stuff all the time. I'm sure it's nothing." My heart hammers against my ribcage, but I ignore it and put my laptop away, grab my snowman pajamas, and march into the bathroom to brush my teeth.

Ten days later, I take the metro to Station Peel to see Dr. Couture for my monthly med check. Sabrina had stopped by our place earlier with Hercule Noirot, telling us she should have the results of the biopsy by the end of the day. I just want to get home to be with Denise and Adam.

In the waiting room, I pick up a magazine. This month's *Elle* advertises a new lipstick called "Acai berry." Another actress comes forward about Harvey Weinstein. There are ten tips for keeping kids' screen time to a minimum. My cell phone pings. I glance down and see a text from Patti.

Got results. Malignant. Major surgery, unsure of prognosis.

My eyes shift focus, back to the magazine, a photo of the kids' room, where everybody is smiling. I start to text Denise and stop. Dr. Couture calls me into her office. I somehow make it through the appointment and leave.

When I get home, Denise is in the kitchen, crying over the sink, washing radishes.

"Claire sent a group email," she says, and grabs me, tightly.

"Mommy, look!" I walk back into the foyer to find Adam descending the carpeted stairs, wearing only his bright new yellow rain boots. He dangles a book over the railing, teasing me.

"Where are your clothes, Boy Wonder?"

"Up. Look!" It's his new favourite, a photographic history of the Montreal Metro, another birthday gift from Mimi. It's open, and he's pointing at a photo of Station Monk on the green line with the two giant sculptures, huge human forms, standing guard.

Parenthood with a preschooler consists of imagination, enthusiasm, and interruption. We swipe at fear with fish sticks, bubble bath, and *Sam and Dave Dig a Hole*.

Finally, he's sleeping, and I climb into bed with Denise. I press my cold hands against her warm back, testing the waters. "T'as les mains froides," she says. When I quickly take them away, she reaches behind her and puts them back.

I reach for my phone on the night table and then immediately put it back, forgetting, as I do so often, that Jessica is gone.

Chapter 69

The next day, I call Patti. "Hey, wanna do a shop for the girls?"
"Yeah mate, Sabrina told me yesterday she's been meaning to get to Rachel-Berri."

I grab my bomber jacket and start up the Honda Fit after scraping ice off the windshield. I look up at the sky. The temps have been hovering around zero which is cold for late April. The sun peeks through the branches of the big maple tree, and I notice tiny leaf buds.

Patti is waiting in front of her apartment when I pull up. She opens the passenger door and for a second, I think I see her eyes tear up. She settles in the seat and takes a breath. Then she looks at me, and we burst out laughing.

"Just drive. We have a mission to complete."

At the store, each of us has a hand on the miniature grocery cart, and we just barely fit walking side by side down the aisle. Every time we pass somebody, we wait until the person is just out of hearing range, and we whisper to the other what kind of animal that person really is.

"Otter."

"Sting ray."

"Wild boar."

Then, after we pile in organic soymilk, carrots, blackberries, and gluten-free bread, we're waiting in line, and we glance outside. There's a boxer tied up with classic black droopy jowls and bug eyes. I notice Patti trying to stifle a laugh. I raise my eyebrows, asking "What?" nonverbally. She gestures with her head to the customer in front of us in line. It's a guy with bug eyes and droopy jowls.

After we bring the groceries to Claire's and I drop Patti back at her place, my body relaxes and I'm able to concentrate on my graphic design clients for the rest of the day. We have supper and then I go back over to Claire and Sabrina's with Denise and Adam and hang out, crying, hugging, throwing the squeaky rubber banana for Hercule Noirot.

The weeks that follow are difficult, but we stay close to our fragile friends. We bring over cauliflower leek soup and bison meatloaf and gluten-free peanut butter cookies. We send texts with emojis. We invite them to see *Mamma Mia Here We Go Again*, to come to our place for Shabbat suppers, and to walk the dogs to Marché Jean-Talon for ice cream. We usually bring Adam because he's full of kisses and stories and giggles.

One Saturday in May, we stop by while we're with Mira on the evening walk. Claire answers the door. She's pale and her eyes are glazed.

"Hi guys. Sabrina's...I mean, she's not really available."

My stomach lurches. "Is she okay?" I start sliding my Star of David up and down the chain.

"Yes, yes, definitely. She's just...well, why don't you come in for a bit."

I look at Denise, and she shakes her head, subtly communicating not to ask, to just go along.

Everything is as it always is except the door to the bedroom is closed.

"Where's Bina?" Adam says.

I look at Claire, who scratches her chin and doesn't make eye contact with my kid.

"She's not feeling good, sweetie."

He starts whimpering and gives Denise the arms up pose. She grabs him, and he buries his face in her neck and starts crying.

Claire's face changes, and she looks more like herself. She rubs Adam's back as Denise does a little rocking motion. "She loves you, beautiful. Her body is just hurting right now. You know that time when you had the tummy sickness, and you had to throw up?"

The back of Adam's head bobs up and down.

"That's kind of the same thing Sabrina's feeling. It's hard to play when our bodies don't feel good."

But she hasn't had chemo yet. Why is she feeling sick? Maybe she has the flu.

Claire kisses Adam's head twice. "This one's from me, and this is from Sabrina." He peels his face away from Denise's shoulder and gives Claire a wet-cheeked smile.

*

My nights become difficult again, even with my medication. I start sketching before bed. I reread *The Tibetan Book of Living and Dying*. Thich Nhat Hanh. Elisabeth Kubler-Ross. My heart is in pieces, and I want to support Sabrina respectfully, quietly, with beauty, something she reveres.

Sharing her passion for ritual, I decide to make and give her an artist's book each week. Drop-off would be before sundown on Friday, when Shabbat officially begins. That ritual had begun to mean something new when we met them. Mom had occasionally picked up a Challah and lit candles, but celebrating with the Itchy Mortals in Montreal had somehow brought the tradition into my adult life in a much more personal and meaningful way. Delivering a book at the beginning would help me feel that ongoing connection with Sabrina, especially because it would probably happen that we wouldn't be doing Shabbat as often because of her not feeling well.

The Friday after I make the first book, I finish supper dishes, leash Mira, grab my bomber jacket, and walk the five blocks to their apartment. I pass Café Dei Campi, the Vietnamese restaurant, the seamstress who keeps cherry lollypops on her counter. Not wanting to intrude, I place the book in their mailbox, walk home, and text Sabrina to let her know it's there.

Her response:

Delicious!

*

Winds blow through the city, and May arrives. It's a Friday evening, and I'm in the living room, helping Adam make an extra-wide log cabin. Realizing it's Shabbat, I text Patti to see if she wants to pull together an impromptu celebration with the Mortals.

She texts back.

Sorry. We have plans.

What?

I go to Denise in the kitchen where she's making her famous seafood salad. I show her the text.

"Am I being paranoid? She never writes to me like that."

"Pas certaine. Maybe she was in a hurry," she says, dipping her wooden spoon into the bowl and holding it out for me to taste.

"Nice." My mind is still on Patti.

"I guess we're not doing Shabbat with the Mortals," she says. "Maybe we could still make the challah?"

After supper, I remember my book for Sabrina. "I'll take Mira and the book and be back for bedtime," I yell up to Denise who is giving Adam his bath.

I make kissing sounds to my dog, wrap the book in a plastic Provigo bag, and head out.

As I turn the corner onto St-Zotique, I finger my creation, imagining my friend flipping pages, noticing details. This week's installment is a collage of flowers, photos taken in Claire and Sabrina's backyard last summer during one of many barbecues the Mortals shared. For the background, I'd glued pieces of torn blue and green paper onto each page. Stuck in a few photo corners. Stamped each blossom's name beneath the pictures. Dripped some wax.

It's warmer as spring approaches, but the night air is sharp with frost. I stop as Mira pees, watching my breath turn to fog. We're just a few houses away and a movement in their front window catches my eye. The dog starts walking again, and I take the package out. I start up the stairs to their door but quickly stop myself. Through the big picture window, I see a group of people inside, in the living room. They're laughing and singing.

The Itchy Mortals.

On Shabbat.

I hear Patti's massive British voice begin a Hebrew chant, just barely muffled by the brick wall between us.

I stand out of view, cheeks burning.

Mira pulls on the leash, desperate to see her other favourite people. Hercule Noirot doesn't bark, thank goodness. I walk up the steps hunched over, quietly open the top of the mailbox, and tuck the book inside. Then I creep away.

Denise opens the door for Mira and me. "Mon Dieu, il fait froid."

I say nothing, unclip the dog's leash, and remove my hat and mittens.

"What's wrong, honey?"

I sit down on the bench in the entryway and cover my wet face with my chilled fingers. For a few moments, I can't speak.

She sits with me, arm around my puffy coat.

"They were all there. Doing Shabbat. Patti was chanting."

"Tabarnak."

"Shhhh!" I look up, hoping Adam didn't hear.

"J'comprends pas, pas pantoute." She shakes her head and scratches her fingernails up and down her thighs, leaving marks on her jeans.

"I don't get it either."

"Why don't you call Claire and ask what's happening?"

"No way. I mean, Sabrina has cancer. It's one of the most awful things that can happen to anyone. They don't even know if it's treatable. So, I'm not going to call and make a fuss about not being included one time."

"You don't have to make a fuss, but you can ask. You can say that you're concerned, and you want to apologize."

"Apologize? What on earth for?"

"Sometimes we hurt people unintentionally. Would it be such a big deal to call and find out?"

I consider it. The idea of having hurt Sabrina or Claire seems absurd. I know it can happen, and I want to be a good friend, to communicate and take responsibility for harm I cause. As always, I imagine asking Jessica and think about what she would say. The knowing is deep in my body and soul. Our mandate as chosen family dictates one option: lighten their load, however possible.

Sometimes the kindest thing you can do for people is to leave them alone.

Chapter 70

Spring makes a grand entrance and quickly morphs into summer. The outside world is flagrantly jubilant: party-pink peonies blooming, people playing chess in the park, kids drawing with chalk on the sidewalks, the three sisters across the street twisting and shaking their new hula hoops.

Sabrina has surgery and spends three weeks recovering at the Royal Victoria hospital. We spend three weeks on Cape Cod at Denise's cousin's cabin. We wait until the last minute to confirm because we want to be available to our friends. Once, in response to my asking endlessly whether there is anything we can do, Claire suggests creating a list of one hundred upbeat films to help them relax. Another time she asks if I could put the garbage and recycling out when she stays overnight at the hospital. I barrel into these tasks with far more force than is needed. Helping, even a little, is like a salve.

After that, we continue offering. And they continue saying "no thank you."

So, we go on vacation.

July becomes August. We stay in touch with Claire and Sabrina. Lightly. One rainy day, Adam rediscovers his Lincoln Logs and constructs three new models. Most sunny days, kids flood the sidewalks and neighbourhood parks and alleyways with balls, bikes, bubbles. I sit in my upstairs studio, overlooking the front of the house, taking breaks from drawing or collage or client work and listening to whizzing scooters, a shrieking toddler, the voices of the three sisters across the street singing "Michaud" or "Mon merle a perdu son bec."

One August afternoon, the air whirring with crickets, Claire stops by. A bunch of us are outside on the sidewalk, our kids drawing a giant castle with chalk. One woman passes around Dixie cups of cherry iced tea, and another offers banana bread. I'm sitting on my front stoop with my next-door neighbour, and I overhear a guy ask Claire how Sabrina is, how things are going. Claire shakes her head and smiles, saying that their biggest problem was having too much support; they had been inventing fake tasks for "overflow" people, like making a list of upbeat movie titles.

"Nice problem," says the man, and they both laugh.

I start to freeze but resist, pushing myself onto my feet. I grab two cups of iced tea and approach Claire. I tap her on the shoulder and smile forcefully when she turns around. I look into her eyes and stop smiling. She takes the tea, flustered.

"Hey, Audrey, Thanks, I didn't see you there. How are things?"

I don't say anything. I just look into her eyes, searching for something familiar and failing.

*

"I miss Patti," Adam says to me one October afternoon. The leaves are turning, as they always do, shimmery gold and dazzling red, nature twirling like a little girl in a tutu.

"Do you want to call her, Boy Wonder?"

He snatches the portable from its cradle and asks me for the number, which I give without looking. The only two phone numbers I'd memorized since moving to Montreal were Patti and Mireille's, and Claire and Sabrina's. He dials and hits speakerphone.

"AAAAdammm!!! How's my little man?" Sportscaster voice, thick cockney accent, thunderous intensity. I can't help smiling. But when they're finished, I don't ask for the phone. And Patti doesn't say, "Put Mummy on, love."

I let go, bit by bit.

On a warm evening, I phone Claire. We hadn't gotten any email updates, and I wanted to offer again, just in case.

"Audrey, it's great to hear your voice."

I finger my Star of David and lick my molars. "You too, Claire. How's Sabrina?"

Silence. Then sobs. "She's so weak, Audrey. She can't even walk to the bathroom by herself. And she's just not getting better. I don't know what I'm going to do."

Everything in my mind whooshes out but Claire and Sabrina. The only thing that makes any sense is to go over. Adam fell asleep early, and Denise is studying for some exam she has at work the next day.

"I'll come over, Claire. Just give me a few minutes."

"No, no, that's okay, Audrey. I'm fine. I just, well, sometimes it catches me off guard, you know, that sadness."

The background sounds grow louder. Voices.

"There's a bunch of people here, so I have plenty of shoulders I can cry on. Stay with Adam and Denise. I'm really glad you called."

I look at the wall in front of me. The framed photo of Denise and me with Mom and my family, with Jessica leaping into the shot and everyone cracking up. We have the body paint, and everyone is dressed up.

Does everything end?

Sabrina's recovery is long. Brutal. Private. From neighbourhood gossip, we learn that there is a small inner circle, first at the hospital and then at home. We learn that Patti and Mireille are part of it and Sabrina's three brothers, but we don't know who else. We know that they do a lot of singing and that they celebrate Shabbat each Friday night.

Occasionally, I phone or email to ask if they need anything. Occasionally, they ask if one of us could walk the dog, which we do. Denise and I go through the process separately, our sadnesses like the two solitudes of Montreal. Sometimes I find Denise perched on the side of the bed, staring off into space. Sometimes she finds me in my studio doing yoga, in tree pose with tear tracks down my cheeks and neck, wet spots on the front of my sports bra. We try not to think about it or talk about it. But the cancer's presence remains in our home, a silent toxin, eroding the structure I thought was solid.

The weeks pass, and Sabrina does recover, bit by bit. She continues chemo and radiation. She sends email updates to the community, the Mortals, and the many others who love and care for her and Claire. She starts to take slow walks around the neighbourhood when the weather is right.

One morning in November, she stops by with Hercule Noirot.

Adam answers the door.

"Hello big guy!"

Adam dives in for a hug. Too hard. I see it from the living room and come over to referee. I peel him off, reprimand him, and send him upstairs. Shrieking.

"Oh my God, I am so sorry. I didn't tell him he needs to be careful

275

with you. Are you okay?" My office phone rings.

Her face is sallow, and I don't know if it's because of Adam or the physical condition she arrived in.

"I'm fine, but it would be great to sit," she says, handing me the leash. I ignore the phone, take the dog and Sabrina's arm, and lead her to the couch. I hear Denise come down the stairs, en route to the post office. She stops suddenly when she sees Sabrina in the living room.

"Bonjour." My wife regains composure, but her voice is chilly.

"Honey, can you get her a glass of water?" I ask, looking to Sabrina for confirmation.

"Actually, tea would be nice if it's not too much trouble," she says. I want to do a cartwheel. I intercept Denise, telling her I'll take care of it, and besides, she has errands to do, doesn't she?

The doorbell rings. The babysitter. Adam flies into her, and there's a flutter of noise. Denise puts down her package and follows me into the kitchen. My office phone rings again.

"Why are you serving her tea?" Denise whispers when we're out of hearing range. I shrug, feeling like a delirious puppy, and fill the kettle.

"I just want to take care of her. She's here."

"Yeah, after months of excluding us."

"But maybe it's over now. I think we have to live in the present. Anyways, you don't have to join in. We can make different choices."

She looks at me, starts to speak, and then changes her mind, picks up her package and leaves.

I'm too giddy to let Denise's reaction bother me. I look in the armoire and find a box she and Claire brought us back from Costa Rica a few years ago: special loose teas from the island. Not being a tea lover, I found myself taken with the gift's whimsical packaging. The box is turquoise, like tropical seawater, with tiny white butterflies. When you take the cover off, you see nine round metal canisters, each sitting in a circular cutout from a piece of cardboard the same colour as the box. When you take out each canister and look through the holes, you can see what's underneath, the bottom of the box, which is white with turquoise butterflies. It comes with a paper describing each flavour. The tea is loose, which means you have to use a tea ball, one of my favourite kitchen implements.

The kettle whistles. I turn off the burner, pour the hot water into the teapot, grab the box, tea ball, mug, milk and spoon, a single daisy from the bouquet on the counter, and put everything on Mom's old silver serving tray. I carry the tray back to Sabrina into the living room and set it down on the coffee table. I recite her choices of tea flavours. She leans back on the couch, sighs, and smiles. "Lovely. Just lovely."

I unleash Hercule Noirot, and he and Mira trot off together, playing. Leto scoots upstairs. My office phone rings again. Adam chases the babysitter down to the basement.

"Maybe I came at a bad time?" Sabrina says hoarsely.

"No, not at all, really, it's fine. It's great. I'm just...just so happy that you're here."

My fingers are cramped and my palms moist. I push any negativity out of my mind and look at Sabrina, who's starting to look a bit more like her usual radiant self.

She asks about our vacation and about Adam. I tell her a few stories. I fill the tea ball with the leaves, clip it shut, and dangle it inside the teapot. It smells like a dark forest.

"How's your artwork going? Are you doing any shows or residencies?"

I laugh. "After work and motherhood, I hardly ever get into my studio. I doubt that will be part of my life again anytime soon."

She looks serious, gazing at me. "You can't let that talent just fizzle. And it won't be good for your relationship with your son."

I squint. "What do you mean?"

She sighs. "If I had a beautiful child like Adam, I would find it difficult too. But nobody is going to advocate for your art. It's like another child. Only nobody will ever be arguing for you spending time on it. Only against it. Those books you made for me...Audrey, you need to be doing that work. It's important."

I feel my cheeks flush. Art has always been my way to be in the world, but I never thought of it as important.

"And you?" I ask, letting the tea steep and avoiding eye contact.

"Not so fast. Promise me you'll let art be important when you make decisions. At least do that for me. I know what it's like not to have much time left."

I pour some tea into her cup and then mine. "Fine, sure, I promise. Now tell me about you!"

"I went back to work a few weeks ago, just part time, and it's been good. I get tired, but there's a lounge I can lie down in if necessary. I had two scans, and they were both clean. Cross fingers and toes."

She wraps her fingers around the ceramic. "I love this mug." It's the one with the multicoloured birds: a toucan, a cockatoo, a macaw.

My whole body is smiling.

I hear the door open and close.

We visit a bit more, and then she takes Hercule Noirot and leaves.

I find Denise upstairs, staring out the window, arms crossed.

"Our friend stopped by to see us," I say, trying to hide my annoyance.

Denise blows her nose and gets up.

"I forgot to pick up the dry cleaning," she says, avoiding my gaze.

Chapter 71

The holidays come and go. We don't see much of the Mortals, but Sabrina and Claire stop by more and more frequently. In February, Claire calls. I put on my headset and answer.

"Hey, Audrey, it's Claire. How's it going?" I'm downstairs in the playroom, sorting Adam's toys in to keep and to give piles.

"Hey, so nice to hear your voice. We're good, you?" I gesture to Denise, who is with Adam doing some numbers project that involves wheel-shaped pieces of uncooked pasta.

"Listen, Sabrina and I realized that Adam's birthday is in a few weeks. We were wondering if you guys are having a party?"

I set down the Lincoln Logs container, slowly.

"Uh, we're, we're not sure yet, we're trying to get organized," I say, opening the canister, fingering one log, and then dropping it.

"Well," Claire said, "we just wanted to let you know that we'd like to be there to celebrate with you. Five is kind of a big deal."

Denise stops what she's doing and looks at me. I hold up one finger.

"That's sweet. Are you sure Sabrina would be up for it?"

"I think so."

Denise mouths "what" from the table, and Adam is trying to toss the pasta wheels into the trashcan across the room.

"That's the nice thing about living so close, that we can always go home if she's tired or whatever." I stand up to go over to Adam, gesturing "no," but accidentally slip on a Lincoln Log and then knock over the whole container.

"Sorry, I'm trying to multitask. Honestly, I'm not sure what we're doing about a party. We'll probably talk about it in the next few days, so I can definitely let you know." As I pick up the spilled logs, Adam is now throwing two wheels at once, trying to get them both into the garbage simultaneously. I say goodbye and hang up the phone.

"Stop that!" I yell at my son and continue picking up the Lincoln Logs. Adam's chin falls to his chest and the tears start. I roll my eyes and then gesture for him to come sit on my lap. I snuggle him, apologizing, and then fill Denise in.

"It seems that they want to reconnect, now that Sabrina is getting better." I tell her about Claire's request. Denise gets up from the table and goes into the living room, sits down on the couch, stares at her thighs.

"I can't."

"Put yourself in their shoes, honey. They miss us. They love us. They want to be close to our boy." Denise turns from the window and looks at me with a blank expression. She nods. I kiss Adam again, take him off my lap, and move over to the couch to hold my wife.

*

We invite Claire and Sabrina to Adam's fifth birthday party. And Patti and Mireille. And on March 28th, they're there, with Denise's extended family. My mom, dealing with my brother who violated his parole, isn't able to make it. But I'm so happy with our little group being present that I don't mind. Like magic: Sprinkle some glitter and the log cabin springs back up, as good as new.

Life regains a sense of forward motion. In May, Patti travels back home to England for her fortieth. It's the first 4-0 in our group, and I remark to Denise that our turn is coming, in just a few short years. In June, Patti comes home to Canada.

The outdoor pool at Parc Père-Marquette opens, and we start taking Adam whenever it's hot. He falls in love with swimming. One day in July, he doesn't need his floatie anymore. One kick. One big splash. He can swim.

Summer temps soar, and we're at the park pool every sunny day. Patti texts me one Saturday: a lesbian couple, friends of hers, had moved to Montreal and their movers had disappeared after some conflict. Could I come and help unload the truck? They're desperate and haven't been able to find anyone to hire last minute. I look at Denise and Adam, splashing around with a big purple beach ball. Then I have a twinge when I imagine myself moving without help on a day like this. I tell Patti I'll be there in an hour and spend the rest of the day sweating and unloading.

The two women are as grateful as they are exhausted. Patti and I agree to organize a welcome supper, with all eight of us Mortals, and we exchange cell numbers. Before I leave, Patti pulls me aside. "Thanks, mate. Really means a lot that you came." I grin and grab her in a sweltering hug.

I return to the pool, high from helping and meeting new friends. Images of barbecues, art openings, and Shabbat suppers with all four couples play in my mind.

In September, Adam has his first day of kindergarten. We pick out a special outfit, buy him a backpack, and take photos of him in front of his new "big boy" school. Sabrina works full time. Her scans are clean. Everybody is busy, but I'm snug and safe, back inside our cabin.

Halloween arrives. I go to Jean-Coutu for Snickers, fake webbing, a string of orange lights. We make trick or treating with our neighbour and her twins. I email the Mortals about stopping by.

Claire responds,

Sure, sounds fun. Maybe on the later side?

Patti texts,

We have supper plans.

I answer,

Anyone I know?

No response.

Well, she must be in the middle of something.

Adam's costume is conceptual. He explains, "The top part is a rainbow. Then under it there's the cloud, and they're both over the house. It's called a rainbow cloud house."

I ask for artistic license, and he grants it. I fetch an old cardboard box from a refrigerator in the basement and gather my paints, twine, and glue. Jean-Coutu has a rainbow mask, a bag of cotton balls, and a purple plastic pumpkin for his candy collecting. I cut out two cardboard sides of a boxy house, punch holes and thread twine in it so he can wear the house. Then I use one side of the cardboard that's left, and I cut out a cloud shape. I paint it white and then glue on the entire bag of cotton balls to make the cloud three dimensional. I finally attach the cloud to the front section of the house on the bottom.

"Wow, Mommy," he gasps when I bring the creation into his room. I step gingerly over five new Lincoln Log cabins, spread out over his floor like a new subdivision. "It's exactly perfect!!!" Denise walks in a moment later and laughs, shaking her head. We look at one another and smile. We'd slowly shed our anxieties and were once again holding hands, snuggling in bed, singing together in the car.

She feeds Mira while I help Adam get into costume, and the three of us leave for our first stop: the corner bakery. As soon as Adam steps out of the house into the windy evening, cotton balls start flying off his costume. But he's so focussed on collecting enough candy to put all of Canada into a diabetic coma that he barely notices when I detach the cloud and toss it into the bakery's trashcan.

We go next door and ring the bell. The twins are dressed as a bear and a fox and are jumping around, sliding down the polished wooden floor on the slippery feet of their costumes. Adam suggests we all get going, "So we can get the candy before people run out."

As we step out into the night, my mind is only partially on Reese's and Smarties. Memories of that winter Shabbat when I peered through our friends' living room window pester my mind. I obsess about Patti's text, her lack of response, and I wonder if we should skip Claire and Sabrina's. I dismiss my feelings as paranoia and try to release the fear with breathing, but instead it pitches a flag and settles right in.

The street life of our Rosemont neighbourhood is especially vibrant on Halloween. Neighbours, with or without children, make a big effort, donning pointy black hats, Frankenstein masks, putty noses. There's a giant cauldron with real steam, stacked bales of hay with a scarecrow who springs to life, a giant glow-in-the-dark toothy pumpkin, a coffin with a bloodied hand hanging out. It's hard being an angsty Jew on such an enchanted evening, but I somehow manage.

After a handful of houses, Marie-Claude says good night and takes the twins back home. They're half-asleep in their stroller.

We approach Claire and Sabrina's, and I look inside the window. A dinner is in progress, with Patti and Mireille and the British couple who had moved to Montreal a few weeks prior. The same couple I'd helped move on that hot Saturday.

Patti's supper plans.

Adam rings the bell, and Sabrina answers.

"Trick or Treat!" Adam says, his smile bursting through his costume.

Sabrina's face lights up. "Who's this big guy?"

Adam tries to roll his eyes behind his mask.

"Not a guy. I'm something else."

Sabrina looks at me, delighted and stuck. "I think I need some help."

I shift my focus back to Adam. "Just tell her, sweetie."

"A rainbow cloud house, of course."

We stand there. Adam holds out his purple plastic pumpkin. Sabrina stares at him and after a few seconds, her gaze changes to something turbulent and sharp. I can't stop staring even though I want to look away.

Then Sabrina shakes her head, apologizes, and invites us inside.

"Happy Halloween Adam, the boy wonder," says Patti. "Do I get my hug with you all dressed up?" Adam runs over, forgetting he's in costume. Patti manages to pick him up and toss him in the air like she used to do when he was little.

"This is a unique costume," says Mireille, winking at me.

"Denise, is that a new haircut?" asks Sabrina. My wife nods, and I notice she doesn't hold eye contact with Sabrina for long.

"Have a seat. Do you want any food?"

Claire unfolds a few chairs.

One of the new women puts a Kit Kat in Adam's pumpkin.

The room buzzes with conversation. Patti asks Adam about his costume. Sabrina gets the lowdown from Denise on the neighbourhood festivities. Claire is trying to talk to me from across the table.

"It's back," she mouths, leaning her head towards Sabrina. "The cancer."

The words strike me like a gong. And I understand immediately that the supper is a distraction—a way to keep minds on life when death has shown up again, like an uninvited guest.

Standing with my mouth hanging open is not a viable option.

Instead, I turn on a bright smile. "We should have dinner together, all of us," I say. Everybody nods enthusiastically.

"Actually, we should get going," says Denise. "Adam has school tomorrow." The room is silent. I look at my wife, notice her rigid mouth. Adam is playing rock, paper, scissors with Patti and doesn't look the least bit tired. But as soon as he hears Denise, he's ready for more trick or treating, so we say our goodbyes and leave.

Things outside have quieted down. We walk down the street without talking. After several more houses, we tell Adam it's time to go home.

I'm so stunned about the cancer's return that Denise has to explain to me that we were excluded again. Even after she says it, I'm doubtful. They were genuinely happy to see us. They knew we were busy trick or treating. It was probably just an oversight.

I get my laptop and set up a Doodle for supper in the coming weeks. I offer twelve options with flexible location. I invite the six women.

Nobody responds.

Chapter 72

By November, we accept that things are back the way they were. We offer but far less frequently. Our visits happen every few weeks instead of days, and we stay for shorter periods of time. And yet, each interaction continues feeling warm. Other than being left out, it's as if nothing has changed.

On a Sunday, we rake leaves in our backyard and jump into the piles. I snap photos of Adam in mid-air over the mounds, his grass-green eyes full of glee. I watch him, reminiscing about my own childhood autumns, the scent of decay in the air, dried leaves tickling my skin, soft crunching of leaves, caws of blue jays. Somehow, in these weeks each year, I was able to immerse myself in nature, in life, without being afraid.

The next Wednesday, Denise spends the morning with Adam at school. I go out for an early afternoon run in the late fall sunshine, and when I return, I find Denise crying at the computer and Adam comforting her.

I put my arm around them both. "What is it?"

Denise points at the screen. It's an email from Claire, explaining that there are no viable treatments left, that Sabrina is officially going into hospice. The doctors are giving her three to five months.

My circulation stops. I'm bloodless, breathless, numb. I stumble back to the futon. Collapse. Denise sobs as the girls across the street jump rope, counting in French. Adam climbs into my lap and starts weeping. Denise joins us on the futon in our hot wet huddle of skin and sweat and heartbreak.

*

The next day, when I finish work, I call Patti for answers.

"I want you to tell me what's going on."

"What do you mean? Sabrina's dying. That's what's going on. But you already know that."

"We're left out of everything. Everything. Were we excommunicated from the Mortals?"

Silence.

"Audrey, I should think you'd stop making it all about you."

"That's completely unfair, and you know it."

"She and Claire are doing what they need to do to survive."

"So why are you there every minute of every day, and we have to stay out? Just tell me what I have to do, and I'll do it. I'm—"

"I have to go now. Call me if you want to have coffee and talk about something else."

She hangs up.

*

I reread "Barn-Raising," an essay by Anne Lamott about illness. Parents of a child with cystic fibrosis, she says, are just like everybody else before the diagnosis, but afterwards, they are suddenly banished to the Land of the Fucked. Wouldn't you want to gather all your closest people to you if this happened? Maybe Denise is right. Maybe I hurt them without knowing it. But so much time had passed that I couldn't imagine starting a conversation that would bring me clarity and also bring me to my most generous and supportive self.

In December, I receive news that I was accepted to another artist colony in May, an application I had filed after Sabrina gave me the pep talk. Claire and Sabrina decide to marry legally to make estate planning simpler. I receive a white e-invitation with a blue Jewish star and a dove.

I tell Denise while she's getting Adam into his pajamas. "One of us should go."

"Why did they invite us?" she asks. I settle in on Adam's bed for reading time.

Tonight, it's *Make Way for Ducklings*, and when we finish, we tuck Adam in and give kisses. "Love you Mommy." He clutches at my neck, poking my Star of David, keeping my cheek pressed to his. "Never gonna let you go." I lie back down with him for a few minutes, skin-to-skin, realizing how seldom we do that now.

When we leave his room, Denise holds my hand, and we stand in the hall together for a few minutes.

I look at her. "Honestly, I'm afraid I'd have a panic attack."

She furrows her eyebrows.

I shake my head. "I don't think I can." Hot tears on my cheeks.

She wraps me in a hug. "I'll go. You stay home with Adam." I lean into my wife, all my weight against her solid frame.

*

The day of the wedding, a Saturday, I take Adam to the Eastern Townships for a sleigh ride. When we get home, Denise is already there, even though the reception was supposed to go much later. Her face is pale, and there are dark grooves beneath her eyes.

"I shouldn't have gone," she says, shaking her head.

Adam twists and turns as I slip off his parka. "What happened?"

Denise sits on the bench in the foyer. "They said hello but then not another word. And the rest of the Mortals were sitting at their table. I was with Sabrina's great uncle and her boss, the guy she hates. Nobody talked, we all just sat there, looking at the rest of the group having a great time."

"MommIE, MommIE!" Adam is chanting and I lift up his paisley turtleneck to give him a zerbert on his belly. He squeals and falls onto me.

"I'm sorry, honey. I should have gone."

"Vraiment. I felt like I crashed some party." My phone buzzes in our bedroom. I dash in to pick it up. It's a text from Claire saying how disappointed they are that I wasn't there.

I throw my phone across the room.

*

January and February come and go. We get reports that Sabrina is trying a new experimental drug. There seems to be some minor progress.

March arrives, and Adam turns six. Sabrina is walking. The tumours have stabilized. In one cautious email, Claire says she's fantasizing of Sabrina coming home.

April is less positive. Sabrina is mostly lying down again. The experimental drug isn't working after all. I call the artist retreat and ask if I can postpone the residency. The director tells me I can't.

On May 2nd, I pack the car and begin the long journey to Scranton, PA. I arrive at Hidden Gardens and immerse myself in nature, the house's ample art collection, its books.

On May 7th, Denise calls me. "Sabrina passed away this morning."

I sit down on the loveseat in the living room. "How's Claire?"

Denise sighs. "I just got an email. I tried Patti and Mireille's phones but got voice mail."

I debate returning a week early for the funeral. That's what a good friend would do. Then I imagine sitting at the service with Denise and Adam, watching Patti and Mireille and the London couple from a distance. My gut wrings itself out like a washcloth. Sabrina's words come back to me about how nobody will be advocating for my art. She, if anybody, would vote for me staying put.

I write six letters to Claire and throw them out. I send an e-card, immediately realizing the weakness of the gesture. The next day, Denise asks if I'll come home early from the residency to attend the funeral. She tells me she's definitely not going. I wonder what Claire wants, expects, needs. I sketch coffins, skeletons holding hands, devastated women huddling together with Denise and I looking on from a distance. I wonder if I even have anything to offer that Claire can't get from her inner circle, which I'm no longer part of.

After several hours of drawing, I decide I need to focus on my artwork. I decide to stay at the residency and miss the funeral. I say out loud, "Sabrina, I hope you meant what you said."

Chapter 73

In between work on my collage and exploring the Pennsylvania hills, I think about a gift for Claire. Flowers. A book. A donation. Nothing seems right.

I get home from the residency. I don't call. A week passes. I still don't call.

Claire unfriends Denise and me on Facebook.

As soon as it happens, I realize that Claire expected us to be there. But how could she? My skin tightens around my bones. And then I imagine it was Denise instead of Sabrina, and the floor drops out from under me. Yes, I'm outside the cabin. But I haven't walked a mile or even a kilometer in Claire's shoes. I might not want to comfort her right now, but I also don't want to hurt her.

I think of the free e-card I sent, and my face flushes.

What would Jessica do?

*

Time moves, uncaring about the details of living and dying. My mom and the boys come up for a week in July. Adam makes a new friend at the park and has his first sleepover. We do a massive toy and game cleanout and consider giving away the Lincoln Logs.

"I think we should keep them," says Denise, standing by the "to go" pile.

"Why? He never plays with them, and neither do we."

"It's the kind of thing he might go back to. He might get interested later."

I give in and start hauling the "to go" boxes into the car.

Since the funeral, we've heard nothing from the remaining Mortals.

In September, I see Claire and Patti walking down the street. I turn around and take another route. In October, I'm pushing Adam on the swings at the park, and I see the five women in the distance, sharing a fall picnic.

*

At Christmas, a card comes in familiar handwriting. I recognize it immediately as Patti's. My pulse jumps and I take it up to my studio to open it in private.

Dear Audrey,

I've been unfair to you and wanted to write. I feel I should help you understand why things happened as they did. I've finally recovered from being angry that you and Denise skipped the funeral, which was devastating to Claire.

What you don't know is how complicated things were with Sabrina. Before the cancer, she and Claire had started talking about having children. Being involved with you and Denise in your fertility process and the birth, and then helping out with Adam, meant so much to them both. Claire realized having a child of her own would feel different than caring for her siblings. And for Sabrina, it gave her the sense that yes, if you could do it, she could do it. They had their first appointment at the clinic, and then the same week, they received the diagnosis.

After that, every time you three came over, she would fall apart. The loss of her own life was one thing, but not having a child was far more devastating. Because she was so private about the whole matter, neither Claire nor I could say anything to you. It left you and Denise in a difficult position, and I'm sorry.

But I also knew we would reconnect eventually because I know you are a real friend and you will understand and forgive. Take whatever time you need. My door is always open. Text me if you want to go for coffee.

Missing you, mate.

-Patti

My hands shake as I read and reread the letter. A crow caws, and I look out the window. The girls across the street are building a snow creature. Denise and Adam are downstairs making rugelach. I realize I haven't looked at the card that's holding the letter. It's a painting of a little tree house, flanked with snow and coloured lights, big windows. Inside there are tiny humans, mistletoe, a tree with glittering presents underneath. On the top, there's a shadow of Santa and the reindeer, just a suggestion of the story and its hero. I see all the light inside the house and think about Hanukkah and the oil and how eight days could feel like eight years. I think about miracles and mythic figures and mending.

I don't share Patti's letter with Denise. I know I'll show her eventually, but something else has to happen first.

Chapter 74

S leep is scarce, and I'm often in my studio when the night is heaviest, at one or two in the morning. One night, I'm roaming the kitchen, foraging. I open the armoire looking for some Life cereal. There, I find the box of teas from Costa Rica in that exquisite packaging.

Yes.

I take the box up to my studio, the skin around my mouth loosening.

The next day, after client appointments, I remove the tea leaves from each metal canister and start fiddling. I jot down notes and measure the circumference of the circle slots and the canisters. Sweat runs down my temples, and my throat is tight.

The next night, after Denise is asleep, I go back into the studio, sinuses pounding. I sort through my photo files on the computer and choose thirty shots of Itchy Mortals gatherings and print them out. I cut the photos out and place them inside the box. When I leave to go to bed, I'm clutching my stomach.

Friday evening is our Hanukkah party, normally one of my favourite nights of the year. I manage to fry up over one hundred latkes and play dreidel with our neighbour and her twins, trying when I'm alone to release my diaphragm muscles enough to breathe freely. Finally, our guests leave, and after Denise and I finish the dishes, I go back into my studio. Breathing is more and more laboured as I hand scratch memories on pieces of paper. I suck in air as I cut one out, roll it tightly into a scroll, and tuck it into one of the nine holes in the cardboard that covers the bottom. I do four until I'm coughing and gasping and have to get out my yoga mat and stretch for an hour to declench.

The next morning, Denise and I are spooning in bed. "What are you working on?" she asks. Her body is so warm and the air so cold.

"Just another collage. Trying some new materials."

"Can I see it?"

I chuckle. "Not much to see yet. I'll tell you when it's ready." Just thinking of the project sends a squirt of adrenaline into my system.

Over the holidays, I make handmade paper from photo scraps mixed with dried flowers and dye from berries, turmeric, beets. In January, once all the paper is dry and set, I tear it up and start gluing the torn pieces onto the cover of the box. I keep at it through the winter. I keep embellishing and embellishing. Glue. Acrylic. Glitter. Stamps. Pastels.

My stomach continues to rebel. The project's momentum pulls me into a swirl of pain and resentment, love and anger, compassion and confusion, self-hatred, and a yearning for wholeness. One night, after working, a burst of nausea pummels me into the bathroom, where I almost miss the toilet.

I push myself, often staying up until 2:00 or 3:00 a.m., tears slowly replacing physical anguish. In early March, my body regains its strength while my psyche becomes distorted, full of severe noise, like an MRI or a rave. The more intricately beautiful the piece becomes, the more desperately sad I feel. But I think about Claire, the beacon of light that is her name, and know that I have to muscle through.

The day Adam turns seven, March 28th, I finish my project.

The second it's done, the box seems to take on a life of its own. Turquoise paint dances with black inked roses, salmon and brick red crayon swirls, bits of white handmade paper ripped in diamond shapes, strips, a spiral. A tiny stamped purple heart punctuates the lower right-hand corner of the box's cover. The scrolls are like portals, revealing bits of the photos beneath them. I hold the box, stroke my fingers along its sides, open and close the top repeatedly, read the scrolls, and put them back.

For the next month, I keep it on a plant stand near the window in my studio. I visit it. I do little tweaks, tiny changes that don't do much and that nobody will ever notice except me.

Finally, I get the project wrapped, address it to Claire, and mail it the Thursday before Easter.

I come home to an empty house. Walk up to Adam's room. Grab the container of Lincoln Logs. Dump them on the floor. I take each of the logs and make a giant circle. I lie down in the middle on my side, curled up. There, I begin to heal.

Chapter 75

Passover arrives, and I imagine Patti and Claire and Mireille and the new Mortals having the big and meaningful Seder we'd been part of for six years. I hadn't heard anything from Claire since sending the package. I reread the Maggid, the Passover story, the story of the miracle, and consider my own life, packed full of small miracles. I'm married. I'm an artist. I have a happy child. I immigrated and can now speak French. None of my counsellors and psychiatrists would have ever believed any of it was possible. I know many people without disabilities who couldn't manage what I do, even if I do struggle and take medication.

Yet still, the absence of Jessica and The Mortals keeps me tense, in between looking at daffodils and hearing the joyful noise of spring birds in the trees of Rosemont.

One evening in May, when Denise and Adam are having supper with Mimi, I'm home finishing an ad for a new company that makes women's tights out of hemp. In the middle of looking for ad clippings in my studio, I find Patti's letter. I take it downstairs and go sit in the blue chair. Leto jumps up on my lap and settles in. I read it and reread it. I think about why I still haven't shown it to Denise.

Maybe because I feel hope perched on my shoulder.

I realize I want to talk to Patti. That I'm ready. That I understand and forgive what happened. My heart is beating fast, but I pick up my phone and call.

"Audrey?"

"Yeah, it's me, surprise, surprise. How's it going?"

Silence. "I'm good, mate."

I clear my throat. "I want to see you. I'm ready to talk."

"Me too. I've been waiting on you, giving you space, that sort of thing."

"What are you doing right now?"

"Not much. Mireille's on a bike ride, and I've only now finished washing up from supper. Want to meet at the park?"

I thought about it. Part of our old routine. She would light up a cigarette, and I would sit on the swing. We'd laugh and it would feel warm and forever.

"I think I'd prefer a café. Maybe that new Turkish place near the laundromat?"

We agree to meet in a half hour.

My hands are shaking, but my feet feel like rocks. I read the letter three more times. I think about giving and taking and healthy connections and how much I've missed Patti and the others. I look in the mirror and think of Jessica when she posted that personal ad for me. "Are you desperate?" I ask my reflection. The reflection shakes her head.

I arrive early and grab a table in the back where there's nobody around. I'm standing in line to order a muffin and a decaf when Patti walks in. She's wearing a paisley scarf I don't recognize, and her hair is longer, but she's clearly still herself.

I take my treats back to the table and smile. She goes to give me one of her bear hugs. I can't say no, but I don't hug back as tightly as I used to.

She steps back. "Sorry, too much?"

"Just don't want to spill my coffee all over you." We both giggle.

She goes and gets a scone and a cappuccino. I watch my hands as they grasp the ceramic mug. They are shaking.

She sits down and organizes herself.

"Thanks for your letter," I say.

"Of course. I didn't know how you'd react. When I didn't hear from you, I thought the worst."

I take a bite and wash it down with decaf.

"At least I felt less crazy. And I understood what you said about protecting Sabrina."

We're both quiet.

"The thing is," I say, wiping my mouth with the little napkin, "I still love you as much as ever."

Patti grins. "That's my Audrey. Good on ya. That's what I kept saying to Claire, that you'd come round, eventually."

"But love isn't the same as trust."

She stops smiling.

I continued. "I kept asking myself why I couldn't let go, why it still bothered me, why, why, why. And once it stopped bothering me, I thought I could just pick up where we were before Sabrina got sick. I wanted that. Part of me still does. But I can't. Trust was broken. There are some things that can't be repaired, no matter how much I want that to happen."

"You're a forgiving person, Audrey. That's all we need, a little forgiveness."

"No, that's actually not true. I forgive you. I forgive Claire and Mireille. I forgave you all months ago. I just can't put things back together. I can't trust you after what happened. I can't be close if I can't trust. I'm sorry. For us both. For all of us."

She's looking down at the table and holding her mug without lifting it. She rubs her eyes under her glasses. I look around the place. There are only two other people. Carla Bruni croons on the stereo. The people behind the counter are playing "Twenty Questions" in French.

Patti's elbows rest on the table and her head is bent forward in her hands. My plate and mug are empty. I look at my watch. Wonder what else to say. Can't think of anything. So, I say goodbye, touch her shoulder gently, and leave.

Chapter 76

May is the last month of touring for TPG, and my heart is lighter. My business is sagging in part because I have so much admin work to do for the company, but I tell myself it's just getting these things into place for the first tour since we've gotten organized. Performances also help me spend less time missing the Mortals and Jessica.

The last Sunday in May is our anniversary. The night before is the final TPG performance, this one at Dawson College. We receive a standing ovation, and we're all high on success afterwards.

"Hey, belle gang," says Stéfanie, "what say we have supper at the sushi place around the corner to celebrate? And some saki, on me?"

Pierre grins and leans in to whisper in my ear. "Now that the money's coming in, she can be generous." I ask him if he got his check in the mail. "Sure, the smallest amount I've ever received via check. Seventeen dollars and eighty-three cents." I don't say anything, but mine was only a bit more.

We eat platters of sushi and tempura and the sake flows.

I get a ride home with Stéfanie, who has also been drinking, and by the looks of it much more than I. This becomes obvious when she nearly runs over a man with a cane in the crosswalk.

"Maybe I should drive?" My heart is pounding so hard I can't swallow.

She pulls over. "Go for it." Her eyes are glassy, and she's picking her cuticles, squeezing her eyebrows together.

She looks sad.

I get in on the driver's side but wait. "Are you okay?"

She brings her face up to her hands. "Brian's gone."

I turn off the car. "What? What do you mean 'gone'?"

"He left last night after we had a huge fight. His work offered him this six-month contract in Japan, and I was against it. I can't come with him, and it's too long to be apart. He says I just want to control him, and that he's going anyway." She leans forwards, arms on the dash, and pushes her head between her arms.

I'm shocked. Nobody in the company had a clue that anything was wrong. We think of Stéfanie as transparent, yet a lot was brewing at home that she had successfully hidden.

I start rubbing her back, little circular motions. She weeps and weeps as we sit together in the parked car.

After a while, she sits up and gives me a tiny smile.

"Merci, Audrey. You're always so kind to me."

She takes my hand in hers and kisses my palm. I feel a pulse between my legs. Try to ignore it. Instead of letting it go, she holds my hand between both of hers.

"I'm here if you need anything," I say weakly.

She nods, lets go of my hand, and looks into the rearview mirror at herself. She smooths her hair and wipes mascara streaks on her cheeks. "J'suis un big mess."

I start her car and take the most direct route I know back to Rosemont. When I get to my house, I give her a quick hug. "Hang in there. Text or call for anything, anytime." She grabs my hand again and gives it a squeeze. "Merci, t'es un amour."

I come inside and Denise is in the living room, reading.

"How was Dawson?"

I take off my jacket and put down my backpack. "Amazing. They gave us a standing ovation and had really smart questions. Then we went for sushi." I put my left hand below my mouth, trying to smell my breath. The scent of alcohol is gone. I breathe in and count to ten. Silently.

I go into the living room and sit on the blue chair.

The hand that Stéfanie squeezed still feels warm.

The words fall out. "I think I have a crush on Stéfanie."

She smiles. "That isn't news."

I stare. "You knew?"

"You're not hard to read. I thought it would pass."

"Me too. But it's been a long time, and it's not passing."

She stops smiling.

"I think she's interested."

"But you told me she was straight! I thought she was with a man."

"Apparently, they've been having problems. He left last night."

Denise looks stunned. "Do you want her like that? I thought everything was fine between us now."

"Me too. But it's like everything is heightened, more intense. I'm not comparing you with her anymore. It's like I'm open to everyone. I don't know. I can't explain it."

I feel Stéfanie's back and the movement of her sobs through my hand.

Denise stands up. She turns to me, face as white as freshly fallen snow.

"Get out."

Chapter 77

I walk the twenty minutes to Stéfanie's. Knock on her door, knuckles buzzing. She takes a while, and then when she opens the door, her face freezes. "What's wrong?"

I whisper that Denise threw me out. I say it's because I had had an affair with a neighbour. It's almost the truth.

"How likely is that? Both of our couples collapse on the same day."

She invites me in and shows me the guest room. "You can stay as long as you like," she says, and I think about the time I'd called on a weekend, and she had refused to speak to me. But I'm so relieved I have a place to sleep that I just thank her, take my evening meds, and collapse on the bed.

*

The next day, I work on my laptop before coming out of the guest room. I hear Stéfanie padding around, making coffee, talking on the phone in French, vacuuming. I decide my teeth are too fuzzy to go without brushing them for another second, so I come out and try to duck into the bathroom without her seeing me. I nearly succeed.

"Bon matin!" She shuts off the vacuum. "Hope I didn't wake you with this monster."

I laugh. "I have a little kid, so I never sleep past seven anyway. I've been up for hours."

"There's coffee, cereal, fruit, yogurt, take whatever you want."

I think about how many times I'd fantasized about this happening, about Stéfanie caring for me, us being together in a cozy warmly-lit sitting room. Now all I can think about is wanting to go home and cuddle with Adam and Denise and how I don't deserve that.

She starts vacuuming and then after a few seconds she turns it off. "House keys are on the kitchen table."

I yell "okay" from the bathroom. I brush my teeth, get dressed, and have some decaf. Then I'm back at my sketchpad, doodling with some concepts for a new graphics client, a company that helps progressive Jews create their own Haggadahs for Passover. I start thinking about my culture, and I wonder for the first time if my bio mom was Jewish.

I turn the page in my sketchpad and start doodling a woman giving birth.

Then I stop and chew my pencil. Look at the indents where my teeth were.

Pick up my phone.

Chapter 78

Lila answers, like she always used to, on the fourth ring.

"Family court records, Lila speaking, how can I help?"

I can't help smiling. "Hi Lila, it's Audrey Meyerwitz."

I hear her suck in her breath. "For the love of God, Audrey, you were the last person I expected to call! How on earth are you?"

There's a tickle in my throat. Then a vice, squeezing. My eyes burn. "I've been better."

Pause. "Is everybody okay?"

I laugh. "Yes, everyone's fine." My siblings. She knows who she's dealing with.

"I'm sure you didn't call to chitchat. What's going on?"

"I wanted to ask if you could get me my adoption records. I want to find my birth mom."

Silence. "Audrey, you know I can't do that."

"Actually, you're the only person who could."

"Yes, but I could lose my job. Forget could, I would lose my job."

"Not if nobody saw."

"It's not that simple. And anyway, I thought you weren't interested in all that."

"I wasn't. Now I am. I've lost so much, and I just have to know...I want to know...who I am, for real. Like, where I came from."

"Have you talked to your mother?"

"No, she would just say the records are sealed. And I don't want to upset her anyway. I know you have access in a way the social workers don't."

I hear a phone ring in the background and some voices. I take a slow breath.

"Can you at least think about it? Like, maybe there's a way you can do it that's discreet."

"I hope nobody is recording this call."

I laugh. "The Department of Social Services doesn't have a budget for that."

"Audrey, are you taking your medication?"

"Yes, this has nothing to do with my anxiety. Really."

Another pause. "I'll think about it."

Chapter 79

A few days later, I'm at Stéfanie's, sketching a Seder plate with recently added elements like the orange and the olive, and my phone rings. It's Denise.

"Hey," I say, carefully.

"Where are you?" she asks. "I've been worried."

I don't say anything.

"You're with her?" Her nose is stuffed up.

"Denise, I don't have any other place to go now that we're out of the Mortals. I couldn't go to Albany because it was too late."

"Are you moving in with her?"

"No! This is silly. Can I come home so we talk about this, face to face?"

Sniffling. "I'm not ready. I just can't believe after all this time—"

"Denise, please. I know you're upset, and I get it, you have every right, but the thing is, I haven't actually done anything with her. We're not together. Really."

She laughs. "You expect me to believe that?"

"Yes, I do. Now you don't trust me?"

"How come it took years to admit you had a crush on her?"

"Because I didn't think it was a big deal. She's straight, and you have a thing about being cheated on. I thought you would be less worried if you didn't know."

"Mon Dieu, you're just like the others."

"Please, Denise, can we at least go to counselling next week? Maybe Gretchen can help us talk it through."

Silence. "Adam misses you."

"I miss him too. And I miss you."

She doesn't respond.

"Can I stop by to pick up some clothes and maybe take him to the park?"

"Fine."

We agree on a time and hang up.

When I arrive at the house, Denise's face is splotchy, and her eyes are swollen. I try not to hate myself but fail. Adam throws himself into my arms and cries. "Why did you leave, Mommy?" I tell him we're trying to figure things out, but that no matter what, he'll have both of us forever.

Forever.

Adam starts tugging at my hand to get going. I pick him up and kiss his belly. He squeals and smells like ketchup and baby shampoo.

Chapter 80

When we get back from the park, Denise is on the land line. "Just a moment, please," I hear her say. When she looks at me, I shake my head, pointing at the door. "I'm sorry. She can't come to the phone right now. Can I take a message?" I see Denise look for a scrap paper and pen. "Okay, Theo, are you calling about graphic design services?" She makes a funny face and looks at me. "Okay, sure, I'll let her know. Thanks, and have a nice day."

She looks at me with her head tilted and arm crossed, an unfamiliar pose. She starts to say something then changes her mind. "Here," she says, handing me the paper. "His name was Theo."

I thank her and look at the note. "Did he say what his business is?"

"Actually, it wasn't a business call."

"Then what was it?"

I notice the edge in my voice. Too many siblings getting in trouble and fielding calls from adults bearing bad news. But mostly Jessica. Always Jessica.

"I don't know. Call him back and ask him yourself."

I study the scrap of paper, trying to figure out the area code. "Honey, did you... "

But she's already gone upstairs.

Chapter 81

I pack a few things in my overnight bag and walk back to Stéfanie's. I lie on the bed and open my laptop. Do a quick email and Facebook check. Then I pick up my phone and call the number on the yellow paper in Denise's handwriting.

A female voice says hello.

"Hi, this is Audrey Meyerwitz. I'm returning Theo's call?" I hear a little gasp on the other end and a muffled voice say, "Hang on."

I roll my eyes, imagining someone somewhere getting my number and wanting to sell me something I don't want or need. Those are the calls that come now in place of the Itchy Mortals and Jessica. I swallow and will myself not to cry. I breathe and start doodling.

I'm tired of my own sadness.

"Hello?" A male voice.

"Hi, Theo. It's Audrey Meyerwitz returning your call."

"Audrey! I...I can't believe it's you."

"I'm sorry. Do we know each other? I have a kid, and I think motherhood slashed my bandwidth in half."

Silence.

"Hello?"

"I'm sorry, Audrey. I've thought about this moment for most of my life."

"I'm sorry. Can you please tell me what this is about?"

I hear him blow his nose. "You're adopted, right?"

"Yes."

"Someone named Lila called telling me you were looking for your birth mother. I don't know how to say this without shocking you. But, here goes. We—we have the same mother. I'm your half-brother."

I don't say anything. I don't think anything.

"Mom passed away ten years ago, and I've been looking for you ever since. I was seven when they took you away to foster care. You were three."

I exhale. "Well, that's not right. My mom adopted me at birth."

"That's what she told you?"

"That's what happened. I have photos of myself as an infant. Not sure how you got this information, but it's definitely not me. You have the wrong person."

"No, I'm sure. Maybe your mom didn't tell you the truth."

My face turns pink. "My mom is a career foster parent and possibly the kindest person on the planet. There's no way she would lie to me about something as important as that."

"There's no way I could know this other than through personal experience. I have photos of us playing together. And we look a lot alike, even if we have different fathers."

I'm shaking my head, heat building in my cheeks. "I'm sorry. Is this fun for you? Do you get your jollies calling me and dumping this story in my lap for no reason? Don't you have a life? I'm hanging up the phone and please don't..."

"Wait, Audrey, please."

His voice is ragged.

"Okay, fine. I'm waiting."

"Will you give me your email address?"

"Why do you want it? Are you going to start stalking me? I have a lot on my plate, and I can't deal with this right now."

"Just look at the pictures. Three pictures. If you still don't believe me, we can drop it. Or you could ask your mom."

I roll my eyes. "This is so scammy."

"The email?"

"Audreydraws@gmail.com."

I hear him typing. We hang up.

In about ten seconds, his email appears on my computer screen. There are three photo attachments. One is presumably Theo, around five years old, holding a baby. It resembles a few photos I have of my infant self. But all babies kind of look alike.

The other two are a different story.

In the second, Theo and a little girl are holding hands and running down a hill. He's looking at her protectively, but she is euphoric, the thrill of a tiny body tearing through space. They are probably six and two. Their faces are practically identical but for her baby fat. And there's no question that the baby fat and the little face are mine.

In the third photo, the one Theo says was taken the day before I left, the little girl is sitting on his lap, and he is sitting on a couch, hugging her around the waist. Her blonde hair is in two pigtails with purple beads. They are looking solemnly at the camera.

I look at the two photos of the two children. They are clearly related. And the little girl looks remarkably like Adam.

My first thought: Call Jessica. Tell Jessica. Send the pictures to Jessica and talk to her about it. We'd had an ongoing conversation for years about my bio family, and she'd never understood my lack of curiosity.

And then I remember she's dead, just like Sabrina.

My heart is thudding so loudly I can hear it. I listen for Stéfanie. Nothing. Her grandfather clock's heavy ticks, the refrigerator's buzz, the wind blowing through a window that's cracked open. No human sounds.

I look in the mirror. Wonder if the adult Theo looks like me.

I dig through my bag and find it: Jessica's purple sweater. I put it on and lay down on the futon, staring at the ceiling.

Chapter 82

The next days are like a dystopian water ballet. There are normal things, like going home to take a nap while Denise is at work or out shopping, taking Adam to the park when the pool opens, giving him a peach yogurt for a snack, a contract for a new client selling special underwear that absorbs blood when you have your period. And then, in the middle of cooking alphabet pasta at Stéfanie's, I'll remember. We're separated. My wife thinks I had an affair with the straight woman I just recently stopped being obsessed with. I'm staying at her place. Theo is out there, somewhere, and I haven't emailed him back. I think about Martha's lies, the sealed records. My sleep is light when it arrives at all.

At my med check in June, I tell Dr. Couture about the separation and about Theo and ask her if we could change anything. She tells me to take a bit more of the Ativan at night when sleep is hard, but she's convinced this is all a normal reaction to two destabilizing situations, and that once I meet Theo and figure out things with Denise and with Martha, I should gradually start feeling normal, or at least normal for me.

One evening I'm finishing a logo and Stéfanie is in her room. "Hey, viens me voir!"

I look up. In her bedroom?

"Pourquoi?"

"Come here and I'll tell you!" Her voice is silly, like a kid playing a trick.

I peek inside her door. "Oui?"

She pats her bed. I hesitate. "Much more comfortable here than holding up the wall," she says.

I walk in and sit on the edge of the bed, as far as I can get from her. "What's up?"

"Lie down next to me!"

This is it. The moment I have dreamed about. But for what? I cannot imagine Stéfanie and I galloping off into the sunset. And what about my family? Yet when she reaches for my hand, I take it.

"Look!" She's holding her tablet, and there are photos from our last show taken by a reporter from Dawson College. I lie down carefully, trying to make a space between our bodies. But she inches over towards me so I can see the pictures better.

The entire right side of my body is in contact with the entire left side of hers.

I admire the photos and feel a burning sensation between my legs. I loosen up. Denise already thinks we're lovers. That I'm a liar. Maybe it would be the best thing, just get it out of our systems.

I roll onto my side and prop myself up with one arm. "Any news from Brian?"

She doesn't look up. "Don't want to talk about it."

I chuckle. "I take that as a no."

"What's your schedule tomorrow?"

"I'm home for the afternoon when Denise goes to her sister's. Morning I was planning to go to the library unless it's okay to be here."

She bonks me over the head with the tablet. "Silly, you have to believe me when I say you can always, always stay here. I like having you here."

She rolls over on her side so that she's facing me and throws her arm around my waist. Okay, well, now I know.

I look at her, and she smiles. I take my hand and cup her cheek and then move my mouth slowly towards hers.

She jerks back immediately. "Franchement. C'est quoi ça?"

Shit.

"I thought—"

"Audrey, I'm straight, you know that. What the hell?" She gets up and sits on the edge of the bed. "Taking advantage of my vulnerability like that. I wouldn't have thought you would stoop that low."

"I'm sorry, but you've been flirting with me for months."

"Flirting? What on earth are you talking about? We're good friends. That's all!"

I realize the futility of the conversation. I get up and head back to the guest room.

"Audrey, I'm sorry, but I don't feel safe with you here. You're going to have to find another solution to your housing problems."

My face burns as I turn around. She has her arms and legs crossed. She's shaking.

"I'm—I'm sorry."

I go into the guest room and call Denise. I tell her that Stéfanie and her husband reconciled, and she needs me to go somewhere else. Our counselling appointment is in a few days, and she agrees to me sleeping at home in my office until I figure something else out.

Chapter 83

Counselling in July brings us both great relief. I am able to convince Denise that I hadn't had sexual contact with Stéfanie nor did I want it, only that I had feelings and that those feelings are finished. We lay out a reunification plan that includes discussing issues for each of us that have been difficult, for Denise, how anxiety affects my parenting, for me, how Denise tries to preempt my mistakes by controlling, for both of us, how we feel isolated after losing our friends, how we hide from each other. On the plan are also steps to communicate better and brainstorming ways to have fun with each other. Until we meet our goals, I would stay with Mimi. Gretchen also encourages me to visit both Theo and Martha, to connect more deeply with the realities of my past and make repairs with the woman who had raised me, regardless of how old I was when I was adopted.

I bring my backpack and overnight bags downstairs, and Adam jumps into my arms. "It's just for a few days, sweetie." My giant child is wrapped around me, his feet kicking the backs of my knees. He grabs my Star of David around my neck and whimpers. I gently peel back his fingers. Denise comes into the foyer and rubs his back singing "Au claire de la lune."

"Mommy is just going to be with Mimi. And we'll see her in a few days."

Denise manages to take Adam off me. He runs into his bedroom wailing.

"Be safe on the road," she says. I go to kiss her, and she steps back. "Sorry."

She nods and gives me a half-smile before closing the door softly.

Chapter 84

It's mid-August, and I'm at Mimi's working on preliminary sketches for the Rainbow Scouts' rebranding. I look up at the clock on a break and realize I feel ready.

I set aside my sketchpad and pull out my laptop. Theo's email is open from the last time I'd been on; each time, I look at the three photographs, studying different details, comparing our faces, trying to discern pieces of this new and old story.

Hello Theo,

Please forgive me hanging up on you and waiting this long to reconnect. You may or may not know that I have an anxiety disorder. This is the kind of situation where I can freak out and act crazy.

This new information changes my entire life story, so it's a big deal. I thought Martha had adopted me at birth. Now I know this isn't true. Now I know that I spent three whole years in another family, a family where you and I were siblings sharing a mother. I have so many questions. Like, why did I get adopted and not you? Did you know my father? Do we have any other siblings? Do you have children?

Please know I am ultimately grateful you reached out, even if my reaction was negative. I take all relationships seriously, and I anticipate being in touch again before too much time has passed.

With awkward gratefulness,

Audrey

*

I visit Theo and his wife, Kimberly, in their Boston home for the first time in September. When I arrive, I pull into a three-story Victorian in Somerville, about fifteen minutes outside the city. There's a big yard, and as I walk up the front steps, I notice there's an office on the first floor, some kind of holistic place, and two apartments above. Theirs is the second.

Theo answers the door. We stand there for a few seconds, staring at each other. I'm looking at a nose with the same little bump as mine, wavy hair the same shade of dirty blonde, the same thick glasses, and the same pointy chin. His body is slender, and his eyes are large. He stands taller than me but not by much. He looks at me with a half-smile.

Something happens to my body, some kind of physical remembering I can't quite understand. This person is made of the same stuff as I am. For a second, I wonder if he is a hologram.

He finally speaks.

"Audrey." His eyes are full of tears.

I pull out some tissues from my backpack and give him one. He laughs. I laugh. Then I hug him. Awkwardly.

"Thank you," I say. He just hugs and hugs and hugs until I'm finding it hard to breathe.

We move into the kitchen where a woman is sitting at the table in a bathrobe. There's an Audubon bird clock, the same one I used to have in my Burlington place, and I notice it's almost 3:00 p.m. I wonder why she isn't dressed and why neither of them is at work. Theo tells me this is Kim, his wife, and we shake hands and smile.

"You must be tired after your long drive. Can I get you something to drink?"

I sit down next to her, turning my neck left and right to stretch. "Some water would be great, thanks."

Kim gives the eye to Theo who gets the water. She gingerly wraps her fingers around the glass that's in front of her.

"You want a straw for that?" Theo asks, his back turned.

"No, I'm really close," says Kim, and her fingers close in a bit more until she's finally grasping. "I'm recovering from Lyme disease," she says to me casually.

My eyes widen. "Oh my God. I'm so sorry."

She smiles. "Don't be. I'm much better than I was a few months ago. It was rough for a while, but Cecelia from downstairs convinced Theo to let us do our thing." Theo puts his hands on his hips. She looks fake-angry, and I can tell this is harmless play.

My brother sets down a glass with ice water in front of me and then sits with us at the table. "Cecelia is a naturopath," he explains, "and she works with a lot of patients with Lyme. They approach it very differently than the medical doctors. No drugs."

My mouth is dry. I try not to look at Kim's finger joints but can't help but peek. They are puffy and purplish.

"We have so much to talk about," says Theo, looking at Kim and then me.

"How can you get better from Lyme without drugs?" I ask.

"It's a long conversation. Why don't I let you two get acquainted? I should have my afternoon nap anyways." She slowly rises to her feet, kisses Theo's shoulder, and shuffles out.

"I'm sorry she's so sick," I say, a pit in my stomach.

"Thanks. It's been really hard for the kids, but they're hanging in there. Pema, our nine-year-old, always wants to entertain Kim, so she brings in her juggling or facts from her favourite nature program. Indigo, our six-year-old, is more sensitive and afraid. She cuddles as much as Kim can manage and is prone to crying jags. We just try to meet their needs as they come up."

I smile. "Do you know about attachment parenting?"

He grins. "Sure. Dr. Sears is great. We still cosleep on occasion, all four of us piled into our double bed." We discuss breastfeeding, baby wearing, and the temperaments of our children. Pema is social and brave, like Adam. Indigo is artistic and sensitive, like me.

"Most people, including Martha, my mom, were pretty skeptical about all of that stuff. Did you and Kim get any negative reactions?"

Theo sighed. "To be honest, I needed convincing. At the beginning, I was like, 'I didn't have half of this stuff, and I turned out fine.' But I honestly think it gave the girls a great foundation, a confidence, and a real intimacy with us that neither Kim nor I had with our parents."

"Will the kids be home from school soon?" I'm excited to see little people, little girls, who might look like me.

Theo grins. "They're at a friend's place for the afternoon. I wanted to make sure we had some adult time together before they descended upon us."

We go into the living room where a yellow photo album is waiting on the coffee table. He opens it, and for the first time, I see a young mother holding a tiny infant.

"That's our mother, Sarah Zimmerman. And the baby is you."

Sarah Zimmerman. My mother's name was Sarah Zimmerman.

Sarah is lying in her bed nursing me, her blonde hair in a pageboy with one barrette holding it back on the left side, and she has a smile that makes me weep.

My beautiful mother. My beautiful young mother.

Theo puts his arm around me. "Is this okay?"

I nod. He passes me a box of tissues.

"Sarah didn't name you Audrey. That was one piece of the puzzle that made it so hard to find you."

"What did she name me?"

Theo taps his fingers on his thighs and looks down. "She named you Delta."

I start laughing. "Get out."

Theo looks at me, completely straight faced.

"It's true."

I'm astonished. "Was she a pilot or something?"

Theo laughs. "No, delta as in math. It's the symbol for change."

I'm speechless.

"She wanted you to be the change. She wanted to break the cycle with you."

One, two, three...

"She was twenty-three when she had you; seventeen when she had me. She always looked so young and full of life when she was sober," said Theo, shaking his head. "She could have made it. Her affair with the man who was your father was the beginning of the end. We aren't a hundred percent sure who he was, but my dad had an idea. He was a dealer."

My father, the drug dealer. I swallow hard.

Then I look more closely at the photo and notice several women in the background.

"It was a home birth," he explains. "Mom was a hippy, a rebel."

"How so?"

"Well, that's a very long story. But in essence, she was always chasing down information and experiences. She was quite smart for someone so uneducated, especially about the natural world, about math, about music. You and I were born at home with a midwife because her best friend happened to be one and lived down the street. She learned a lot about women owning their pregnancies and births and was apparently very proud of herself." I think of the home birth I had longed for. Sarah looks so relaxed and happy. I remember feeling stressed and uncomfortable at the hospital, the harsh fluorescent lighting, the cold temperatures, the dirty recovery rooms.

"Can I make copies of some of these photos?" I ask.

"Actually, Audrey, I made this for you. I have one exactly like it on that shelf over there."

My brother made me a photo album. Of our family history. "I don't know what to say. That's so generous."

He shows me the guest room upstairs, and I change into a fresh t-shirt. There are three intricate drawings of different plants in frames on one wall, and on another is a large photo of the whole family on a beach. Kim is shockingly heavier, a normal weight as compared to the gaunt version I met earlier. Her cheeks are ruddy, and she's got a devilish look as she gives both girls bunny ears. I look more closely at the children. Pema has a darker complexion, more like her mom, but the face shape and glasses evoke her father. Indigo is fair and looks much more like Theo, which means more like me.

I come downstairs, and he's still looking at the album.

"Audrey, do you know anything about Sarah from your adoptive mother?"

"No, nothing. Nothing at all."

Theo looks up from the photos and out the window, away from me. "She was a heroin addict. She was clean for three whole years, including when she was pregnant with you. Then she relapsed, which is why you went to foster care and eventually got adopted. I stayed with my dad. I tried so hard to help her." He shakes his head slowly. "From after you left until I graduated from high school, she was on and off using, living mostly on the street. She used to come around our place and ask Dad for money. I wanted to run away with her. But she also terrified me. Her hair was clumped, and her arm was covered with red sores. She was my mother and not my mother. Once when I pushed past my dad and hugged her legs, she screamed at me to get away."

I'm staring at him, trying to picture Sarah and little Theo and jail and arms with sores. My ribcage swells, and my lungs shrink. Realizing that fainting isn't an option, I get on the floor and begin to stretch.

"Sorry, I need to do this to relax."

"It's fine. Do you want a break, Audrey?"

Tears flutter in my eyelashes. "Nope."

"I graduated and got a job as director of a house for developmentally disabled men. It wasn't great money, but it was odd hours so I could spend daytime on the phone with police precincts, courthouse records departments, rehab treatment facilities, and homeless shelters for women. I finally tracked her down when I was twenty-five. She answered an email I'd sent months earlier. Apparently, it was forwarded. She was in a halfway house, sober, and looking for work."

"Did she ever have a profession?"

Theo smiles. "That's an interesting question. She grew up in a highly orthodox Jewish sect. When she and my dad got pregnant at seventeen, her parents disowned her, her community kicked her out, and she had to find a place to live fast. My dad was a pianist and doing great in school, so they lived in my grandparents' basement for a while."

"Sarah's parents were orthodox?"

"Yes, her parents were Lubavitcher, or Chabad."

I stare.

"That was a huge part of her being a rebel. But the heroin...it was too strong, even for her."

My mother, an orthodox intellectual hippy junkie rebel.

"You asked about work. She was a singer. That's how she made money at first."

"What?"

"She realized she had a good voice when she apparently started singing to me while she was pregnant. My dad thought she was talented, so he introduced her to one of his pianist friends and got her a fake ID. They started playing in some local nightclubs."

"Don't tell me: Your real name is Thelonious?!?"

He blushes and chuckles. "Yes, that's right. I haven't told a lot of people, but Dad is a huge Monk fan, and I think Sarah must have been, too."

"How did she do, with the singing?"

"Pretty well. She didn't make tons of money or get famous, but she was able to work even after she had me, very part time. My dad said in those first months, she had maybe two or three gigs a week."

"Is that how she got into heroin?"

"Dad thinks so. She started hanging out with musicians and drinking and partying as long as he was home with me. My father wanted her to get counselling because of being excommunicated from her family and community, but she always told him she was too busy loving life."

I fold myself into pigeon pose.

"Did she make any records?"

"I haven't found any. I did have a journal from when she was pregnant, and in one entrée, it says they did some kind of demo tape, but I never found it, and the studio didn't have any information going back that far. But I did find this. I think it's lyrics."

I hear him shuffling paper, and I sit up. He hands me a yellow legal-sized sheet with lines and faintly penned words. Sarah's writing. She wrote a song. This song.

Falling Through the Night

Falling through the night,
I'm reeling from another blight.
The souls around me covering their ears.

Falling through the night,
My heart's a comet, fast and bright,
The wind around me wipes away my tears.

Ohhhh,
The sky is endless black,
Ohhhh,
Can I turn things back?

Falling through the night,
I long to recreate the light,
To help me find the many things I lack.

The front door opens and slams shut. "We're home!" says a little voice, and then a littler one, "Daddy, can I have a cheese stick?"

The girls.

I put the paper back in the folder. Theo excuses himself and gets up. I stand, unsure of what to do. Do they know about me? What should I say to them?

Theo is quick: he intercepts Pema and Indigo before they have a moment to get busy. The three walk into the living room and stand, looking at me.

They are stunning and ordinary, the two little bodies with the big body in between, smiling at me bathed in the sun's rays.

Pema has Kim's dark straight hair and olive skin, but the nose is Theo's. She is tall and slender and wears glasses. Indigo is chubbier with light hair that waves like Theo's and mine. She has huge marble green eyes, which remind me of Adam's, along with her heart-shaped face and fragile expression.

Theo has one arm around each daughter. A twinge: Theo gets to raise girls.

"Pema, Indie, meet your Aunt Audrey."

Aunt Audrey. Of course.

They are mine, too.

Pema comes to me, holds out her fist. "I picked this out for you. Daddy told me you're an artist, and I thought maybe you would want to draw it." She unfolds her fingers revealing a white rock. I cradle it in my hand like a chick and thank her, smiling into her earnest face.

Indigo is hiding behind Theo's legs, so I get on my hands and knees and scurry behind the couch. I peek slowly above the back cushions and catch Indigo doing the same from behind Theo. She giggles as I pop down. We scamper around for a few more minutes until she asks for a snack again.

The rest of the afternoon is play. Pema shows me a complicated card game called Wizard, her shark posters, her sparkly amber nail polish, her trundle bed, "For when I have sleepovers because that's what big girls do," she says, face sombre.

Indie is much more physical than her sister. We have a pillow fight, and then I suggest airplane, hoist her into the air with my feet pushing against her little tummy, telling her about how I play this game every day with Adam, her cousin.

Theo and Kim prepare supper. When I ask if I can help, they both say that playing with the kids is more than enough. We all sit at the table with zebra placemats and black ceramic plates full of barbecued chicken, asparagus, sweet potato mash, and quinoa. I realize I haven't seen one slice of bread since arriving. Before we eat, we all hold hands. The four of them close their eyes.

Theo: "I'm grateful for Audrey, for this beautiful reunion."

Kim: "I'm grateful for my family, which just got bigger and better."

Pema: "I'm grateful for having a sleepover tonight even though Aunt Audrey won't sleep in my room."

Indie: "I'm grateful for dessert."

Me: "I'm grateful...just grateful."

After supper, the girls clean up their rooms, and we then look at their baby books. Indie's face so strongly resembles both Adam's and mine that I ask to make a photocopy. Theo says he's included several in my album. Then the girls change into pajamas, brush teeth, and the four of them pile onto Kim and Theo's bed and pick up a worn copy of *Mary Poppins*. I stand in the doorway, wishing I had my camera, and at the same time knowing I would never be so intrusive.

"Aunt Audrey, come read with us!" Indie hops off the bed, takes my hand, and leads me in.

After the girls are tucked in with goodnight kisses and hugs, Theo makes tea, and he and Kim and I share stories. Kim tells me about Lyme. The couple had gone through a big rift because he decided that conventional medicine was best when she was so sick, and she didn't have the strength to fight him. But finally, after two years of antibiotics and little progress, she told him, simply, that she was going off all medication and with Cecelia's guidance, she was going to follow a protocol developed by her colleague. That was just two months ago.

"I'd been in bed for most of the last year. Now, I'm up and down but mostly up, at least sitting. My Bell's palsy is gone, my memory's better, and I don't have the flares and pain as bad as before. I probably seem very sick to you, but this is nothing compared to what it was."

I shake my head. "I don't know how you did that. I would be so scared to go off my medication."

"What do you take medication for?"

"It's kind of a long story."

She smiles. "I've got time." I look over at Theo, and he nods, encouraging me.

I tell her about my diagnosis. About school, about my aides, my psychiatrists. My medication. They both listen and don't say anything. When I pause, Kim speaks.

"Audrey, I don't want to be rude, but Cecelia's taught me a lot about health and thinking about it differently. Would you be comfortable telling her about your history? She might have some different ideas about healing."

I don't say anything. My skin prickles, like someone just ripped off my shirt. I try to think of an excuse to take a drive. Theo's face changes as the panic creeps up inside me. "Kim's enthusiastic, Audrey. She wants to share her knowledge because her healing was a miracle, truly. This doesn't mean you have to say yes."

"I think—I'm already overwhelmed."

"That's fine," says Kim. "And believe me, you're not that different from most people. If you get home and you're still interested, we can talk whenever you want. I know you're a graphic designer with your own business, so scheduling shouldn't be hard. Just email Theo, or we can be Facebook friends."

Realizing how exhausted I am, I announce that I'm turning in. They ask me about my departure tomorrow and if I'd like breakfast before I leave.

"I hope we can visit again soon," says Theo. He's looking at me like a dressing room mirror, seeing what fits, what doesn't. He's not quite the male version of me, but suddenly I have a vision of all five of us under the same roof, a strange one I don't recognize but that is warm and real.

"I'd love you guys to meet Denise and Adam."

Kim grins. "I would love it, too. I'm not quite ready for travel, but that day is coming."

"We could take a vacation together, maybe. Adam loves the beach."

"Super idea."

We're all smiling at each other. I stand up, and then they stand up. We walk into the centre of the living room, and for a second, we just look at each other. Then we hug, heads awkwardly clunking, a little circle of relatives. I think of Sarah's song, "Falling Through the Night," and how lonely she must have been. I hope she can see us from where she is.

Chapter 85

When I get back to Montreal, I stop at the house. Denise pecks my cheek and asks a lot of questions. I tell her I need time to process. But I can't resist telling her my given name.

At first, she thinks I'm joking. "Like that song from the 1970s, 'Delta Dawn, what's that flower you have on?'"

I nod, and when my face stays serious, she stops. "That's really what she named you?"

Yep.

Denise shakes her head. "Well, Martha may be a liar and all kinds of bad things, but thank goodness she adopted you because you get to go through life as Audrey." I roll my eyes. She smiles, and when her kind eyes meet mine, a little rocket takes off in my belly, the first time in months.

*

Fall is in full swing. Adam's in first grade, and Denise has taken on extra hours. I start marketing and am soon maxed out with clients. I stay in touch with Kim and Theo and Pema and Indie and think a lot about healing. Finally, in October, I get up the courage to go see my mother.

Albany is less than a four-hour drive and a beautiful if desolate one, with I87 going straight through the Adirondacks. Because I leave on a Wednesday morning, the border is quick, and there's little traffic. In my head, I go over what I want to say to Martha, over and over and over. I want to be sane, calm, and factual, and at the same time, my anger is like a cooped-up child who only gets louder as I try to ignore her.

When I arrive, it's one of those crisp fall days where the sun patches feel like bath water and shady patches like ice. Martha, being addicted to projects, is out trimming one of the side hedges while the boys are at school, a cigarette jammed between her lips. Pulling up into the driveway, I feel the air thin out and my armpits go greasy with sweat. *I can do this.* The neighbours' stereo is blasting, as it frequently does; on this day it's "Yellow Submarine" by the Beatles. If they hadn't had such great taste in music, I think Martha would have spent her days in a different courtroom.

I open the car door, and she turns.

"Audrey! What are you doing here?"

I lean against my car, unable to smile, to speak, to move.

"What's wrong? Is it Denise? Adam?"

The blue metal of my Honda Fit heats the backs of my thighs, but I stay frozen. Stare at her. Fury bubbles up in my stomach.

"What's the matter?" She leans down to put the cigarette out on a rock.

And then I watch something happen to my mother. It's like a trap door opens that had been closed, locked, and covered with a massive antique rug, a coffee table, and five of the heaviest photo books in the universe. The furniture and rug start levitating. The lock breaks. And the trap door pops open.

I take my backpack and move towards the house, step by step, passing Martha, holding a gaze with her for a moment, my face hard. I walk into the house and up to my old room, which now has two single beds, since there's usually a foster kid or two staying there.

I put down my backpack and sit on the edge of one of the beds. Martha's old grandfather clock ticks insistently. I notice she's moved one of our three menorahs onto my bookshelf. Tears are stuck somewhere in the dungeon of my body, but I pre-empt them, knowing my adoptive mother would soon be up to face the music.

I hear the screen door slam and the sounds of Martha changing her clothes in the foyer. I think about Lyme and tick checks and Kim. I think about Theo and Pema and Indie and Sarah Zimmerman.

My heartbeat pumps like far-off thunder.

Footsteps on the stairs.

A knock. "Can I come in?"

I close my eyes. I came to talk to her. But my words have fled the scene.

"Okay."

When she opens the door, her face is drained of colour. Her hand trembles on the doorknob.

"I'm guessing Theo found you."

I stare at her. She knew. She's known the whole time. And for once in my life, I'm able to speak up for myself.

"You lied to me, Martha. You lied for my entire life. Our relationship is a big fucking joke." My voice is even, but heat swirls through my cheeks and sweat drips from my neck to my back. I picture my baby blanket at the foot of my bed in Burlington and feel ashamed. That blanket hadn't touched my baby self, not once.

She's quiet, standing there holding the doorknob. "I can see you're upset. Do you want to talk or vent? Either is fine."

I stand up, shaking my head. "Either is fine? What a crock. Your life is a lie, Martha. This 'helping hurting kids' is just a way to make yourself feel better. Why do you even do it? Is it for the money? For an ego boost? Tell me what role I play in your little Greek tragedy. Because I want out. You probably don't even know the real definition of trust."

I turn towards the window, knowing I'm being unkind but also honest in a conflict with my mother for the first time in my life. I hear her breathing, checking her pockets for cigarettes. Finally, she comes over to me. She puts an arm out to touch my shoulder, but I brush it away.

She sighs. "I'll be in the kitchen starting supper."

I spend the rest of the afternoon in my old room with the door closed. I stare at the ceiling, at the cobwebs in the corners. At my art books on the bookshelf. I look out the window at the fenced in yard, the deck that the boys built with their Big Brothers, Martha's flower gardens with black-eyed Susans and sedum.

The room light grows grey with the evening. I hear the boys come home from school, drop their backpacks, clunk around looking for food, laughing about some guy's ugly dog at the park. I smile and want to run in and join what's happening in the kitchen. But I don't go.

I don't know what's mine anymore.

Martha knocks on my door to tell me supper is ready. I tell her I'm not hungry. The boys come in and give me delicate hugs, knowing something is wrong but not knowing how to ask what. After things quiet down in the kitchen, I open my door and check their bedrooms. Both closed. I creep out, make myself a peanut butter and jelly sandwich, and tiptoe back to my room.

The next day, I text Denise when I get up to tell her I'll be staying longer. She writes back to take my time, that this is important. I write that I'm so grateful we're working on our relationship. I think of trust and lies and why people tell them. I wonder if she's ever lied to me, and then I think probably not. I think about us in twenty-five years and the kind of trust that's necessary to have something that's different, better than what Martha gave me. I decide I want that with both Adam and with Denise. And I know what I have to do to get it.

*

It's after 10:00 a.m. and the boys are off to school. I hear Martha in the kitchen reading the paper. Yoga, drawing, getting dressed.

A knock on my bedroom door.

Martha hears me and knocks again. "Auddy, are you okay?"

Can't speak. But a crack opens in my heart.

"Can I come in, hon?"

I walk over and slowly open the door.

She looks so sad.

"It's awful to find out someone you trust has been lying to you."

I go sit back on the bed. Hands fly up to protect my face. Nose runs. She offers a tissue. I grab it. "How do you know? Nobody has ever lied to you about your life story."

"Auddy, I know you're angry. But there are things you don't know about me that—"

"Mom, stop. This is my story, and you lied about it. Can you at least just be honest about that?"

She hands me another tissue. I take it.

We sit on the little bed not talking. The crickets and birds and the breeze give me a quiet soundtrack. My sobs eventually turn to hiccups.

"Water?" she asks.

I nod.

She's back with my favourite mug, the one with Snoopy dancing exuberantly while Schroeder plays the toy piano.

I sip and set the mug down on my night table. I turn and look at her. Her face is calm. She's been waiting for this.

"I'm sorry, sweetie. I thought this would be the best way for you as a child. I knew it would be hard later, but I wanted you to feel wanted and unburdened by your past."

"Unburdened? What does that even mean?"

She sighs. "Can I put my arm around you?"

Part of me wants to punch her. But my strength is flagging, and I nod.

"There's something you don't know about me."

I turn to look at her. "More lies?"

"Remember when Grandma Rose and Grandpa Sid died, and you asked me if there was any money, and I said no?"

"Of course. What does that have to do with anything?"

Martha takes a breath. "That wasn't the truth. There was actually over a million dollars. The lawyer called and told me that everything went to Esther and Josh."

I thought of my aunt and uncle and their families, how different they were from us. My four cousins, Harvard and Princeton grads, three doctors and one lawyer, each of them with two kids, huge houses, expensive bar and bat mitzvahs, fancy parties, cleaning ladies, not a foster child or an adoption in sight. The only times we saw them were weddings and funerals. I had never questioned why; things at our house were always so chaotic and over-peopled that I was thankful there weren't tons of extended family obligations.

But this story is new information. I look at Martha who is staring at the wall.

"It's not like that event was so different from history. I was unplanned, Audrey. The only reason Rose didn't have an abortion is because the rabbi found out somehow that she was planning to get one, and he told her it was against the religion. And she made sure I knew it, day after day it seemed."

I look at her, dazed. We only saw my grandparents a few times a year, but we all thought her parents just got along better with Esther and Josh. That it was a personality thing, a happenstance, not a good fit.

"They never wanted me. Everything good went to Esther and Josh, no matter how hard I tried. I was an outcast my entire life until I finally got into college early, thanks to an English teacher in high school. If I hadn't had a full scholarship for undergrad, I would probably still be waiting tables."

All those years, I had secretly envied Martha having a "real" family who were genetically related. Even if they were snobby.

"I thought about that all my life. They chose to tell me I was unplanned. Maybe if they hadn't, they wouldn't have thought about it every time they looked at me. And maybe I would have been happier."

Maybe she's right.

"Audrey, the situation with Sarah was a nightmare. I knew about her history from a social worker friend who told me because she knew I was Jewish and that I fostered. I wanted to shield you from that. I wanted you to have a simple story–that I loved you from your first breath. I thought it was best. Maybe I was wrong."

I collapse on the bed. Martha reaches out from her position on the bed and scoops me up. She used to do this when I was little; I'm not sure her back can handle my adult body. But she's a strong woman. Next thing I know, she's hoisting me onto her lap, and my arms wrap around her, cheek pressed into her neck, the way Adam does with me. For a second, I think about biting her, but my rage melts away with the warmth of her skin against mine.

Martha leans her head back and looks at me. She grabs two tissues and wipes both of my cheeks at the same time, like she's done since I was three. We sit like that until it's time for lunch.

*

Martha and I spend the rest of that second day together. We walk around the neighbourhood, we bake pumpkin muffins, we sit out back on lounge chairs, her reading, me sketching. We don't talk much more about my past, although occasionally I think of a question, and she answers, seemingly truthfully. When Ian and Brandon come home from school, we do our usual antics, playing charades and ping pong in the basement, making popcorn sprinkled with parmesan, watching reruns of "Days of Our Lives" and doing imitations of the characters.

The next morning, I call Denise. She asks how the visit is going. I ask her how things are at home. We both listen.

Chapter 86

It's November, and we're all busy. I'm still at Mimi's, and we're still working with Gretchen. My anxiety is heightened despite reconciling with Mom and running ten kilometres twice a week. I average five to six hours of sleep a night and have trouble staying awake all day, which makes it even harder to fall asleep and stay asleep at night.

But in between med checks, couples counselling, playing cards with Adam, and doing public service ads for the Humane Society, I keep thinking about Kim and Cecelia and healing with no medication.

One day, I email Kim and tell her I'm interested in learning more. We immediately schedule a Zoom chat.

"I'm so happy I can share this with you," she says, as we warm up to one another. "Theo cut sugar and gluten just after we saw you, and he's already sleeping better."

"I didn't know he had insomnia," I said. Would we ever have enough time to make up for what we had missed?

"The thing is, in North America, we've blindly accepted that good health means we have to take certain medicines. Especially with psychological issues, we've been given a story that leads us to fill the pockets of the pharmaceutical companies. Nobody is getting better, and lots of people are getting worse."

"Well, I know I'm better on my meds," I say quickly. And then I think, do I? I've been taking medication for most of my life since childhood.

"Bear with me, Audrey."

*

I'm at Mimi's through the first week of Christmas. I read all the books Kim sends me, and I do a phone appointment with Cecelia. I take a big breath and commit to the drastic dietary changes that can decrease inflammation of the brain, the new theory floating around the holistic healing world. I cut dairy, sugar, and gluten. I cut corn, soy, and anything processed. I eat as much organic produce as possible. Some months are easier than others, when design work is abundant. I learn about vitamins and minerals, about herbs, about meditation. I continue my running and yoga and add strength training. I stop screen time before 8:00 p.m. every night.

The first Friday in March, I'm having a roasted chicken with Mimi when my phone rings. It's Denise.

"Comme ça va?"

"Good. I finished the website for the doggie photographer, and the badminton coach says she put the check in the mail. How are you and Boy Wonder?"

"Not bad. He lost another tooth at school, but he got to bring the attendance down to Mr. Patenaude, so he was in a great mood when I picked him up. We're having tacos."

A meal close to a hundred percent processed, I think, but I stay quiet. Honesty doesn't mean I have to speak every truth from minute to minute.

I clear my throat. "Can we talk about me coming home?"

"That's actually the reason I called."

Pause.

I get up the courage. "I want to have a clearing conversation. Trust is what matters and making repairs. I still have a few repairs."

"Do you want to do it now, on the phone?"

I think about Denise, her beautiful auburn hair, and honey-brown eyes. "I think it's better in person."

"Do you want to come over and read with us before bedtime?"

I look around at the guest room, my clothes stacked up in neat piles. There's a foot of snow on the ground, it's minus eleven Celsius, and I'd have to take the metro.

"I'd love it."

In a half hour, I open the door to our home. I walk in as quietly as I can. But Adam hears, and he yells down, "Mommy, it's really you!"

I take off my boots and coat and hat and gloves, smiling to myself. "I saw you yesterday, sweetie." He races to the top of the stairs in his dolphin pajamas. I trot up the steps and grab him, tickle him until he squeals.

We read two chapters of a book in the *Dolphins Ahoy* series.

"Can we do gratitudes?" he asks.

"I thought you hated gratitudes. Who are you, and what have you done with my son?"

He giggles. "I'll start. What was hard was François imitating my voice on the playground. What I'm grateful for is that Mommy read with us, that I got to deliver the attendance, and that we had tacos. Oh yeah, and that Mommy is here now."

I take a breath. "What was hard is not knowing when I can come home to stay. I'm grateful for Mimi for taking me in. I'm grateful for Theo and Kim and Pema and Indie, and I can't wait for you guys to meet them. And I'm most grateful to Denise for second chances."

Adam kisses my elbow. I look at Denise. A tear is rolling down her cheek.

"I'm grateful for Adam and Audrey. And nothing was hard."

We cuddle up, Denise on one side, Adam in the middle. We're both cuddling Adam, but our arms are too long, and we end up wrapping our arms around each other too, squishing our beautiful boy. "Adam sandwich!" he says ecstatically. I look at Denise who is biting her lip to keep from laughing.

We go downstairs together once Adam is dozing and sit on the sofa. It's quiet at first.

"Well, I want to tell you that I'm sorry for everything I've done. I should have quit TPG when I realized I was attracted to Stéfanie."

She shifts and puts a pillow behind her. "I don't agree. I don't think any of that was wrong. We'll always be attracted to others. It's what we do that matters."

"But it upset you so much when I told you."

"Because I thought it had finished."

"Me too. I think it was that night, after Dawson. It was such a high. But that's not what I want, Denise. I want you and Adam."

Her face is soft. "I want that, too. But I don't know if I can trust you."

"I know. Believe me, I know. This is one of the reasons I knew we had to talk. There's another thing I've never told you. And maybe you'll hate me, but I can't have secrets from you."

Her body tenses visibly. "What?"

I take a breath. "When I put my profile up, when Jess and I did, I had been thinking about coming to Canada. I had just found out that Congress had axed Wellness funding and they were considering getting rid of the Affordable Care Act. With my disability, I couldn't afford to not have health insurance."

She scrunched up her eyes. "I don't understand. You married me to get to Canada?"

"It was an idea. The dating site had a tab where you could pick a country. The first search I did was in Canada. But I had a few dates with women in Vermont, too. There's no way I could fake being in love with you, Denise. All the secrets and lies I just found out about in my life...I want you to know everything. If you're upset with me and want to break up, I could accept that, but I couldn't accept keeping anything from you. Everything I've always wanted is only possible by being honest."

She's smiling now. "I don't think it's a big deal. But I'm really glad you told me."

I take her hand. "Denise, I want to marry you all over again. But I want to expect more from myself, and I want you to expect more of me. I want to be my best for you."

She folds me into her. "Je t'aime. Mon amour, je t'aime."

Chapter 87

L ately, I find my bearings at night. At my computer after supper, I think about the day. Denise and I fought over my worrying and then talked it through when we calmed down. Eight-year-old Adam swam with our neighbour's grandson, Philippe, and the kids shared almond butter and apple jelly sandwiches for lunch while I ate my salad. We all played a rousing game of Name That Tune. When Adam cried because Philippe had to go home, I scooped up all seventy pounds of him onto my lap, dabbed both cheeks with tissues at the same time, and stroked his arm, humming little cartoonish melodies in his ear.

We Zoomed with Martha and the gang, and Adam asked if Ian and Brandon could come to Six Flags Great Escape when we visit in Albany in a few weeks.

The three of us ate a homemade pesto pizza on cauliflower crust and then slow-raced up the stairs. Denise read another chapter of *Le chasseur de monstres* out loud before lights out.

Thinking about the day's highlights, I lie down next to my son and kiss him, feeling his breathing become rhythmic as he drifts off. His scalp smells of heat and grass and wrestling. I leave his room and go downstairs.

I answer emails on my laptop, including one from Eve. "I'm engaged! Bet you'd never thought you'd be getting this news from me. Wondering if you would be my maid of honour, kind of stepping in for Jess?" I want to shout up to Denise but don't, not wanting to wake Adam.

As I'm opening messages, a new one comes in, from Theo. It's full of photos from our week at Virginia Beach together. I see Pema and Indie with Adam, collecting shells, riding the waves, burning marshmallows at campfires. There is one of all seven of us on the last day, in movie star poses in front of the ocean.

I close the laptop and pick up my sketchpad. I draw a sun but anthropomorphized, with legs and arms and a smile and, of course, shades. He's doing a little dance.

Upstairs later, I undress, pull on my pregnancy tee shirt with the purple octopus, and brush my teeth. The diet recommended by Cecelia has surprised me. I still see Dr. Couture every month, but I seem to be getting my delta sleep regularly because my days are good. I'm off all but one of my medications with only two short panic attacks in three months. Medication might always be a part of my life, and that would be fine, too. My healing is full of surprises and is seldom linear.

I wonder at that moment how my life would have been different if I had grown up with Theo, with my brother. I wonder if I no longer have an anxiety disorder, or whether I had one in the first place. I wonder if how I address it has changed my symptoms. I wonder if any of that even matters.

I crawl into bed and cuddle up next to Denise, who is already asleep. On my nightstand is the cup of chamomile tea she's left me. Waiting for it to cool, I open the nightstand's little drawer to put away my wedding ring for the night, and I glance at my new Canadian passport, the family photo with Jessica barging in, my old red thread bracelet from the baby shower. It's bunched and balled but still with me since the ritual with my old friends, the Mortals, the night that connection enveloped me, pushing away the drifting.

Then I look under the passport where there's my favourite photo of Jessica and me at Pride the summer before I met Denise. She had just cut her hair, and half of her head looked like a dandelion gone to seed. She was looking up and shrugging while I pointed at the hair with one hand, the other arm around her. You can see her semicolon tattoo and her three skinny braids.

I finger the photo then lean it against the lamp on my night table. I then tuck the bracelet and family photo inside the passport, put them in the drawer, and slide it closed.

I turn out my light and close my eyes. Later, Adam crawls into bed with us, adding his nasal breathing to the sleeping sounds. It's postmodern jazz, better than Mozart or Monk, wind or waves, the call of loons on Lake Eden. Mira sighs, and Leto jumps up and curls into a ball at our feet. I remember Sarah and her song and my old name, Delta, as I slip into sleep and join the quintet.

Acknowledgements

Portions of this novel appeared in the following publications as essays and short stories, and I'm very grateful for the support.

- *The New Quarterly*, issue 147 Summer 2018: "Crocodile in the Elevator"
- *Lilith Magazine*, December 2017: "Chosen"
- *Swelling with Pride: Queer Conception and Adoption Stories* (Caitlin Press, October 2018): "Loving Benjamin"
- *How to Expect What You're Not Expecting: Stories of Pregnancy, Parenthood, and Loss* (TouchWood Editions, September 2013): "Loving Benjamin"
- *Hotch Potch Literature and Art*, Volume 1 Issue 2: "Logs in a Circle"

Special thanks to Monika Proffitt, former director of Starry Night Artist Retreat, as well as Madrono Ranch and Soaring Gardens Artists' Retreat, where much of this novel was written.

Thank you to Andrea and Jesse and everyone at Demeter; obviously, the book would not exist without you, and I'm grateful you chose to nurture it to maturity.

Talia Weisz provided wonderfully generous and thought-provoking feedback and questions as a beta reader.

Glo Harris, Jenn Marlow, and Lori Shwydky were generous enough to read the manuscript through and offer articulate and passionate blurbs that are helping with promotion; those friends and their words also lifted my spirits and confidence during moments of doubt, so double thank-yous all around.

Betsy Warland gave me a wonderful manuscript consultation many years ago when this book was just a bunch of personal essays about queer motherhood; she was the one who suggested it might want to be a novel, and she was right.

My parents, Terry and Brad Schwartz, gave me the best gift of all, of course...

Christine Ma-Kellams, a Hotch Potch colleague, is my novel promotion collaborator; her book, *The Band,* was born the same year as mine and is as utterly fabulous as she is. Thank you.

Chris Tebbetts, author, longtime friend, and occasional collaborator, helped with the blurb and title and general moral support. Much appreciated, dear one.

To my real-life Mortals: Lilli, Larissa, and Louise, as well as Diana, Verena, and Eleanor, may they rest in peace.

To the Wordies from Inked Voices, thanks for helping keep me on track during the time I was with you in our accountability group. Brooke McIntyre, a special thanks to you for your consistent presence, openness, and support, which all help keep my writer self thriving.

Lucie Gagnon co-created most of the experiences that this book was based on. She was and still is my family, best friend, co-parent, and collaborator, and I would never have grown up as much as I have without her. She also provided French proofreading, which I desperately needed. Finally, she made me laugh until I peed, at too many points to count, during the writing of this book, something essential for profound literary inspiration.

Alexi Gagnon-Schwartz made me a mother and has been the second most wonderful gift in my life, besides life itself. This boy has brought me so much happiness, challenge, surprise, learning, and belly laughs. He's helped make me a better mother, a better writer, and a better human. Just because he can pick me up now doesn't mean he'll ever win at arm wrestling. So glad we can agree that I am, and always have been, the funniest.

And finally, Erin Needham, my partner, love, and cover designer extraordinaire, has encouraged me in a multitude of ways during the submitting and publishing part of this journey. Thanks for helping me stay on the path of growth and for showing up authentically again and again and again. I am too poor a writer to adequately express how much I love and appreciate you.

Deepest appreciation to
Demeter's monthly Donors

DEMETER

Daughters
Tatjana Takseva
Debbie Byrd
Fiona Green
Tanya Cassidy
Myrel Chernick

Sisters
Amber Kinser
Nicole Willey

Grandmother
Tina Powell